DARKER THAN YOU THINK

BOOKS BY JACK WILLIAMSON

The Legion of Space
Darker than You Think ★
The Green Girl
The Cometeers
One Against the Legion
Seetee Shock
Seetee Ship
Dragon's Island
The Legion of Time
Undersea Quest
(with Frederik Pohl)
Dome Around America
StarBridge
(with James Gunn)
Undersea Fleet
(with Frederik Pohl)
Undersea City
(with Frederik Pohl)
The Trial of Terra
Golden Blood
The Reefs of Space
(with Frederik Pohl)
Starchild (with Frederik Pohl)
The Reign of Wizardry
Bright New Universe
Trapped in Space
The Pandora Effect
Rogue Star
(with Frederik Pohl)
People Machines
The Moon Children

H. G. Wells: Critic of Progress
The Farthest Star
(with Frederik Pohl)
The Early Williamson
The Power of Blackness
The Best of Jack Williamson
Brother to Demons,
Brother to Gods
The Alien Intelligence
The Humanoid Touch
The Birth of a New Republic
(with Miles J. Breuer)
Manseed
Wall Around a Star
(with Frederik Pohl)
The Queen of the Legion
Wonder's Child: My Life in
Science Fiction
(memoir)
Lifeburst
Firechild ★
Land's End ★
(with Frederik Pohl)
Mazeway
The Singers of Time
(with Frederik Pohl)
Beachhead ★
The Humanoids ★
Demon Moon ★
The Black Sun ★
The Silicon Dagger ★

★ Available from Tor Books

DARKER
THAN YOU
THINK

Jack Williamson

A Tom Doherty Associates Book
New York

This is a work of fiction. All the characters and events portrayed in this novel are either fictitious or are used fictitiously.

An Orb Edition
Published by Tom Doherty Associates, LLC
175 Fifth Avenue
New York, NY 10010

www.tor.com

Library of Congress Cataloging-in-Publication Data

Williamson, Jack.
  Darker than you think / Jack Williamson.
    p. cm.
  "A Tom Doherty Associates book."
  ISBN 0-312-86992-4
  I. Title.
PS3545.I557D3 1999
813'.52—dc21   99-046758
                                                      CIP

First Orb Edition: December 1999

Printed in the United States of America

0   9   8   7   6   5   4   3   2   1

CONTENTS

List of Full-Page Illustrations
by David G. Klein

Darker than Ever

"Why, gentlemen, is evil?"

The darkness of night is never as fearful as the greater darkness of the unknown . . . or the unknowable. Yet the defining element of humanity, our one certain distinction from the beast, is the desire to explore that greater darkness. Religion, mythology, art, and literature provide glimpses into that abyss. Although they offer no sure answers, we can experience hope or horror (and sometimes both) while in their thrall—and, on occasion, we can find new questions to ask.

The ageless quandary—what is evil?—troubles our priests and psychiatrists and politicians, but it is known, at least instinctively, by the least of animals as they confront, fight, flee from, or succumb to predators. In nature, killing may have a purpose—food, shelter, territory—yet for the victim, murder is murder, a kind of evil. But the animal, although it knows or senses the existence of evil, does not seem capable of asking the next question, the one so expertly framed by Jack Williamson in his classic novel, *Darker than You Think*: "Why? Why is evil?"

Darker than You Think originally saw print as a 40,000-word "complete novel" in the December 1940 issue of the legendary pulp magazine *Unknown*. Williamson revised and expanded the text in the fall of 1947 while working as wire editor for the *Portales Daily News*, a job that he soon abandoned to write full-time. The book version, published by Fantasy Press in 1948, more than doubled the length of its prior incarnation, but without significant changes in characters or plot. It is arguably the best, and certainly the best remembered, American novel about lycanthropy.

The werewolf took its pride of place in the pantheon of monsters with a stealth particularly fitting for a creature of the night. Although many of our most famous monsters—including Count Dracula and Frankenstein's monster, the Phantom of the Opera, and even the Mummy—may trace their popularity to a single work of fiction, the werewolf leapt from folklore into film without the intervention of a defining novel or short story. Its fangs were bared in literature dating back to the *Satyricon* of Petronius (60 A.D.) and Marie de France's *Lay of the Bisclavret* (circa 1175), and it thrived in the late stages of the gothic novel, prowling through the pages of Frederick Marryat's *The Phantom Ship* (1839), G. W. Reynolds's *Wagner: The Wehr-Wolf* (1846), and Erckmann-Chatrian's *Hugues-Le-Loup* (1869); but its seminal expression, until this century, was in the oblique: Robert Louis Stevenson's *Strange Case of Dr. Jekyll and Mr. Hyde* (1886), which offered a pseudoscientific splintering of id and ego that brought life to the brute (rather than the beast) in man.

Guy Endore's *The Werewolf of Paris* (1933) and Jessie Douglas Kerruish's *The Undying Monster* (1936) carried the legend of the *loup garou* into the twentieth century, but it was two classic Universal horror films, Stuart Walker's *Werewolf of London* (1935) and George Waggner's *The Wolf Man* (1940), that elevated the werewolf to an undying icon of the monstrous. The latter film also gave Lon Chaney, Jr., his definitive role as the tormented shape-shifter Larry Talbot—a role later essayed by such popular and prominent actors as Michael Landon, Oliver Reed, Michael J. Fox, and Jack Nicholson. The werewolf soon became an instantly recognizable monster (invoked most recently on U.S. postage stamps) that specifically symbolized all that is bestial in humanity.

Darker than You Think was a crucial turning point in this grand and complex history: a werewolf novel that is not truly a werewolf novel, but something more, a sublime evocation of the dark fantastic that seeks to explore the primal motif that powered the folklore and, in turn, the fiction and film.

Reporter Will Barbee, a dreamy cynic, awaits the arrival of an airplane carrying Dr. Lamarck Mondrick and his team of archeologists on their return from a lengthy, mysterious dig in the Gobi Desert. The assignment is ironic: Mondrick had been Barbee's professor and mentor, but he turned suddenly against him, dashing his hopes for a career in the sciences—and dispatching him into the bitter realm of journalism.

Mondrick and his team plan to announce a find of astonishing historical significance—one that will answer that ultimate question: "Why, gentlemen, is evil?" But Barbee's attention is diverted by the presence of another reporter: the comely and mysterious April Bell, wrapped in white fur and carrying a tiny black kitten. Her "trimly cool" features, and her flame-red hair and green eyes, tug at Barbee's heart—but it is her perfectly white teeth that invoke a most peculiar reaction: "It occurred to him that the spectacle of April Bell gnawing a red bone would be infinitely fascinating." Barbee soon compares her to the mythic Circe: "[I]n the legend, she had a disturbing way of changing the men she fascinated into unpleasant beasts."

This feral vision ushers in a primal dread that imbues the remainder of the novel. When the scientists finally emerge from the airplane, their much-anticipated announcement is absent of joy: "Every wary movement whispered out their abiding terror. They were not elated victors returning to announce a new conquest at the dark frontier of the known. They were tight-lipped veterans instead . . . moving steadily into a desperate action."

The analogy to combat is intense and apt. The Mondrick Expedition has uncovered evidence of a conflict more terrible, and terrifying, than the recently concluded Second World War. They bear witness to a battle between mankind and an elder race that has echoed down the ages in the folklore concerning werewolves and other shapeshifters: "a hidden enemy, far more insidious than any of your modern fifth columns that scheme the ruin of nations." Their discovery coincides with a rumored escalation of the violence, and an end to humanity's reign on earth: "I'm going to tell you of the expected coming of a Black Messiah—the Child of Night—whose appearance among true men will be the signal for a savage and hideous and incredible rebellion."

Dr. Mondrick is the first casualty of the renewed war, and Barbee, the reluctant prodigal, investigates a most curious form of murder. The death leaves the expedition's secret—a carved wooden box—in the unsteady hands of the remaining scholars and their one source of strength, Mondrick's wife, Rowena, who was blinded by a leopard on an earlier sojourn to Africa, where she "saw too much." Yet nothing is as it seems. Shapes, like shadows, shift with the onset of night; and the disturbing enigma unearthed by the Mondrick Expedition is only one of the mysteries to be revealed.

Barbee's naiveté is self-imposed, a way of avoiding a truth that he knows, if only instinctively. Despite the mounting evidence of a peril that is both physical and spiritual, he insists that his former mentor "was harmless—just a scientist, digging for knowledge." Yet Mondrick's studies were resolutely the stuff of überscience, striving to shore up breaches in human wisdom about unnatural phenomena like psychokinesis and witchcraft—and lycanthropy. His findings, echoed later in another classic text, Nigel Kneale's *Quatermass and the Pit* (1959), propose that myth is far more than a convenient metaphor or, indeed, a collective memory, but the imprint of an elder race: "We aren't all human—and that alien inheritance haunts our unconscious minds with the dark conflicts and intolerable urges that Freud discovered and tried to explain."

Exiled from the modern priesthood of science, it is Barbee, a resolute dreamer, who personifies the central conflict presented by Jack Williamson, in which the irrational flame of emotion—and especially passion—burns against the cold sterility of rational explanations. In the world of the imagination, Williamson urges, there is danger, but there is also the delight of possibility; while in the world of logic, there is only "a dim nightmare of bitter compromise and deadly frustration."

In a visionary finale, Williamson inverts the traditional and seemingly inevitable outcome of his drama, concluding with a defiant liberation that prefigured, by more than three decades, the subversive strain of "anti-horror" that powers the best contemporary fiction of the dark fantastic. Indeed, with its undercurrent of violence and sexual tension, and its yearning for transformation and transcendence, *Darker than You Think* is a cornerstone for the bestselling work of writers from Clive Barker and Stephen King to Anne Rice and Peter Straub.

Order, Williamson reminds us, is the fantasy—and chaos, that presumed signifier of evil, is in fact the reality. The monstrous is not an invader from some other realm, an underworld or distant planet, but a part of the very impulse of being. It cannot be exorcised, at least not for long; and stories that suggest otherwise are more often than not escapist lies, useful only for lulling children—or ourselves—to sleep.

Why, gentlemen, is evil? The answer lies . . . within.

DOUGLAS E. WINTER
Oakton, Virginia
March 1999

DARKER THAN YOU THINK

1
The Girl in White Fur

The girl came up to Will Barbee while he stood outside of the glass-and-stucco terminal building at Trojan Field, Clarendon's new municipal airport, hopefully watching the leaden sky for a glimpse of the incoming planes. There was no reason for the sudden shiver that grated his teeth together—unless it was a fresh blast of the damp east wind. She looked as trimly cool and beautiful as a streamlined electric icebox.

She had a million dollars' worth of flame-red hair. White, soft, sweetly serious, her face confirmed his first dazzled impression—that she was something very wonderful and rare. She met his eyes, and her rather large mouth drew into a quick pleasant quirk.

Barbee turned to face her, breathless. He looked again into her gravely smiling eyes—they were really green. He searched her for the cause of that cold shudder of intuitive alarm, and became aware of an

1

equally illogical attraction—life had turned Barbee a little cynical toward women, and he liked to consider himself totally immune.

Her green gabardine business suit was modishly severe, plainly expensive, and cunningly chosen to accent the color of her eyes. Against the windy chill of this overcast October afternoon, she wore a short coat of some heavy white fur that he decided must be Arctic wolf—bleached, perhaps, or albino.

But the kitten *was* unusual.

She carried a snakeskin novelty bag, with the double handle over her arm, like two thick coils of a diamondback. The bag was open, like a flattened basket, and the kitten peered contentedly out of it. It was a perfectly darling little black kitten, less than half grown. It wore a wide red silk ribbon, neatly tied in a double bow.

They made a striking picture, but the kitten, blinking peacefully at the lights coming on in the cloudy dusk, just didn't seem to fit. The girl didn't look quite the type to shriek with delight over such a clever pet. And the slick chick she appeared to be, the chic young businesswoman, simply wouldn't include even the very cutest black kitten in her street ensemble.

He tried to forget that odd little shiver of alarm, and wondered how she knew him. Clarendon was not a large city, and reporters get around. That red hair was something you wouldn't forget. He looked again, to be sure her disturbing eyes were really fixed on him. They were.

"Barbee?"

Her voice was crisp and vigorous. The soft, throaty vitality of it was as exciting, somehow, as her hair and her eyes. Her manner remained casually impersonal.

"Will Barbee," he admitted. "Leg man for the *Clarendon Star.*"

More than ever interested, he enlarged upon that modest fact. Perhaps he hoped to discover the cause of his brief shiver. He didn't want her to go away.

"My editor wants two birds with one stone tonight," he told her. "The first is Colonel Walraven—twenty years since he wore the uniform, but still he likes the title. He has just quit a cushy berth in the Washington bureaucracy and come home to run for the senate. But he won't have much to say for the papers. Not till he sees Preston Troy."

The girl was still listening. The black kitten yawned at the lights flashing on, and the little crowd of waiting relatives and friends clustered along the steel-mesh barrier that kept the public off the field, and the white-clad attendants beyond, busy preparing to service the planes. But the girl's intense green eyes still watched his face, and her magical voice murmured softly:

"Who is your other bird?"

"A big one," Barbee said. "Dr. Lamarck Mondrick. Kingpin of the Humane Research Foundation, out by the university. He's due here tonight, on a chartered plane from the West Coast, with his little expedition. They've been to the Gobi—but probably you know all about them?"

"No." Something in her voice stirred his pulse. "What about them?"

"Archeologists," he said. "They had dug in Mongolia before the war. When the Japs surrendered, in '45, they cut all sorts of diplomatic red tape to get back again. Sam Quain, who is Mondrick's right hand man, had served on some war mission to China, and he knew the ropes. I don't know exactly what they went to look for, but it must be something special."

She looked interested, and he went on:

"They're our home-town boys, coming back tonight, after two years of perilous tangles with armies and bandits and sandstorms and scorpions, in darkest Mongolia. They're supposed to be bringing home something that will rock the world of archeology."

"And what would that be?"

"My job tonight is to find that out." Barbee still studied her with gray puzzled eyes. The black kitten blinked at him happily. Nothing about her explained that brief tingle of intuitive alarm. Her green-eyed smile seemed still aloofly impersonal, and he was afraid she would go away. Gulping, he asked desperately:

"Do I know you?"

"I'm a rival." She was suddenly less remote; her voice held a purring chuckle of friendliness. "April Bell, of the *Clarendon Call*." She showed him a tiny black notebook, palmed in her left hand. "I was warned to beware of you, Will Barbee."

"Oh." He grinned and nodded toward the little groups of passengers inside the glass front of the terminal building, waiting for the airliner. "I was afraid you had just stopped off, on your way back to Hollywood or Broadway. But you aren't really on the *Call*?"

He looked at that flame-colored hair, and shook his head in admiration.

"I'd have seen you."

"I'm new," she admitted. "In fact, I took my journalism degree just last summer. I only began Monday on the *Call*, and this is my first real assignment." Her voice was childishly confidential. "I'm afraid I'm pretty much a stranger in Clarendon, now—I was born here, but we went to California when I was still a little girl."

Her white teeth gleamed, in a smile innocently hopeful.

"I'm so new," she confided softly, "and I want so much to make good on the *Call*. I do want to turn in a good story on this Mondrick expedition. It all sounds so strange and thrilling, but I'm afraid I didn't learn many ologies in college. Would you mind, Barbee, if I ask you a few silly questions?"

Barbee was looking at her teeth. They were even and strong and very white—the sort of teeth with which beautiful women in dentifrice advertisements gnawed bones. It occurred to him that the spectacle of April Bell gnawing a red bone would be infinitely fascinating.

"Would you really mind?"

Barbee gulped and called back his thoughts. He grinned at her, beginning to understand. She was a fresh cub, new to the newspaper game—but clever as Lilith. The kitten was doubtless intended to complete a touching picture of helpless femininity, and annihilate any male resistance that her appealing eyes and devastating hair had failed to conquer.

"We're rivals, lady," he reminded her, as sternly as possible. Her look of hurt reproach tugged at him, but he kept the gruff abruptness in his voice. "And your name couldn't really be April Bell."

"It was Susan." Her greenish eyes turned dark, pleading hopefully. "But I think April will look so much nicer on my first by-line." Her voice was small and husky. "Please—about the expedition—Dr. Mondrick must be pretty important, if all the papers want a story on him?"

"He'll make good copy," Barbee agreed. "His whole expedition is only four men, and I'm sure they had quite an adventure, just getting to those sites in the desert and back again, in times like these. Sam Quain has Chinese friends, and they must have helped."

With a tiny fountain pen, she made flowing marks in the little black

4

notebook. The deft smooth grace of her white hands, oddly, made him think of some wild creature, unfettered and shy.

"Chinese friends," she murmured as she wrote, and looked up beseechingly. "Really, haven't you any idea what it is they're bringing back?"

"Not even a hint," he told her. "Somebody at the Foundation just called the *Star* this afternoon, and tipped us off that they'd be here in a chartered plane, by seven. The Foundation man said they'd have a hot story—some big scientific announcement. He wanted photographers, and scientific staff writers, but the *Star* doesn't go in for heavy science. I'm supposed to cover Walraven and the expedition, too."

He was trying to remember the name of a certain mythological lady. She had been fascinating—as lovely, no doubt, as April Bell. But, in the legend, she had a disturbing way of changing the men she fascinated into unpleasant beasts. What was her name—Circe?

Barbee hadn't spoken that name aloud—he was certain of it. But a quick, humorous quirk of the girl's red mouth, and a gleam of slightly malicious amusement in her eyes, gave him a brief, rattled impression that he had—though he didn't even know what had made him think of that mythical sorceress.

For an uncomfortable instant, he tried to unravel the association. He had read a little of Menninger and Freud, and sampled Frazer's *Golden Bough*. The symbolism of such folktales, he knew, expressed the fears and hopes of early man, and the notion popping into his own head must betray something about his own unconscious. Exactly what, he didn't want to know.

He laughed abruptly, and said: "I'll tell you anything I can—though I'll probably get it in the neck when Preston Troy reads my story in the *Call*, too. Or shall I write it out for you?"

"My shorthand is very good, thank you."

"Well, Dr. Mondrick was a big-shot anthropologist at Clarendon University, before he resigned, ten years ago, to establish his Foundation. He's not one of your narrow specialists, and he doesn't blow his own horn. But any of his associates will tell you that he's about the greatest all-around student of mankind in the world today. Biologist, psychologist, archeologist, sociologist, ethnologist—he seems to know everything that matters about his pet subject, mankind.

"Mondrick is the big shot of the Foundation. He raises the jack and spends it—without much publicity about the exact projects he's at work on. He led three expeditions to the Gobi, before the war interrupted, and then he rushed right back. The digs are in the Ala-shan section of the southwestern Gobi—just about the driest, meanest, hottest desert going."

"Go on," the girl prompted eagerly, pen poised above her tiny notebook. "Haven't you any idea what they're after?"

"We start even there—and the best man wins!" Barbee grinned. "But, whatever it is, Mondrick has been after it for twenty years. He organized the Foundation, just to find it. It's his life work, and the life work of such a man is apt to be important."

The little groups of spectators stirred expectantly outside the steel fence, and a small boy pointed excitedly into the gray overcast. The damp wind shuddered to the drum of mighty motors. Barbee looked at his watch.

"Five forty," he told the girl. "The airliner isn't due till six, the dispatcher says. So this must be Mondrick's plane coming in early."

"Already?" Greenish eyes shining, she seemed almost as breathless as the pointing boy. But she watched him, not the sky. "You know the others?" she asked. "The men with Mondrick?"

A flood of memories slowed Barbee's reply. His mind saw three once-familiar faces, and the murmur of the waiting crowd became the haunting echo of once-known voices, ringing down the years. He nodded, a little sadly.

"Yes, I know them."

"Then tell me."

April Bell's crisp voice broke his brief reverie. She waited, with her quick pen ready. He knew he shouldn't spill all his background material to a rival from the *Call*, but her hair was sullen flame, and the dark warmth of her oddly long eyes thawed his reluctance.

"The three men who went back to Mongolia with Mondrick in '45 are Sam Quain and Nick Spivak and Rex Chittum. They're the oldest friends I have. We were all freshmen together at the university, while Mondrick still was teaching there. Sam and I boarded two years at Mondrick's house, and afterwards the four of us were all suitemates in Trojan Hall on the campus. We all took Mondrick's courses, and—well—you see—"

Barbee stammered, and halted awkwardly. An old pain awakened, throbbing at his throat.

"Go on," whispered April Bell, and the quick flash of her sympathetic smile made him resume.

"Mondrick was already gathering his disciples, you see. He must already have planned this Research Foundation, though he didn't organize it until after I graduated. I believe he was picking men, then, to train for this search in the Gobi, for whatever it is."

Something made him gulp.

"Anyway, we all took his courses—in what he called the 'humane sciences.' We worshipped him. He got scholarships for us, and gave us all the special help he could, and took us with him on his summer field trips to Central America and Peru."

The girl's eyes were uncomfortably penetrating.

"What happened to you, Barbee?"

"I was somehow left out," he admitted awkwardly. "I never quite knew why—because the same bug had bitten me. I loved all the work, and my grades were higher than Sam's. I'd have given my right arm to be with them on the first dig in the Gobi."

"What happened?" the girl insisted, without mercy.

"I never knew." He swallowed hard. "Something turned Mondrick against me—I never knew what. At the end of our senior year, Mondrick was giving us all inoculations and blood-group tests, to get us ready for another field trip. He called me into the lab, one day, and told me not to plan on going."

"But why?" the girl whispered.

"He wouldn't say why." Barbee spoke huskily, wincing from that old injury. "Of course he saw how hurt I was, but he wouldn't explain. He just turned gruff—as if the thing hurt him too—and promised to help me get any other job I wanted. That was when I went to work on the *Star*."

"And your friends went on to Mongolia?"

"That same summer," Barbee said. "With the first Foundation expedition."

Her green eyes searched him.

"But still," she said, "the four of you are friends?"

He nodded, faintly puzzled.

"Yes, we're friends. I felt a little bitter toward old Mondrick because he wouldn't tell me why he didn't want me. But I never had any quarrel at all with Sam and Nick and Rex. They're okay. Just the same, every time I run across them. The Four Muleteers, Sam used to call us, when we made those muleback summer jaunts into Mexico and Guatemala and Peru. If Mondrick ever told them why he kicked me out, they never spoke about it."

Barbee looked uncomfortably past the girl's bright hair into the cold leaden dusk that now was throbbing to the engines of the unseen plane.

"They didn't change," he said. "But of course we drifted apart. Mondrick was training them into a team of specialists in different departments of his 'humane sciences'—grooming them to look for that something in the Ala-shan. They didn't have much time for me."

Barbee caught his breath.

"Miss Bell," he demanded abruptly, to end that aching memory of old defeat, "how did you know my name?"

Her eyes lit with a teasing mockery.

"Perhaps that was just a hunch."

Barbee shivered again. He knew that he himself possessed what he called the "nose for news"—an intuitive perception of human motivations and the impending events that would spring from them. It wasn't a faculty he could analyze or account for, but he knew that it wasn't unusual. Most successful reporters possessed it, he believed—even though, in an age of skepticism for everything except mechanistic materialism, they wisely denied it.

That dim sense had been useful to him—on those summer field trips, before Mondrick turned him out, it had led him to more than one promising prehistoric site, simply because he somehow knew where a band of wild hunters would prefer to camp or to dig a comrade's grave.

Commonly, however, that uncontrolled faculty had been more curse than blessing. It made him too keenly aware of all that people thought and did around him, kept him troubled with an uneasy alertness. Except when he was drunk. He drank too much, and knew that many other newsmen did. That vague sensitivity, he believed, was half the reason.

That same formless intuition, perhaps, could account for his brief shudder at the first glimpse of April Bell—though nothing about her long, warm eyes and flame-colored hair seemed at all alarming now.

And her own hunch about his name wasn't completely surprising—except that it went too far.

A good deal too far. Barbee grinned at her and tried to relax that instinctive alarm. Doubtless her own editor had briefed her on the story he expected her to get and told her how to get it. Probably she was tantalizing men with her own irresistible mixture of wide-eyed innocence and guile. The strangest incongruity always had a sane explanation, if only you could find it.

"Now—please, Barbee—who are they?"

Her red head nodded eagerly toward a little group filing out of the terminal building, beyond the steel barrier. A thin little wisp of a man gestured excitedly toward the dull, thrumming sky. A tiny child cried to see, and her mother took her up. A tall blind woman came behind, guided by the leash of a huge tawny German shepherd.

"If you have such wonderful hunches," Barbee retorted, "why ask me?"

The girl smiled repentently.

"I'm sorry, Barbee. It's true I just came back, but I do have old friends in Clarendon, and my editor told me you used to work with Mondrick. These people must be waiting to welcome the expedition home. I'm sure you know them. May we talk to them?"

"If you like." Barbee didn't want to resist. "Come along."

Her arm slipped through his. Even white fur, where it touched his wrist, felt somehow electric. This girl did things to him. He had believed himself impervious to women; but her warm allure, balanced with that queer, lingering sense of unease, disturbed him more deeply than he wanted her to guess.

He guided her through the terminal building, pausing beside a clattering teletype machine to ask the busy dispatcher:

"Is that the Mondrick plane?"

"In the pattern, Barbee." The dispatcher nodded, frowning at a wind indicator. "Landing on instruments."

Still he couldn't see the plane, however, when they came outside again to the edge of the taxiway, and the drum of it seemed fainter in the gloomy murk.

"Well, Barbee." The girl nodded hopefully toward the people waiting. "Who are they?"

Barbee wondered what made his voice unsteady.

9

"The tall woman with the dog," he began. "The one standing there alone, with the black glasses and the lonely face. She's Dr. Mondrick's wife. A lovely, gracious person. A gifted pianist, even though she's blind. She has been a friend of mine ever since the two years Sam Quain and I lived in her house when we were in the university. I'll introduce you."

"So that's Rowena Mondrick?" Her voice seemed hushed, oddly intense. "She wears strange jewelry."

Puzzled, Barbee glanced back at the blind woman who stood very straight, silent and lonely and aloof. As always, she wore plain black. It took him a moment to see her jewels, simply because he knew them so well. Smiling, he turned to April Bell.

"That silver, you mean?"

The girl nodded, her eyes fixed on the old silver combs in Rowena Mondrick's thick white hair, the silver brooch at the throat of the black dress, the heavy silver bracelets, and the worn silver rings on the white and youthful-seeming hands that held the dog. Even the dog's leather collar was heavy with massive silver studs.

"It's odd, perhaps," Barbee agreed. "Though it never struck me that way, because Rowena loves silver. She says she likes the cool feel of it. Touch, you know, is important to her." He looked at the girl's set face. "What's the matter? Don't you like it?"

Her burnished head shook slightly.

"No," she whispered solemnly, "I don't like silver." She smiled at him quickly as if in apology for her long stare. "Forgive me. I've heard of Rowena Mondrick. Will you tell me about her?"

"I think she was a psychiatric nurse at Glennhaven when she met Dr. Mondrick," Barbee said. "That was probably thirty years ago. She was a brilliant girl and she must have been beautiful then. Mondrick rescued her from some unhappy love affair—I never heard the details of that—and got her interested in his work."

Watching the blind woman again, the girl listened silently.

"She went to Mondrick's classes and became an able ethnologist herself," Barbee went on. "She used to go with him on all his expeditions until she lost her sight. Since, for the last twenty years or so, she has lived very quietly here in Clarendon. She has her music, and a few close friends. I don't think she takes any more part in her

10

husband's researches. Most people consider her a little odd—and I suppose that was a dreadful experience."

"Tell me about it," the girl commanded.

"They were in West Africa," Barbee said slowly, thinking wistfully of the other days when he had been on expeditions to search for lost fragments of the puzzle of the past. "I think Dr. Mondrick was hunting proof of a notion that modern man first evolved in Africa—that was long before he found those sites in the Ala-shan. Rowena was taking the chance to gather some ethnological data on the Nigerian tribal societies of human alligators and human leopards."

"Human leopards?" The girl's greenish eyes seemed to narrow and turn darker. "What are they?"

"Only the members of a secret cannibalistic cult, who are supposed to be able to turn themselves into leopards." Barbee smiled at her taut intentness. "You see, Rowena was preparing to write a paper on lycanthropy—that's the common belief among primitive tribes that certain individuals are able to transform themselves into carnivorous animals."

"Is that so?" the girl whispered breathlessly. "Tell me!"

"The animals are usually the most dangerous ones found in the locality," Barbee went on, eager to keep her interested and glad to find some use at last for the dry facts he had learned in Mondrick's classes. "Bears in the north countries. Jaguars in the Amazon basin. Wolves in Europe—the peasants of medieval France lived in terror of the *loup-garou*. Leopards or tigers in Africa and Asia. I don't know how the belief could have spread so widely."

"Very interesting." The girl smiled obliquely, as if in secret satisfaction. "But what happened to Rowena Mondrick's eyes?"

"She would never talk about it." Barbee lowered his voice, afraid the blind woman might hear. "Dr. Mondrick told me all I know—once we were talking in his study, before he fell out with me."

"Well, what did he say?"

"They were camped deep in Nigeria," Barbee said. "I believe Rowena was looking for data to connect the human leopards of the cannibal tribes with the leopard familiars of the Lhota Naga medicine men of Assam and the 'bush soul' of certain American tribes."

"Yes," the girl whispered.

"Anyhow, Rowena had been trying to get the confidence of the natives and asking questions about their rituals—too many questions, Mondrick said, because their bearers got uneasy and one of them warned her to look out for the leopard men. She kept on, and her investigations led her to a valley that was taboo. She found artifacts there that interested Mondrick—he didn't say what they were—and they were moving camp into that valley when it happened."

"How?"

"They were on the trail at night, when a black leopard jumped on Rowena out of a tree—it was actually a leopard, Mondrick said, and not a native in a leopard skin. But I guess the coincidence was a little too much for the native bearers. They all lit out, and the beast had Rowena down before Mondrick's shots frightened it away. Her wounds were infected, of course, and I think she very nearly died before he got her back to any sort of hospital.

"That was her last expedition with him, and he never went back to Africa—I believe he gave up the idea that Homo sapiens originated there. After that, do you think it's any wonder if she seems a little strange? The leopard's attack was so tragically ironic—huh?"

Glancing at the taut white face of April Bell, he had caught an expression that shocked him—a look of burning, cruel elation. Or had the gray dusk and the harsh light from the building merely played an unkind trick with her unusual features? She smiled at his startled grunt.

"It does seem ironic," she whispered lightly, as if not much concerned about Rowena Mondrick's old disaster. "Life plays queer tricks sometimes." Her voice turned grave. "It must have been a dreadful blow."

"It was, I know." Barbee felt relieved at her solicitude. "But it didn't break Rowena. She's a charming person, really. No self-pity. She has a sense of humor, and you soon forget she's blind."

He caught the girl's arm, feeling the sleek softness of that snowy fur. The black kitten blinked at him with huge blue eyes from the snakeskin bag.

"Come along," he urged. "You'll like Rowena."

April Bell hung back.

"No, Barbee!" she whispered desperately. "Please don't—"

But he was already calling heartily:

"Rowena! It's Will Barbee. The paper sent me down to get a story on your husband's expedition, and now I want you to meet my newest friend—a very charming redhead—Miss April Bell."

The blind woman turned eagerly at the sound of his voice. Nearing sixty, Mondrick's wife preserved a youthful slenderness. The thick coils of her hair had been entirely white since Barbee first knew her; but her face, flushed now with excitement and the cold, seemed firm and pink as a girl's. Used to them, Barbee scarcely saw her opaque black glasses.

"Why, hello, Will." Her musical voice was warm with pleasure. "It's good to know your friends." Shifting the dog's short leash to her left hand, she held out the right. "How do you do, Miss April Bell?"

"Very well." The girl's voice was sweetly remote, and she made no move to take the blind woman's extended hand. "Thank you."

Flushed with embarrassment for Rowena, Barbee tugged sharply at the girl's fur sleeve. She jerked stiffly away. He peered at her face and saw that her cheeks had drained colorless, leaving her lips a wide red slash. Narrowed and darkened, her greenish eyes were staring at Rowena's thick silver bracelets. Nervously, Barbee tried to save the situation.

"Careful what you say," he warned Rowena with attempted lightness. "Because Miss Bell is working for the *Call*, and she'll put every word down in shorthand."

The blind woman smiled, to Barbee's relief, as if unaware of April Bell's puzzling rudeness. Tilting her head to listen again at the whispering sky, she asked anxiously:

"Aren't they down?"

"Not yet," Barbee told her. "But the dispatcher says they're in the landing pattern."

"I'll be so glad when they're down safe," she told him uneasily. "I've been so dreadfully worried, ever since Marck went away. He isn't well, and he insists on taking such frightful risks."

Her thin hands quivered, Barbee noticed, and clutched the dog's short leash with a desperate tenseness that turned the knuckles white.

"Some buried things ought to stay buried," she whispered. "I tried to get Marck not to go back to those digs in the Ala-shan. I was afraid of what he would find."

April Bell was listening intently, and Barbee heard the catch of her breath.

13

"You," she whispered, "afraid?" Her pen shuddered above the tiny notebook. "What did you expect your famous husband to find?"

"Nothing!" The blind woman gasped the word, as if alarmed. "Nothing, really."

"Tell me," the girl insisted sharply. "You may as well, because I believe I can already guess—"

Her low voice broke into a stifled scream, and she stumbled backward. For the shepherd's leash had slipped out of the blind woman's fingers. Silently, the huge dog lunged at the cowering girl. Barbee kicked desperately, but it rushed past him, fangs bared viciously.

Barbee spun, snatching for the dragging leash. The girl had thrown up her arms instinctively. Her snake-skin bag, flung out in an accidental arc, fended the slashing jaws from her throat. Savagely silent, the animal tried to spring again, but Barbee had caught the leash.

"Turk!" Rowena called. "Turk, to heel."

Obediently, still without a growl or bark, the big dog trotted toward her. Barbee put the leash back in her groping hand, and she drew the bristling animal to her side.

"Thank you, Will," she said quietly. "I hope Turk didn't hurt your Miss Bell. Please tell her that I'm extremely sorry."

But she didn't scold the dog, Barbee noticed. The huge tawny beast stood close against her black skirt, snarling silently, watching April Bell with baleful eyes. Pale and shaken, the girl was retreating toward the terminal building.

"That nasty dog!" A sallow, sharp-featured little woman came back from the group ahead, scolding in a plaintive nasal whine. "Now remember, Mrs. Mondrick, I begged you not to bring him. He's getting ugly, and he'll hurt somebody."

Calmly, the blind woman stroked the dog's head. She caught the wide collar with a small deft hand, gently fingering the heavy silver studs. Rowena, Barbee recalled, had always loved silver.

"No, Miss Ulford," she murmured softly. "Turk was trained to guard me, and I want him with me always. He'll not attack anybody, unless they're trying to harm me." She listened to the throbbing sky again. "Isn't the plane down yet?"

Barbee had seen no threatening gesture from April Bell. Shocked

14

and puzzled by Rowena's behavior, he hurried back to the red-haired girl. Standing beside the glass door of the bright-lit waiting room, she was caressing the black kitten, murmuring softly:

"Be still, darling. That big, bad dog doesn't like us, but we needn't be afraid—"

"I'm sorry, Miss Bell," Barbee said awkwardly. "I didn't know that would happen."

"My fault, Barbee." She smiled at him contritely. "I shouldn't have taken poor little Fifi so near that evil brute of a dog." Her greenish eyes glowed. "Thank you so much for pulling him off me."

"Turk never acted that way before," he said. "Mrs. Mondrick wants to apologize—"

"Does she?" April Bell glanced obliquely at the blind woman, her long eyes quite expressionless. "Let's forget the incident," she said briskly. "The plane's coming in, and I want you to tell me about those others waiting."

She nodded eagerly at the little group beyond the blind woman, all hopefully watching the low, ragged cloud bases that now began to glow with a soiled pink from the reflected lights of the city.

"Okay." Barbee was glad to ignore that awkward and somewhat baffling occurrence. "The sharp-nosed little woman who came back to Rowena is her nurse, Miss Ulford. She's the one that's usually ailing, though, and Rowena actually does most of the nursing."

"And the others?"

"See the old gent just lighting his pipe—only he's too excited to get the match struck? That's old Ben Chittum. Rex's granddad, and the only relative he has. Runs a newsstand down on Center Street, just across from the *Star* building. He put Rex through school, until Mondrick got him that scholarship."

"And the rest?"

"The little fellow in the long overcoat is Nick Spivak's father. The proud-looking, dark-haired woman is Mrs. Spivak. They have a tailor shop in Brooklyn, on Flatbush Avenue. Nick's the only son. He's got over saying 'woik' and 'goil,' but he still thinks the world of them. They've been awfully upset ever since Nick went back with the expedition. They must have written me a dozen letters, wanting to know if I had heard anything. They came down to meet Nick on the morning plane. I suppose he wired them from the coast.

"Most of the others are friends, and people from the Foundation. There's Professor Fisher, from the anthropology department at the university. And Dr. Bennett, who has been in charge out at the Foundation—"

"Who's the blonde?" interrupted April Bell. "Smiling at you."

"Nora," Barbee said softly. "Sam Quain's wife."

He had first met Nora the same night Sam did—at the freshman mixer during registration week at Clarendon. Fourteen years hadn't dimmed the friendly sparkle of her eyes; the smiling matron now, he thought, waiting for her husband, looked as happily breathless as that slim girl had been, excited over the bright new world of the university.

Barbee started toward her with April Bell, circling cautiously wide of Rowena Mondrick's watchful dog. Nora glanced hopefully again at the murmuring clouds and came to meet them, leading little Pat.

Patricia Quain had just turned five years old and was very proud of that accomplishment. She had her mother's wide blue eyes and cornsilk hair, but her pink stubborn face showed a reflection of Sam's square chin. She was tugging back, peering hungrily into the darkening sky.

"Will Daddy be safe, up there in the cold night?"

"Of course, darling. Nothing could happen to them now." But Nora's warm voice was not so cheerful as she tried to make it, and she called anxiously: "Do you think they'll be much longer, Will? We can hardly wait. I made the mistake of looking up the Ala-shan country in Sam's library, and after that I could hardly sleep. Two years is such a long time. I'm afraid Pat won't know her father."

"Yes, I will, Mother." The child's firm voice showed Sam's own determination. "I'll know my own Daddy."

"There!" Barbee heard the bark of wheels scuffing the runway. The anxious tension of those breathless watchers had got into him, and he smiled at Nora, sharing her glad relief. "They're down safe, and they'll taxi in now."

Holding the girl's fur sleeve, he glanced watchfully at Rowena Mondrick's great dog, standing against his mistress and glaring ominously at April and the blue-eyed kitten.

"Nora, this is Miss April Bell. She's learning to be a sob sister on the *Call*. Anything you tell her may be quoted against you."

"Really, Barbee!"

April made that protest with a charming little laugh. When the eyes of the two women met, however, Barbee sensed fire—something like the sudden shower of sparks when hard metal meets the grinding wheel. Smiling with angelic sweetness, they shook hands.

"Darling! I'm so happy to meet you."

They hated each other, Barbee knew, savagely.

"Mother!" little Pat cried eagerly. "May I touch the dear little kitten?"

"No, honey—please!"

Nora caught hastily at the child, but her small pink hand was already reaching eagerly. The black kitten blinked and spat and scratched. With a sob of pain, that she stubbornly tried to stifle, Pat drew back to her mother.

"Oh, Mrs. Quain," purred April Bell. "I'm so sorry."

"I don't like you," Pat declared defiantly.

"Look!" Old Ben Chittum limped past them, pointing with his pipe into the gloomy dusk, shrill with excitement. "There's the plane, rolling down the taxi-strip."

The Spivaks ran after him.

"It's our Nick, Mama! Our Nick—safe at home from that cruel desert across the sea."

"Come on, Mother." Pat tugged impatiently at Nora's hand. "Daddy's back—and I will too know him."

Rowena Mondrick followed that breathless group, proud and straight and silent. She seemed entirely alone, even though little Miss Ulford held her arm to guide her and the huge tawny dog stalked stiffly at her side. Barbee glimpsed her face under the opaque black lenses, and its white agony of hope and terror made him look hastily aside.

He was left with April Bell.

"Fifi, you were very naughty!" She patted the kitten reprovingly. "You spoiled our interview."

Barbee felt an impulse to follow Nora and explain that April Bell was a stranger. He still had a tender spot for Nora—sometimes he wondered, wistfully, how different life might have been if he and not Sam Quain had drawn her to be his partner at that freshman mixer. But April's long eyes smiled again, and her voice chimed contritely:

"I'm sorry, Barbee—truly I am."

"That's all right," Barbee told her. "But how come the kitten?"

Her eyes turned greenish black again, strangely intense, as if some secret fear had dilated the pupils. For an instant he glimpsed a wary alertness, as if she were playing an obscurely difficult and dangerous game. He didn't understand that. A cub reporter, of course, might be jittery about her first big assignment. But April Bell seemed too briskly competent to suffer any such misgivings, and the thing he glimpsed was something more than mere timidity. It was desperate, deadly.

Barbee recoiled a little from that look of fearful searching. After the briefest instant, however, the girl's white, frozen face came alive again. She straightened the kitten's red ribbon, and smiled at him warmly.

"Fifi belongs to my Aunt Agatha," she cooed brightly. "I live with her, you know, and she came out with me today. Auntie went shopping with the car and left Fifi with me. She's to meet me in the waiting room. Excuse me, and I'll see if she's come—and get rid of the little beast before it makes another scene."

She hurried away from him, into the bright-lit building. Barbee looked after her, through the glass doors, with a puzzled and uneasy interest. Even the lithe free grace of her walk fascinated him. She seemed untamed.

Barbee tried to shrug off that vague conflict of attraction and formless apprehension, and followed Nora Quain to the little group watching the chartered transport roaring toward them on the taxi-strip, huge and ungainly in the gloom. He was tired, and probably he had been drinking more than was good for him. His nerves seemed on edge. It was only natural for him to feel a strong response to such a girl as April Bell. What man wouldn't? But he resolved to control that reaction.

Nora Quain turned her attention from the incoming plane long enough to ask him:

"Is that girl important?"

"Just met her." Barbee hesitated, wondering. "She's . . . unusual."

"Don't let her be important," Nora urged quickly. "She is—"

She paused as if to find a word for April Bell. The warm smile left her face, and her hand moved unconsciously to draw little Pat to her side. She didn't find the word.

"Don't, Will!" she whispered. "Please!"

The engines of the taxiing transport drowned her voice.

2
The Kitten Killing

Two white-uniformed attendants were waiting with a wheeled gangway to land the incoming passengers. The big transport, however, looming dark and monstrous in the floodlights on the field, stopped a full hundred yards from the terminal building. The great motors died in a silence that seemed breathless.

"Marck!" In that sudden stillness the voice of Mondrick's blind wife was a thin, frantic cry. "Can anybody see Marck?"

Old Ben Chittum led the eager rush toward the transport, waving his pipe wildly and shouting unanswered greetings to his son. Papa and Mama Spivak ran behind him, calling for Nick, and burst into tears when their son didn't appear. Nora Quain picked up the toddling child and held her apprehensively tight.

Rowena Mondrick was left behind, with her huge dog and the bewildered-looking little nurse. The dog had ceased to bristle, with

April Bell's departure. It glanced at Barbee with friendly golden eyes, and then ignored him.

"The plane stopped pretty far out," he told Rowena. "I don't know why. But Dr. Mondrick and the others should be out to meet us in a moment."

"Thank you, Will." She smiled toward him gratefully, her face turning smooth and youthful again for an instant under the blank lenses, before her bleak unease came back. "I'm so afraid for Marck!"

"I can understand that," Barbee murmured. "Sam Quain told me about the Ala-shan—a desert that makes Death Valley look like a green oasis, so I gather. And I know Dr. Mondrick's health isn't good—"

"No, Will, it's nothing like that." Her thin, straight shoulders shrugged uneasily. "Marck does have that trick heart, and his asthma seems worse every year. But he's still vigorous, and he knows his deserts. It isn't that at all."

Her small hands tightened on the shepherd's leash, and Barbee thought they shuddered. She drew the huge dog to her again. Her light fingers moved quickly over its fine tawny head, and then dwelt upon the polished silver studs that knobbed its collar, as if she found a sensuous pleasure in feeling the cold white metal.

"I used to work with Marck, you know," she whispered slowly. "Before I saw too much." Her thin left hand came quickly up, as if moved with an unforgotten horror, to cover for an instant her dark lenses and the empty scars behind them. "I know what his theory is, and what Sam Quain found for him under that old burial mound in the Ala-shan on the last expedition before the war. That's why I tried to persuade him not to go back."

She turned abruptly, listening.

"Now where are they, Will?" Apprehension breathed in her low voice. "Why don't they come?"

"I don't know," Barbee told her, himself uneasy. "I don't understand it. The plane's just standing, waiting. They've put the gangway against it, and now they're opening the door, but nobody comes out. There's Dr. Bennett, the Foundation man, going aboard."

"He'll find out." Holding fast to the dog, Rowena turned back toward the terminal building, listening again. "Where's that girl?" Alarm edged her whisper. "The one Turk chased away."

"Inside," Barbee said. "I'm sorry anything unpleasant happened.

April's charming, and I hoped you'd like her. Really, Rowena, I couldn't see any reason—"

"But there is a reason." The blind woman stiffened, her face taut and pale. "Turk didn't like her." She was patting the huge dog's head; Barbee saw its intelligent yellow eyes look warily toward the building, as if alert against April Bell's return. "And Turk knows."

"Now, Rowena," Barbee protested. "Aren't you carrying your trust in Turk a little too far?"

Her blind lenses stared at him, somehow ominous.

"Marck trained Turk to guard me," she insisted solemnly. "He attacked that woman because he knows she's . . . bad." Her taut fingers quivered on the silver-knobbed collar. "Remember that, Will!" she begged huskily. "I'm sure that girl would be charming—very. But Turk can tell."

Barbee stepped back uncomfortably. He wondered if the black leopard's claws, ripping out her sight, had left unhealed mental scars as well. Rowena's apprehensions seemed somewhat beyond the rational. He was glad to see the gangling figure of the Foundation manager coming back down the steps from the silent plane.

"There's Bennett," he said. "I suppose the others will come off with him."

Rowena caught her breath, and they waited silently. Barbee watched to see Sam Quain's bronzed head, his blue-eyed face. He looked for Nick Spivak, dark and slight, frowning wistfully through his glasses and moving always with a nervous haste, as if knowledge had almost eluded his zealous pursuit; and he pictured Rex Chittum, who for all his scholarship still appeared as robustly ignorant as another Li'l Abner. His mind saw old Mondrick himself, ruddy and stout and bald, chin massively aggressive and mild eyes distant with rapt preoccupations.

But they didn't come.

"Where's Marck?" Rowena whispered sharply. "And the others?"

"I don't see them." Barbee tried not to sound uneasy. "And Bennett seems to be shooing everybody away from the plane. Now he's coming this way."

"Dr. Bennett?" Her piercing call startled Barbee. "What's keeping Marck?"

Striding back toward the terminal building, the gaunt scientist paused. Barbee could see the lines of worry bitten into his frowning face, but his voice was reassuring.

"They're all safe, Mrs. Mondrick," he told her. "They're getting ready to come off the plane, but I'm afraid there'll be a little delay."

"Delay?" gasped Rowena. "Why?"

"Dr. Mondrick has this announcement, on the results of the expedition," Bennett said patiently. "I gather that his finds were extremely important, and he wishes to make them public before he leaves the field."

"Oh—no!" Rowena's pale left hand flashed fearfully to her throat, the light glowing cold on her paler silver rings and bracelets. "He mustn't!" she sobbed. "They won't let him."

Bennett frowned with momentary puzzlement.

"I can't see why there should be so much fuss about any research announcement," he said briskly. "But I assure you that you needn't worry over any possible danger, Mrs. Mondrick. The doctor appears rather unduly concerned about some trouble—precisely what, I didn't gather. He has asked me to send for a police escort to guard his person and his finds until the announcement is safely made."

Rowena shook her proud head, as if in fearful scorn of police protection.

"Don't you worry, Mrs. Mondrick," Bennett insisted. "Your husband told me what to do, and I'll take care of everything. I'll arrange for the press to meet him as he steps off the plane. All the reporters will be searched for weapons, and there'll be police enough to stop any possible attempt at interference."

"They can do nothing!" the blind woman snapped bitterly. "Please go back and tell Marck—"

"I'm sorry, Mrs. Mondrick," Bennett broke in with veiled impatience. "But the doctor told me what he wants, and the arrangements must be made at once. He asked me to hurry—as if he feels there is danger in delay."

"There is." She nodded bleakly, clutching the dog's collar. "Go on!"

The frowning Foundation man strode on toward the terminal building, and Barbee fell in step beside him, angling hopefully:

"Clarendon's such a peaceful little city, Dr. Bennett—what sort of trouble do you suppose Mondrick could expect?"

"Don't ask me," Bennett rapped. "And don't you try to beat the gun.

Dr. Mondrick doesn't want any premature leaks, or any fantastic journalistic guesses. He says this is a big thing, and he wants the people to get it straight. The *Life* photographers and the AP staffers should be here now, and I'm trying to get a radio reporter. Everybody will get an even break on the hottest story of the year."

"Maybe," Barbee murmured silently, for he had learned to be cynical about elaborate press releases. He would wait and see. Strolling through the terminal building, he glimpsed April Bell's vivid hair in a phone booth. Nobody in sight looked like her Aunt Agatha, and he reminded himself to be skeptical of women, too.

He drank two cups of hot coffee at the lunch counter in the waiting room; but the chill in him came from something colder than the raw east wind, and it was still unthawed when a croaking loudspeaker announced the arrival of the regular airliner. He hurried out to catch Walraven.

The airliner taxied on past the dark transport where Mondrick waited, to stop opposite the terminal building. Two or three businessmen got off, and a dreamily sedate honeymoon couple. Walraven strutted heavily down the steps at last, his brassy voice booming impressively as he told the pert little air hostess about his contacts in Washington.

Walraven struck an inflated pose for the *Star* photographer, but he wouldn't be quoted on anything when Barbee tried to interview him. Off the record, he was planning a strategy conference with his great good friend, Preston Troy. He asked Barbee to stop at his old law office for a drink just any time, but he had nothing for the record. He tried to push his weak chin out again for the photographer, and got into a taxi.

Preston Troy would supply the strategy, Barbee knew, and hire somebody to write suitable words for the record. The truth about Walraven, as the empty false front for Troy's own political ambitions, would make real news. But not for the *Star*. Barbee let him go and hurried back to Mondrick's transport.

"Mama, I'm afraid!" He heard the high voice of little Pat Quain from the uneasy waiting group, and saw her held close in Nora's arms. "What has happened to my Daddy?"

"Sam's all right." Nora didn't sound too sure. "Just wait, dear."

Three police cars had pulled up outside the steel fence. Half a dozen uniformed men were already escorting the impatient reporters and photographers toward the huge chartered plane, and two of them turned to herd back the anxious relatives and friends.

"Please, officer!" Rowena Mondrick sounded almost frantic. "You must let me stay. Marck's my husband, and he's in danger. I must be near, to help him."

"Sorry, Mrs. Mondrick." The police sergeant was professionally firm. "But we'll protect your husband—not that I see any cause for all this alarm. The Foundation has asked us to clear the field. Everybody except the press and radio people will have to move back."

"No!" she cried sharply. "Please—you can't understand!"

The officer took her arm.

"Sorry," he said. "Please come quietly."

"You don't know anything," she whispered bitterly. "You can't help—"

Firmly, the officer led her away.

"Please stay, Mother," little Pat was whispering stubbornly. "I want to see my Daddy—and I will too know him."

Herself as pale as the frightened child, Nora Quain carried her back toward the lights of the terminal building. Mama Spivak uttered a low wailing cry and began to sob on the little tailor's shoulder. Old Ben Chittum shook his black pipe in the other policeman's face, quavering hotly:

"Look here, officer. I've been praying two years for my boy to get back alive from them dern deserts. And the Spivaks here have spent more than they could really afford to ride the planes all the way down from New York City. By golly, officer—"

Barbee caught his indignant arm.

"Better wait, Ben."

The old man limped after the others, muttering and scowling. Barbee showed his press credentials, submitted to a swift search for concealed arms, and joined the reporters gathered beneath the vast wing of the transport. He found April Bell beside him.

The black kitten must have been returned to Aunt Agatha, after all, for the snakeskin bag was closed now. Pale and breathless, the girl was watching the high door of the plane with a feverish-seeming intentness. She seemed to start when she became aware of Barbee's glance. Her flaming head had turned to him abruptly. For an instant, he thought he could feel the tense, desperate readiness of some feral thing, crouched to leap. Then she smiled, her long, greenish eyes turning warm and gay.

"Hi, reporter." Her soft voice was comradely. "Looks like we've got ourselves a page-one story. Here they come!"

Sam Quain led the way down the gangway. Even in that first breathless instant, Barbee saw that he had changed. His square-jawed face was burned dark, his blond hair bleached almost white. He must have shaved aboard, but his worn khakis were wrinkled and soiled. He looked tired and somewhat more than two years older.

And there was something else.

That something else was stamped also upon the three men who followed him down the wheeled steps. Barbee wondered if they had all been ill. Dr. Mondrick's pale heavy face, under the stained and battered tropical helmet, sagged shockingly. Perhaps that old asthma was troubling him again, or that trick heart.

Even very ill men might have been smiling, Barbee thought uneasily, upon the moment of this triumphant return to their country and their friends and their wives, with a great work accomplished. But all of these weary, haggard men looked grimly preoccupied. None of them spared a wave or a smile for those who met them.

Nick Spivak and Rex Chittum came down from the transport behind old Mondrick. They also wore wrinkled, sun-bleached khaki, and they were lean and brown and grave. Rex must have heard old Ben Chittum's quavering hail from the guarded group at the terminal building, but he gave no sign.

For he and Nick were burdened. They carried, between them, a green-painted rectangular wooden box, lifting it by two riveted leather handles. Barbee thought it showed the careful workmanship of some simple craftsman in a remote village bazaar. Thick iron straps bound it, and a heavy padlock secured the hand-forged hasp. The two weary men leaned against its weight.

"Careful!" Barbee heard Mondrick's warning voice. "We can't lose it now."

Nervously, the haggard-cheeked anthropologist reached to steady the box. His attention didn't leave it until the men carrying it were safely down the steps. Even then, he kept his hand on it as he nodded for them to bring it on toward the waiting reporters.

These men were afraid.

Every wary movement whispered out their abiding terror. They were not elated victors returning to announce a new conquest at the dark frontier of the known. They were tight-lipped veterans instead, Barbee felt, calmly disciplined, moving steadily into a desperate action.

"I wonder—?" whispered April Bell, her long eyes narrowed and dark. "I wonder what they really found?"

"Whatever it is," breathed Barbee, "the find doesn't seem to have made them very happy. A fundamentalist might think they had stumbled into hell."

"No," the girl said, "men aren't that much afraid of hell."

Barbee saw Sam Quain's eyes upon him. The curious tension of that moment checked his impulse to shout a greeting. He merely waved his hand. Sam nodded slightly. That desperate, hostile alertness didn't leave his dark, hard face.

Mondrick stopped before the waiting photographers, under the plane's long wing. Flashbulbs flickered in the windy gloom as he waited for the younger men to close in beside him and set down the heavy box. Barbee studied his face, revealed by the pitiless flashes.

Mondrick, he saw, was a shattered man. Sam and Nick and Rex were tough. That burden of dread, whatever its origin, had merely drawn and sobered and hardened them. But Mondrick was broken. His weary, unsteady gesture betrayed nerves worn beyond the point of failure, and his sagging face was haunted.

"Gentlemen, thank you for waiting."

His voice was low and hoarse, ragged. Dazzled from the flashbulbs, his sunken eyes roved fearfully across the faces before him and flickered apprehensively toward the waiting people beyond the two policemen, outside the terminal building. He must have seen his blind wife there, standing a little apart with her tawny dog, but he ignored her. He glanced back at his three companions around the heavy box, as if for reassurance.

"Your wait will prove worthwhile, because"—and it seemed to Barbee that his rasping voice was desperately hurried, as if he were somehow fearful of being stopped—"because we have something to tell mankind." He caught a gasping breath. "A dreadful warning, gentlemen, that has been hidden and buried and suppressed, for the most wicked ends."

He gestured, with the jerky stiffness of desperate tension.

"The world must be told—if the time for the telling is not already past. So get what I'm going to tell you. Please broadcast my statement, if you can. Film a record of the evidences we brought back." His worn boot touched the wooden box. "Get it on the air and into print tonight—if you can."

"Sure, doc." A radio announcer grinned, moving up his microphone. "That's our business. I'll make a wire recording, and rush it back to the studio—if your story is politically okay. I suppose you're going to give your angle on the Chinese situation?"

"We saw a great deal of the war in China," Mondrick told him solemnly, "but I'm not going to talk about it. What I have to say is more important than the news of any war—because it will help you understand why wars are fought. It will explain a good deal that men have never understood, and a good many things we've been taught to deny."

"Okay, doc." The radio man adjusted his equipment. "Shoot."

"I'm going to tell you—"

Mondrick coughed, and caught his breath again. Barbee heard his laborious wheezing, and saw the quick alarm on Sam Quain's drawn face. Quain offered a handkerchief and Mondrick wiped sweat off his forehead—while Barbee, hunched in his topcoat, stood shivering in the moist east wind.

"I'm going to tell you some stunning things, gentlemen." Mondrick stumbled hoarsely on. "I'm going to tell you about a masked and secret enemy, a black clan that plots and waits unsuspected among true men—a hidden enemy, far more insidious than any of your modern fifth columns that scheme the ruin of nations. I'm going to tell you of the expected coming of a Black Messiah—the Child of Night—whose appearance among true men will be the signal for a savage and hideous and incredible rebellion."

That weary, shattered man gasped painfully again.

"Prepare yourselves for a jolt, gentlemen. This is a terrible thing—and you may doubt it, at first, as I did. It is really too dreadful to believe. But you'll have to accept it, as I did, when you see the unpleasant things we have brought back from those pre-human burial mounds in the Ala-shan.

"My discoveries there—or, rather, ours—solve many enigmas." His haggard eyes moved gratefully toward the three men guarding the iron-strapped box, and he bowed a little to them. "We've found the answers to riddles that have baffled every science—and to other mysteries so obvious, so much a part of our daily lives, that most of us are never even conscious they exist.

"Why, gentlemen, is evil?"

His lead-hued face was a mask of pain.

"Have you ever sensed the malignant purpose behind misfortune? Are you ever puzzled by the world's discord, by the shadow of war abroad and the clamor of strife at home? Reading the daily news of crime, are you ever shocked and appalled at the monstrosity of man? Have some of you wondered, sometimes, at the tragic division in yourselves—at the realization that your unconscious minds hold wells of black horror?

"Have you wondered—"

Mondrick choked and bent. He labored to breathe again, pressing both quivering hands against his sides. An ominous blue touched his face. He coughed into a handkerchief, and mopped his face again. His voice, when he could speak again, was strained and shallow, pitched in a higher key.

"I've no time to catalog all the dark riddles in our lives," he gasped. "But—listen!"

Disturbed by a sense of a veiled and monstrous tension mounting, Barbee looked uneasily around him. A photographer was slipping a fresh film pack into his camera. The radio man was fussing with his tape recorder. Mechanically, the bewildered reporters were taking notes.

April Bell, beside him, stood in a frozen pose. White with pressure, both her hands gripped the top of her snakeskin bag. Dilated, greenish black, her long eyes were staring at Mondrick's sick face, fixed with a peculiar intensity.

Briefly, Barbee wondered about April Bell. Why did she frighten him? What was the key to her strong attraction for him—what stronger call than the flaming lure of her bright hair had overbalanced his vague alarm? How much of what Mondrick would call good was in her, and how much of evil, and what was the point of conflict?

Unconscious of Barbee, she kept staring at Mondrick. Her pale lips moved silently. Her white hands twisted the snakeskin bag with a kind of savagery—as if it were something alive, Barbee felt uneasily, and her fingers were rending claws.

The gasping old man seemed to win his fight for breath.

"Remember, gentlemen," he wheezed laboriously, "this is no whim of the moment. I first suspected the frightful facts thirty years ago— when a shocking incident made me see that all the work of Freud, with his revealing new psychology of the unconscious, was merely a penetrating description of the minds and behavior of men, not really an explanation of the evil we see.

"I was then a practicing psychiatrist, out at Glennhaven. I gave up my medical career—because the truth I suspected made a mockery of all I had been taught and a cruel sham out of my efforts to aid the mentally ill. Unfortunately, I quarreled rather bitterly with old Dr. Glenn—father of the Glenn who heads Glennhaven now—because of that unfortunate incident.

"I turned to other fields—looking for evidence to disprove the thing I feared. It didn't exist. I studied abroad, and finally accepted a faculty position at Clarendon University. I tried to master anthropology, archeology, ethnology—every science bearing on the actual nature of mankind. Item by item, my research turned up facts to confirm the most dreadful thing a man has ever feared."

The sick man stooped and sobbed for breath again.

"For years," he whispered painfully, "I tried to work alone. You will presently understand just what that meant—and how extremely difficult it was for me to find aid. I even allowed my dear wife to help me, because she already shared my secret. She lost her eyes—and proved by her great sacrifice that all our fears were well founded.

"But I did, at last, find men whom I could trust." Mondrick's pallid face briefly tried to smile. His hollowed eyes glanced once more at the hard, taut faces of Sam Quain and Nick Spivak and Rex Chittum, warm with a deep affection. "And I trained them to share—"

The old man's voice sobbed and stopped. He bent double, livid-faced, laboring to breathe. Sam Quain held him to keep him from falling until that hard paroxysm ended.

"Forgive me, gentlemen—I'm subject to these attacks." His voice seemed fainter; he daubed weakly with the handkerchief at his sweat-drenched face. "Bear with me, please," he gasped. "I'll try to hurry on—through all this background that you must have—if you're to understand."

Sam Quain whispered something, and he nodded heavily.

"We had a theory," his shallow voice rasped hastily, as if racing with time. "We wanted proof—to warn and arm true mankind. The evidence we needed could exist only in the ashes of the past. Ten years ago I gave up my chair at the University to search the old cradles of the human and semihuman races—to find that convincing proof.

"You can guess a few of the difficulties and the perils we had to face—I've no time to list them. The Torgod Mongols raided our camps. We almost perished of thirst, and we all but froze to death. Then the war drove us out—just when we had located the first pre-human sites."

He toiled to breathe again.

"It used to appear that those dark huntsmen already knew that we suspected them and were trying to cut us down before we could expose them. The State Department didn't want us to go back. The Chinese government tried to keep us out. The Reds held us as spies—until we convinced them we were after something bigger than military information. Man and nature stood against us.

"But these are tough boys with me!"

The old man bent, heaving to another paroxysm.

"And we found what we were after," he whispered triumphantly. "Found it—and brought it safely home, from those prehuman sites." Once again his boot touched the green wooden box that his three companions guarded. "We brought it back—and here it is."

Once again he straightened, struggling to breathe, painfully searching the faces before him. Barbee met his dull, haggard eyes for an instant and saw in them the stark conflict of dreadful urgency and deadly fear. He understood that long preamble. He knew that Mondrick wanted desperately to speak—to blurt the bald facts out—and knew that a sick dread of disbelief restrained him.

"Gentlemen, don't condemn me yet," he croaked laboriously. "Please forgive me, if all these precautions appear unnecessary. You'll understand them when you know. And now that you're somewhat prepared, I must speak the rest abruptly. I must break the news, before I'm stopped."

His blotched face twitched and shivered.

"For there is danger, gentlemen. Every one of you—every person

30

who hears this news—is himself in deadly danger. Yet I beg you to listen . . . for I still hope . . . by spreading the truth . . . too far for them to kill enough to stamp it out entirely . . . to defeat those secret clansmen."

Mondrick fought for breath again, doubled and shuddering.

"It was a hundred thousand years ago—"

He strangled. His own frantic hands came up to his throat, as if he strove to open a way for his breath. A bubbling sound rattled in his throat. His contorted face and clawing hands turned a cyanotic blue. He swayed to his knees, sagging in Sam Quain's arms, gagging on words he couldn't speak.

"That couldn't be!" Barbee caught Quain's shocked whisper. "No—there are no cats here!"

Blinking, Barbee shot a bewildered glance at April Bell. She stood stiffly motionless, staring at the gasping explorer. Dilated in the gloom, her eyes were strange and black. White as her white fur, her fixed face held no expression. Both her hands clutched her snakeskin bag, twisting savagely.

But where was any cat?

The bag was closed now, and he saw nothing of her happy black kitten. Anyhow, why should the stricken man be gasping anything about a cat? Shivering to the cold east wind, Barbee peered back at Mondrick.

Sam Quain and Nick Spivak had laid the struggling man on his back. Quain ripped off his own khaki shirt and folded it under Mondrick's head for a pillow. But Rex Chittum, Barbee noticed, stayed beside that heavy wooden box, his roving eyes warily alert—as if its contents were more important than the old explorer's last agony.

For Mondrick was dying. His wild hands fought for air again and fell. His mottled face turned lax and lividly pale. He kicked convulsively and lay still again. As surely as if the garroter's iron collar were being screwed down against his throat, he was strangling to death.

"Back!" Sam Quain shouted. "He's dying for air."

A flashbulb detonated blindingly. Policemen pushed back the news photographers, crowding nearer for a better shot. Somebody shouted for the crash truck, but Mondrick had already ceased to move.

"Marck!"

Barbee heard that piercing scream. He saw Mondrick's blind wife

31

dart away from that guarded group by the terminal building, the huge dog beside her, running as surely as if she could see again. One of the officers tried to stop her and fell back from the dog's silent snarl. She reached the fallen man and knelt to dwell upon his splotched face and lax hands with her desperately searching fingers. Light shone cold on her silver rings and bracelets and burned in the tears streaming from the empty scars under her dark lenses.

"Marck, my poor blind darling!" Barbee heard her stricken whisper. "Why didn't you let me come with Turk to guard you? Couldn't you see them closing in?"

3

The White Jade Wolf

The man sprawled dead on the taxiway didn't answer that bitter whisper, and the huddled blind woman made no other sound. With a shaken gesture, Barbee beckoned the other newsmen back. His throat hurt and something cold had touched his spine. Silently, he turned to Sam Quain.

Quain's blue eyes were staring vacantly at the man on the ground. Beneath a thin undershirt, his goose-pimpled flesh was shuddering. He didn't seem aware of the clamoring reporters, and at first he made no sign when Barbee stripped off his own topcoat to fling around him.

"Thanks, Will," he murmured emptily at last. "I suppose it's cold."

He caught his breath, and turned to the newsmen.

"There's a story for you, gentlemen," he said quietly, his dry voice oddly flat and slow. "The death of Dr. Lamarck Mondrick, noted anthropologist and explorer. Be sure you get the spelling right—he was always particular about the *c* in Lamarck."

Barbee snatched at his taut arm.

"What killed him, Sam?"

"Natural causes, the coroner will say." His voice stayed flat and dull, but Barbee felt him stiffen. "He had had that asthma, you know, for a great many years. He told me out there in the Ala-shan that he knew he was suffering from a valvular heart disease—and knew it before we ever started. Our expedition was no picnic, you know. Not for a sick man, at his age. We're all pretty tired. When this attack struck, I guess his old pump just couldn't take the strain."

Barbee glanced at the still form on the ground and the woman in black sobbing silently.

"Tell me, Sam—what was Dr. Mondrick trying to say?"

Sam Quain swallowed hard. His blue eyes fled from Barbee's face into the cold gloom, and came back again. He shrugged in the borrowed topcoat, and it seemed to Barbee that he tried to shake off the horror that hung like a dark garment on him.

"Nothing," he muttered hoarsely. "Nothing, really."

"Huh, Quain?" rapped a hard voice over Barbee's shoulder. "You can't give us any runaround now."

Sam Quain gulped again, hesitant and visibly ill.

"Spill it, Quain!" demanded the radio reporter. "You can't tell us all that build-up was just for nothing."

But Sam Quain nodded his sun-bleached head, seeming to make up his mind.

"Nothing worth big headlines, I'm afraid." Pity touched and softened the horror lingering on his square-jawed face. "Dr. Mondrick had been ill for some time, you see, and I'm afraid his splendid mind had lost its old acuity. Nobody can question the accuracy and originality of his work, but we had tried to restrain him from this rather melodramatic manner of making it public."

"You mean," the radio man snarled indignantly, "that all this talk about your discoveries in Mongolia is just a crazy gag?"

"On the contrary," Sam Quain assured him, "Dr. Mondrick's work is both sound and important. His theories, and the evidences we have gathered to support them, are worth the attention of every professional scientist in the anthropological fields."

Sam Quain kept his haunted eyes away from the old man's body and the silent woman. His taut, dry voice was carefully calm.

"Dr. Mondrick's discoveries are quite important," he insisted flatly. "The rest of us tried to persuade him, however, to make the announcement in the usual way—in a formal paper, presented before some recognized scientific body. And that, since this tragedy, is what we shall doubtless do in time."

"But the old man kept hinting about some danger," rapped a photographer. "About somebody that didn't want him to talk. And then he conked off, right in the middle of what he had to say. That's pretty damn funny. You aren't just possibly frightened off, Quain?"

Sam Quain gulped nervously.

"Naturally, we're upset," he admitted huskily. "But where's any tangible proof that Dr. Mondrick had any enemy here?" His own haggard eyes peered away into the thick dusk, narrowing as if to hunted fear. "There's none," he insisted. "Dr. Mondrick's death at this moment can be nothing more than a tragic coincidence. Perhaps it was less. The fatal attack was doubtless brought on by his own excitement."

"But what about his 'Child of Night'?" the radio reporter broke in. "His 'Black Messiah'?"

Sam Quain's bleak face tried to smile.

"Dr. Mondrick read detective stories. His Child of Night, I believe, is merely a figure of speech—a personification of human ignorance, perhaps. He was given to figurative language, and he wanted to make his announcement dramatic."

Sam Quain nodded toward the wooden box.

"There lies your story, gentlemen. I'm afraid Dr. Mondrick chose an unfortunate publicity device. After all, the theory of human evolution is no longer frontpage news. Every known detail of the origin of mankind is extremely important to such a specialist as Dr. Mondrick, but it doesn't interest the man in the street—unless it's dramatized."

"Hell!" The radio man turned away. "That old buzzard sure took me for a ride." An ambulance drew up beside the plane, and he watched the blind woman bidding her husband a final farewell. Barbee was glad she couldn't see the flashbulbs flickering.

"What are your plans now, Mr. Quain?" demanded a hawk-faced man in black—a science reporter, as Barbee knew him, for one of the press associations. "When are you going to give us the rest of this interrupted announcement?"

"Not soon." Sam Quain patiently turned his head for a photographer and blinked at the cruel flashbulbs. "We all felt, you see, that Dr. Mondrick was speaking prematurely. I think all my associates in the Foundation will agree with me that the objects we brought back from the Ala-shan must be studied carefully in our own laboratory, along with all Dr. Mondrick's notes and papers, before we have any statement for the public. In due time, the Foundation will publish a monograph to present his work. That may take a year. Perhaps two."

Somebody in the impatient group made an impolite sound through his lips.

"We've got a story, anyhow." The science reporter grinned at him cheerfully. "If that's the way you want it, we'll use what we have. I can see the tabloid heads already—'Prehistoric Curse Clips Grave Robber.'"

"Print what you like." Sam Quain peered around him in the windy gloom, and Barbee could see his veiled unease. "But we have no further statement now—except that I want to offer our apologies, on behalf of the Foundation, for this tragic anticlimax. I do hope you will be generous in anything you write about Dr. Mondrick. He was truly great—if sometimes a trifle eccentric. His work, when fully published, will place him securely among the honored few of the humane sciences, along with Freud and Darwin."

His weary jaw set stubbornly.

"That's all that I—or any of us—will have to say."

The photographers flashed a final bulb at his set face, and began packing their equipment. The radio man coiled up his cable and took down his microphone. The newsmen scattered reluctantly, to file their stories of an obscure and unresolved event.

Barbee looked for April Bell and glimpsed her entering the terminal building. She had slipped away, he supposed, to telephone her story to a rewrite man on the *Call*. But Barbee's own deadline was midnight, for the early edition of the *Star*. He still had time to try to solve the riddle he felt in Mondrick's death.

He pushed impulsively forward to seize Sam Quain's arm. The tall explorer recoiled from his unexpected touch with a little gasping cry, and then manufactured a tortured grimace of a smile. Naturally he was nervous after that tragic ordeal. Barbee led him aside, toward the tail of the huge silent plane.

"What's the matter, Sam?" he demanded huskily. "Your deflation of the suspense was good—but not good enough. Old Mondrick's build-up rang true. I know you were all scared spitless. What is it you're afraid of?"

Dark and wild, Sam Quain's blue eyes looked into his. They searched him, Barbee thought, as penetratingly as if to discover and unveil some monstrous enemy. Sam Quain shivered, hunching his wide shoulders in the tight borrowed coat, yet his patient, weary voice seemed calm enough.

"We were all afraid of exactly what happened," he insisted. "We all knew Dr. Mondrick was ill. We had to climb over a cold front on the flight here from the coast, and the altitude must have strained his bad heart. He insisted on making his statement here and now—probably just because he knew his time was nearly up."

Barbee shook his head.

"That makes sense—almost," he said slowly. "But asthmatic attacks aren't commonly fatal, nor heart attacks predictable. I can't help believing you were all afraid of something else." He caught Quain's arm. "Can't you trust me, Sam? Aren't we still friends?"

"Don't be a fool, Will." A quivering urgency began to mar Quain's forced calm. "I don't think Dr. Mondrick quite trusted you. There were few he did trust. But of course we're still friends."

He shrugged uneasily, and his hunted eyes fled to the locked box with Spivak and Chittum tautly alert beside it.

"Now I must go, Will. Too many things to do. We must arrange about Dr. Mondrick's body, and take care of the box, and get the rest of our freight hauled out to the Foundation." He shucked off the tight coat, shivering. "Thanks, Will. You need it, and I had a coat on the plane. Excuse me now."

Barbee accepted the topcoat, urging:

"Take time to see Nora—you know she's here to meet you, with little Pat." He nodded toward the lights of the terminal building. "Old Ben's over there, to see Rex, and the Spivaks came all the way from Brooklyn to meet Nick." Bewilderment echoed in his voice. "What's the matter, Sam? Can't you take a moment to meet your own families?"

Quain's eyes turned dark, as if with agony.

"We'll see them when we can, Will." He paused to find a worn leather coat in the pile of battered luggage and stout wooden crates unloaded from the transport. "My God, Will!" he whispered hoarsely. "Don't you think we're human! It's two years since I've seen my wife and baby—but we must take care of Dr. Mondrick's box."

Nervously impatient, he started to turn.

"Hold on, Sam." Barbee caught his arm again. "Just one more question." He dropped his voice, too low for the group about the ambulance to hear, or the men unloading the plane. "What has a cat to do with Mondrick's death?"

"Huh?" He felt Quain's arm jerk. "What cat?"

"That's what I want to know."

Quain's sick face turned very pale.

"I heard him whisper—when he was dying—but I saw no cat."

"But why, Sam?" Barbee insisted. "What would a cat matter?"

Quain's eyes searched him, narrowed and strange.

"Dr. Mondrick's asthma was due to an allergy," Quain muttered huskily. "An allergy to cat fur—he took sensitivity tests which proved that. He couldn't go in a room where a cat had been kept without getting an attack."

The frightened man caught his breath.

"Will, have you seen a cat here?"

"Yes," Barbee nodded. "A black kitten—"

He felt Sam Quain stiffen and saw April Bell coming back from the terminal building. The lights caught her red hair, and she looked strong and quick and graceful as some prowling jungle cat—he wondered why that comparison struck his mind. Her dark warm eyes found Barbee, and she smiled gaily.

"Where?" Sam Quain was whispering urgently. "Where was any kitten?"

Barbee looked at April Bell's long eyes, and something decided him not to tell Sam Quain that she had brought the kitten. Something about her stirred and changed him, in ways he didn't want to define. In a lowered, hasty voice, he finished lamely:

"Somewhere about the building yonder, just before the planes came in. I didn't notice where it went."

Quain's narrowed eyes seemed hard with suspicion. He opened his mouth as if to ask some other question, and closed it with a gulp when he saw April Bell beside them. It seemed to Barbee that he crouched a little, like a fighting man ready for a dreaded opponent.

"So you're Mr. Quain!" the girl cooed softly. "I want to ask you just one thing, if you please—for the *Clarendon Call*. What have you got in that green box?" Her long eyes glanced eagerly at the iron-strapped chest and the two wary men on guard beside it. "A bushel of diamonds? Blueprints for an atom bomb?"

Poised like a boxer on the balls of his feet, Sam Quain said softly:

"Nothing so exciting, I'm afraid. Nothing that would interest newspaper readers, I'm sure. Nothing you'd bother picking up on the street. Just a few old bones. A few odds and ends of rubbish, broken and thrown away before man's history dawned."

She laughed at him gently.

"Please, Mr. Quain," she protested. "If your box has no value, then why—"

"Excuse me," Sam Quain rapped abruptly. The girl caught his arm, but he shrugged himself free and strode away, without looking back, to join the two men beside the wooden strongbox.

Quain murmured something to one of the officers, gesturing at the anxious people still waiting by the terminal building. Barbee stood aside with April Bell, watching as old Ben Chittum and the Spivaks and Nora Quain came back to the transport. The spry old man shook his handsome grandson's hand. Stout Mama Spivak sobbed in the arms of her thin, spectacled Nick, and Papa Spivak hugged them both.

Sam Quain waited for Nora by the wooden chest. He kissed her hungrily and lifted little Pat in his arms. The child was laughing now. She called for her father's handkerchief and scrubbed furiously at the tearstains under her eyes. Nora tried to draw her husband away, but he sat down firmly on the green box and took the child on his knee.

Mama Spivak, with both arms around her son, abruptly began wailing piercingly.

"Maybe there's nothing in that box, except what he said," April Bell purred in Barbee's ear. "But they would all of them give their own lives, along with old Mondrick's, just to protect it." Her long eyes peered off into the gloom above the field lights. "Wouldn't it be funny," she whispered faintly, "if they did?"

"But not very amusing," Barbee muttered.

Something made him shiver again. Perhaps he had got chilled, while

40

Quain had his coat. He drew a little away from the girl because suddenly he didn't want to touch that sleek white fur. He couldn't help wondering about the kitten. There was a slight, uncomfortable possibility that this red-headed girl was an extremely adroit murderess.

Barbee didn't like that word. He had seen female criminals enough, on the police court beat, and none had ever looked quite so fresh and bright as April Bell. But now a man was dead, killed by the airborne protein molecules from a kitten's fur as efficiently as if a strangler's cord had done it; and this tall, alluring red-head was responsible for the presence of the kitten.

Barbee was startled, when he looked automatically for the snakeskin bag in which she had carried the kitten, to see that it was gone. The girl seemed to follow his eyes. Her own turned dark again, and her face seemed pale as the fur she wore.

"My bag!" She spread her empty, graceful hands. "Must have mislaid it, in all the excitement of filing my story. It's one that Aunt Agatha gave me, and I simply must find it. There's a family heirloom in it—a white jade pin. Will you help me look, Barbee?"

Barbee went with her to look where the departing ambulance had stood, and then about the telephone booths in the waiting room. He wasn't very much surprised, somehow, when they found no trace of the lost bag. April Bell was simply too efficient and intensely awake to mislay anything. At last she glanced at a diamond-crusted watch.

"Let's give it up, Barbee," she cooed, without visible regret. "Thanks awfully, but perhaps I didn't have it anyhow—Aunt Agatha probably picked it up without thinking when I gave little Fifi back to her."

Barbee tried not to lift his eyebrows, but he still suspected Aunt Agatha to be entirely imaginary. He remembered seeing the bag, savagely twisted in the girl's long fingers as old Mondrick lay struggling on the ground, but he didn't say so. He didn't understand April Bell.

"Thanks, Barbee," she said. "Now I've got to phone the desk again. Forgive me if I scoop you."

"'For the whole truth, read the *Star.*'" Barbee quoted his paper's slogan, grinning. "I still have till midnight to find out what they brought back in that green box, and why old Mondrick died when he did." His grin sobered, and something made him gulp. "Shall I—may I see you again?"

41

He waited painfully for her answer, staring at her sleek white coat. He wanted desperately to see her again—was it because he was a little afraid she had murdered Mondrick, he wondered, or because he hoped very much that she hadn't? For a moment, a little frown of puzzlement creased her smooth forehead. He breathed again when she smiled.

"If you like, Barbee." Her voice was all velvet and moonbeams. "When?"

"For dinner—tonight?" Barbee tried not to seem too breathless. "Would nine be too late? Right now I want to find out what Sam Quain and Company are going to do with that mysterious box, and then I must write my story."

"Nine isn't late," she cooed. "I love the night. And I too must watch that box."

Dark again, her long greenish eyes stared at the three weary men, carefully loading the heavy wooden chest into Dr. Bennett's car. The little group of relatives stood back to watch, puzzled and distressed. Barbee touched April Bell's white fur, and shivered in the icy wind.

"At nine?" he said huskily. "Where shall I meet you?"

April Bell smiled abruptly, with a quizzical lift of her penciled brows.

"Tonight, Barbee?" she purred. "Nora will think you've lost your head."

"Perhaps I have." He touched the snowy fur, and tried not to shiver again. "All this is quite a jolt to me—Rowena Mondrick is still a friend of mine, even since her husband fell out with me. I do feel upset, but Sam Quain will take care of everything. I hope you'll decide to dine with me, April."

I hope you'll tell me, he added silently, why you brought that black kitten here, and why you felt it necessary to invent Aunt Agatha, and whether you had any reason to desire Dr. Mondrick's death. Something made him gulp again, and he waited hopefully.

"If I can manage." Her white teeth smiled. "Now I must run—I have to call the city desk, and then I'll ask Aunt Agatha."

She did run—as gracefully, he thought, as some creature never tamed. He watched her to the phone booth, aware of a vague surprise that any woman could stir him so. The caress of her liquid voice lingered in his mind. He filled his lungs and drew down his chin and flexed his fingers. Suddenly he wished he had drunk less whisky and kept himself more fit. He could see the gleam of her white fur inside the lighted booth. He shivered again; perhaps he was taking cold. Resolutely, he turned away. How would it make him feel, he wondered, if he should discover that April Bell really were a murderess?

Quain and his companions had taken the wooden box away in Dr. Bennett's car. Nora and the others, left behind, were trailing despondently back through the terminal building. Mama Spivak was still wailing thinly, with Papa trying clumsily to console her.

"It's all right, Mama." The little tailor patted the quivering bulges of her shoulder. "Nickie should come back to Brooklyn with us, when he has such great things to do for the Foundation? He surely knows how you cleaned and cooked for him till the whole flat is shining and rich with good smells. He knows his round-trip fare is paid already, but the love is what matters. Don't cry, Mama."

"I should mind the food?" she sobbed. "The cleaning? Even the fare to Brooklyn? No, Papa. It's that awful thing that was buried in that desert. That old, bad thing they brought back in that green box—the thing my Nickie won't whisper its name, even!"

Her shuddering arms clung to the tiny tailor.

"I'm afraid yet, Papa!" she wailed. "That thing they took to Sam's house in the box, it killed poor Dr. Mondrick. I'm afraid it will get Sam and Nora yet. I'm afraid it will take our own little Nickie, too!"

"Please, Mama." Papa Spivak tried to laugh at her. "Nickie says you're just an old silly."

His laugh wasn't successful.

Nora Quain carried little Pat, holding the child against her with a frightened-seeming tightness. Nora's face looked empty with distress, and she didn't see Barbee. Blinking, Pat was trying to smooth Nora's yellow hair. Barbee heard the child urge softly:

"Now, Mother—don't *you* cry!"

The hurt on old Ben Chittum's dried-up face moved Barbee to call impulsively: "Come along with me, Ben—I'll drive you back to town."

"Thanks, Will, but I'm okay." The old man managed a stiff little grin. "Don't worry about me. I know Rex will come on out to see me when they get that box safe to Sam's place. Of course I'm disappointed, but I'll be okay. Hell, I'm spry as a spring lamb!"

Barbee glanced back to be sure that April Bell was still in the telephone booth, and followed a hunch. He walked quickly to the big trash can behind the terminal building and fumbled under discarded newspapers and candy wrappers and a crushed straw hat.

It was the same sort of hunch that had led him to a hundred news stories—the sort of intuition, arising from nowhere and yet oddly certain, which Preston Troy called the essential equipment of the good reporter. The nose for news. Once he had mentioned it to Dr. Glenn, and that suave psychiatrist told him that the faculty was nothing more than logical reasoning, working below the level of his conscious mind. Glenn's glib explanation didn't quite satisfy him, but he had come to trust his hunches.

Under the broken hat, he found the snakeskin bag.

Two ends of red ribbon fluttered beside the clasp, crushed and twisted as if they had been wrapped around straining fingers. Barbee snapped open the bag. Inside was the small, limp body of Aunt Agatha's black kitten.

The red ribbon, tied in a slip knot, was drawn into a noose so tight it had almost cut off the little swollen head. The pink mouth was open, the tiny tongue exposed, the blue eyes glazed and bulging. The kitten had been expertly garroted. A single drop of blood on the white silk lining of the bag led Barbee to something else.

Stirring the lax little body with his forefinger, he found something hard and white buried in the tangled black fur. He pulled it carefully away and whistled silently as he turned it under the light from the building. It was April Bell's lost heirloom—that white jade pin. The ornamental part was carved into a little running wolf, set with a polished eye of green malachite. The work was very delicate and true—the tiny wolf looked as slim and graceful, he thought, as April Bell herself.

The clasp behind it was open, and the strong steel pin had been thrust into the kitten's body. A drop of dark blood followed when he drew it out. The point, he thought, must have pierced the kitten's heart.

4
The Witch Child

Barbee remembered a little he had learned long ago in Dr. Mondrick's classes about the theory and practice of magic among primitive mankind, but he was no student of what are termed the occult sciences. That wasn't necessary. The black kitten and the aged scholar had both died at the same time, in precisely the same way. April Bell must have killed the kitten. Had she thereby—ignoring whatever part in Dr. Mondrick's death might be due to that fashionable new biochemical magic called allergy—intended murder?

Barbee believed she had.

But what was he to do about it? His first impulse was to carry the snakeskin bag and its disquieting contents out to Sam Quain's house—perhaps he could use it for a wedge, to get a glimpse inside that guarded wooden coffer. But he dropped the idea. Witchcraft might be a fruitful subject for the technical monographs of such scholars as

Mondrick, but Sam Quain would only laugh, he felt, at any suggestion of a chic modern witch with penciled brows and enameled nails practicing her black arts in a live American town. Sam's distant curtness had annoyed him, besides—and he felt a curious reluctance to get April Bell involved.

Perhaps she hadn't killed little Fifi, after all—one of the small boys he had seen watching the airliner come in would be a more likely assassin. Perhaps her Aunt Agatha actually existed. Anyhow, if she decided to dine with him, he might learn a little more about her. Somehow, he knew he had to end the shocked uncertainty that tortured him.

His mind was made up. He wiped the blood from that steel point on the lining of the bag and dropped the little jade wolf in his coat pocket. He closed the snakeskin bag again and buried it once more under the broken straw hat. Briefly he wondered what the refuse collectors would think if they happened to salvage the bag, and supposed they were used to such minor mysteries.

The bitter wind, as he hurried back around the bright-lit building, set him to shivering again. The cloudy night seemed suddenly darker. He mopped his sweaty hands, and heard a ripping sound and looked down to see that he had torn his handkerchief across.

He strode eagerly to meet April Bell in the waiting room when she came out of the telephone booth. Her face looked flushed—perhaps only from the excitement of completing her first big assignment for the *Call*. Certainly she didn't look like a murderess. Yet he still had to find out why she had brought the black kitten here, and whether she had really stabbed and strangled it in a magical effort to stop the heart and breath of Dr. Mondrick.

"Ready?" he called. Her greenish eyes were bright, and she met him with a smile of what seemed to be warm comradeship. He nodded hopefully toward the parking space where his shabby coupe waited. "May I drive you back to town?"

"Sorry, but my car's here." She seemed to catch her breath. "Aunt Agatha had a bridge party, and she went back to town on the bus."

"Oh." He tried not to show his disappointment, or his doubt of Aunt Agatha's reality. "Then how about our date for dinner?"

"I called Auntie, and she says I may go." Her gay smile warmed him.

"Wonderful!" he whispered. "Where do you live?"

"The Trojan Arms," she told him. "Apartment 2-C."

"Huh!" He couldn't help blinking. That swank apartment-hotel was another business enterprise of Preston Troy, and Barbee had written puffs about it for the *Star*. The cheapest suite in it, he knew, would cost two hundred a month. April Bell was doing very nicely for a cub reporter—unless, of course, Aunt Agatha should happen to be both real and wealthy.

"But I'll meet you." The tall redhead didn't seem to see his bleak astonishment, and something in her soft, husky voice made him forget it. "Where shall we go?"

"The Knob Hill?" he suggested hopefully—although that suburban night spot was really too expensive for reporters on the *Star's* scale of pay.

"I'd love it," she purred.

He walked with her out through the windy night to her own parked car. It was a long maroon convertible, worth four thousand, he estimated uncomfortably, on the black market. Not many cub reporters drove such opulent machines. Perhaps, he hoped, it belonged to Aunt Agatha.

He opened the door and she stepped in quickly, as graceful in her white fur as the tiny jade carving in his pocket. She took his hand for an instant, and the touch of her strong cool fingers was exciting as her voice. He put down the impulse to kiss her, afraid that would spoil everything. His breath hastened. Murderess or not, April Bell was going to be a fascinating girl to know.

"Bye, Barbee," she whispered. "Till nine."

Barbee drove back to town in his prewar coupe, and stopped at his desk in the long city room to hammer out his stories for the *Star*. Writing, he was glad of the terse, stereotyped objectivity of modern journalese.

Dr. Lamarck Mondrick, famed anthropologist and founder of the Humane Research Foundation, just returned from two years of excavating prehistoric sites in the remote Ala-shan desert, fell dead last night at the municipal airport, dramatically cut off as he attempted to tell newsmen what his expedition had discovered.

That was the lead. He went on with the simple facts of the tragedy, filled out with his own knowledge and biographical facts culled from the file in the morgue. He was glad that a formal obituary had no space for anything about April Bell, or the assassinated kitten in the trash can.

Eagerness hurried him back to the battered old coupe. Sliding under the wheel, he found himself emptyhanded, and realized he had forgotten to buy a bottle. It was months since he had passed the Mint Bar, he thought, without stopping for a shot and maybe a bottle to take along. April Bell might be good for him.

His own apartment was two shabby rooms, with kitchenette and bath, in a run-down two-story building on Bread Street. The decayed neighborhood was too close to the mills, but the rent wasn't too high for his pay and the landlady didn't seem to care how much he drank.

He bathed and shaved, and discovered himself whistling happily as he looked for a clean shirt and a suit that wouldn't be too shabby for the Knob Hill. April Bell might be what he needed. He had closed the door behind him at eight forty when he heard the telephone ring inside. He hurried back to answer it, shaken with a sudden apprehension that she had decided not to see him.

"Will?" The voice was a woman's, calm and yet intense. "I want to talk to you."

It wasn't April Bell, and that quick dread relaxed its grasp. In a moment he recognized the clear, gracious voice of Mondrick's blind wife, serenely sweet, reflecting nothing of the shock he knew she must feel.

"Can you drive out to see me, Will?" she asked. "Right away?"

He frowned at his watch. The Knob Hill was forty blocks out Center Street, beyond the river and outside the city limits. The old Mondrick house, just off the university campus, was forty blocks in the other direction.

"Not right now, Rowena," he stammered awkwardly. "Of course I want to do everything I can to make things easy for you. I can come out in the morning, or maybe later tonight if you need me. But right now I have an engagement that I can't break—"

"Oh!" The sound seemed almost a cry of pain. The receiver was silent for a moment, and then Rowena Mondrick's calm sweet voice asked very softly: "With that Bell woman?"

"With April Bell," Barbee said.

"Will, who is she?"

48

"Huh!" Barbee caught his breath. You had to hand it to Rowena. She certainly kept up with the world, in spite of all her tragedies. "Just a fresh girl reporter," he said, "on the evening paper. I had never met her before tonight. Turk didn't seem to like her, but I thought she was pretty slick."

"You didn't!" the blind woman protested, and then begged urgently: "Break your date, Will! Or put her off, until you have time to come and talk with me. Won't you? Please!"

"Sorry," he muttered awkwardly. "But I really can't, Rowena." A faint resentment edged his tone, in spite of him. "I know you don't like her—and your dog doesn't. But I find her very interesting."

"I'm sure you do," Rowena Mondrick said quietly. "It's true I don't like her—for an excellent reason, that I want to tell you whenever you have time to listen. So please drive out when you can."

He couldn't speak of all the reasons behind his interest in April Bell—he wasn't even sure that he fully understood them. Yet a flood of pity for the blind woman in her bereavement made him regret his impatience, and he said clumsily:

"Sorry, Rowena. I'll come to see you as soon as I can."

"Watch yourself, Will!" cried that sweetly urgent voice. "Watch yourself with her tonight. Because that woman plans to injure you—dreadfully!"

"Injure me?" he whispered unbelievingly. "How?"

"Come out tomorrow," Rowena said, "I'll tell you."

"Please explain—" Barbee gasped before he heard her hang up. He put the receiver back, and stood a moment wondering what she could have meant. He could see no possible reason behind her words—unless she had turned her dog's savage lunge at April's kitten into a personal antagonism.

Rowena Mondrick, he remembered, had been given to spells of moody strangeness ever since he knew her. Usually serene and normal as any seeing person, keenly alive with her friends and her music, often even gay—sometimes she left her piano and ignored her friends, seeming to care only for the company of her huge dog and the caress of the odd silver jewelry she wore.

Her strangeness must be a natural aftermath of that ghastly event in Africa, Barbee supposed, and Mondrick's sudden death had awakened her old terrors. He'd see her in the morning, and do what he could to

49

soothe her irrational fears. He'd try to remember to take her a couple of new records for the automatic phonograph Sam and Nora Quain had given her.

But now he was going to meet April Bell.

The bar at the Knob Hill was a semicircular glass-walled room, indirectly lit with a baleful, dim red glare. The seats were green leather and chromium, too angular for comfort. The whole effect was sleek and hard and disturbing—perhaps it was intended, Barbee thought, to goad unsuspecting patrons into buying drinks enough so they wouldn't be aware of it.

April Bell flashed her scarlet smile at him from a tiny black table under an arch of red-lit glass. The white fur was tossed carelessly over the back of another chair, and she somehow looked utterly relaxed in the angular seat, as if this deliberately jarring atmosphere didn't disturb her. Indeed, her long oval face reflected a satisfaction that seemed almost feline.

Her rather daring evening gown was a deep green that accented the eager green of her slightly oblique eyes. Barbee hadn't even thought of wearing dinner jacket or tails, and for a moment he was uncomfortably aware of his gray year-old business suit, a little too loose on his lank frame. But April didn't seem to mind and he forgot, in his instant appreciation of all the white-wolf coat had hidden. The white, well-groomed flesh of her seemed infinitely desirable, yet something made him think of the blind woman's warning.

"May I have a daiquiri?" she asked.

Barbee ordered two daiquiris.

He sat looking at her across the little table, so close he caught her clean perfume. Almost drunk before the drinks came with the sheen of her red hair and the dark intensity of her long eyes, the warm charm of her eager-seeming smile and the lithe vitality of her perfect body—he found it hard to recall his plan of action.

The velvet caress of her slightly husky voice made him want to forget that he suspected her of murder—yet he knew he could never forget, until he learned the truth. The frantic unrest in him, the sharp conflict of bright hope and vaguely dreadful terror, would not be stilled.

He had tried, driving across the long river bridge, to plan his inquiry. Motivation, it seemed to him, was the essential point. If it were true that she knew nothing of Mondrick, and had no reason to wish him harm, then the whole thing became fantastic nonsense. Even if the kitten's accidental presence had actually caused the fatal attack, that unfortunate coincidence should trouble neither him nor the law.

Barbee didn't like to consider the other alternative. This tall redhead, smiling with her intoxicating hint of special comradeship through a foot or so of smoke-hazed air, seemed to offer him more than a lonely, faintly embittered newspaperman could quite dare dream of, and he didn't want to knock her gift into the dust. He wanted her to like him.

He didn't want to find a motive; he shrank from trying to discover why she might have desired Mondrick's death. Yet a score of unsolved riddles came crowding to haunt him, each casting its sinister shadow across the girl's gay smile. Who had been Mondrick's "secret enemy," awaiting the coming of a "Child of Night"?

Suppose April Bell were a member of some desperate conspiracy? In this seething postwar world, when nations and races and hostile philosophies still battled to survive, when scientists fashioned another more shocking agency of death each day, it wasn't hard to picture that.

Suppose Mondrick and his party, on their long trip home across the battlegrounds of Asia, had secured evidence about the identity and aims of those conspirators—and brought it back in that wooden box? Taking extreme precautions—fully aware of some danger they couldn't avoid—they had attempted to broadcast their warning. But Mondrick, before he could name the menace, had fallen dead.

April Bell had killed him—he couldn't quite escape the cold finality of that. Whether it was freakish accident or premeditated homicide, the black kitten she had brought to the plane in her snakeskin bag must have been the fatal instrument. He didn't like the implication, yet there it was.

Their daiquiris came, and her white teeth smiled over the glass. She was warm and real and near, and he tried desperately to shake off the hard constraint of his suspicion. After all, he told himself, it was utterly fantastic. In a world which afforded such efficient instruments of homicide as knives and cyanide and tommy guns, no serious murderer would think of depending on the protein dust from the fur of a black kitten carried across the victim's path. No efficient modern killer, he assured himself, would place any reliance on a strangling ribbon knotted around a kitten's throat and a pin thrust through its tiny heart.

That is, unless—

Barbee shook his head and raised his glass, with an awkward little smile, to clink against April Bell's. The longer he let himself brood over those vague improbabilities surrounding Dr. Mondrick's death, the less pleasant they appeared. He determined to devote himself entirely to the more attractive business of an evening with the most fascinating woman he had ever met.

What if she were a witch?

That is, he amended the phrase, what if she had wished to bring about Mondrick's death and expected to accomplish it by garroting little Fifi? After all, he was fully fed up with his life as it had been. Eighty hours a week on Preston Troy's dirty yellow rag for a wage that hardly paid for his rent and meals and whisky. He had been drinking nearly a fifth of cheap bourbon a day. April Bell, even if she believed herself a witch, might prove to be a more exciting escape.

She looked at him as their glasses chimed, and her long dark eyes held a cool, smiling challenge.

"Well . . . Barbee?"

He leaned across the tiny octagonal table.

"To . . . our evening!" Her vital nearness took his breath. "Please, April—I want to know about you—everything. Everywhere you've been, and everything you've done. Your family and your friends. What you dream about, and what you like for breakfast."

Her red lips curved in a slow feline smile.

"You ought to know better, Barbee—a woman's mystery is her charm."

He couldn't help noticing again the even white strength of her perfect teeth. They reminded him of Poe's weird story—something about a man haunted by a dreadful compulsion to pull his sweetheart's teeth. He tried to shake off that untimely association, and started to lift his glass. A shudder made it tremble in his hand, and the pale drink splashed on his fingers.

"Too much mystery is alarming." He set the glass down carefully. "I'm really afraid of you."

"So?" She watched him wipe the cold stickiness of the spilled drink off his fingers, the smile on her white mobile face seemingly faintly malicious, as if she were laughing at him secretly. "Really, Barbee, you're the dangerous one."

Barbee looked down uncomfortably, and sipped his drink. Until tonight, he had thought he knew about women—far too much about them. But April Bell baffled him.

"You see, Barbee, I've tried to build an illusion." Her cool voice mocked him with that secret laughter. "You've made me very happy, accepting it. Surely you wouldn't want me to shatter it now?"

"I do," he said soberly. "Please, April."

She nodded, and red lights burned in her sleek hair.

"Very well, Barbee," she purred. "For you, I'll drop my painted veil."

She set down her glass, and leaned toward him with her round arms crossed on the tiny black table. The white curves of her shoulders and her breasts were near him. Faintly, he thought he caught the natural odor of her body, a light, dry, clean fragrance—he was glad it had escaped the advertising crusades of the soap manufacturers. Her husky voice dropped to match his own soberness.

"I'm just a simple farmer's daughter, really," she told him. "I was born here in Clarendon county—my parents had a little dairy up the river, just beyond the railroad bridge. I used to walk half a mile every morning to catch the school bus."

Her lips made a quick half smile.

"Well, Barbee—does that shatter my precious illusion enough to suit you?"

Barbee shook his head.

"That hardly dents it. Please go on."

Her white expressive face looked troubled.

"Please, Will," she begged softly. "I'd rather not tell you any more about me—not tonight, anyhow. That illusion is my shell. I'd be helpless without it, and not very pretty. Don't make me break it. You might not like me without it."

"No danger." His voice turned almost grim. "But I do want you to go on. You see, I'm still afraid."

She sipped her daiquiri, and her cool green eyes studied his face. That secret laughter had left them. She frowned a little, and then smiled again with that air of warm accord.

"I warn you—it gets a little sordid."

"I can take it," he promised her. "I want to know you—so that I can like you more."

"I hope so." She smiled. "Here goes."

Her mobile face made a quick grimace of distaste.

"My parents didn't get on together—that's all the trouble, really." Her low voice was forced and uneven. "My father—but there's no use digging up the unpleasant details. The year I was nine, Mother took me to California. Father kept the other children. It's that cheap, ugly background that I built my illusion to hide."

She drained her glass nervously.

"You see, there wasn't any alimony." Her flat voice turned bitter. "Mother took her own name back. She worked to keep us. Hash-slinger. Salesgirl, stenographer, carhop. Movie extra. Finally she got a few character bits, but it was pretty rough sledding for her. She lived for me, and tried to bring me up to play the game a little shrewder.

"Mother had a poor opinion of men—with reason enough, I'm afraid. She tried to fit me to protect myself. She made me—well, call me a she-wolf." Her fine teeth flashed through an uneasy little smile. "And here I am, Barbee. Mother managed to put me through school. Somehow, all those years, she kept her insurance paid up. I had a few thousand dollars when she died. By the time that's gone, if I do as she taught me—"

She made a wry little face, and tried to smile.

"That's the picture, Will. I'm a ruthless beast of prey." She pushed her empty glass aside abruptly—the gesture seemed nervous, somehow defiant. "How do you like me now?"

Shifting uncomfortably before the penetrating keenness of her faintly Oriental eyes, Barbee was grateful for the waiter's approach. He ordered two more daiquiris.

In a lower voice that seemed to hold a faint bitter mockery—perhaps of herself—April Bell asked, "Does the ugly truth behind my poor, torn illusion make you any less afraid of me?"

Barbee contrived to grin.

"As a beast of prey," he said as lightly as he could, "your equipment is splendid. I only wish that reporters on the *Star's* payroll were fair financial game." A hard earnestness came back into his uneasy voice. "But it's something else that I'm afraid of."

He stared at her. For he thought her white, perfect body had imperceptibly tensed. He thought her long greenish eyes had narrowed alertly. Even the faint, fragrant scent of her now carried a subtle warning, it seemed to him—as if she had been an actual thing of prey, crouching beyond that tiny black table, wary and deadly. Her instant smile didn't quite erase that startled impression.

"Well?" Her voice seemed hoarse with tension. "What *are* you afraid of?"

Barbee gulped the rest of his own drink. His fingers drummed nervously on the table—he noticed how large and gnarled and hairy his hand seemed, beside hers. His mind had rebelled against the intolerable conflict of frantic hope and desperate doubt, and a reckless impulse told him to blurt out the truth.

"April—"

He checked himself, and caught his breath. Because her white oval face had turned remote and cold. Her long greenish eyes had narrowed alertly—almost as if she had already heard what he was going to say. He made himself go on.

"April—it's about what happened at the airport." He leaned across the little table. Something made him shiver. His voice turned suddenly hard, accusing. "You killed that black kitten—I found the body. You did it to cause the death of Dr. Mondrick."

Barbee had expected a violent denial. He had prepared himself to face her slashing anger. A bewildered lack of comprehension was what he had hoped for—if some youthful assassins had really kidnapped and destroyed little Fifi. He was completely at a loss when the girl covered her face with her hands, elbows propped on the little table, and began sobbing silently.

He stared at the red splendor of her hair, and bit his lip. Her despair and pain were terribly real, and a sharp knife of contrition twisted in his breast. He couldn't endure tears. All his cruel suspicions became utterly fantastic. He had been a complete fool, even to mention Aunt Agatha's kitten.

"April—really—" he floundered. "I didn't mean—"

He subsided while the stony-faced waiter set down two fresh daiquiris and went away with his two dollar bills and the empty glasses. He wanted desperately to touch April Bell's white trembling shoulder, somehow to soothe her hurt. Suddenly he didn't care what she was or what she had done. Instead, a tremendous excited curiosity to know how and why she had done it rose in him.

"Please, April," he begged faintly. "I'm very sorry."

She lifted her head, and looked silently at him out of her wet, slightly slanted eyes—or was it only that her thin brows had been artfully plucked to make them look oblique? Her eyes were huge and dark and solemn, and tears had smeared the smooth makeup on her cheeks. Her red head nodded slightly—in a hopeless little bow of tired defeat.

"So you know." It was a statement, bitterly final.

Barbee reached impulsively to take her slender hands, but she drew them back and dropped them wearily in her lap. She sat looking at him, waiting, defiantly submissive, almost haggard with her ruined makeup, for once not building any illusions—or was this just a new one?

"I don't know anything." His hurried voice was anxious and bewildered. "This is all a nightmare—too many things I can't believe, or understand. I—" He blinked, and swallowed hard. "I didn't mean to hurt you so. Please, April—believe that. I like you . . . a very great deal. But . . . well, you know how Mondrick died."

Her wet eyes dropped wearily. She found a handkerchief in the green leather bag that matched the gown and lent its color to her eyes. She dabbed away her tears, and unobtrusively flicked powder on her cheeks again. She sipped deliberately at her cocktail, and he saw the glass quivering in her long, slender fingers. At last she looked up solemnly.

"Yes, Will." Her voice was low and grave. "You've found me out—I guess it's no use trying to fool you any longer. The truth is hard to say, and I know it will upset you.

"But I'm a witch, Barbee."

Barbee half rose, sat down again, and nervously tossed off his daiquiri. He blinked at her hurt, earnest face and shook his head savagely. He caught his breath and opened his mouth and shut it again. At last he demanded breathlessly:

"What the devil do you mean?"

"Just what I said," she told him soberly. "I didn't tell you what my parents quarreled about—I couldn't. But that was the cause. I was a witch child, and my father found it out. My mother had always known, and she stood by me—he'd have killed me if she hadn't. So he drove us both away."

56

5

The Thing Behind the Veil

April Bell leaned across the little eight-sided table, her strained white face floating close to his in the thick haze of hot blue smoke and alcohol that the Knob Hill's patrons paid so well to breathe. Her husky voice was very low, and her long eyes watched his startled expression with a painful intensity, as if to estimate the impact of her words.

Barbee had a queer, numbed feeling in the pit of his stomach; it was amazingly like the effect of a tremendous slug of whisky—he was numbed, yet with a foreknowledge of warmth to come. He gulped and breathed again and nodded anxiously. He didn't quite dare speak—he didn't want to challenge the girl's confession, nor could he yet accept it.

Her white, troubled face smiled slightly, relaxing to a faint relief.

"You see," she told him slowly, "Mother was my father's second wife. Young enough to have been his daughter. I know she never loved him—I never really understood why she married him. Such a

57

disagreeable brute, and he never had any money. Certainly she wasn't following the rules she laid down for me."

Barbee reached for a cigarette. He didn't want to interrupt the girl, and he thought she would stop if she knew the agonized intensity of his own interest. He needed something to do with his nervous hands. She shook her head when he offered the worn case to her, and her slow, hushed voice went on.

"But Mother had been in love with some other man—she never told me his name. Maybe that explains her marriage and the way she felt about men. My father never did much to make her love him. Perhaps he knew something about that other man. I know he suspected that I wasn't really his."

Careful not to let his fingers tremble, Barbee lit his cigarette.

"Father was a stern man," the girl went on. "A Puritan, really—he belonged back in old Salem. He was never actually ordained—he couldn't quite agree with any denomination—but he used to preach his own harsh faith on street corners here in town on market Saturdays, whenever he could get a few idlers to listen. He considered himself a righteous man, trying to warn the world away from sin. Actually, he could be monstrously cruel.

"He was cruel to me."

Old pain made a shadow on the girl's pale face.

"You see, I was a precocious child. Father had older children, by his first marriage, who were not. I could read a little by the time I was three. I understood people. Somehow, I could just sense what people would do, and things that would happen. My father wasn't pleased to see me more clever than my older brothers and sisters—the ones he knew were his own."

She smiled faintly.

"I think I was pretty, too—my mother always told me so. No doubt I was spoiled and vain, and sometimes nasty to the others. Anyhow, I was always in some quarrel with the older children, with my mother taking sides with me against them and my father. Of course they were all much bigger, but even then I think I was pretty clever in finding ways to hurt them."

Her oval face turned very white.

"And Father, too," she whispered. "I used to flaunt my red hair at him—it was lighter then, and my mother kept it in long curls. It happened that he and Mother were both dark-haired, and now I'm sure that other man, the one he suspected, must have been a redhead. Then I only knew that the color of my hair goaded him to fury. I was just five years old the first time he called me a witch child—and snatched me out of Mother's arms to whip me."

Her greenish eyes were dark and dry. To Barbee they seemed hard as emeralds, ruthless with an old and unforgotten hate. Her face, except for the scarlet bows of her lips, seemed white as the wolf fur flung over the chair beside her. Her hushed, hurried voice was bitter and dry—as cruel, he thought, as the parching winds of the Ala-shan must be.

"My father always hated me," she told him. "His children did—no, I never believed that I was really his. They hated me because I was different. Because I was prettier than any of the girls, and quicker than any of the boys. Because I could do things none of them could. Yes— because I was already a witch!"

She made a savage little nod.

"They all stood against me—all except Mother. I had to defend myself and strike back when I could. I knew about witches from the Bible—Father used to read a chapter at every mealtime, and then chant an endless grace before he would let us eat. I asked questions about what witches could do. Mother told me some things, and I learned a lot from the old midwife who came when my married sister had a child—she was a queer old woman! By the time I was seven years old, I had started to practice the things I had learned."

Barbee sat listening, half incredulous and yet fascinated. The girl's taut face swam close to him in the thick blue haze, mirroring all she said, a white enigma of old pain and hate and occasional glee, sullen-lipped and yet strangely lovely.

"I began with small things," she whispered. "As a child would. The first serious incident came later, when I was nearly nine. My half brother Harry had a dog named Tige. For some reason Tige always hated me. He would growl when I tried to touch him—like that Mondrick woman's ugly dog did today. Another sign, my father said, that I was a witch child sent to visit the wrath of God upon his house.

"One day Tige bit me. Harry laughed at me and called me a wicked little witch. He was going to let Tige chase me—that was what he said. Maybe he was just teasing. I don't know—but I said I'd show him that I really was a witch. I told him I'd put a spell on Tige and kill him. I did my best."

Her long eyes narrowed, and her nostrils seemed to pinch.

"I remembered all the old midwife had told me. I made up a little chant about Tige dying, and whispered it during family prayers. I gathered hairs out of his blanket and spit on them and burned them in the kitchen stove. And I waited for Tige to die."

Barbee tried to ease her painful intensity.

"You were just a child," he murmured. "Just playing."

"Tige went mad the very next week," she said quietly. "Father had to shoot him."

Her quiet seemed more startling than a scream. Barbee moved uneasily and caught his breath.

"Coincidence," he muttered.

"Maybe." A brief amusement lit the girl's face, as if she had seen his apprehensive start. "I don't think so." That shadow of old bitterness came back. "I believed in my power. Harry did. So did my father, when Harry told him. I ran to Mother, where she was sewing. Father dragged me outside, and whipped me again."

Her long trembling fingers lifted her glass, but she set it back untasted, absorbed in her narrative.

"Father hurt me cruelly, and I felt that he was savagely unjust. While he was whipping me, I screamed that I would get even. As soon as he let me go, I tried to. I slipped out to the dairy and pulled hairs out of the three best cows and the bull my father had just bought for the herd. I spat on the hairs and burned them with a match and buried them behind the barn. I made another chant."

Her long dark eyes peered somberly through the smoke.

"Promptly a week afterward, the bull dropped dead."

"Coincidence," Barbee whispered faintly. "It must have been coincidence."

Her scarlet lips twisted to a wry, slight smile.

"The veterinarian said it was hemorrhagic septicemia," she said softly. "The three cows died, too, as well as the best yearling heifer and two steer calves. My father remembered the threats I had screamed, and Harry had watched me digging behind the barn. Harry tattled, and Father whipped me until I confessed that I had tried to kill the cattle."

Abruptly, with a swift, catlike grace of motion, she tossed off her drink. Her greenish eyes looked straight at Barbee, glazed and hard as if she didn't see anything. Nervously, her tense fingers started twirling the glass. The thin stem snapped, and the bowl splintered on the floor. Without seeming to notice, she went on huskily:

"That was a dreadful night, Barbee. Father sent all the other children to stay at my married sister's house—to escape the taint of witchcraft, he ranted, and avoid the dreadful wrath of God. Just he and Mother and I were left, to pray it out together, Father said, and let me suffer the just retribution for my sin."

Nervously, her red-nailed fingers spun the stem of the shattered glass.

"I'll never forget that night. Mother cried and tried to make excuses for me and begged for mercy—I remember her down on her knees, on the splintered pine floor before my father, as if he had been another angry deity. But he didn't pay much attention to her prayers. He stamped up and down that gloomy little room, and shouted his questions and his cruel accusations at Mother and me, and read from the Bible by the light of a smelly coal-oil lamp. Again and again he read that terrible line: *Thou shalt not suffer a witch to live.*"

Afraid she might cut her trembling hand on the daggerpoint of the broken glass, Barbee lifted it out of her fingers. She didn't seem to notice.

"It went on all night," she whispered. "Father would make us kneel and pray. He would walk the floor and sob, and curse my mother and me. He would jerk her up when she knelt at his feet and cuff her about the room and warn her not to shelter a witch child in her bosom. Finally he would snatch me out of her arms, and whip me again, until he nearly killed me. And then he would read out of the Bible.

"Thou shalt not suffer a witch to live."

She paused, her long eyes staring at his hands. Barbee looked down and saw a bright red drop on his finger. Carefully, he set the broken glass stem in the ash tray. He wiped the blood on his handkerchief, and lit another cigarette.

"He would have killed me, too," the girl's hoarse, bitter voice went on. "Mother fought him, the last time, to make him let me go. She broke a chair over his head, but that didn't seem to hurt him much. He dropped me on the floor, and started for his shotgun leaning by the

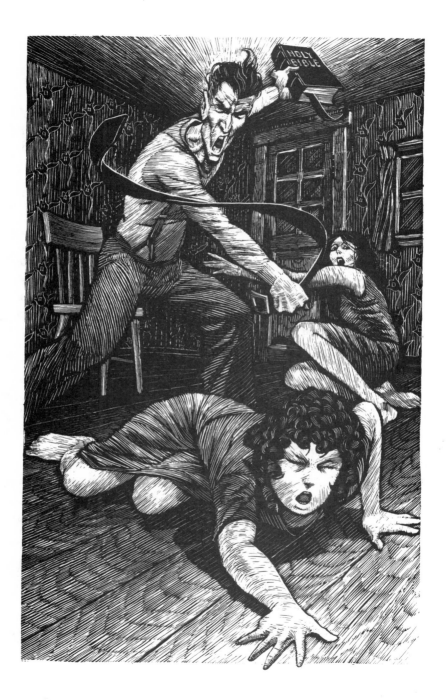

door. I knew he meant to kill us both, and I screamed out a chant to stop him."

Her husky voice caught, and she swallowed hard.

"It worked. He fell on the floor, just as he reached the gun. The doctors said later that it was a cerebral hemorrhage. They told him he had better learn to control his temper. I don't suppose he ever did, because he dropped dead the day he got out of the hospital and heard that Mother had taken me and run away to California."

Barbee was a little startled to discover that the waiter had swept up the shattered glass and set two fresh daiquiris on the tiny table. April Bell lifted her drink thirstily. Barbee found two more dollars in his flat pocketbook, and wondered briefly what the dinner check would come to. He sipped at his own drink, and carefully held himself from interrupting.

"I never knew exactly what Mother believed." That answered the question he hadn't dared to ask. "She loved me. I think she could have forgiven me anything. She only made me promise, when we were safe out of Father's house, that I would never try to make another spell. I didn't—so long as she lived."

She set back her empty glass, her white fingers steady again.

"Mother was all right—you'd have liked her, Barbee. You couldn't really blame her for not trusting men, and she did all she could for me. As the years went by, I think she almost forgot all that had happened back here at Clarendon. I know she wanted to. She would never talk of coming back, even to visit her old friends here. I know it would have shocked her horribly to know what I was—what I really am."

That hardness had melted from the girl's greenish eyes; they seemed liquid now, huge and dark and queerly eager. "I kept my promise not to work any more spells," she told him softly. "But nothing could stop my knowledge of the powers awakening and growing within me. Nothing could keep me from feeling what other people thought and foreseeing things that were going to happen."

"I know." Barbee nodded. "That's what we call the nose for news."

She shook her bright head gravely.

"It's more than that," she insisted quietly. "Other things happened. I didn't work any more spells—not on purpose. But things happened that I couldn't help."

He listened, and tried not to let her see him shiver.

"There was a girl at school," she said. "I didn't like her, anyhow—she was too nasty-nice, always quoting the Bible and meddling in other people's lives like those half sisters I hated. Once she won a journalism scholarship that I had set my heart on. I knew she had cheated to get it. I couldn't help wishing something would happen to her."

"And," Barbee breathed, "did it?"

"It did," April told him gently. "The day that girl was supposed to accept the scholarship, she woke up ill. She tried to go to the auditorium anyhow and fainted on the way. It was acute appendicitis— the doctors said. She nearly died. If she had—"

Nearly black, her long eyes stared straight at Barbee. He saw the bleak memories in them, of dread and pain. He saw her white body shudder in the daring gown.

"Another coincidence, you can say. That's what I wanted to think, Barbee. Because I didn't really hate that girl. I thought I'd lose my mind until the doctors said she would pull through. But that wasn't the only incident. Other things kept happening, almost as serious. I grew to be afraid of myself."

Her voice sank.

"Don't you see, Barbee?" Her dark eyes begged him to understand. "I didn't make any conscious spells, but still that power was working in me. When such seeming accidents always follow the acts and wishes of a person, it gets to be beyond the realm of coincidence. Can't you see?"

Barbee nodded. After a while he remembered to breathe again. At last he muttered huskily, "I guess so."

"Please try to see my side of it," the girl urged softly. "I didn't ask to be a witch—I was born this way."

Barbee drummed nervously on the table with his knuckles. He saw the waiter coming back and impatiently waved him away. He gulped, and said uneasily: "Look here, April—do you mind if I ask a few more questions?"

Her white shoulders shrugged with a mute and weary bitterness.

"Please," he said. "Perhaps I can help—I do want to."

"Now that I've told you," she whispered faintly, "what does anything matter?"

"There are things that still might matter a good deal—to you and me." Her white face seemed dull and sad, but this time she let him take her hand across the tiny table. Earnestly he asked: "Have you ever talked about this thing to anybody who might understand—a psychiatrist, I mean, or a scientist like old Mondrick was?"

Her bright head nodded apathetically.

"I have a friend who knows about me—he knew my mother and I think he used to help us, back when times were hard. Two years ago, he persuaded me to go to Dr. Glenn. Young Dr. Archer Glenn, you know, here at Clarendon."

Barbee tried to smother an instant jealous desire to know more about that friend. His fingers tightened on the girl's limp, cool hand, but he managed to nod calmly.

"I know Glenn," he said. "Interviewed him once, while his father was still working with him—I was writing up Glennhaven for a special medical edition of the *Star*. Glennhaven is supposed to be about the best private mental hospital in the country. What—?"

Anxiety caught his voice, and he had to swallow.

"What did Glenn tell you?"

Her pale face reflected a faint, defiant amusement.

"Dr. Glenn doesn't believe in witches," she purred gently. "He tried to psychoanalyze me. I spent an hour a day for nearly a year, lying on a couch in his office at Glennhaven and telling him all about me. I tried to cooperate—you have to, at forty dollars an hour. I told him everything—and still he doesn't believe in witches."

She chuckled softly.

"Glenn thinks everything in the universe can be explained on the basis that two and two make four. If you put any kind of spell on anything, he always insisted, then wait long enough, some accident is sure to happen to it. He used big words to tell me that I was unconsciously kidding myself. He thought I was a little bit insane—a paranoiac. He wouldn't believe that I was a witch."

A faint malice curved her crimson lips.

"Not even when I showed him!"

"Showed him?" Barbee echoed. "How?"

"Dogs don't like me," she said. "Glennhaven's out in the country, you know, and the dogs off the farms across the road used to come and bark at me when I got off the bus, and chase me into the building. One day I got tired of that—and I wanted to show Glenn.

"So I brought a little modeling clay. I mixed it with dust from around

65

a bench at the corner, where the dogs used to stop. When I got to Glenn's office, I molded it into rough little figures of five of the dogs. I whispered a little chant and spat on them and smashed them on the floor. Then I told Glenn to look out the window."

Glee danced in the girl's long eyes.

"We waited ten minutes. I pointed out the dogs. They had followed me to the building. They hung around a little while, barking at the window. Then they all started away after a little terrier bitch—she must have been in heat. They ran out into the highway, all together, just as a speeding car came around the curve. The driver tried to swerve but he didn't have time. The car hit them and turned over as it skidded off the road. All the dogs were killed—I'm glad the driver wasn't."

Barbee shook himself uneasily, and caught his breath.

"What did Glenn say?"

"He seemed to be delighted." April Bell smiled enigmatically. "It turned out the bitch belonged to a chiropractor who lives down the road, and he said the dogs had been digging up the grounds. He doesn't like either dogs or chiropractors—but still he wouldn't believe in witches."

The girl shook her burnished head.

"The dogs had died because the chiropractor's bitch happened to slip her leash, he said, and not because of any spell of mine. He went on to say that I didn't really want to give up my psychosis and we couldn't make any progress until I changed my attitude. He said my gift was just a paranoid delusion. He charged me another forty dollars for that hour, and we went ahead with the analysis."

Barbee exhaled blue smoke into the thick blue air, and moved uncomfortably in the angular seat. He saw the waiter watching imperatively, but he didn't want another drink. He looked uncertainly back at April Bell. Her brief amusement had vanished; her face seemed tired and sad. Slowly she drew her cold hands out of his fingers.

"And you think he was right, Barbee."

He gripped the edges of the little table.

"My God!" he whispered explosively. "It would be no great wonder if you showed some tendencies of insanity, after all you've lived through!"

A warm surge of pity rose in him, and turned to burning anger against all her old misfortunes, against the ignorance and the cruel fanaticism of her stern father who had forced her to accept such pitiful delusions. He felt an imperative urge to shelter her, to help her back toward complete sanity. The hot, foul atmosphere of the crowded bar began to choke him. He coughed to hide his feelings. Too much show of pity would only offend her.

Quietly she said: "I know I'm not insane."

So, Barbee understood, did all lunatics. He didn't know what to say next. He wanted time to think—to analyze her curious confession and check all these evasive uncertainties against the ruthless fact of Mondrick's death. He looked at his watch, and nodded toward the dining room.

"Shall we eat?"

She nodded eagerly. "I'm hungry as a wolf!"

That word checked Barbee—reminding him of Aunt Agatha's odd jade pin. She was already reaching, with her swift feline felicity of action, for the white fur beside her, but Barbee sat heavily back in the angular chair.

"Let's have another drink." He signalled the waiter and ordered two more daiquiris before he turned to face her slight frown of puzzlement. "It's late," he said, "but there's one more thing I've got to ask about." He hesitated and saw that wary, dangerous alertness come back to her white, taut face. Reluctantly, he demanded:

"You did kill that kitten?"

"I did."

His hands gripped the table until the knuckles snapped.

"And you did it to cause the death of Dr. Mondrick?"

In the haze of smoke, her bright head nodded slightly.

"And he died."

The calm matter-of-factness of her tone sent a shiver down Barbee's spine. Darkly greenish, her watchful eyes seemed flatly opaque. Her oval face was a lifeless, waxen mask. He couldn't guess what she thought or what she felt. The bridge of confidence was swept away, and it left a chasm of peril between them.

"Please, April—"

Quick sympathy quivered in his voice. He wanted urgently to reach and comfort the defiant loneliness he knew she felt, but his impulsive effort failed to penetrate her hostile citadel. Barbee dropped to a note as cool and gravely impersonal as hers had been, asking:

"Why did you want to kill him?"

Across that tiny table her low and toneless voice was as distant as if it called from within a far-off fortress tower.

"Because I was afraid."

Barbee's brows went up.

"Afraid of what?" he demanded. "You said you didn't even know him. And how could he have harmed you? I did have an old grudge against him, of course—for dropping me from his little circle of disciples when he organized the Foundation. But he was harmless—just a scientist, digging for knowledge."

"I know what he was doing." The girl's voice was hard and cold and still remote. "You see, Barbee, I always wanted to know about myself—and the power born in me. I didn't study psychology in college, because all the professors seemed stupidly wrong. But I've read nearly everything that has been published on such unusual cases as mine."

Her eyes were hard as polished malachite.

"Did you know Mondrick was an outstanding authority on witch-craft? Well, he was. He knew all the history of the witch persecutions, and a great deal more besides. He had studied the beliefs of every primitive race—and those beliefs were something more to him than strange fairy stories.

"You know the myths of Greece, for instance—full of illicit love affairs between the gods and human girls. Nearly all the Greek heroes—Hercules and Perseus and the rest—were supposed to have illegitimate immortal blood. They all had remarkable powers and gifts. Well, years ago Mondrick wrote a monograph analyzing those legends as racial memories of conflict and occasional interbreeding between two prehistoric races—the tall Cro-Magnons, perhaps, he suggested in that first paper, and the brutish Neanderthalers.

"But you worked under him, Barbee—you must know the range of his interests. He dug up graves and measured skulls and fitted broken pots together and deciphered old inscriptions. He looked for differences in the people of today—tested their blood and measured their reactions and analyzed their dreams. He had an open mind for everything that most scientists throw out because it doesn't fit their own preconceptions. He was an authority on extrasensory perception and psychokinesis before anybody else thought of the words. He tried every avenue to find what he wanted."

"That's true," Barbee said. "So what?"

"Mondrick was always cautious in what he wrote," the girl's far, cold voice went on. "He covered up his real meaning with harmless scientific words—to keep from exciting too many people, I suppose, before his proofs were ready. Finally, a dozen years ago, he quit publishing anything at all—he even bought up and burned the copies of his early monographs. But he had already written too much. I knew what he was doing."

April Bell paused while the slow waiter brought the change out of Barbee's lone twenty, automatically sipping at her drink. That made three, he thought—no, it must be four. She held them well enough. When the waiter was gone, she resumed in the same flat voice:

"Mondrick believed in witches."

"Nonsense!" Barbee started. "He was a scientist."

"And he still believed in witches," she insisted.

"That's what frightened me today. Most scientists, so-called, reject the evidence without a look, but Mondrick had spent his whole life trying to put witchcraft on a scientific basis. He went to the Ala-shan to find new evidence. And I knew today—from the way everything happened, from the fear on those men's faces and Mondrick's cautious first remarks—that he had found what he wanted."

"But—not that!"

"You don't believe, Barbee." Her dry voice was edged again with a veiled mockery. "Most people don't. That fact is our chief protection— for we are the enemies of people." Her red lips curved at his incredulous amazement. "You can see why men must always hate us— because we are different. Because we have inborn powers greater than are given men—and yet not great enough!"

A savage spark of wild hostility lit her greenish eyes, as she half whispered that. In a moment they were dark again, expressionless and hard, but Barbee had glimpsed a naked, stark ferocity that he couldn't forget. His own glance dropped uneasily, and he deliberately drained his cocktail.

"Mondrick was trying to expose us—so that men could destroy us," her hard voice rapped. "That's what frightened me tonight. Perhaps he had invented a scientific test to identify witches. Years ago, I remember, he wrote a scientific paper on the correlation of blood groups and introversion—and *introvert* is one of the harmless scientific terms he used to use when he was really writing about witches.

"Can't you understand, Barbee?"

Her low, husky voice was suddenly pleading, and that hard blankness had gone from her eyes. Perhaps the alcohol had affected her, after all, to dissolve the barriers of normal reserve. Now her eyes seemed warm, as intimately appealing as her voice.

"Don't you see, Will, that I was fighting tonight for my life? Can you blame me for using all my own poor weapons against such a great and cunning enemy as old Mondrick? For he was my enemy—as that stupid dairy man was, and all true men must be. Men aren't to blame. I know that, Barbee. But then—am I?"

Tears wet her limpid eyes.

"I can't help it, Barbee. The trouble began when the first witch was hounded and stoned to death by the first savage man. It will go on till the last witch is dead. Always, everywhere, men must follow that old Biblical law: *Thou shalt not suffer a witch to live.*"

Her naked shoulders shrugged hopelessly.

"That's me, Will," she whispered bitterly. "You wanted to break the pretty little shell of my illusion. You weren't satisfied with my performance as a human woman—though I can't believe it's really so bad. You had to see the thing beyond my veil."

Wearily, she reached for her white fur again.

"So here I am," she told him quietly. "A hunted enemy of all the human breed. Old Mondrick was the ruthless human hunter—cunningly seizing every resource of science to track down and wipe out me and my kind. Can you blame me if I made a feeble little spell to save myself? Can you blame me if it worked?"

Barbee moved to rise, and sat back abruptly. He shook himself, as if to break the fascination of her liquid eyes and shining hair and softly pleading voice.

"Your kind?" he echoed sharply. "Then you aren't alone?"

The warmth left her long eyes; again they narrowed, flat and cruel and wary, the eyes of a pursued and desperate animal. Her face went whiter, and her voice turned coldly toneless.

"I'm quite alone."

Barbee leaned forward, grimly intent.

"Mondrick spoke of a 'secret enemy.' Do you think he meant—witches?"

"He did."

"Do you know any others?"

Her answer, he thought, was a fractional second delayed. Her eyes were screens for thought, opaque and hard. Her tense white face showed nothing.

"No." Suddenly her whole body trembled, so that he knew she was fighting back tears. In the same flat and lifeless voice, she asked: "Must *you* persecute me?"

"I'm sorry," Barbee whispered. "But now, when you have told me so much, you must go on and tell me everything. How else can I judge?" His hands closed hard on the edges of the little table. "Do you know what Mondrick meant when he spoke of a leader coming—the Child of Night?"

He half glimpsed, for a tiny instant, a queer little smile—too swiftly come and gone for him to be sure she had smiled at all. Her fine shoulders lifted above the strapless gown.

"How could I know?" she said. "Is that all?"

"One more question—and then we'll eat." Barbee's gray eyes strove to pierce those hard screens of unfeeling malachite. "Do you know what proteins Dr. Mondrick was allergic to?"

Her wary hostility gave way to a genuine bewilderment.

"Allergic?" Her voice was puzzled. "That has something to do with hay fever and indigestion, hasn't it? Why no, of course I don't. Really, Will, I didn't know Mondrick personally—only his work. I don't think I ever saw him before tonight."

"Thank God!" breathed Will Barbee.

He stood up and filled his lungs gratefully with the heavy bar fumes, smiling down at her.

"That was a pretty cruel grilling," he said. "Forgive me, April—but I just had to know those things."

She remained seated, and her tired face failed to reflect his eager smile.

"Forgiven," she said wearily. "And we'll skip the dinner. You may go when you wish."

"Go?" he protested quickly. "Lady, you have promised me the

evening. You said you were hungry as a wolf, and the Knob Hill chef is famous for his steaks. We can dance after dinner—or maybe take a drive in the moonlight. You don't *want* me to go?"

The hard screens vanished from her eyes, and he saw a tender delight.

"You mean, Barbee," she whispered softly, "even after you've seen the strange, poor thing behind my veil—"

Barbee grinned, and suddenly laughed. His tension had somehow evaporated completely. "If you're a witch, I'm completely under your spells."

She rose with a smile that grew slowly radiant.

"Thank you, Will." She let him take her fur coat, and they started toward the dining room. "But, please," she whispered huskily, "just for tonight—won't you try to help me forget that I'm—what I am?"

Barbee nodded happily.

"I'll try, angel."

6
As a Wolf Runs—

They stayed at the Knob Hill until closing time. The steaks were perfect. The dance band played, he felt, for the two of them alone; and April Bell moved in his arms with a light, smooth grace that made him think of some wild creature. They spoke of nothing graver than the music and the wine, and she seemed to forget that she might be anything more dangerous than a very gorgeous redhead. So did Barbee—most of the time.

The white flash of her perfect teeth, however, reminded him now and then of the white jade pin he had brought in his pocket—he knew it must be hers, but still he didn't quite dare return it. The greenish mystery of her long eyes shocked him more than once with a disquieting awareness that the haunting riddle of Mondrick's death was still not really solved, that her own strange confession had only added another new enigma.

He wanted to drive her home, but her own maroon convertible was parked on the lot behind the nightclub. He walked her to it, opened the door for her, and then caught her arm impulsively as she started to slide under the wheel.

"You know April—" He hesitated, not quite certain what he meant to say, but the bright expectancy on her face made him go on. "I've a feeling about you that I don't understand. A funny feeling—I can't explain—"

He paused again, awkwardly. Her white face was lifted to him; he wanted to kiss her, but that sudden peremptory emotion demanded expression.

"An odd feeling that I've known you somewhere, before tonight." His voice was bewildered, groping. "That you are part of something— old and somehow very important—that belongs to us both. A feeling that you wake something sleeping in me."

He shrugged, helpless.

"I want to tell you," he whispered. "But I can't quite pin it down."

She smiled in the darkness, and her velvet voice hummed a bit of a song to which they had danced: "Maybe It's Love."

Maybe it was. Years had passed since the last time Barbee had really thought himself in love, but as he recalled the experience it had never seemed quite so disturbing as this. He was still afraid—not of the dark-lipped girl who seemed to be waiting for his kiss, not even of the twentieth-century sorceress she pretended to be, but rather of that vague and strangely terrifying feeling she aroused, of awakening senses and powers and old half memories in himself. There was nothing he could actually put into words, but he couldn't help shivering again.

"This wind's still cold!" He didn't try to kiss her. Abruptly, almost roughly, he pushed her into the car and shut the door. "Thanks for a wonderful time." He was trying to cover the unresolved conflict of his emotions, and his voice turned brisk and cool. "I'll call you tomorrow at the Trojan Arms."

She looked at him from the wheel. The slow, tantalizing smile on her dark lips suggested an amused and pleased awareness of all the disturbed emotion she aroused in him.

" 'Night, Barbee," she purred gently, and bent to start the motor. Barbee stood watching as she drove away, fingering the white jade wolf in his pocket. He wondered why he hadn't dared return it. The bitter wind struck him, and he turned uneasily toward his own shabby car.

Barbee covered Mondrick's funeral for the *Star*. The simple services were held at two, next day. Although the wind had shifted toward the south, the day was blustering and raw, and only the blind widow and a few close friends from the university and the Foundation braved it to watch the graveside ceremony.

Nick Spivak and Rex Chittum were among the pallbearers, looking very taut and grim. Surprisingly, Sam Quain was absent. Barbee walked up to Nora, who stood alone near where Rowena Mondrick waited with her nurse and her great tawny dog, to ask concernedly:

"Is Sam ill, Nora?" He saw her start, as if from grave preoccupation. "I thought he'd be here."

"Hello, Will." She gave him a little wan smile; Nora had always seemed friendly, even since Sam and Mondrick changed. "No, Sam's all right," she said. "He just stayed at the house to watch that green box they brought back from Asia. Can you imagine what they have in it?"

Barbee shook his head; he couldn't imagine.

Rowena Mondrick must have heard their voices, for she turned quickly toward them—her attitude, Barbee thought, oddly alarmed. Her taut face was colorless beneath her opaque black glasses; the grasp of her thin fingers on the huge dog's leash and its silver-studded collar seemed somehow almost frantic.

"Will Barbee?" she called sharply. "Is it you?"

"Yes, Rowena," he said, and paused to fumble for some word of consolation that wouldn't merely mock her grief. She didn't wait for that.

"I still want to see you, Will," she said urgently. "I hope I'm not too late to help you. Can you come to the house this afternoon—say, at four?"

Barbee caught his breath, staring uncertainly at the stern purpose which had almost erased even the grief from her thin white face, turning its sad, patient sweetness into something almost terrible. He recalled her telephoned warning against April Bell, and wondered again what Mondrick's death had done to her mind.

"At four," he promised. "I'll come, Rowena."

At five minutes of four, he parked in front of the rambling old red-brick house on University Avenue. It looked rundown and shabby—the Foundation had taken most of Mondrick's own fortune, besides the sums he raised from others. The shutters needed repair and naked spots showed through the unraked lawns. He rang the doorbell and Rowena herself came to let him in.

"Thank you for coming, Will." Her low, gracious voice seemed entirely composed. Tears had stained her face, but her grief had not overwhelmed her. Moving as confidently as if she could see, she closed the door and pointed to a chair.

He stood a moment looking around the gloomy, old-fashioned front room that he had known ever since he and Sam Quain boarded here as students. The room was faintly perfumed from a huge bowl of roses set on her grand piano—he saw the names on the card beside them, Sam and Nora Quain. A gas fire glowed in the dark cavern of the old fireplace. The huge dog Turk lay before it, regarding Barbee with alert yellow eyes.

"Sit down," Rowena Mondrick urged softly. "I've sent Miss Ulford out to do some shopping, because we must talk alone, Will."

Puzzled and rather uncomfortable, he took the chair she indicated.

"I want you to know that I'm terribly sorry, Rowena," he said awkwardly. "It seems so awfully ironic that Dr. Mondrick should die just at the moment of what must have been his greatest triumph—"

"He didn't die," she said softly. "He was murdered—I imagined you knew that, Will."

Barbee gulped. He didn't intend to discuss his suspicions and perplexities with anybody else—not until he had managed to make up his own mind about April Bell.

"I wondered," he admitted. "I didn't know."

"But you saw April Bell last night?"

"We had dinner," Barbee said. He watched the blind woman as she came with her almost disconcerting certainty of motion to stand before him, tall and straight in her severely cut black suit, resting one thin hand on the piano. A faint resentment stirred him to say defensively: "I know Turk didn't seem to like April Bell, but I think she's something pretty special."

"I was afraid you would." Rowena's voice seemed gravely sad. "But I talked to Nora Quain, and she doesn't like the woman. Turk doesn't, and I don't. There's a reason, Will, that you should know."

Barbee sat erect, uncomfortable in his chair. Mondrick's widow and Sam Quain's wife weren't picking girl friends for him, but he didn't say so. Turk stirred before the fire, keeping baleful yellow eyes on Barbee.

"That woman's bad," Rowena whispered. "And bad for you!" She leaned a little toward him, cold lights glowing on her old silver necklace and her heavy silver brooch. "I want you to promise me, Will, that you won't see her any more."

"Why, Rowena!" Barbee tried to laugh—and tried not to think of April Bell's queer confession. "Don't you know I'm a big boy now?"

His attempted lightness brought no smile.

"I'm blind, Will." Rowena Mondrick's white head tilted slightly, almost as if her black glasses could see him. "But not to everything. I've shared my husband's work since we were young. I had my small part in the strange, lonely, terrible war he fought. Now he's dead—murdered, I believe."

The blind woman stiffened.

"And your charming new friend April Bell," she said very softly, "must be the secret enemy who murdered him!"

Barbee caught his breath to protest—and knew there was nothing he could say. A frightened impulse urged him to defend April Bell. But he remembered Mondrick's gasping death and that strangled kitten with the needle in its heart. He remembered her own confession. He swallowed hard and murmured uneasily:

"I can't believe she did that."

Rowena Mondrick stood taut and straight.

"That woman killed my husband." Her voice turned sharp, and the big dog rose uneasily behind her. "But Marck's dead. We can't help that. You're the one in danger now."

She came slowly toward Barbee, holding out both her thin hands. He stood up and took them silently. They felt tense and cold, and they clung to his fingers with a sudden desperate pressure.

"Please, Will!" she whispered. "Let me warn you!"

"Really, Rowena!" He tried to laugh. "April's a very charming girl, and I'm not allergic."

Her cold fingers quivered.

"April Bell won't try to kill you, Will," she told him quietly. "Your danger is something other than death, and uglier. Because she will try to change you—to arouse something in you that should never be awakened."

The big dog came bristling, to stand close against her black skirt. "She's bad, Will." The blind lenses peered at him disquietingly. "I can see the evil in her, and I know she means to try to claim you for her own wicked breed. You had better die like poor Marck, than follow the dreadful path where she will try to lead you. Believe me, Will!"

He dropped her cold hands, trying not to shudder.

"No, Rowena," he protested uncomfortably, "I'm afraid I can't believe you. I think your husband's death was probably just the unfortunate result of too much excitement and fatigue for a man seventy and ill. I'm afraid you're dwelling too much on it."

He crossed hopefully to the piano.

"Do you feel like playing something? That might help."

"I've no time for music now." She patted the dog's great tawny head, nervously. "Because I'm going to join Sam and Nick and Rex in poor Marck's unfinished battle. Now won't you think about my warning— and stay away from April Bell?"

"I can't do that." In spite of him, resentment edged his voice. "She's a charming girl, and I can't believe she's up to any ugly business."

He tried to warm his tone.

"But I'm truly sorry for you, Rowena. It seems to me that you've just been brooding too much. I don't suppose there's much I can do, since you feel this way, but you do need help. Why don't you call Dr. Glenn?"

She stepped back from him, indignantly.

"No, Will," she whispered. "I'm entirely sane." Her thin fingers clung fiercely to the dog's collar; and the huge beast pressed close to her, watching Barbee with unfriendly yellow eyes. "I need no psychiatrist," she told him softly. "But I'm afraid you may—before you're through with April Bell."

"Sorry, Rowena," he said abruptly. "I'm going."

"Don't, Will!" she called sharply. "Don't trust—"

That was all he heard.

He drove back to town, but it was hard to keep his mind on his reportorial chores. He took no stock in Rowena Mondrick's crazy warning. He really meant to call April Bell's apartment, but somehow he kept putting it off. He wanted to see her, yet daylight had failed to dispel any of his tortured uncertainties about her. Finally, as he left the city room, he decided with an uneasy relief that now it was obviously too late to make the call.

He stopped for a drink at the bar across the street, and had more than one, and took a bottle with him when he drove back to his lonely apartment in the dilapidated old house on Bread Street. A hot shower, he thought, might help the alcohol relax him. He was taking off his clothing when he found the white jade pin in his pocket. He stood a long time, absently turning the tiny object on his sweaty palm, staring at it—

Wondering—

The tiny malachite eye was the same color as the eyes of April Bell— when she was in her most wary and alarming mood. The fine detail of the running wolf's limbs and snarling head had been cut with careful skill. From the worn sleekness of the white jade, he knew it must be very old. A very old trinket, it was cut in a wiry, lean-lined style of workmanship he had never seen before.

Remembering the white wolf coat, he wondered suddenly what the wolf, as a symbol, meant to April Bell. Dr. Glenn must have found her, he thought, a remarkably interesting analytic subject—he wished for an instant that it were possible to get a look at Glenn's private records of her case.

He started and blinked, trying to rid himself of a disconcerting impression that the malachite eye had winked at him maliciously. He was almost asleep, standing half undressed in his narrow bedroom beside the ramshackle chiffonier. The damned pin had almost hypnotized him. He resisted a sudden, savage impulse to flush it down the commode.

That would be insane. Of course, he admitted to himself, he was afraid of April Bell. But then he had always been a little afraid of women—perhaps Dr. Glenn could tell him why. Even the most approachable female made him a little uneasy. The more they mattered, the more afraid he was.

His hunch about the pin couldn't mean anything, he assured himself. The damned thing got on his nerves just because it stood for April Bell. He'd have to taper off the whisky—that was all his trouble, as Glenn would surely tell him. If he obeyed that panicky impulse to dispose of the pin, it would only be an admission that he believed April

Bell to be—actually—just what she said she was. He couldn't accept that.

He put the pin carefully in a cigar box on the chiffonier, along with a thimble and his old pocket watch and a discarded fountain pen and a number of used razor blades. His uneasy thoughts of April Bell were not so easy to put away. He couldn't escape considering the faint but infinitely disturbing possibility that she really was—he felt reluctant even to think the word—a witch.

A being born a little different, he preferred to phrase it. He remembered reading something about the Rhine experiments at Duke University. Some people, those sober scientists had proved, perceived the world with something beyond the ordinary physical senses. Some people, they had demonstrated, displayed a direct control over probability, without the use of any physical agency. Some did, some didn't. Had April Bell been born with that same difference, manifest in a more extreme degree?

Probability—he recalled a classroom digression of Mondrick's on that word, back in Anthropology 413. Probability, the bright-eyed old scholar said, was the key concept of modern physics. The laws of nature, he insisted, were not absolute, but merely established statistical averages. The paperweight on his desk—it was an odd little terra-cotta lamp which he must have dug out of some Roman ruin, the black-glazed relief on the circular top of it showing the she-wolf suckling the founders of Rome—the lamp was supported, Mondrick said, only by the chance collisions of vibrating atoms. At any instant, there was a slight but definite probability that it might fall through the seemingly solid desk.

And the modern physicists, Barbee knew, interpreted the whole universe in terms of probability. The stability of atoms was a matter of probability—and the instability, in the atomic bomb. The direct mental control of probability would surely open terrifying avenues of power—and the Rhine experiments had seemingly established that control. Had April Bell, he wondered uneasily, just been born with a unique and dangerous mental power to govern the operation of probability?

Unlikely, he told himself. But nothing at all, old Mondrick himself had insisted, was completely impossible in this statistical universe. The remotest impossibility became merely remotely improbable. Barbee shrugged impatiently, and turned on the shower—the new physics, with its law of uncertainty and its denial of all the comfortable old concepts of matter and space and time, and its atom bombs, became suddenly as disquieting as the dark riddle of Mondrick's death.

In the shower, he fell to wondering what that terra-cotta lamp had meant to Mondrick. What racial memory could be represented in the legend of those Roman heroes mothered by the wolf bitch? Barbee couldn't quite imagine.

He toweled himself wearily, poured himself a generous nightcap and went to bed with a magazine. His mind refused to be diverted, however, from those disquieting channels. Why had Mondrick and his obviously frightened companions taken such elaborate precautions at the airport and yet failed to take enough? That must indicate, he thought, a peril even greater than those four fearful men had believed.

Something far more alarming than one exotic redhead.

If April Bell were indeed a witch, his unwilling speculations ran on, there might very reasonably be others—more powerful and less charming to go dancing with. There might be other parapsychological experimenters, to phrase it differently, busy discovering their inborn gifts and developing scientific techniques for the mental control of probability. If so, they might be organized, preparing for the time to test their power, awaiting the appearance of an expected leader—the Child of Night—to lead their Saturnalian rebellion.

Barbee's aching eyes had closed, and he pictured that coming dark Messiah. A tall, lean, commanding figure, standing amid shattered rocks, terrible and black in a long hooded robe. He wondered what manner of being it could be—and why April Bell had smiled. Breathlessly, he peered under the black hood to see if he could recognize the face—and a white skull grinned at him.

He awoke with a start—yet it wasn't the shock of that ghastly dream that roused him, but rather the quivering intensity of some vague eagerness that he couldn't quite define. A thin little pain shuddered in the back of his head, and he took a second nightcap to ease it. He turned on the radio, heard the oily beginning of a singing commercial and turned it off again. He was suddenly desperately sleepy—

And afraid to sleep.

He couldn't understand that dim terror of his bed. It was a slow, creeping apprehension, as if he knew that the vague unease which haunted him now would possess him entirely when he slept. But it

wasn't completely—fear. Mingled with it was that unresolved eager yearning which had roused him, the breathless expectancy of some obscure and triumphant escape from all he hated.

Neither could he quite understand the way he felt about April Bell—and that feeling was somehow a part of the other. He thought he ought to have a shocked horror of her. After all, she was either the witch she claimed to be, or else more likely a lunatic. In one way or another she had almost certainly caused Mondrick's death. But the thing that haunted him was his puzzled dread of that frightful, chained and yet dangerous something she awakened in himself.

Desperately, he tried to put her out of his mind. Certainly it was too late to telephone her now. He wasn't sure he wanted to see her—though that dimly dreadful yearning insisted that he did. He wound up his alarm clock, and went to bed again. Sleep pressed upon him with an urgency that became resistless.

And April Bell was calling to him.

Her voice came clearly to him, above all the subdued murmur of traffic noises. It was a ringing golden chime, more penetrating than an occasional beep of a driver's horn or the far clamor of a streetcar. It shimmered out of the dark, in waves of pure light as green as her malachite eyes. Then he thought he could see her, somehow, far across the slumberous town.

Only she wasn't a woman.

Her urgent velvet voice was human, still. Her long, dark eyes were changed, with that same exotic hint of a slant. Her white wolf coat was evidently part of her now. For she had become a white she-wolf, sleek and wary and powerful. Her clear woman-voice called to him, distinct in the dark.

"Come. Barbee. I need you."

He was aware of the cracked, dingy plaster of his narrow bedroom, of the steady tick of his alarm clock and the comfortable hardness of the mattress beneath him and the sulphurous odor of the mills that came through his open window. Surely he wasn't actually asleep, yet that calling voice was so real that he tried to answer.

"Hello, April," he murmured drowsily. "I'll really call you tomorrow. Maybe we can go dancing again."

Strangely, the she-wolf seemed to hear.

"I need you now, Barbee," her clear voice replied. "Because we've a job to do together—something that can't wait. You must come out to me right away. I'll show you how to change."

"Change?" he muttered heavily. "I don't want to change."

"You will," she said. "I believe you have my lost heirloom—that white jade pin?"

"I have it," he whispered. "I found it with that murdered kitten."

"Then take it in your hand."

In a numbed, groping, sleep-drugged way, Barbee thought he got up and went to the chiffonier and fumbled in that box of odds and ends for the tiny jade pin. Dimly, he wondered how she knew he had it. He carried it back, and sprawled heavily on the bed again.

"Now, Will!" Her vibrant voice called across the shadowy void between them. "Listen, and I'll tell you what to do. You must change, as I have changed. It should be easy for you, Will. You can run as the wolf runs, trail as the wolf trails, kill as the wolf kills!"

She seemed nearer in the misty dark.

"Just let go," she urged. "I'll help you, Will. You *are* a wolf, and your pattern is the jade pin in your hand. Just turn loose, and let your body flow—"

He wondered dimly how the mental control of probability could mold a man into the four-footed kind of wolf she clearly meant, but his brain seemed too numb and slow for thought. He clutched the pin and made a groping effort to obey. There was a curious, painful flux of his body—as if he had twisted into positions never assumed, had called on muscles never used. Sudden pain smothered him in darkness.

"Keep trying, Will." Her urgent voice stabbed through that choking blackness. "If you give up now, halfway changed, it may kill you. But you can do it. Just let me help, till you break free. Just let go, and follow the pattern, and let your body change. That's it—you're flowing—"

And suddenly he was free.

Those painful bonds, that he had worn a whole lifetime, were abruptly snapped. He sprang lightly off the bed, and stood a moment sniffing the odors that clotted the air in the little apartment—the burning reek of whisky from that empty glass on the chiffonier, the soapy dampness of the bathroom, and the stale, sweaty pungence of his soiled laundry in the hamper. The place was too close; he wanted fresh air.

He trotted quickly to the open window and scratched impatiently at the catch on the screen. It yielded after a moment, and he dropped to the damp, hard earth of Mrs. Sadowski's abandoned flower bed. He shook himself, gratefully sniffing the clean smell of that tiny bit of soil, and crossed the sidewalk into the heavy reek of burned oil and hot rubber that rose up from the pavement. He listened again for the white she-wolf's call, and ran fleetly down the street.

Free—

No longer was he imprisoned, as he had always been, in that slow, clumsy, insensitive bipedal body. His old human form seemed utterly foreign to him now, and somehow monstrous. Surely four nimble feet were better than two, and a smothering cloak had been lifted from his senses.

Free, and swift, and strong!

"Here I am, Barbee!" the white bitch was calling across the sleeping town. "Here by the campus—and please hurry!"

He heard her, and he had already started toward the campus, when a sudden impulse of perversity made him turn back south, on Commercial Street, toward the railroad yards and the open country beyond. He had to escape the chemical fumes from the mills that lay in a burning pall over the city, suffocating and intolerable. And he wanted to explore this new existence, to find his powers and their bounds, before he came face to face with that sleek she-wolf.

Loping easily along the pavement in the silent warehouse district, he paused to sniff the rich perfumes of coffee and spices that floated from a wholesale grocery, and checked himself abruptly as a sleepy policeman met him at the corner. Caught full in the street light, he turned to run for the nearest alley—the bored cop would doubtless welcome a bit of diversion and a chance to try his gun, and an unmuzzled gray wolf would certainly be fair game.

The officer merely yawned, however, staring straight at him, and flung a foul-smelling cigarette butt before him on the street, and shuffled wearily on his beat, pausing to try the warehouse door. Barbee trotted back ahead of him, just to be sure. Still the cop didn't see him. He ran on out the odorous street, too elated to wonder why.

He crossed the railroad yards ahead of a smelly, pounding locomotive, and loped west along the highway beyond, to escape the reek of wet steam and cinders and hot metal. He dropped into the ditch beside the acrid asphalt, and the earth felt cool and damp beneath his springy pads.

"Barbee! Why don't you come on?"

He heard the she-wolf's call behind him, but he wasn't ready to heed her yet. The night refreshed him with the clean chill of autumn. A breath of wind swept away all the sharp traffic odors of the road and brought him a delicious symphony of farmyard and woodland scents.

He rejoiced in the aroma of wet weeds and the redolence of decaying leaves. He liked even the cold dew that splashed his shaggy gray fur. Far from the too-loud clank and wheeze of the locomotive, he paused to listen to the tiny rustlings of field mice, and he caught a cricket with a flash of his lean forepaw.

April called, but he still ignored her.

Elation lifted him: a clean, vibrant joy that he had never known. He raised his muzzle toward the setting half moon and uttered a quavering, long-drawn howl of pure delight. Somewhere beyond a dark row of trees a dog began to bark in a frightened and breathless way. He sniffed the cold air and caught the noisome scent of that ancient enemy, faint and yet sickeningly unpleasant. His hackles lifted. Dogs would learn not to bark at him.

But the white wolf's call came again, suddenly more urgent:

"Don't waste time on a stray dog, Barbee—we've more deadly enemies to deal with tonight. I'm waiting on the campus, and I need you, now."

Reluctantly, he turned back north. The dark world flowed, and the furious barking of that angered dog was lost behind him. In a moment, he was passing Trojan Hills—as Preston Troy had named his baronial country place southwest of Clarendon, on the rolling uplands above the river valley that held the town and Troy's mills. The lights were out in the big house beyond the trees; but a lantern was bobbing about the stables, where perhaps the grooms were tending a sick horse. He heard a soft, uneasy whicker and paused a moment to sniff the strong, pleasant pungence of the horses.

"Hurry, Barbee!" begged April Bell.

He loped on, unwillingly, toward the uneasy murmuring and the clashing, violent odors of the city. Presently, however, he caught the she-wolf's scent, clean and fragrant as pine. His reluctance faded, and he ran eagerly along the deserted streets toward the campus, searching for her.

Somewhere among the dark, crowded houses, a dog made one thin yelp of alarm, but he ignored it. Her scent guided him, and she came trotting out of the fragrant evergreens on the campus to meet him on the wet grass. Her long greenish eyes were bright with welcome. He sniffed the clean, sweet redolence of her, and she touched his muzzle with a tingling cold kiss.

"You're late, Barbee!" She sprang away from him. "You've wasted too much of the night already, and we've enemies to meet. Let's go!"

"Enemies?" He stared at her lean white sleekness, puzzled. Somewhere to the south, the way he had come, a dog was barking nervously. He snarled toward the south. "That, you mean?" he whispered. "Dogs?"

Her greenish eyes glittered wickedly.

"Who's afraid of those curs?" Her white fangs flashed in scorn. "Our enemies are men."

7
The Trap in the Study

The white bitch ran, and Barbee followed. He hadn't realized how late it was, but much of the night had fled. The streets were empty, save for a few late motorists who seemed to drive with an apprehensive speed. Most of the traffic signals were out; only the one at the corner of the campus, where Center Street crossed the highway, was blinking a warning yellow. Loping after the fleet white wolf, Barbee called uneasily:

"Hold on, here—I want to know where we're going."

She leapt gracefully out of the path of a drumming car—the driver didn't seem to see them. Running on with an easy feral lightness, she looked back at Barbee. Her long red tongue was hanging out of her mouth, and her clean fangs shone.

"We're going to call on some old friends of yours." He thought she grinned maliciously. "Sam and Nora Quain."

"We can't harm them," he protested sharply. "Why should they be—enemies?"

"They are enemies because they are human," the white bitch told him. "Deadly enemies, because of what is in that wooden box that Quain and old Mondrick brought back from Asia."

"They're my friends," Barbee insisted, and whispered uneasily: "What's in that box?"

Her long eyes narrowed warily as she ran.

"Something deadly to our kind—that's all we have been able to discover," she said. "But the box is still at Sam Quain's house, though he's ready to move it to the Foundation tomorrow—he had been clearing out the top-floor rooms for it, and hiring guards, and arranging his defenses against us there. That's why we must strike right now. We must have a look inside tonight—and destroy whatever weapons they brought back from those prehuman mounds to turn against us."

Barbee shivered a little as he ran.

"What sort of weapons?" he whispered uneasily. "What can hurt us?"

"Silver can," the white bitch said. "Silver blades and silver bullets—I'll tell you why when we have a little time. But the contents of that box must be something more lethal than silver—and the night's going fast!"

They passed the yellow-blinking signal, and ran on through solid walls of odor—the sulphurous bite of settling fumes from the industrial district and a piercing reek of garbage smouldering in some incinerator, the crisp fragrance of a bakery, and a thin bitter stench trailing from the packing plant across the river, and the stale unpleasant human fetors seeping out of the silent houses.

She turned off the highway, crossing a corner of the campus toward the broad grounds of the Research Foundation and Sam Quain's little house beyond. The leaf-strewn grass made a cool, pleasant cushion for Barbee's pads, rustling very faintly, and his sniffing nostrils found a new orchestra of odors so intriguing that he almost forgot the task and the peril before them.

The grass and the walks still reeked of the students who had thronged them during the day, the human body smells rank and rancid, very different from the clean, friendly fragrance of the racing wolf beside him. An explosive purple malodor of hydrogen sulphide burst from the chemistry lab, and a pleasant pungence of manure drifted from the model dairy barn of the agriculture department beyond the highway.

The Foundation building was a slender tower of white concrete, aloof beyond its lawns and hedges, nine stories tall. Barbee wondered for a moment at the dogged intensity of old Mondrick's secret purpose—at the tireless drive that had overcome his age and illness to build this stern citadel and then ransack the cradlespots of mankind for the archeological treasures he had hoarded and studied here.

The white, graceful spire was enveloped in the turpentine-and-linseed-oil smells of new paint, mingled with a faint, jarringly unpleasant scent that Barbee couldn't identify. Light shone from the top-floor windows, and he flinched from a sudden blue flicker, painfully intense, that must come from a welding arc. The snarl of a power saw came down to him, and the muffled thudding of a carpenter's hammer.

Racing on beside him, the white wolf pricked up her ears.

"They're at work tonight," she said. "It's too bad we had to strike so openly against old Mondrick, but he gave us no time for the niceties we prefer. Now I'm afraid we've tipped our hand too far—Quain must know about what we expect, because he's having that top floor rebuilt into a fortress against us. We must get at that box, tonight!"

Down the wind, Professor Schnitzler's collie began to howl.

"Why is it?" Barbee asked apprehensively. "Men don't seem to see us, but dogs are always frightened."

April Bell snarled toward the howling.

"Most men can't see us," she told him. "No true man can, I think. But dogs have a special sense for us—and a special hatred. The savage man who domesticated the first dog must have been an enemy of our people, as cunning and terrible as old Mondrick or Sam Quain."

They came to the little white bungalow on Pine Street that Sam Quain had built for Nora the year they married—Barbee remembered drinking too much at their housewarming party, perhaps to dull his own unspoken disappointment. The she-wolf led him warily around the silent house and the garage, listening, sniffing uneasily. Barbee heard soft breath sounds from a lifted window, and then he caught the scent of little Pat from the sand pile in the back yard, where she had played.

He sprang before the white wolf with a growl in his throat.

"They mustn't be hurt!" he protested sharply. "I don't understand all of this—and it seems like fun. But these people are friends of mine—Sam and Nora and Pat. It's true Sam has acted a little funny, but still they're the best friends I have."

The bitch grinned redly over her hanging tongue.

"Both Sam and Nora?" Her greenish eyes mocked him. "But they're the dangerous ones." She crouched a little, fine ears lifted, sniffing the wind. "The thing in that box must be the key to some power more deadly than all our little spells—or they would never have dared defy us as they did."

Still he blocked her way.

"But I don't think we'll have to harm them now," she said. "They're both truly human—they won't be aware of us, unless we wish to make them so. The contents of the box are what we must reach and destroy."

"All right," Barbee yielded unwillingly. "So long as we don't injure them—"

Hot dog scent struck his nostrils. Inside the house there was a sudden small, shrill yelping. The she-wolf sprang back fearfully. Barbee shuddered to a deep, ungovernable alarm, and he felt his gray hackles rise.

"That's Pat's little dog," he said. "She calls it Jiminy Cricket."

The wolf bitch snarled. "She'll call it dead tomorrow."

"Not Jiminy!" Barbee cried. "Pat would be heartbroken."

A screen door banged. A fluff of white fur hurtled out into the back yard, barking furiously. The she-wolf sprang away from it apprehensively. It leaped at Barbee. He tried to cuff it away, and angry little teeth grazed his forepaw. The pain woke a latent savagery in him that drowned his regard for little Pat.

He crouched and sprang. His powerful jaws caught that bit of fur, and shook it until the thin yelping ceased. He tossed it upon the sand pile and licked the evil-tasting dog hair off his fangs.

The white wolf was trembling.

"I didn't know about the dog," she whispered uneasily. "Nora and the child were out when I came this evening to see what Sam was up to, and it must have been with them." Her lean shape quivered. "I don't like dogs. They aided men to conquer us once."

She slunk toward the back door.

"We must hurry now—the night is already too far gone."

Barbee tried to forget that little Pat would cry.

"The daylight?" he asked apprehensively. "Is it dangerous?"

The white wolf turned back quickly.

"I had forgotten to warn you," she whispered urgently. "But you must never try to change by day—or let dawn find you changed. Because any strong light is painful and likely to be injurious when we are changed; and the sun's rays are deadly."

"Why?" he asked uneasily. "How can light be harmful?"

"I used to wonder," she told him. "I talked about it once, to one of us who has quite a name in physics. He told me his theory. It sounds good—but we'd better look for that box."

Her deft, slender forepaw opened the screen, and Barbee led the way through the back door into the hot stuffiness of the little house. The air was heavy with cooking smells and the sharpness of an antiseptic Nora must have used to clean the bathroom and the warm body scents of Sam and Nora and the child, all overladen with the noisome, sickening rankness of the little dog he had killed.

They paused in the narrow hall beyond the little kitchen, listening. A clock ticked softly. The refrigerator motor started suddenly behind them, so loud they started. Above its steady drumming, he could hear Sam's strong, even breathing from their room and Nora's breath, slower and more quiet. Pat turned uneasily in her bed in the nursery and whimpered in her sleep:

"Come back to me, Jiminy!"

The she-wolf sprang toward the nursery door, snarling silently, but the child didn't quite wake. Barbee had started after her, alarmed for Pat. She turned back to him, her white fangs smiling.

"So Quain's asleep!" A taut elation rang in her tone. "Quite exhausted, I imagine. It's lucky you got that nasty little cur outside—he must have counted on it to wake him if we came. Now for the green box—I think it's in his study."

Barbee trotted to the study door, and rose against it to try the knob with his supple forepaws. It didn't yield. He dropped back to the floor and turned uncertainly toward the white wolf.

She stood listening, snarling toward the nursery, and he heard little Pat whimpering in her sleep. A sharp pang of concern for the child struck Barbee; a surge of his old loyalty to Sam and Nora impelled him to abandon this queer project and get the wolf bitch out of the house before she could harm them. That brief humane impulse died, however, against the stronger urgencies of this exciting new existence.

"I'll look for Sam's keys," he offered. "He must have them in his trousers—"

"Wait, idiot!" He had started toward the bedroom; the she-wolf's fang caught the scruff of his neck to stop him. "You'll wake him—or trip some trap. His keys are probably protected with a silver ring that it would poison us to touch. The padlock on that box is silver-plated, I saw. And I don't know what other weapons Quain has lying by his hand—deadly relics they dug up of that old war our people lost.

"But we don't need the keys."

Barbee blinked at the locked study door, bewildered.

"Stand still," she whispered. "I see I must tell you a little more of the theory of this change of state—if Quain stays asleep. Ours is a precious and useful power, but it has its limitations and penalties attached. If you fail to regard them, you can very easily destroy yourself—"

The sudden creak of bedsprings checked her. She whirled warily, greenish eyes blazing, silken ears lifted. Barbee heard Nora's sleepy voice—and a cold terror shook him, that he might be forced to injure her.

"Sam?" she said. "Where are you, Sam?" Then she must have found him beside her, for the bed creaked again, and she murmured faintly. "'Night Sam."

When the breath sounds were regular again, Barbee whispered uneasily:

"Why don't we need the keys?"

"I'll show you," the white wolf said. "But first I'm going to explain a little of the theory of our free state—to keep you from killing yourself. You must understand the dangers—"

"Silver?" he said. "And daylight?"

"The theory joins it all together," the wolf bitch told him. "I don't know physics enough to explain all the technical ramifications, but my friend made the main point seem simple enough. The link between mind and matter, he says, is probability."

Barbee started a little, remembering old Mondrick's lecture.

"Living things are more than matter alone," she continued. "The mind is an independent something—an energy complex, he called it— created by the vibrating atoms and electrons of the body, and yet

93

controlling their vibrations through the linkage of atomic probability—my friend used more technical language, but that's the idea of it.

"That web of living energy is fed by the body; it's part of the body—usually. My friend is a pretty conservative scientist, and he wouldn't say whether he thinks it's really a soul, able to survive long after the body is dead. He says you can't prove anything about that."

Her greenish eyes smiled secretly, as if she knew more than she said.

"But that vital pattern, in us, is stronger than in true men—his experiments did prove that. More fluid, and less dependent on the material body. In this free state, he says, we simply separate that living web from the body, and use the probability link to attach it to other atoms, wherever we please—the atoms of the air are easiest to control, he says, because the oxygen and nitrogen and carbon are the same atoms that establish the linkage in our bodies.

"And that explains the dangers."

"Silver?" Barbee said. "And light? I don't quite see—"

"The vibrations of light can damage or destroy that mental web," she told him. "They interfere with its own vibration. The mass of the body protects it, of course, when we are in the normal state. But the transparent air, when we are free, gives no shelter at all. Never let the daylight find you free!"

"I won't." Barbee shivered. "But how does silver harm us?"

"Vibration, again," the white wolf whispered. "No common matter is any real barrier to us in this free state. That's why we don't need Quain's keys. Doors and walls still seem real enough, I know—but wood is mostly oxygen and carbon, and our mind webs can grasp the vibrating atoms and slip through them, nearly as easily as through the air. Many other substances we can possess for our vehicles, with a little more effort and difficulty. Silver is the deadly exception—as our enemies know."

"Huh?" Barbee gasped. "How is that?"

Yet he scarcely listened, for something made him think of blind Rowena Mondrick, with her heavy silver rings and bracelets, her quaint old silver brooches and her silver beads, and the silver-studded collar she kept on her great tawny dog. Something lifted the gray shaggy fur along his spine, and something made him shudder.

"Different elements have different atomic numbers and different periods of electronic vibration," the white wolf was saying. "My friend explained it all, but I don't remember the terms. Anyhow, silver has the wrong vibration. There is no probability linkage. We can't claim silver, to make it a path or a tool for our free minds. Instead, the electronic vibrations of silver clash with ours; they can shatter the free pattern. So silver's poison, Will. Silver weapons can kill us—don't forget!"

"I won't," Barbee whispered uneasily.

He shook out his gray fur, trying vainly to dislodge that clinging chill. The white she-wolf stood listening again to the breath-sounds in the house, poised alertly, one graceful forefoot lifted. He moved toward her quickly.

"I won't forget," he said. "But I want to know the name of your physicist friend."

She laughed at him suddenly, red tongue hanging.

"Jealous, Barbee?" she taunted softly.

"I want to know," he insisted grimly. "And I want to know the name of this expected Child of Night."

"Do you, Barbee?" Her red smile widened before it sobered. "You'll find out," she promised, "when you have proved yourself. But now I think you understand our free state and its dangers well enough. Let's get to work, before Quain wakes."

She trotted back to the study door.

"Now you understand," she whispered, "and I can help you pass. My friend taught me how to smooth the random vibrations from the heavier elements in the wood and the paint that otherwise would be something of a barrier."

Her greenish eyes fixed intently on the lower panels of the door— and Barbee remembered old Mondrick's lecture on probability. All matter was mostly empty space, he said; only the random collisions of vibrating atoms kept the little black lamp from falling through the seemingly substantial desk. Nothing in the universe was absolute; only probabilities were real. And the mind web, according to this theory of April's unknown friend, governed probability.

"Wait," the she-wolf whispered. "Follow me."

Before her greenish stare, the bottom half of the study door melted into misty unreality. For an instant Barbee could see the dark screws that held the hinges, and all the mechanism of the lock, as if in an X-ray view. Then the metal faded also, and the slender bitch glided silently through the door.

Uneasily, Barbee followed. He thought he felt a slight resistance, where the wooden panels were. He felt as if something brushed his gray fur lightly as he stepped carefully through. He stopped inside with a stifled growl. The white wolf cowered back against his shoulder.

For something in that room was—deadly.

He stood sniffing for the danger. The close air was thick with odors of paper and dried ink and decaying glue from the books on the shelves, strong with the mothball reek from a closet, perfumed with the fragrant tobacco in the humidor on Sam's desk. It was musky with the lingering scent of a mouse that once had dwelt behind the books. But the queer, powerful malodor that frightened him came from the battered, iron-strapped wooden chest on the floor beside the desk.

It was a piercing, musty reek, as if of something that had moldered for a very long time underground. It was alarming in a way he couldn't understand—though it reminded him of that undefinable evil scent about the Foundation tower. The white bitch stood taut beside him, frozen in her snarl, with hatred and stunned fear in her eyes.

"It's there in that box," she whispered faintly. "The thing old Mondrick dug from the graves of our race in the Ala-shan—the weapon that destroyed our people once, and Quain plans to use again. We must dispose of it—somehow—tonight."

But Barbee shook himself, retreating apprehensively.

"I don't feel good," he muttered uneasily. "I can't breathe. That stink must be poisonous. Let's get back to the open."

"You're no coward, Barbee." The bitch curled her lip, as if to stir him with a hint of scorn. "The thing in that box must be deadlier than dogs, or light, or even silver—our people could have dealt with all of them. We must get rid of it—or else our kind must die again."

Crouching, white fur bristled, she moved toward the massive coffer. Unwillingly, sick with that unknown fetor, Barbee followed her. That lethal reek seared his nostrils. He swayed, shivering to an insidious chill.

"Padlocked!" he gasped. "Sam must have expected—"

Then he saw the narrowed eyes of the crouching bitch fixed upon the carved side of the green-painted chest, and he remembered her control of atomic probability. The wooden planks turned misty, revealing all the iron screws that fastened them. The screws dissolved, and the wide iron bands, and the heavy hasp. The white wolf growled, quivering to a cold ferocity.

"Silver!" she gasped, cowering back against him.

For inside the vanished wood was a lining, of hammered white metal, which refused to dissolve. The atoms of silver had no linkage with the web of mind. The reeking contents of the chest were still concealed.

"Your old friends are clever, Barbee!" White fangs flashed through the she-wolf's snarl. "I knew the box was heavy, but I didn't guess it had a silver lining. Now, I suppose, we must look for the keys and try the padlock. If that fails, we must attempt to burn the house."

"No!" Barbee shuddered. "Not while they're all asleep!"

"Your poor Nora!" The white bitch mocked him. "Why did you let Sam take her?" Her red grin turned grave. "But fire is the last resort," she told him, "because the vibrations are so deadly to us. First we must search for the keys."

They were creeping back toward the door and the faint murmurings of sleep from the bedroom beyond, when Barbee started to a sudden drumming clamor. To his acute senses, it seemed as if the whole house shuddered. Whimpering with shock, the white bitch sprang back from him toward Sam Quain's cluttered desk. That peremptory clatter paused, and he realized that it had been the telephone.

"What fool is calling now?" the white bitch snarled, hoarse with urgency and terror. Barbee heard the bed groan again and the sleep-muffled sound of Sam Quain's voice. That silent room seemed suddenly a closing trap, and he was frantic to escape. The next ring of the phone, he knew, would finish waking Quain. He darted toward the dark opening in the locked door, calling back to his companion:

"Let's get away—"

But the snarling bitch was already crouching. One clean leap carried her to the top of the desk. Silently, before the telephone could ring again, she caught the receiver in her deft forepaws, and lifted it carefully.

"Quiet!" she commanded softly. "Listen!"

A breathless hush filled the tiny house. A clock ticked on the desk, oddly loud. Barbee heard Sam Quain's sleep-dulled voice again, uncertainly interrogative, and then his even breathing. The refrigerator motor in the kitchen stopped its muffled whirring. He heard the thin voice in the receiver, calling frantically:

"Sam?" It was Rowena Mondrick. "Sam Quain—can you hear me?"

Barbee heard an uneasy little groan from the bedroom, and then the heavy breathing of Sam Quain's tired, uneasy sleep.

"Nora, is it you?" Barbee heard that small voice from the receiver on the desk, shrill with fright. "Where is Sam? Have him call me, won't you, Nora? I've a warning for him—tell him it's about Barbee."

The white bitch crouched over the receiver, her long fangs bared as if to slash the instrument. Her silken ears were pricked up delicately to listen, and her slanted eyes were narrowed greenish slits of hate.

"Who—?" Terror seemed to choke that tiny voice. "Sam?" it gasped faintly. "Nora? Won't you—speak—"

A thin little scream came out of the instrument, so penetrating Barbee was afraid it would reach the bedroom. The receiver clicked as the frightened woman at the other end hung up. Leaving the receiver down, the white bitch sprang back to Barbee's side.

"That wicked widow of old Mondrick's!" she gasped faintly. "The woman knows too much about us—she saw too much, before she lost her eyes. Her knowledge, I'm afraid, could make the thing in that green box more deadly to us than it is already."

Her long ears flattened, and she snarled again.

"There's another job for us, Barbee," she said softly. "I think we had better dispose of Rowena Mondrick, before she ever talks to Sam Quain."

"We couldn't hurt an old blind woman!" Barbee protested sharply. "And Rowena is my friend."

"Your friend?" the white bitch whispered scornfully. "You've a lot to learn, Barbee." Something seemed to clot her whisper, to turn it thick and low. "When you're the very one she's trying to betray—"

She swayed and sank down on the worn carpet.

"April?" Barbee touched her icy muzzle anxiously. "What's the trouble, April?"

The slender wolf shuddered where she lay.

"—trapped!" Barbee had to crouch to hear her faint whisper. "Now I see why your old friend Quain went on to bed and left the back door open so invitingly. That green box is the bait—he must have known we couldn't get in it. And that old, evil thing inside it is the deadfall."

Barbee had nearly forgotten that penetrating odor from the box, which at first had seemed so noxious. He raised his muzzle heavily to sniff for it again. It seemed fainter now, and it was almost pleasant. Drowsily, he sniffed again.

"Don't breathe it!" the she-wolf whispered frantically. "Poison. Quain left it—to kill us." She shivered on the floor, and he could scarcely hear her whisper. "We must leave the box—and pay our visit to your dear friend Rowena. If we ever get out of here—"

She lay limp and still.

"April!" yelped Barbee. "April!"

She didn't move.

8

The Huntress in the Dark

Barbee swayed beside the flaccid form of the slim she-wolf and awkwardly spread his four legs to keep from falling. He sniffed the odor of the thing in the wooden coffer. That was a secret thing, older than remembered history, which had lain long-buried under the Ala-shan with the bones of the race it had killed. It was going to kill him too. Yet somehow the emanations of it were now fragrantly sweet; drowsily, he wondered why it had ever seemed so foul.

He inhaled again.

He was going to sleep beside the sleeping bitch. He felt very tired, and that old, queer perfume seemed to ease away all his worry and strain and aching weariness. He breathed it deep, and prepared to lie down. But the white wolf shivered on the floor, and he heard her tiny whisper:

"Leave me, Barbee! Get out—before you die!"

That awoke a faint awareness of her peril. He liked that ancient, strange perfume from the box behind them, but it was killing April Bell. He must get her out, to the open air. Then he could come back, and breathe it, and sleep. He caught the loose fur at the back of her neck, and dragged her laboriously toward the opening she had made in the locked door.

A vague consternation took hold of him, and her limp body dropped from his relaxing jaws. For the way was closing. The dark screws and the metal of the lock appeared again, and then the ghostly outline of the wooden panels turned suddenly real. This quiet study room indeed had been a baited trap—his drowsy thoughts grasped that much. And the trap was sprung.

Weakly, he blundered against the door. It flung him back, solid as it seemed. He tried to remember old Mondrick's lecture and that theory of April's friend. All matter was mostly emptiness. Nothing was absolute; only probabilities were real. His mind was an energy web, and it could grasp the atoms and electrons of the door by the link of probability. It could smooth the random vibrations which made the door a barrier.

He pondered that, laboriously—but the door was still a barrier. The slender bitch lay still at his feet, and he braced himself to keep from going down beside her. The old, sweet fragrance of that thing in the box seemed to thicken in the air. He was breathing hard, his tongue hanging. That old perfume would end all his trouble and his pain—

Faintly, the she-wolf whimpered at his feet:

"Look at the door. Open the wood—I'll try to help—"

Reeling, he stared at the solid-seeming panels. Gropingly, he tried to dissolve them again. Only probabilities were real, he remembered—but those were merely words. The door remained solid. He felt a faint quiver of effort in the she-wolf's body, and he tried to share her action. Slowly, in a fumbling way, he got hold of a curious, novel sense of extension and control.

A misty spot came in the wood. Uncertainly, he widened it. The she-wolf shuddered at his feet and seemed to stiffen—and still the opening was too small. He tried again, swaying to the sweet caress of that perfume. The space came wider. He caught her fur, stumbled at the door, and sprawled through it with her.

The effluvium of the box was left behind. For an instant Barbee wanted desperately to go back to it, and then a sick revulsion seized him. He lay on the floor in the narrow hallway, shaken with nausea. Faintly, in the locked room behind him, he heard a telephone operator's impatient tones in the dropped receiver on Sam Quain's desk. Then Nora's voice sobbed suddenly through the house, muffled with terror and sleep:

"Sam—Sam!"

The bed groaned as Sam Quain turned uneasily, but neither quite awoke. Barbee staggered to his feet, panting gratefully for the clean air. Nuzzling the still white wolf, he caught that foul malodor seeping under the door, and disgusted nausea staggered him once more.

He lifted the she-wolf again and flung her limp body over his gaunt, gray shoulders. Lurching and trembling under her slight burden, he stumbled back through Nora's clean-smelling kitchen and pushed out through the unlatched screen.

They were safely out of Sam's queer trap, he thought, uneasily shaking out his shaggy fur as he ran with the she-wolf on his back. He couldn't quite outrun the sickening memory of that lethal effluvium, but the clean chill of the night wind cleared it from his nostrils. His strength came back.

He carried the white bitch back down the street to the campus and laid her on the white-frosted grass. The zodiacal light was already lifting its warming pillar of pale silver in the east. On the farms beyond the town he could hear roosters crowing. A dog was howling somewhere. The peril of dawn was near—and he didn't know what to do for April Bell.

Helplessly, he started licking her white fur. Her slender body shivered, to his immense relief, and began heaving as she breathed again. Weakly, she swayed to her feet. She was panting, her red tongue drooping. Her eyes were dark with terror.

"Thank you, Barbee!" She shuddered. "That was horrible. I'd have died there in your old friend's cunning little trap if you hadn't brought me away." Her feral eyes narrowed. "That thing in the box is deadlier than I ever dreamed. I don't think we can ever destroy it, really. We can only strike at those who hope to use it—until it is buried again—and forgotten as it was under those mounds in the Ala-shan."

Barbee shook his pointed head reluctantly.

"At Sam?" he whispered. "And Nick? And Rex?"

The white panting bitch grinned at him wickedly.

"You're running with the black pack now, Barbee," she told him. "You have no human friends—for all men would kill us, if they knew. We must destroy the enemies of the Child of Night before we die. But Quain isn't first on the list—not since that phone rang. Now we must dispose of old Mondrick's widow, before she talks to him."

Barbee started back from her.

"Not—Rowena!" he breathed urgently. "She has always been a true friend to me—even since Mondrick changed. So generous, and always kind. You forget her blindness, because she's such a real human being—"

"But you aren't, Barbee!"

The white bitch grinned at him, and turned suddenly grave.

"I don't think the widow is, either," she added soberly. "She has just enough of our blood, I believe, to make her dangerous to us. That's why we must stop her, before she can tell—"

"No!" Barbee whispered violently. "I'll do no harm to a poor old woman."

"She won't be such easy game," the sleek bitch panted. "She learned too much from old Mondrick, and she saw too much in Africa. You've seen that silver she wears against us. She must have other weapons, besides that great ugly dog that Mondrick trained. She'll be tough, but we must try—"

"I won't!"

"You will," she told him. "You'll do what you must, Barbee, because you are what you are. You're free tonight, and all your human inhibitions are left behind with your body on the bed. You're running with me tonight, as our dead race used to run, and we've human game to hunt."

Her red laugh mocked at his restraint.

"Come along, Barbee—before the daylight."

The white bitch ran, and the feeble fetters of Barbee's human constraints fell from him. He raced after her across the grass, feeling the pleasant crispness of crunching frost beneath his pads, alert to every murmur and odor of the slumbering town—even the hot fumes from the motor of a passing milk truck seemed almost fragrant now, since he had smelled that poisonous thing from the mounds of the past.

West of the campus, on University Avenue, they came to the old brick house on the ill-kept lawn. Barbee hung back when he saw the black crepe on the front door, but the slender she-wolf trotted on ahead of him, and her clean scent swept away his lingering compunctions.

For his body lay far away, and his human bonds were broken. The sleek white bitch was near him, alive and exciting. He ran with her pack now, and they followed the Child of Night. He paused beside her on the stoop, waiting for the panels of the front door to dissolve.

"Rowena shouldn't suffer," he whispered uneasily. "She was always a gracious friend to me. I used to come and let her play the piano for me—usually pieces she had composed, weird and sad and beautiful. Surely she deserves some clean, easy end—"

The white wolf started beside him. His nostrils caught a faint pungence, penetrating and hateful—the odor of dog. The hair rose on his neck. Beside him the lean bitch bristled and snarled. Her greenish eyes were fixed on the door, and she made no reply to his interrupted plea.

Crouching beside her, Barbee saw the bottom of the door fade into misty unreality. Briefly, he glimpsed the familiar room beyond—the black cavern of the fireplace and the dark bulk of Rowena's grand piano. He heard the shuffle of hurried steps and saw vague shadows move. The latch clicked, and that ghostly shadow of a door was flung abruptly open.

The she-wolf cowered back beside him, snarling silently.

A flood of odors poured out of that open door, more immediate and real than anything he heard or saw. He caught the thin, bitter reek of gas burning in the old fireplace, and the thick sweetness of the roses Sam and Nora Quain had sent in the vase on the piano. There was the lavender perfume and the mothball sharpness of Rowena Mondrick's clothing, and the hot, acrid, frightened odor of her body. And there was the dog scent, overwhelming.

The dog reek was less evil than the emanations of that thing in Sam Quain's box, but still it sickened him again. It chilled him with a terror older than mankind, and it steeled him with a racial hatred. His hair stood up and his lips curled back. He gathered his feet and caught his breath and crouched to face an immemorial enemy.

Rowena Mondrick walked out past that ghostly door, her great leashed dog stalking close beside her, stiff-legged and growling softly. Wrapped in a long black silk robe, she stood tall and sternly straight. A

distant street light gleamed pale on the silver brooch at her throat and on her massive silver rings and bracelets. It glittered cruelly on the point of a thin silver dagger in her hand.

"Help me!" whispered the crouching bitch. "Help me pull her down!"

That thin blind woman, clutching her dagger and her huge dog's leash, once had been his friend. But she was human, and Barbee crouched beside the snarling she-wolf. Bellies low, they crept upon their prey.

"I'll try to hold her arm," the white bitch breathed. "You tear out her throat—before she can use that silver blade."

Rowena Mondrick waited in the dark doorway, the ghostly panels of the open door growing slowly real again beside her. Her growling dog was straining forward on the leash; she drew it firmly back and caught its silver-studded collar. Her thin white face looked tired and sad. Her head tilted, and Barbee shivered to a disconcerting impression that her opaque black lenses could see him.

"Will Barbee." She spoke his name softly, looking down as if she saw him. Still quietly gracious, her voice held a hurt reproach. "I knew your danger, and I tried to warn you away from that slick little witch—but I hardly expected you to forget your humanity so soon!"

Barbee felt hot with shame. He crouched back, turning to whimper an uneasy protest to the creeping she-wolf. The ferocious scorn of her white snarl silenced him.

"I'm truly sorry this must be you, Will," the woman's wounded voice continued gently. "But I know you've surrendered to the dark blood in you—I had always hoped you would master it. All who have the black blood aren't witches, Will—I know that. But I see I was wrong about you."

She paused a moment, stiffly straight in her stern black.

"I know you're here, Will Barbee!" He thought she shuddered, clutching her thin silver blade—it had been hammered and filed, he saw, out of a sterling table knife. "And I know what you want."

Her tawny dog was straining forward against the silver-bossed collar, following every movement of the creeping wolf bitch with savage yellow eyes. Rowena clung with a taut white hand to its collar, her blind lenses watching.

"I know," she whispered bitterly. "But I won't be easy to kill!"

The crouching bitch grinned at Barbee, and crept closer.

"Ready, Barbee," she breathed. "When I get her elbow!"

Barbee gathered his pads and hugged the cold floor, measuring the space to Rowena's throat. He shook off a lingering reluctance, knowing he had to obey—because this was real, and the lithe bitch his companion, and his lost humanity a dim dream.

"Now!" the she-wolf called. "For the Child of Night!"

She sprang silently. Her slender body made a flowing gleam of white, her bared fangs slashing at the blind woman's arm. Waiting for her to drag down the dagger, Barbee felt a sudden black savagery mount in himself, and a hot thirst for the sweetness of blood.

"Will!" Rowena was sobbing. "You can't—"

He caught his breath to spring.

But the dog Turk had yelped a frightened warning. Rowena Mondrick let the collar go, swaying back and slashing with her silver dagger.

Twisting in the air, the leaping she-wolf evaded the blade. The heavy silver bracelets on the blind woman's arm, however, struck her sleek, narrow head. She fell, trembling from the blow, and the huge dog caught her throat. She twisted helplessly in its jaws, whimpered once, and went limp.

Her whimpered appeal freed Barbee from his last compassion for Rowena. His fangs ripped at the dog's tawny throat and struck the silver-studded collar. Numbing pain flashed through him from the cold metal. He staggered back, sick from the shock of silver.

"Hold her, Turk!" Rowena gasped.

But the great dog had already dropped the white wolf as it whirled to meet Barbee's charge. She lurched to her feet, and stumbled painfully off the stoop.

"Let's go, Barbee!" she cried apprehensively. "The woman has too much of our own dark blood—she's stronger than I thought. We can't beat her, and silver, and the dog!"

She fled across the lawn.

Barbee ran after her. And the blind woman followed, moving with a swift confidence that was terrible now. The far street light shone cold on the brooch and the beads and the bracelets that were her invulnerable armor and pale on her deadly blade.

"Take 'em, Turk!" she called fiercely to the dog. "Kill 'em!"

They fled together, gray wolf and white, back down the empty street toward the silent campus. Barbee felt numbed and ill from the shock of silver against his jaw, and he knew the tawny dog would overtake him. Its savage baying crept up close behind him, and he turned at the corner of the campus to make a desperate stand.

But the white bitch flashed back, past him. She ran in front of the dog and danced away as it followed. She mocked its angry baying with her own malicious yelping. Grinning redly, she lured it away from Barbee, toward the empty highway beyond the dark campus.

"Take 'em, Turk!" the blind woman was screaming behind him. "Keep 'em for me!"

Barbee shook himself and retreated uneasily from her. The racing wolf and the pursuing dog were already gone from his sight, but her clean scent and the dog's foul reek floated in the motionless cold air behind them. He could hear the dog's deep-throated baying far ahead, a dull note of frustration already marring its hot eagerness.

The blind woman followed Barbee, running recklessly. Glancing apprehensively back as he came to the highway, he saw her a full block behind. She came to a drive that curved across the frosty lawn as he watched her. Her black, staring lenses must not have seen the curb, for she stumbled on it and fell full length on the concrete.

Barbee felt a brief impulse of pity. The unexpected fall, he knew, must have bruised her painfully. In another moment she was up, however, limping after him desperately. He saw the glint of starlight on her bright blade and ran again, turning right down the highway on the hot mingled scent of the wolf and the dog.

The next time he paused to look back, under the blinking traffic signal where Center Street crossed the highway, the blind woman was far behind. A lone car was drumming down the road toward them. Barbee ran hard from the glare of its headlights until they became too painful, and then crouched in an alley until it roared past. When he rose to look back again, he couldn't see Rowena.

The doleful baying of the dog had drawn far ahead of him, and presently he lost it under the rumble of the mills and the steam-hiss and steel-clatter of the railroad yards. Still he could follow the trailing scents of the pursuit, and they led east through a maze of poor cross streets, until he came into the yards.

The odors of dog and wolf were thinned there with the hot stink of engine grease and the dry bite of cinders and the reek of creosoted ties, diluted with the sharp sulphurous acid of coal smoke. Yet he kept the trail until a switch engine came chuffing down the tracks to meet him, a brakeman standing on the step.

Barbee sprang side, but an accidental blast of steam roared around him, sweeping away every scent except its own hot, wet reek of oil and metal. Blind to him, the brakeman spat accidentally near him, but even that sharp tobacco pungence was carried away by the steam. The trail was broken.

He trotted in a weary little circle on the parallel tracks, sniffing hopefully. His nostrils found nothing except steam and steel and creosote and the bitterness of half-burned diesel fuel, all overladen with the settling chemical stenches from the industrial district.

He cocked his shaggy ears, listening desperately. The clangor of the switch engine was diminishing down the tracks. Steam hissed and machines clattered in the roundhouse. The rumbling of the mills made a dull background of sound. Far in the east, beyond the river, he heard the whistle of a train coming in. But he couldn't find the voice of the dog.

Sharp pain struck his eyes as he looked at the east; warning pangs throbbed through his head. The tall mill stacks were long black fingers, spread against the first greenish glow of dawn. The white bitch was lost from him, and deadly day was near; it suddenly occurred to him that he didn't know how to go home to his body.

He was trotting aimlessly on across the bright cold rails when the baying came again, slow and hopeless now, from toward the mills. He ran down the yards toward the sound, keeping between two lines of standing boxcars that shut out part of the increasing, painful light.

He could see the white bitch at last, loping back toward him with a lithe and lazy-seeming grace. She had led the chase in a clever circle, but she must be exhausted now, or weakening before the lethal light, because the dog was gaining swiftly. The baying turned sharper, quicker in tempo. It became an eager yelping, triumphantly excited.

Barbee ran out from the standing cars to meet the bitch.

"You rest," he gasped. "I'll lead the dog."

He wasn't sure he could lead it far, because the dawn stung through him with its cruel, increasing radiation, and his weary body still felt stiff from that shock of silver. But the sleek she-wolf was his own kind, and he dropped back to draw the chase away from her.

"No, Barbee!" she called quickly. "It's late—we must stay together now."

He ran on beside her, too weary to ask what she meant to do. The glare of the east was mounting, and Barbee turned aside toward the river lowlands, when they came out of the yards, thinking to gain a little shelter from the light in the tangled thickets there.

"This way, Barbee!" The she-wolf stayed on the tall embankment. "Keep with me."

Frantically he scrambled back up the weed-grown slope, and raced to overtake her. The tawny dog was close behind, yipping breathlessly with each leap, the gray light glinting on its deadly collar. Barbee fled from it, straining to keep up with the white wolf's lazy fleetness.

The dark river was close ahead. The stale reek of its muddy banks caught his nostrils, and the sharpness of rotting leaves. The wind brought him a rank whiff of the city disposal plant, and he could smell the acrid unpleasantness of chemical wastes from the mills in the flat, black water.

Beyond the river, the white flame of dawn became terrible in the sky. His eyes dimmed and burned, and his body shrank from the driving light. Grimly, he raced to overtake the lean white bitch. Somewhere far ahead, the train wailed again.

They came to the narrow bridge, and the white wolf trotted out across the ties with delicate, sure feet. Barbee hung back, filled with an old, vague terror of running water. The great yelping dog, however, was almost upon him. Shuddering, careful not to look down upon the black sleekness of the far water, he picked his way out across the bridge. The dog followed recklessly.

Barbee was midway of the span when the rails began to sing. The train's whistle screamed again, and its cruel headlamp burst around a curve, not a mile ahead. An impulse of panic checked him, but the plunging dog was close behind. Frantically, he raced on to beat the train.

All the seeming weariness of the white bitch had vanished, now. She drew far ahead, a fleet white shadow. He ran desperately after her, beside the purring, shivering steel. The air trembled, and the bridge

shuddered. He saw her waiting for him, sitting on her haunches beside the pounding track, laughing at the dog.

He flung himself down beside her in the dusty wind of the thundering train. Faintly, he heard the dog's last howl of fear. The bitch smiled redly at the small splash of its tawny body in the black water, and shook the cinders out of her snowy fur.

"That will do for Mr. Turk," she murmured happily. "And I think we can take care of his wicked mistress just as neatly, when the time comes—in spite of all her silver weapons and her mongrel blood!"

Barbee shuddered, cowering down beside the embankment, away from the burning east. The steamy dust was thinning, and the humming of the rails began to fade. He thought of Rowena Mondrick falling on the drive and limping on again; and pity struck him, sharp for an instant as his fear of her silver dagger.

"We can't!" He shivered. "Poor Rowena—we've already hurt her enough."

"This is war, Will," the white bitch whispered. "A war of races, old as mankind and our own. We lost it once; we won't again. Nothing is too cruel for such mongrel traitors to our blood as that black widow. We've no more time tonight, but I imagine we've already upset her plan to warn Sam Quain."

She stood up gracefully.

"Now it's time to go home." She trotted away from him, along the tracks. "'Night, Barbee!"

Barbee was left alone. The flame of the east was searing through him now, and a cold dread possessed him, for he didn't know how to go back. Uncertainly, he groped for his body.

He didn't know the way. Yet he was dimly aware of his body, somehow, lying stiff and a little chilled across the bed in his little place on Bread Street. He tried awkwardly to possess and move it, a little as if he sought to awake from a dream.

That first effort was feeble and fumbling as a child's first step. Somehow it was intolerably painful, as if he overtaxed some faculty never used before. But the very pain spurred him. He tried again, frantic to escape the greater pain of day. Once more he felt that curious change and flow—and he sat up painfully on the edge of his own bed.

The narrow little bedroom had grown cold, and he felt chilled and stiff. A queer, heavy numbness possessed him, and all his senses were strangely dulled. He sniffed eagerly for all those odors that had been so richly revealing to the gray wolf, but his human nostrils, choked with cold, caught nothing at all. Even the whisky scent was gone from the empty glass on the chiffonier.

Aching with fatigue, he limped to the window and put up the blind. Gray daylight had dimmed the street lamps—he shrank back from the bright sky, as if it had been the dreadful face of death.

What a dream!

He mopped uncertainly at the cold film of terror-sweat on his forehead. A nagging ache throbbed in his right canine tooth—that was the fang, he recalled uncomfortably, that he had struck against the silver studs of Turk's collar. If a rum hangover did such things to him, he had better stick to whisky—and maybe less of that.

His throat felt raw and dry. He limped into the bathroom for a drink of water and found himself reaching awkwardly for the glass with his left hand. He opened his tight-closed right with a nervous start, and found himself still clutching Aunt Agatha's white jade pin.

Jaw sagging, he stood peering incredulously at his numbed hand and that odd trinket. Across the back of his lean fist was a long red scratch—precisely where Jiminy Cricket's sharp little tooth had grazed the gray wolf's forepaw in his dream. He tried to shake off an uncomfortable prickling sensation.

Nothing really strange about it, he tried to tell himself. He recalled some of old Mondrick's classroom discussions on the psychology of dreams; such phenomena of the unconscious, he recalled Mondrick saying, were always less extraordinary and instantaneous than they appeared to the dreamer.

His own troubled doubts about April Bell and her curious confession had caused him to get up in his sleep, the sane solution came to him, to fumble in that cigar box on the chiffonier for that odd pin. He must have scratched his hand on one of the used razor blades there, or perhaps on the pin itself. And all the rest could be nothing else than his own unconscious effort to explain that trifling accident with the material of his own buried desires and fears.

That must be! With a wan little grin of relief, he rinsed his dry mouth, and then reached eagerly for the whisky bottle to help himself to a hair of the dog—He grimaced at the phrase, remembering the disgusting taste of dog hair in the dream, and firmly set the bottle back.

113

9

Nightmare's Aftermath

Barbee wanted to forget that dream. He went shivering back to bed, and tried to sleep again. He couldn't sleep. Every detail of that long nightmare lingered to haunt him, horribly vivid and real. He couldn't rid his mind of the wolf bitch's crimson grin, or the flimsy feel of Jiminy Cricket's vertebrae snapping in his own powerful jaws, or the sight of Mondrick's widow stumbling in her frantic pursuit, pitiable in her blindness and yet terrible with that silver blade.

He got up again, and limped unthinkingly to pull the blinds against the cruel light of day. He poured antiseptic on that enigmatic scratch, and shaved carefully, and took an aspirin to dull that ache in his jaw.

Dreams were logical results of normal causes, he kept insisting to himself, and he didn't need Dr. Glenn to help him unravel this one. The obvious dislike of Nora Quain and Mrs. Mondrick for April Bell might very plausibly have planted the suggestion in his own unconscious that the charming redhead was a bitch, and his own indignant revolt against the suggestion seemed motive enough for the gray wolf's part. With all the bizarre details of the Mondrick tragedy for background, and his own nervous fatigue, the nightmare seemed natural enough.

Yet he wasn't quite satisfied with such efforts at rational self-analysis. He decided to call Rowena Mondrick. He wanted to assure himself that she was really safe in the old house on University Avenue, and her dog Turk with her.

He dialed her number with a numb forefinger. For a long time there was no answer—perhaps, he hoped, everybody was safely asleep. At last he heard the high-pitched voice of Mrs. Rye, the housekeeper, asking sharply what he wanted.

"I'd like to speak to Mrs. Mondrick, if she's up."

"She ain't here."

"Huh!" He gulped, trying to swallow his instant panic. "Then give me Miss Ulford, please."

"She ain't, either."

"What—?" he croaked feebly. "Where—?"

"Miss Ulford went in the ambulance, to see after poor Mrs. Mondrick."

He nearly dropped the receiver.

"How's that?"

"Mrs. Mondrick—the poor old dear—she must have gone out of her head last night. The shock of her husband called so sudden, you know. And she has always had them funny spells, you know, ever since that varmint clawed out her eyes across the water."

Barbee swallowed hard.

"What happened?" he gasped impatiently.

"She got up in the night, and slipped out of the house with that ugly dog she insists on keeping. I guess she thought she was hunting something—that same varmint, might be, as got her eyes. Anyhow, she carried one of her good sterling table knives, that she had gone and sharpened like a dagger. Lucky thing the dog started barking. That woke Miss Ulford, and she got up and followed."

Barbee listened, mute and shivering.

"The dog must have run off and left her. Mrs. Mondrick was stumbling after it through the streets—poor blind thing—as hard as she could run. The nurse said she had to chase her nearly twenty blocks—I don't see how she ever got so far."

Mrs. Rye seemed to find a morbid satisfaction in her own narrative.

"Miss Ulford was all worn out herself, but she finally brought Mrs. Mondrick home in a cab. Dear blind thing—she was all skinned and bleeding from falling in the streets, and quite out of her head. She wouldn't let go that sharpened knife till we twisted it away, and she kept screaming something about the things Turk was after.

"Miss Ulford called the ambulance from Glennhaven, and woke me to pack a few of Mrs. Mondrick's things. They took her away, not an hour ago—she struggled with the keepers, poor old dear, till I was afraid she'd kill herself."

"I—I think Glenn has treated her before." Barbee tried desperately to make his voice sound calm. "Why didn't she want to go?"

"She kept begging us to take her to Mr. Sam Quain's house. She was so frantic about it, that I finally tried to telephone Mr. Quain for her—but the operator told me he had left his receiver off the hook. The men in the ambulance kept telling her they'd take care of everything, and they took her on to Glennhaven."

"So she ain't here," Mrs. Rye concluded. "Anything I can do?"

Barbee stood woodenly, too dazed to reply.

"Hello?" said Mrs. Rye. "Hello?"

He couldn't find his voice, and she hung up impatiently. He stumbled to the bathroom and poured himself half a tumbler of whisky—and dashed it untasted, on a terrified impulse, into the lavatory. If whisky had anything to do with such disturbing occurrences as this, it was high time to quit.

Little Miss Ulford was a smart nurse, he told himself stubbornly, to take her patient to Dr. Glenn. That queer tragedy at the airport had clearly been too much for Mrs. Mondrick, and his own fears for her sanity must have played a part in shaping that grotesque dream. Grimly, he resolved not to ponder the too-many coincidences between fact and dream—that road to madness Mrs. Mondrick herself must have travelled.

On abrupt impulse, he called the Trojan Arms.

He couldn't quite dare ask April Bell if she had got home safe from the railroad bridge. He knew very well that people didn't get hurt in other people's dreams. But he wanted to hear her voice, and know where she was. He could make his excuses for not calling yesterday and ask her for another date. His voice turned eager as he asked for Miss Bell.

"Sorry, sir," the clerk told him. "We can't disturb Miss Bell."

"I'm a friend," Barbee insisted. "I don't think she'd mind."

The clerk was firm, and Barbee asked for the manager. Publicity is important to hotels, and Gilkins was commonly cooperative with the working press. April Bell, however, appeared to be the uncommon case.

"Sorry, Mr. Barbee," he murmured politely, "but we really can't disturb her. Sorry, old man—but Miss Bell always sleeps till noon, and she has left strict orders not to be bothered for anything less than fire or bloody murder."

Barbee tried not to shiver at that last phrase. The tall redhead kept pretty luxurious hours, it seemed to him—for a cub reporter on an afternoon paper. Barbee left a message that he had called, and determined not to brood about his nightmare.

He dressed hastily, stopped for a cup of coffee at the Dainty Diner on the corner, and drove on downtown. He wanted people around him. Human people. He wanted familiar voices and the clatter of type-writers and the steady thump of teletypes and the jingle of mats in the composing machines and the deep rumble of the presses. He stopped across the street from the *Star* at old Ben Chittum's newsstand, and asked about Rex.

"He's all torn up." The lean old man seemed moodily depressed. "It must have hit him pretty hard, the way Dr. Mondrick went. He stopped to see me yesterday after the funeral, but he didn't have much to say. Had to get back to the Foundation."

He paused to straighten a rack of papers, and then peered sharply at Barbee.

"Why didn't the papers print more about it?" he wanted to know. "I know you were out there, and this girl from the *Call*. It seems important to me—when a man like Dr. Mondrick dies that way. But there's hardly anything."

"Huh?" Barbee was vaguely puzzled. "I thought it was a page-one story, and I turned in six hundred words. I guess I was too upset myself to notice what they used."

"See." The old man showed him a copy of yesterday's *Star*. Not a word of his story had been printed. On an inside page, he found the bare announcement of Mondrick's funeral at two in the afternoon.

"I don't get it," he said, and shrugged off his brief perplexity. He had more disquieting riddles than that to solve. He crossed the street, glad to get back to the ordered confusion of the newsroom.

On his desk was a familiar blue-paper memo requesting him to report to Preston Troy. The *Star* was not the greatest among Troy's enterprises—which included the mills and the Trojan Trust and the radio station and the baseball club. The newspaper was his favorite child, however, and he handled most of his affairs from his spacious corner office on the floor above the city room.

Barbee found the publisher dictating to a svelte titian-haired secretary—Troy was famous for the sophisticated good looks of his secretaries. He was a squat, florid man, with a thin fringe of reddish hair around the pink dome of his head. He looked up at Barbee with shrewd blue eyes, and rolled his thick cigar across his wide, aggressive mouth.

"Find me the Walraven file," he told the girl, and his cold eyes came to Barbee. "Grady says you're a good legman, Barbee. I want to give you a chance at some feature stuff—under your own by-line—to build up Colonel Walraven for the senate."

"Thanks, Chief," Barbee said without enthusiasm for Colonel Walraven. "I see Grady didn't run my story yesterday on Mondrick's death."

"I told him to kill it."

"Will you tell me why?" Barbee watched Troy's pink-jowled face. "I thought it was page-one stuff. Strong human interest, with a swell mystery angle. Old Mondrick died, you see, right in the middle of telling what they had brought back from Asia in that green box.

"And it's still a good story, Chief." Barbee curbed his eagerness, trying to sound sanely calm. "The coroner's verdict was death from natural causes, but the old man's associates act as if they don't believe a word of that. They're hiding whatever is inside that green box, and they're still afraid to talk."

Barbee gulped and tried to slow his voice.

"I want to follow up the story, Chief. Give me a photographer, and I'll file some features that will put Clarendon on the map. I want to find why Mondrick went to the Ala-shan. And what those men are afraid of. And what they're hiding in that box."

Troy's eyes were hard and blank.

"Too sensational for the *Star*." His rasping voice was abruptly dictatorial. "Forget it, Barbee. Get to work on the colonel."

"Too sensational, Chief?" Barbee echoed. "You always said murder was the cornerstone of the *Star*."

"I set our editorial policy," Troy snapped. "We're printing nothing about the Mondrick case. Neither, you will find, is any other large newspaper."

Barbee tried to swallow his puzzled unease.

"But I can't forget it, Chief," he protested. "I've got to find out what Sam Quain is hiding in that box. It haunts me. I dream about it."

"You'll have to work at that on your own time—and at your own risk." Troy's voice was flat and cold. "And not for publication." He studied Barbee with penetrating eyes, rolling the thick perfecto back across his mouth. "Another thing—just keep in mind you aren't a fish. Better lay off the booze."

He opened the desk humidor, and his hard face thawed.

"Have a cigar, Barbee." His voice turned easily genial. "Here's the Walraven file. I want a biographical series. His early hardships, his military heroism, his secret philanthropies, his happy domestic life, his public-spirited service in Washington. Play down anything the voters wouldn't like."

That would be plenty, Barbee thought.

"Okay, Chief."

He went back to his desk in the noisy city room, and began to finger through the pile of clippings. But he knew too much the clippings didn't say, about the sewer bonds and the highway department scandal and the reason the Colonel's first wife had left him. It was hard to keep his mind on the unsavory task of whitewashing such a man for the senate, and he found himself staring over his typewriter at the picture of a lean wolf howling at the moon on a calendar, thinking wistfully of the splendid freedom and power he had enjoyed in that dream.

To hell with Walraven!

Barbee knew suddenly that he had to get the facts behind the bizarre riddles of Mondrick's death and Rowena's madness and April Bell's queer confession. If he were only building haunted castles out of whisky and coincidence, he wanted to be certain of it. If not—well, even insanity would break the monotonous grind of a legman on the *Star.*

He stuffed the Walraven papers into his desk, got his coupe out of the parking lot, and drove out Center Street toward the university. He still couldn't understand why the Mondrick case didn't fit the editorial policy of the *Star*—nothing had ever been too sensational for Preston Troy before. Anyhow, for print or not, he had to know what was in that box.

Sam Quain must have moved it already, he supposed, from his study to the place he was arranging on the top floor of the Foundation building. He wondered what those carpenters and welders had been doing there—and realized that once more he was accepting the dream as fact.

He turned right at the traffic light, and left on Pine Street, and parked in front of Sam Quain's little white bungalow. It looked exactly as it had in the nightmare—even to the same rusted tin bucket and toy spade on Pat's sand pile in the back yard. He knocked, trying to ignore an uneasy tingling sensation, and Nora came from the kitchen to open the door.

"Why, Will—come in!"

A mild astonishment widened her blue eyes—they looked dull, he thought, and the lids a little swollen, as if she hadn't slept well.

"Is Sam at home?" A sudden pang of icy dread halted him inside the door, as if this quiet and friendly seeming dwelling concealed some deadly trap. He couldn't help sniffing, as that panic caught his breath, for the seeping, lethal malodor of the thing in Sam Quain's box. His nostrils found nothing more noxious, however, than the pleasant aroma of a roast in the oven; and he saw Nora's faintly puzzled expression.

"I'm looking for Sam, for another interview," he told her. "I want to ask more about the Foundation expeditions, and what they found at those sites in the Ala-shan."

Her tired face frowned.

"Better forget it, Will." Her hurried voice seemed dry and uneasy. "Sam won't talk about it, not even to me. I don't know what they brought back in that mysterious box, and there isn't a chance Sam would let you see it. He kept it here in his study the last two nights—and woke up this morning dreaming about it."

"Huh?" Barbee gulped. "He did?"

"He thought somebody was trying to take it." Nora shivered a little, and her blue eyes looked dark-shadowed with worry. "I guess the thing is getting on my nerves as well as Sam's because we both had a bad night. It seems I almost remember—"

She checked herself, looking sharply at Barbee.

"A funny thing," she added, without saying what she almost remembered. "The telephone receiver in Sam's study was off the hook this morning. I'm pretty sure it wasn't last night, and Sam had the door locked. I can't imagine how that happened."

Barbee offered no solution for that puzzle. He looked away from her troubled face, trying to swallow the sudden tightness in his throat, and asked abruptly:

"Where is Sam now?"

"Down at the Foundation," she said. "He has had a crew of men working day and night there since he got back—installing the fixtures in a new lab, he told me. He telephoned them when he woke up this morning, and Nick and Rex came in a station wagon for him and the box. He didn't even have time for his breakfast."

Her tired eyes looked appealingly at Barbee.

"Sam told me not to worry," she said, "but I just can't help it. He telephoned just a few minutes ago that he won't be home tonight. I suppose it is a really big discovery, that will make them all famous when it's announced, but I don't quite understand the way they act. They all seem so—frightened!"

She shuddered a little, and added hopefully:

"Maybe Rex will tell—"

She caught herself.

"Tell what?" Barbee demanded.

Her soap-reddened hands twisted uncertainly at the corner of her kitchen apron.

"Sam warned me not to say anything about it." Freckles stood out from the worried pallor of her round face. "I know I can trust you, Will—but I didn't mean to mention it. Please don't let your paper get hold of it." Her eyes were afraid. "Oh, Will—I'm so upset—I don't know what to do."

Barbee patted her plump shoulder.

"I won't print anything you tell me," he promised.

"It's nothing much, really." Her sleepy, uncertain voice seemed grateful. "Just that Sam sent Rex back, after they left this morning, to get our car. I was going to take it to have the brakes tightened this morning. But they were in such a hurry. Rex is going to take it, Sam told me on the phone, to drive to State College tonight to make a radio broadcast."

"What about?"

"I don't know—Sam just told me the Foundation is buying time for a special program tomorrow. He asked me to listen. But not to speak about it. I hope they explain some of this horrid mystery." Her voice turned anxious. "You won't say anything, Will?"

"I won't," he promised. "Good morning, Pat—how are you?"

Little Patricia Quain came slowly from the nursery and clung to Nora's soapy hand. Her blue eyes were redder than Nora's, and ringed with grime. Her pink, square-jawed face seemed stubbornly set against any more tears.

"I'm all right, thank you, Mr. Will." Her low voice struggled not to break. "The tragedy is poor little Jiminy Cricket. He was killed last night."

Barbee felt a frigid breath blow out of the darkness of his mind. He turned and coughed in an effort to cover his terrified start.

"That's mighty bad." His voice rasped huskily. "How did it happen?"

Pat's wet blue eyes blinked.

"Two big dogs came in the night," she told him soberly. "One was white and one was gray. They wanted to take Daddy's box out of the study. Little Jiminy ran out to stop them, and the big gray dog bit his back and killed him."

Mute and shaken, Barbee turned to Nora.

"That's what Pat says." Her own tired voice seemed bewildered. "Anyhow, her little dog is dead. We found it lying on the sand pile this morning—right where she told me to look, when she woke up crying."

Her plump shoulder shrugged vainly at the inexplicable.

"I really think a car struck the little dog," she insisted resolutely. "Some of those college boys drive so recklessly at night. Probably he crawled back to the sand pile before he died, and Pat must have heard him whining."

Pat set her pink, grimy jaw.

"Please, Mother—no!" she protested stubbornly. "That big gray dog did it with his long, ugly teeth. I did too see him, and the pretty white dog with him, like I do in dreams. Didn't I, Mother? Didn't Daddy believe me?"

"Maybe he did, darling." Nora turned her round troubled face to Barbee. "It's true Sam turned white as a sheet when Pat told about her dream. He wouldn't go with us to look for Jiminy—just ran to see about his box in the study."

Her tired eyes were suddenly concerned.

"You look pale, Will—do you feel all right?"

"I had a funny dream myself." He tried to laugh. "Something I ate, maybe. I'm going to run on over to the Foundation now and talk to Sam." He put his hand around the child's small back. "That's too bad about Jiminy."

The child shrank from his hand, and hid her stained face in Nora's apron.

"I don't think Sam will tell you anything," Nora was saying. "If he does, Will—won't you let me know?" she walked outside the door with him, and dropped her voice below Pat's earshot. "Please, Will—I'm so afraid, and I don't know anything to do about it."

10

A Friend of April Bell

Autumn-fire still burned in the trees on the campus and the adjoining grounds of the Humane Research Foundation, and all the lawns were red and gold with fallen leaves. Barbee recalled the scents that had been so vivid in his dream and sniffed the cool air. All he could smell was a faint pungence of leaves burning in some back yard.

He met six freshmen marching down University Avenue, escorted by six sophomores with paddles and burdened with the cage that held the Clarendon tiger—this was homecoming week, he recalled, and the daily march of the tiger was part of the traditional preliminary ceremonies before the football game with State College.

That mascot was the life-size model of a saber-tooth, complete with tawny stripes and ferocious snarl, which had been merely an exhibit in the university museum until it was first abducted years ago by raiders from State College. The sight of it brought back wistful memories to Barbee.

For the Muleteers had been the four heroes who crossed the mountains west of Clarendon in Rex's ancient, stripped-down Cadillac on the eve of another homecoming game, disguised themselves successfully with the red war paint of the State College Indians, and snatched the stolen tiger out of the very midst of a State war dance.

But that was many years ago, before old Mondrick turned against him. Wistfully, for a moment, he wondered why—but the problems of the present were large enough without brooding over old slights. He parked around the corner, and strode firmly up the walk to the tall new Foundation building.

That lingering, nameless malodor of the night had fled, and the sounds of nighttime carpentry had ceased. The austere hush of the dim corridors seemed almost ominous. Instead of the girl he expected to see at the information desk, he found a thick-set man who looked many years too mature for his university sweater.

"Sorry, mister." The man scowled. "Library and museum not open today."

"That's all right," Barbee said pleasantly. "I only want to see Mr. Quain."

"Mr. Quain's busy."

"Then I'd like to speak to Mr. Spivak or Mr. Chittum."

"Busy." The man scowled harder. "No visitors today."

Barbee was reviewing his gate-crashing technique when he saw the two men idling in the automatic elevator. They also seemed too old to be wearing sweaters splashed with the yellow-and-black of the Clarendon tiger, and they looked back at him too sharply. He saw the bulges at their hips and remembered that Sam Quain had been hiring guards for the Foundation.

He scrawled on a card: "*Sam, it will save us both trouble if you will talk to me now*" and pushed the card and a dollar bill across the information desk. He smiled at the cold-eyed watchman.

"Please send that to Mr. Quain."

Silently, the bleak-faced man pushed back the dollar and carried the card to the elevator. He limped like a tired policeman, and Barbee found the bulge his gun made. Sam Quain evidently intended to protect that box.

Barbee waited ten uncomfortable minutes under the guard's cold stare before Sam Quain stepped abruptly out of the elevator. Barbee was appalled to see the stark intensity of his contained desperation—no wonder Nora had been upset. He was coatless; his shirt sleeves were rolled up and his big hands had a vague chemical odor, as if he had been interrupted in some laboratory task. His unshaven face was gray and harsh with strain.

"This way, Will."

His haggard eyes recognized Barbee without friendship, and he led the way brusquely across the corridor to a long room which briefly puzzled Barbee. The walls were hung with huge maps of all the continents and others which bewildered him until he recognized them as restorations of the different coastlines and vanished land masses of the geologic past. A battery of card-punching and card-sorting machines occupied the end of the room, with long rows of gray steel filing cabinets beyond.

Barbee wondered for a moment what sort of data old Mondrick and his associates had assembled and analyzed here. The rivers and mountains of those lost continents older than legendary Atlantis and Lemuria were shown in convincing detail; colored boundaries across them puzzled him again. The work of the room had been either completed or suspended, because the sleek machines were silent today, the dim-lit aisles deserted.

Sam Quain shut the door behind them and turned beside a desk to face Barbee. There were chairs, but he didn't ask Barbee to sit. He knotted one gaunt fist in an unconscious gesture of restrained emotion.

"Better lay off, Will!" His quiet voice was vibrant with a controlled vehemence. "For your own sake."

"Tell me why," Barbee challenged.

A spasm as if of anguish twisted Quain's stiff face. His dark, tortured eyes looked up for a moment at those maps of the far past. He coughed, and his voice seemed to choke.

"Please, Will—don't ask me that!"

Barbee sat down on the corner of the desk.

"We're friends, Sam—or we used to be. That's why I came out here. You can tell me some things I've got to know—for very urgent reasons."

Quain's face set.

"I can't tell you anything."

"Listen, Sam!" A quivering urgency turned Barbee's voice imperative. "What was old Mondrick trying to say when he died? What did you find in the Ala-shan—and what have you got in that wooden box?" He studied Quain's bleak, gray face. "And who is the Child of Night?"

He paused, but Quain stood woodenly silent.

"You might as well answer, Sam," he rasped bitterly. "I'm in the newspaper game, remember. I know how to deal with unwilling sources. I'm going to find out what you're hiding—whether you like it or not."

Quain's blue eyes narrowed and his Adam's apple jerked to an uneasy gulp.

"You don't know what you're meddling into." His abrupt, low voice was harsh with pain. "Won't you just leave us alone with this—while there's something left of our old friendship? Can't you forget you're a snooping newshawk?"

"This isn't for the *Star*," Barbee protested huskily. "The paper isn't interested. But things are happening that I can't understand. I've got to solve some riddles, Sam, before they drive me nuts!"

His voice shuddered.

"I know you're afraid of something, Sam. Why else did you take all those useless precautions to guard old Mondrick at the airport? And why have you turned this building into a fortress?" He swallowed. "What's the danger, Sam?"

Stubbornly, Sam Quain shook his head.

"Better forget it, Will," he said. "The answers wouldn't make you any happier."

Barbee rose trembling from the edge of the desk.

"I know a little already," he said hoarsely. "Enough to drive me nearly out of my mind. I feel that you are putting up a terrific fight against—something. I'm involved in it—I don't know how. But I want to be on your side, Sam."

Sam Quain sat down heavily in the chair behind the desk. He fumbled nervously with a paperweight—it was that little Roman lamp of Mondrick's, Barbee saw, the one whose blackglazed design showed Romulus and Remus, twin sons of dark Mars and a human vestal, sucking at the dugs of a wolf bitch.

"Anything you know may be very unfortunate, Will—for both of us."

He pushed the terra-cotta lamp away from him abruptly, and sat a long time motionless beyond the desk, searching Barbee with hollowed, pain-shadowed eyes.

"I think you're imagining things," he said softly at last. "Nora was telling me you've been working too hard, and drinking too much. She was worried about you, Will, and I'm afraid she's right. I think you need a rest."

He put his hand on the desk telephone.

"I think you ought to get out of town for a few days, Will—before you drive yourself into a complete breakdown. I'll arrange it for you—so nothing will cost you a cent—if you'll promise to catch the afternoon plane today for Albuquerque."

Barbee stood frowning and silent.

"You see," he explained, "the Foundation has a little party working in New Mexico—excavating a cave dwelling for remains that may tell us why Homo sapiens was extinct in the western hemisphere when the Amerinds arrived. But you needn't bother with their work."

A hopeful smile warmed his harsh face.

"Won't you take a week off, Will?" he urged. "I'll call Troy and fix it with the paper—you might even do a feature story on the trip. Get plenty of sunshine and a little exercise—and forget about Dr. Mondrick."

He started to lift the phone.

"Will you go—today—if we arrange the reservations?"

Barbee shook his head.

"I don't bribe, Sam." He saw Quain's angry flush. "I still don't know what you're trying to cover up, but you can't ship me out of town that way. No, I'm going to stick around and see the fun."

Quain stood up stiffly.

"Dr. Mondrick decided not to trust you, Will—a long time ago." His voice was flat and cold. "He never told us why. Maybe you're all right. Maybe you aren't. We simply can't afford to take chances."

His stubborn face was bleak and dangerous.

"I'm sorry you choose to be so unreasonable, Will. I wasn't trying to bribe you—but I have to warn you now. Lay off, Will. If you don't stop this presumptuous investigation of affairs that don't concern you—we'll have to stop you. I'm sorry, Will. But that's the way it is." He shook his raw-boned, sun-bronzed head regretfully. "Think it over, Will. Now I've got to go."

He strode to open the door.

"Wait, Sam!" Barbee protested sharply. "If you can only give me one sane reason—"

But Sam Quain shut the door of that enigmatic room behind them and turned abruptly away. Barbee attempted to follow, but the elevator doors shut in his face. Uneasily conscious of the cold-eyed guard at the reception desk, he retreated from that stern tower that had become a citadel of the inexplicable.

Beside his shabby car at the curb, he turned to look up at those high windows behind, where he had seen the blue glare of welding torches in that nightmare, as Quain's men prepared a strongroom for the box. He couldn't help shivering, or sniffing again for that peculiar fetor. His nostrils caught nothing now. Yet the perfect fit between dream and reality frightened him—and his very sanity, he felt, was locked inside that guarded wooden box.

A sudden, illogical panic swept him into the car. He raced the motor and clashed the gears and lurched around the turns getting back to the highway. Foolish, he told himself. But Sam Quain, with that curious mixture of desperate intensity and solemn regret and sheer terror, had somehow shaken him.

He drove around the campus until that irrational spasm of dread had passed, and then started back to town. He glanced hopefully at his watch, but it wasn't time to call April Bell. He was still supposed to be working for the *Star*, he recalled, and the Walraven file was waiting in his desk in the city room. His troubled brain, however, revolted at the unpleasant chore of renovating Walraven for the voters, and suddenly he knew that he had to see Rowena Mondrick.

Why did she wear those quaint old silver heirlooms—in reality and in his dream? What, precisely, had she and Dr. Mondrick been digging for in Nigeria—and what had been the exact circumstances of that black leopard's attack? What did she know of Mondrick's later work? Did she know of any enemies who might have conspired to murder him at the airport? Did she know the name of the Child of Night?

If she could answer even one of those restless questions that stalked the darkness of his thoughts, her answer might be the touchstone he needed to distinguish between fact and whisky-bred illusion.

Passing the office, he drove on to the foot of Center Street and north on the new river road. Glennhaven occupied a hundred well-kept acres on the hills above the river, four miles out of Clarendon. Trees still gaudy with autumn screened the hospital buildings and the occupational therapy shops away from the highway.

Barbee parked on the gravel lot behind the long main building, an impressive three-story prison of yellow brick. He walked around the building into the cool, dim-lit hush of a wide reception room. Austere and opulent as the foyer of a bank, it seemed a temple to the new god Freud. The slim girl sitting at a switchboard behind a massive mahogany desk was its virginal priestess. He gave her his card.

"I've come to see Mrs. Rowena Mondrick," he said.

Her fragile loveliness reminded him of a portrait of some princess of old Egypt that he had seen in the university museum. Her eyes and hair were very black; her skin was pale ivory, her brow very low, her skull oddly long. She leafed swiftly through a black-bound book, and gave him a dreamy smile.

"I'm sorry, sir, but I haven't your name." Her voice was a sleepy caress. "All visits to our patients must be arranged in advance, you see, through the doctor in charge of the case. If you wish to leave your request—"

"I want to see Mrs. Mondrick, now."

"I'm very sorry, sir." Her slow smile was hauntingly exotic. "I'm afraid that would be impossible to arrange, today. If you wish to return—"

"Who is her doctor?"

"One moment, sir." Her slender ivory fingers riffled gracefully through the black book. "Mrs. Rowena Mondrick was admitted at eight this morning, and she's under—" The girl's limpid voice quivered melodiously, intoning the name of a minor deity. "She's under Dr. Glenn."

"Then let me see him."

"Sorry, sir," she purred. "But Dr. Glenn never sees anyone without an appointment."

Barbee caught his breath, and stifled an angry impulse to stalk past the girl and see what happened. She was watching him with dark misty eyes, and he knew she could call enough husky attendants to preserve the temple's solemn sanctity.

He gulped uneasily, trying to swallow the dry apprehension in his throat. Glennhaven, he knew, was rated as one of the country's finest psychiatric hospitals. There was no good reason, he told himself, for his old dim terror of all mental institutions.

"Mrs. Mondrick is a friend of mine," he told the girl. "I only want to find out how she is."

"Any discussion of our patients is against the rules," that fragile priestess cooed. "With Dr. Glenn himself in charge of the case, however, you may be certain that Mrs. Mondrick is receiving the best care possible. If you wish to ask permission for a visit—"

"No," he muttered. "Thanks."

He fled from the girl's exotic smile and that well-ordered, ruthless hush. The blind woman was not a sacrificial victim imprisoned in this efficiently conducted twentieth-century temple, he tried to tell himself. Actually, Glenn was a distinguished psychiatrist; his treatment would surely be kind and skillful.

Barbee was glad to get outside again, however. He filled his lungs thankfully with the cold autumn air, and hurried back to his car. One more effort had failed, but there was still April Bell. Eagerness hurried his breathing when he thought of that vivid redhead. It was almost time to call her hotel. He was going to return the jade wolf and find out, somehow, whether April Bell had dreamed—

Sight of Miss Ulford broke his thought. A gray little wisp of a woman, the nurse was sitting on a bench at the bus stop on the corner. He pulled to the curb and offered to drive her home.

"Thank you so much, Mr. Barbee." Smiling gratefully with yellow false teeth, she got in the car beside him. "I just missed the bus," she said plaintively, "and I don't know when the next one is. I suppose I could have asked the girl to call a taxi—but I hardly know what I'm doing, I'm so upset about poor Rowena."

"How is she?" Barbee whispered huskily.

"Acutely disturbed—that's what Dr. Glenn wrote on her chart." Worry rasped in the nurse's dry nasal voice. "She's still hysterical—she didn't want me to leave, but Glenn said I must—and they're giving her sedatives to calm her."

"What—" Barbee's hoarse voice caught. "What seems to be the trouble?"

"She has this obsessive dread, as Glenn calls it, and this queer compulsion."

"Huh?" Barbee frowned uneasily. "About what?"

"You know how she always was about silver? Glenn calls that an obsession, and it's worse after last night. You see, we took off that quaint old silver jewelry this morning when we were dressing her scratches and bruises from falling on the pavement, and she was perfectly frantic, poor dear, when she found she didn't have it. Dr. Glenn let me go back to the house and bring her beads and bracelets, and she thanked me like I had saved her life."

Barbee tried not to show his shudder.

"This compulsion?" he asked faintly. "What's that?"

"I don't understand it." The bent little nurse looked up at him with sad, bewildered eyes. "She wants to see Mr. Sam Quain. There is something she must tell him, she says, but she's quite unreasonable about it. She won't use the telephone. She won't write a note. She won't even trust me with her message. She did beg me to get him to come to see her—she wanted me to tell him she had a warning for him—but of course she isn't allowed any visitors."

Barbee tried to swallow the harsh dryness in his throat and decided not to ask any more questions, for fear the nurse should notice his own disturbance. The car, he discovered, was still in second gear. He shifted nervously into high, driving back to Clarendon along the river road.

"I'm so terribly sorry for poor Rowena," that plaintive whine went on. "Blind and all, and her husband hardly cold in the ground. She's still so dreadfully upset. She kept begging us to look for Turk—her big dog, you know. She let it out last night, and it didn't come back. Now she says she needs it with her, to guard her in the dark. Glenn kept asking her what she's afraid of, but she would never say."

Barbee sat taut and cold, shivering at the wheel. He dared not look at the nurse again. He was staring straight ahead but his eyes must have been blind to the road. He heard Miss Ulford's stifled shriek, and saw a huge truck looming close ahead on the narrow Deer Creek bridge. Somehow, he had got to driving far too fast. He whipped around the truck on screaming tires and grazed safely past the concrete railings and slowed beyond, still shuddering.

"Sorry," he whispered to the frightened nurse. "I was thinking about Rowena."

It was fortunate, he thought, that Miss Ulford couldn't know what he was thinking. He left her at the shabby old house on University Avenue and drove back to town. It was almost noon, and he waited at his desk, fumbling impatiently with the Walraven clippings, for the time to call the Trojan Arms again.

All his breathless eagerness to see April Bell again seemed to dry up, however, when he took hold of the telephone. He stubbornly refused to believe that she was anything more dangerous than any other alluring redhead, but he couldn't stop the panic that possessed him. Abruptly, he put the receiver back.

Better wait until he got hold of himself, he decided. Maybe he'd be smarter not to call at all, but just drop in unannounced. He wanted to be watching her face when he mentioned that white jade pin.

It was time for lunch, but he wasn't hungry. He stopped in a drugstore for a dose of bicarbonate, and in the Mint Bar for a shot of bourbon. That picked him up, and he went to the offices of Walraven's law firm, hoping to escape all his tormenting uncertainties for a little while and so find a fresh perspective on the alarming riddle of April Bell.

The bland-faced politician gave him another drink, and started telling dirty stories about his political rivals. Colonel Walraven's genial good humor evaporated, however, when Barbee mentioned sewage bonds. He suddenly recalled a pressing appointment, and Barbee went back to his desk.

He tried to work, but he couldn't put that guarded box out of his thoughts, or Sam Quain's unhappy threat. He couldn't forget Rowena Mondrick in that haunting dream, clutching her silver knife as she stumbled blindly after him. He couldn't stop wondering what she wanted to tell Sam Quain. And a green-eyed wolf bitch kept grinning at him from the blank page in his typewriter.

There was no use stalling any longer, he decided suddenly. He shrugged off that irrational dread of April Bell as he hastily put away the Walraven file—and a new fear seized him, that he had waited too long.

For it was almost two o'clock. She should have been gone from her apartment hours ago, he knew—if she were actually a reporter on the

Call. He hurried down to his car, went back to his own apartment to get the white jade pin, and drove too fast out North Main Street to the Trojan Arms.

It didn't surprise him to see Preston Troy's big blue sedan in the parking lot behind the apartment-hotel. One of Troy's more gorgeous ex-secretaries, he knew, had an apartment on the top floor.

Barbee didn't stop at the desk—he didn't want to give April Bell warning enough to make up any more tales about Aunt Agatha. He meant to drop the little jade wolf in her hand, and watch the expression in her greenish eyes. He didn't wait for the elevator but climbed the stairs to the second floor.

Still, he wasn't surprised when he saw Troy's squat figure waddling down the corridor ahead of him—the ex-secretary, he supposed, must have moved down into a new apartment. He started looking for the numbers. Here was 2-A, and 2-B; the next should be 2-C—

His breath went out.

For Troy had stopped ahead of him, at the door of 2-C. Barbee stood slack-jawed, staring. The heavy little man in the sharp-creased double-breasted suit and shrieking purple tie didn't knock or touch the buzzer. He opened the door with his own key. Barbee caught the haunting velvet huskiness of April Bell's voice, intimate and low, and the door closed again.

Barbee stumbled back to the elevator and punched the down button savagely. He felt sick, as if from a blow in the stomach. It was true, he reminded himself, that he had no claim whatever upon April Bell. She had mentioned other friends, he remembered, besides Aunt Agatha. Obviously she couldn't live here on her newspaper earnings.

But he couldn't help feeling sick.

11

As a Saber-Tooth Slays—

Barbee went back to the noisy city room—there was nothing else to do. He didn't want to think any more about April Bell, and he sought relief from all the cruel perplexities that leered from the shadows of his mind in his old anodynes: hard work and raw whisky.

He got out the Walraven file again and hammered out a feature article on the boyhood hardships of "Clarendon's First Citizen," numb to the sordid facts that had to be omitted. He went out to cover a stop-Walraven meeting of indignant citizens, and put tongue in cheek to write it up the way Grady said Troy wanted it written, as a sinister gathering of the evil henchmen of unspecified interests.

He was afraid to go home.

He tried not to let his thoughts dwell upon the reasons, but he loitered about the newsroom until the third edition went to press, and then stopped to have a few drinks with some of the gang in the bar across the street.

Somehow, he was afraid to go to sleep. It was long past midnight, and he was reeling with whisky and fatigue, when he tiptoed down the creaking hall and let himself into his little apartment in the gloomy old house on Bread Street.

He hated the place suddenly, with all its vague musty smells and the faded, dingy wall paper and the cheap, ugly furniture. He hated his job on the *Star* and the cynical dishonesties of his article on Walraven. He hated Preston Troy. He hated April Bell, and he hated himself.

He felt tired and lonely and bitter, and suddenly very sorry for himself. He couldn't do the lying stuff that Troy demanded of him, and yet he knew he lacked the fortitude to quit. It was Dr. Mondrick who had killed his pride and confidence, he thought bitterly, years ago when that gruff old scientist abruptly shattered his planned career in anthropology and refused to state a reason. Or was that idle blame-laying, and the fatal fault a part of himself? Anyhow, his life was wrecked and squandered. He could see no future—and he was afraid to sleep.

He dawdled in the bathroom, and tilted up the bottle on the chiffonier to drain the last gulp of whisky. With the vague hope that it might somehow explain his dream, he took one of his old textbooks from the shelves and tried to read the chapter on lycanthropy.

The book cataloged the queerly universal primitive beliefs that human beings could change into dangerous carnivorous animals. He skimmed the list of human wolves and bears and jaguars, human tigers and alligators and sharks, human cats and human leopards and human hyenas. The were-tigers of Malaysia, he read, were believed invulnerable in the transformed state—but the careful, objective language of the academic authority seemed very dull and dry beside the remembered reality of his dream. His eyes began to blur and ache. He laid the book aside and crawled reluctantly into bed.

A were-tiger, it occurred to him, would make a peculiarly satisfactory transformation. Enviously, he recalled the tawny ferocity of the Clarendon tiger—the reconstructed saber-tooth he had seen the freshmen carrying down University Avenue that morning. Dozing, he dwelt wistfully upon the deadly power of that extinct predator, lingering longingly upon each remembered detail of its ferocious claws and the terrible, cruel snarl of its white saber-fangs. And all his dread of sleep was changed into burning eagerness.

This time it was easier. The flow of change was scarcely painful. He sprang to the floor beside his bed, landing in that awkwardly narrow space with a cat-like, silent ease. Curiously he turned to look back at the slumbering form between the sheets, a gaunt, shrunken thing, deathly pale and still.

For a moment he stood wondering how that feeble, ugly husk could ever have been a dwelling for all the splendor of raw power that he felt within him now. But the odors of the room were foul to him, the rank smells of moldering books and neglected laundry and stale tobacco and spilled whisky; and the narrow walls too close for his magnificent dimensions.

He squeezed into the shrunken front room, and padded across it to the door—his new eyes saw everything in the room with a wonderful clarity, even by the faint light that seeped under the drawn blinds from the street lamp on the corner. He fumbled with his huge paw for the key in the lock—and then remembered the art April Bell had taught him.

Nothing anywhere was absolute, and only probabilities were real. His free mind was a moving pattern, an eternal complex of mental energy that grasped atoms and electrons by the linkage of probability to be its vehicle and its tools. That mental web could ride the wind, and slip through wood or common metal—the only barrier was lethal silver.

He made the effort he remembered. The door grew misty. The metal of screws and lock and hinges appeared and dissolved again. He slipped through the opening and padded carefully down the hall past the slow breath-sounds of Mrs. Sadowski's other tenants.

The street door yielded also. A late drunk weaving uncertainly up the sidewalk outside brushed against his tawny coat and peered through him vacantly, hiccoughed once, and staggered happily on. He stalked out into the evil reeks of burned rubber and dropped cigarettes on the pavement and trotted away toward the Trojan Arms.

April Bell came down to meet him beside the tiny, ice-rimmed lake in the little park across the street. This time she wasn't wolf, but woman. He knew, however, as soon as he saw her slip out through the unopened front door of the apartment-hotel, that she had left her real body sleeping behind. She was entirely nude, and her hair fell in loose red waves to her white breasts.

"You must be strong, Will, to take such a shape!"

Admiration warmed her velvet voice and danced in her limpid greenish eyes. She came to meet him, and her tall body felt smooth and cool against his fur. She scratched playfully behind his ears, and he made a deep pleased purr.

"I'm glad you're so powerful," she whispered. "Because I'm still not feeling well—your old friend Quain nearly killed me with that clever trap in his study. And I was just about to try to call you, Will. You see, we have another job to do tonight."

He lashed his tail in sudden dim alarm.

"Another?" He thought of blind Rowena Mondrick falling on the pavement as she chased him with her silver blade in that other dream. He growled softly at the woman beside him. "I don't want another job."

"Nor did I." She tickled him below the ears. "But I just found out that Rex Chittum drove out of town an hour ago in Sam Quain's car. He was working with Quain all day at the Foundation, and now I've found out that he had arranged to broadcast tomorrow from the radio station at State College. I'm afraid he's planning to finish that scientific announcement that old Mondrick started at the airport."

Her low voice was a crystal melody.

"We must stop him, Will."

"Not Rex!" Barbee protested sharply. "Rex is an old, good friend—"

His scalp tingled to her cool, caressing fingers.

"All your old, good friends are human beings, Will," she purred. "They are enemies of the Child of Night, cunning and ruthless and strong. They are grasping every resource of science to seek us out and strike us down. We must use the few feeble weapons in our hands."

She chucked him lightly under his mighty jaw.

"Surely you see that, Will?"

He nodded his massive head, yielding to her inexorable logic. For this was life, with the white frost crisp beneath his huge pads and the woman's soft hand brushing sparks from his tawny coat. The world in which Rex Chittum once had been his friend was now no more than a dim nightmare of bitter compromise and deadly frustration. Recalling the desperate eagerness for escape that had shaped his flow into the saber-tooth's form, he growled again in glad relief.

"Then let's go," she urged, and he let her leap astride him. She was no burden to his new and boundless strength. He carried her back down Main to Center Street, and out past the yellow-blinking signal at the corner of the campus, and on toward the mountain road.

They passed dark sleeping houses beside the highway. Once a dog began to howl impotently behind them. The moon was down and the clear sky frosted with the autumn constellations. Even by the colorless light of the stars, however, Barbee could see everything distinctly— every rock and bush beside the road, every shining wire strung on the striding telephone poles.

"Faster, Will!" April's smooth legs clung to his racing body. She leaned forward, her breasts against his striped coat, her loose red hair flying in the wind, calling eagerly into his flattened ear. "We must catch them on Sardis Hill."

He stretched out his stride, rejoicing in his boundless power. He exulted in the clean chill of the air, the fresh odors of earth and life that passed his nostrils, and the warm burden of the girl. This was life. April Bell had awakened him out of a cold, walking death. Remembering that frail and ugly husk he had left sleeping in his room, he shuddered as he ran.

"Faster!" urged the girl.

The dark plain and the first foothills beyond flowed back around them like a drifting cloud. He found a limit, however, even to the saber-tooth's power. As the road wound up the dark, tree-dotted flanks of the higher foothills, his pounding heart began to ache.

"I know this country," he gasped. "Sam Quain's father used to have a little ranch up here before he died. I used to come out here to ride and hunt with Sam. And this is the road we took—the four Muleteers, Sam called us—when we rescued the Clarendon tiger from State. We rolled boulders on the road to stop the Indians while we changed a tire on Sardis Hill."

His mighty flanks heaved to his labored breathing.

"It must be twenty miles ahead," he wheezed. "The grades are steep—I'm afraid we can't get there."

"The grades are steeper for your old friend's car," the urgent girl called back. "And there's a reason we must catch him on Sardis Hill—or let him go unharmed."

"What reason?" he breathed.

"We're never quite so powerful as we feel in this free state," she whispered in the rushing wind. "Because our usual bodies are left behind, and our moving mind complexes can draw only upon the chance energies that they happen to grasp from the atoms of the air or other substances we possess, by the linkage of probability. All our power lies in that control of probability, and we must strike where it will serve."

He shook his immense sleek head, impatient with the intricacies of her explanation. The involved paradoxes of mathematical physics had always baffled him; now he felt content with the saber-tooth's surging might, without troubling to analyze the atomic structure of power.

"What probability?" he said.

"I think Rex Chittum is quite safe from us," whispered the girl on his back, "so long as he is driving carefully along a straight, level road—Quain must have briefed him and armed him against us, and the probability of any harm to him is too slight for us to grasp.

"So go faster!" Her slim cool fingers clutched his tawny fur. "We must catch him on Sardis Hill, because the probability of his death will be far greater when he starts down that double curve—I've a sense for such things, and I can tell. The man's afraid. He'll drive too fast, in spite of all Quain told him."

The girl lay flat upon his wide, striped shoulders.

"Faster!" she screamed on the screaming wind. "And we'll kill Rex Chittum on Sardis Hill!"

He shuddered beneath her and lay closer to the black road as he ran. The dark hills wheeled beside them, as if carried on two turning platforms. They passed the first pines; he caught the clean fragrance, and his eyes could see every needle and cone, distinct in the starlight.

Beyond the pines, red tail lamps winked and disappeared again.

"There!" the white girl called. "Catch him, Barbee!"

He stretched himself again, and the dark hills flowed. His long muscles ached and his pads were bruised and his heaving lungs breathed raw pain, but he overtook the glaring red tail lamps that fled toward Sardis Hill. He came up behind the car, grinding up the last long grade toward the saddle of the pass.

It was the little tan convertible, he saw, that Nora had bought while Sam was away. The top was down in spite of the chill of the night—it didn't work well, he remembered. Hunched over the wheel, bundled in a black overcoat, Rex Chittum looked scared and cold.

"Good work, Barbee," the girl purred. "Just keep up, till he starts down the curve."

He bounded on obediently. Gears snarled ahead as the little car labored up the grade, and the air behind it was foul with hot rubber and half-burned gasoline. Rex Chittum turned once at the wheel to peer back apprehensively. His dark head was carelessly bare—Barbee's eyes could see every curly hair, ruffled by the cold wind. For all the gray fatigue on his face and the black stubble on his chin and the shadow of dread in his narrowed eyes, he still looked handsome as another Li'l Abner.

Barbee growled at the girl astride him.

"Must we kill Rex?" he protested. "He always was such a good kid, really. We went to school together, you know. We neither had much money—Rex was always trying to lend me his last dollar, when he needed it more than I."

"Run, Barbee," the girl murmured. "Keep up."

He turned to snarl with deadly sabers.

"Think of poor old Ben Chittum at the newsstand," he growled softly. "Rex is all old Ben has left. He worked at all sorts of odd jobs and went dressed like a tramp when they first came to Clarendon to keep Rex in school. This will break his heart."

"Keep running, Barbee." The white girl's voice was clear and sweet and limpidly pitiless. "We must do what we must, because we are what we are." Her cool fingers scratched his mighty shoulders. "To save our own kind, and defend the Child of Night."

She flattened against his fur.

"Run Barbee!" she screamed. "Keep in reach—we'll have to stand the motor fumes. Wait now—stay just behind. Wait till he's on the hairpin—till he's going a little faster. Wait till the linkage of probability is strong enough to grasp—can't you feel it growing? Wait! Wait—"

Her long body stiffened against him. Her cool fingers tightened in his shaggy fur, and her bare, clinging heels dug deep into his heaving flanks. She was sweet against him, and the clear logic of this new life conquered the dreary conventions of that old, dim existence where he had walked in bitter death.

"Now," she screamed. "Spring!"

Barbee sprang, but the little car drew away from him, speeding on the down grade. His reaching claws caught only asphalt and gravel, and the hot fumes choked him.

"Catch him!" shrieked the girl. "While the link is strong enough!"

The fever of the chase burned away his lingering compunctions. He spurned the road and sprang again. His extended claws scratched and slipped on enameled metal, but he managed to catch the leather upholstery. His rear feet found the bumper. He clung to the lurching car, crouching.

"Kill him!" screamed April Bell. "Before the linkage snaps!"

Rex Chittum turned again, below him at the wheel, peering back with dark, anxious eyes. He shuddered in his bulky coat, to the bitter wind or something else. He didn't seem to see the snarling saber-tooth. A brief, stiff smile lighted his haggard, stubbled face.

"Made it," Barbee heard his thankful murmur. "Sam said the danger was—"

"Now!" the girl whispered. "While his eyes are off the road—"

Swiftly, mercifully, the long sabers flashed. Rex Chittum had been a loyal friend to him in that dead, dim world behind, and Barbee didn't want to cause him pain. The linkage of probability was still a dry technical phrase to Barbee, but he could feel the warm yielding tissues of the human throat his sabers slashed. He forgot the words, tasting the hot salty sweet of spurting blood and giddy with its odor.

The man's lifeless hands let go the wheel. The little car had been going too fast—somehow, Barbee sensed, that fact had intensified the link that let his long fangs strike home. Tires smoked on the pavement and danced on the gravel, and the car left the road where the hairpin bent.

Barbee flung himself away from the plunging machine. He twisted in the air, and dropped cat-like on all four pads, clinging to the slope with his claws. The girl had lost her seat as the car lurched over beneath them. She came down on the loose rocks beside him, clinging to his fur with both frantic hands. He heard her gasp of pain, and then her awed whisper:

"Watch, Barbee!"

The hurtling car, the motor still drumming and wheels spinning against the empty air, seemed to fly almost above them. It turned three times in empty space, and first struck the long rockslide a hundred feet below them. It flattened and crumpled and rolled until finally a boulder stopped it. The red, torn thing half under it made no movement.

"I thought the linkage would be strong enough," the tall girl purred. "And you needn't worry over your own part, Barbee—the police will never know that the broken windshield didn't slash his throat. Because, you see, the probability that it would was all that forged the linkage to enable your fangs to do it."

She tossed the long red hair impatiently back of her bare shoulders, and bent to feel her ankle. Her white face set with pain, and her long greenish eyes turned uneasily toward the pale silver point of the zodiacal light, rising in the dark hollow of the pass behind them.

"I'm hurt," she whispered, "and the night is nearly gone. Darling, you must take me home."

Barbee crouched beside a boulder to help her mount again, and he carried her back over the pass and down the long dark road toward Clarendon. Light as his own footfalls when they set out, she now felt heavy as a leaden statue. He lurched and swayed to her weight, shivering to a sickening chill.

That hot sweet taste of Rex Chittum's blood was a lingering bitterness in his mouth. All his mad elation had fled. He felt cold and ill and strangely tired, and he was afraid of the glowing east. He hated that narrow, ugly prison sleeping on his bed, but he had to go back.

He shook himself as he limped wearily on toward the greenish glow of day, until April Bell protested sharply. He couldn't quite dislodge his memory of that dull shadow of horror in Rex Chittum's eyes, looking back through him before he struck, or forget the grief that old Ben would feel.

12
Hair of the Tiger

Barbee woke late. The white glare of sunlight in the bedroom hurt his aching eyes, and he rolled shuddering away from it before he remembered that its deadly power was only a dream. He felt stiff and vaguely ill. A dull, leaden weariness ached in all his body, and a clamor of agony started in his head when he sat up.

The shadowy dread in Rex Chittum's dark, unseeing eyes still haunted him, and he couldn't forget the feel of soft skin and firm tendons and the stiff tissues of the larynx slicing to his long sabers. He blinked apprehensively about the narrow room, glad to see no evidence that any saber-tooth had ever walked there.

He stood up uncertainly and tottered into the bathroom, holding his head. The shower, as hot as he could bear it and then as cold, washed some of the stiff pain out of him. A teaspoon of baking soda, stirred in a glass of cold water, eased the queasy feeling in his stomach.

But the face in his mirror shocked him. It was a bloodless gray, seamed and drawn, the eyes deep-sunken and red-rimmed and glittering. He tried to smile, just to light the dark strangeness of it, and the pale lips twitched at him sardonically. That was a lunatic's face.

He reached a shuddering hand to change the angle of the cheap mirror, hoping to correct some accidental distortion. The result was still unpleasant. The putty-colored face looked too gaunt, the raw-boned skull too long. He had better get more vitamins, he told himself uneasily, and drink a good bit less. Even a . . . shave might help, if he could manage not to nick himself too deeply.

The telephone rang as he fumbled with his razor.

"Will? . . . This is Nora Quain." Her voice was sick. "Brace yourself, Will. Sam just called me from the Foundation—he worked there all night. He called to tell me about Rex. Rex started to drive to State College last night—in our car, remember. He must have been driving too fast—too nervous, maybe, about that broadcast he meant to make. Anyhow, the car turned over on Sardis Hill. Rex was killed."

The telephone fell out of Barbee's hands. He dropped weakly on his knees, and groped for it with queerly numb fingers, and picked it up again.

"—ghastly," Nora's low, hoarse voice was rasping. "Anyhow he died instantly, the state police told Sam. His head was cut almost off. The edge of the windshield, the police said. It's a terrible thing, and I—I almost blame myself. You know the brakes weren't very good—and I didn't think to tell him."

Barbee nodded at the receiver mutely. She didn't know how terrible it was. He wanted to scream, but the stiff constriction in his dry throat wouldn't even let him whisper. He shut his aching eyes against the cruel white glare from the window, and saw the handsome haggard face of Rex again, grown bitterly reproachful in his recollection, the brown fearful eyes still peering through him unseeingly.

He felt the receiver vibrate and listened again.

"—all he had," Nora's shaken voice was saying. "I think you're his best friend, Will. He's been waiting for two years in that little newsstand for Rex to come home. He's bound to take it pretty hard. I think you ought to break the news. Don't you think so?"

He had to swallow twice.

"All right," he gasped huskily. "I'll do it."

He hung up the telephone and stumbled back into the bathroom and took three long gulps out of a bottle of whisky. That took hold of him and steadied his quivering hands. He finished shaving and drove downtown.

Old Ben Chittum lived in two small rooms behind the newsstand. He was already open for business when Barbee parked at the curb, arranging magazines in a rack outside the door. He saw Barbee and gave him a cheery, snaggle-toothed grin.

"Hi, Will!" he called brightly. "What's new?"

Barbee shook his head, gulping mutely.

"Busy tonight, Will?" Noticing nothing, the old man ambled across the sidewalk to meet him, digging his pipe out of a bulging shirt pocket. "Reason I ask, I'm cooking dinner tonight for Rex."

Barbee stood swaying, feeling cold and bad inside, watching the spry old man strike a light for the pipe.

"Haven't seen much of Rex since he got back from over the water," old Ben went on. "But I reckon he'll have his work caught up by now, and I know he'll want to come. He always liked my beef mulligan, with hot biscuits and honey, ever since he was a kid, and I remember you used to eat with us now and then. Welcome, Will, if you'd like to come. I'm going to call Rex—"

Barbee cleared his throat harshly.

"I've got bad news for you, Ben."

The man's spry vitality seemed to drain away. He gasped and stared and began to tremble. The pipe dropped out of his gnarled fingers, and the stem broke on the concrete sidewalk.

"Rex?" he whispered.

Barbee gulped, and nodded again.

"Bad?"

"Bad," Barbee said. "He was driving over the mountains on some business for the Foundation late last night. The car went out of control on Sardis Hill. Rex was killed. He—he didn't suffer."

Ben Chittum stared a long time, blankly, out of slowly filling eyes. His eyes were dark like Rex's, and when they went out of focus, staring vaguely past Barbee, they were suddenly Rex's own, as they had been in that dreadful dream, peering with a fear-shadowed vacancy through the crouching saber-tooth.

Barbee looked hastily away, shivering.

147

"I've been afraid," he heard the old man's broken whisper. "They just don't seem quite right—none of them—since they got back from over the water. I tried to talk to Rex, but he wouldn't tell me anything. But I'm afraid, Will—"

The old man stooped painfully to pick up the pipe and the broken stem; his quivering fingers fitted the pieces awkwardly back together.

"I'm afraid," he muttered again. "Because I think they dug up something in that desert that should have stayed under the ground. You see, Rex told me before they ever left that Dr. Mondrick was looking for the true Garden of Eden, where the human race came from. I'm afraid they found it, Will—and things they shouldn't have found."

Wearily, he stuffed the pieces of the pipe back in his pocket.

"Rex ain't the last that's going to die."

His dark, unseeing eyes came back into focus, looking at Barbee. He seemed to become conscious of his tears and wiped at them with an angry sleeve. He shook his head and limped heavily back to move his rack of magazines inside the door.

Barbee stood watching, too shaken even to offer any aid.

"Rex always liked my beef mulligan," the old man murmured softly. "Especially with buttered hot biscuits and honey. You remember that, don't you, Will? Ever since he was just a kid."

Dazedly, he locked up the newsstand. Barbee drove him to the morgue. The ambulance hadn't come back with the body—Barbee felt mutely grateful for that. He left the stunned old man in the kindly hands of Parker, the county sheriff, and turned automatically toward the Mint Bar.

Two double slugs of bourbon, however, failed to stop the throbbing in Barbee's head. The daylight was too bright, and that queasy sickness came back to his stomach. He couldn't forget that vacant blankness of unseeing horror in Rex's eyes, and a frenetic tension of terror crept upon him from that dark recollection.

Desperately, he fought that terror. He tried to move deliberately, tried to smile disarmingly at the casual witticisms of another early drinker. He failed. The man moved uneasily to a farther stool, and Barbee saw the bartender watching him too keenly. He paid for his drinks and stumbled back into the glare of day.

He had the shakes, and he knew he couldn't drive. He left his car where he had parked it, and took a taxi to the Trojan Arms. The front door through which April Bell had slipped so easily in his dream was unlocked now. He staggered through it and lurched straight to the stair, before the clerk could stop him.

A card hung on the doorknob of 2-C said, "Don't Disturb," but he knocked vigorously. If the Chief's still here, he thought grimly, let him crawl under the bed.

April Bell was slim and tall and lovely in a sea-green robe nearly as revealing as that dream had been. Her long hair, brushed to a coppery luster, was loose about her shoulders. Her face was a pale smooth oval; she hadn't painted her lips. Her greenish eyes lighted as she recognized him.

"Will—come on in!"

He came in, grateful that the clerk hadn't overtaken him, and sat down in the big easy chair she pointed to beside a reading lamp. His employer wasn't in sight, but he wondered if this weren't Troy's chair—for April Bell would hardly be interested in the new copy of *Fortune* on the little table beside it, or care to smoke the cigars in that heavy gold case he thought he must have seen somewhere before.

He looked away from those things almost guiltily—they stirred a hot, illogical resentment in him; but he hadn't come here to quarrel with April Bell. She was moving, with the easy feline grace that he remembered in the dream, to sit on the sofa across from him. It was easy to picture her as she had ridden the racing saber-tooth, nude and white and beautiful, her red hair streaming in the wind—and he started to the uneasy impression that her flowing felicity of motion concealed a very slight limp . . .

"So you turned up at last, Barbee?" Her slow voice was huskily melodious. "I was wondering why you didn't call again."

Barbee pressed his hands against his thighs to stop their shaking. He wanted to ask her for another drink—but he had already had too many, and they didn't seem to help. He rose abruptly from the chair that must be Preston Troy's, stumbling a little on the footstool, and stalked to the other end of her sofa. Her long eyes followed him, bright with a faintly malicious interest.

"April," he said hoarsely, "the other night at the Knob Hill you told me you were a witch."

Her white smile mocked him.

"That's what you get for buying me too many daiquiris."

Barbee clenched his cold gnarled hands together to stop their shuddering.

"I had a dream last night." It was hard to go on. He peered about uncomfortably at the quiet luxury of the room. He saw a framed painting of a frail, gray, resolute little woman who must have been April's mother; and he flinched again from the business magazine and the gold cigar case beside the chair. His throat felt raw and dry.

"I had a dream." He brought his aching eyes back to the long-limbed girl; her silent smile somehow made him think of the white bitch's grin in that first dream. "I thought I was a tiger." He forced the words out, rasping and abrupt. "I thought you were—well, with me. We killed Rex Chittum on Sardis Hill."

Her dark-penciled brows lifted slightly.

"Who's Rex Chittum?" Her greenish eyes blinked innocently. "Oh, you told me—he's one of your friends who brought back that mysterious box from Asia. The one who belongs in Hollywood."

Barbee stiffened, scowling at her unconcern.

"I dreamed we killed him." He almost shouted. "And he's dead."

"That's odd." She nodded brightly. "But not so unusual. I remember I dreamed of my own grandfather the night he died." Her voice was lightly sympathetic, silk and cream and the chime of golden bells, but he thought he heard a secret mockery within it. He searched her greenish eyes again, and found them limpidly clear as mountain lakes. "The road men ought to fix that curve on Sardis Hill," she added absently, and so dismissed his dream.

"The clerk told me you phoned yesterday morning." With lazy grace she tossed back her shining hair. "I'm sorry I wasn't up."

Barbee gulped down an uneasy breath. He wanted to sink his fingers into her satin shoulders and shake the truth out of her—or was that veiled mockery all his own imagining? He felt cold and tense with terror of her—or was it the terror of some dark monster in himself? He rose abruptly, trying not to show his shuddering.

"I wanted to bring you something, April." Her long eyes brightened expectantly, and she seemed not to notice the shaking of his hand as he felt for the little jade pin still in his coat pocket. He held it concealed, cold in his hand, and watched her face as he dropped it into her extended palm.

"Oh, Barbee!" She saw it, and the dark wonder in her eyes changed to innocent delight. "That's my precious lost pin—the one Aunt Agatha gave me. A family heirloom, and I'm so glad to have it back."

She moved the little running wolf upon her palm, and Barbee thought its tiny malachite eye winked at him again, as subtly malicious as he imagined her own. Eagerly she breathed:

"Where did you ever find it?"

Barbee thrust his face at her, watching grimly.

"In your lost bag," he rapped flatly. "Stuck in a dead kitten's heart."

Her long body shuddered in the green robe, as if with mock horror.

"How gruesome!" Her low voice was warmly melodious. "You seem so morbid today, Barbee." Her limpid eyes studied him. "Really, you don't look well at all. I'm afraid you're drinking more than is good for you."

He nodded bitterly, ready to admit his defeat in the game they had played—if the girl indeed had played a game. He searched her sweetly sympathetic face for any sign of secret triumph, and attempted one last feeble sally, asking:

"Where is your Aunt Agatha today?"

"Gone." Her fine shoulders tossed carelessly beneath the flowing hair. "She says the winter here in Clarendon hurts her sinuses, and she went back to California. I put her on the plane last night."

Barbee made a wry little bow, yielding the game—still uncertain whether Aunt Agatha had ever existed outside April Bell's imagination. He couldn't help swaying a little as he stood, and the girl came to him sympathetically.

"Really, Barbee," she urged, "don't you think you ought to see a doctor? I know Dr. Glenn, and he has been very successful with alc— with people who drink too much."

"Go on," Barbee rasped bitterly. "Call me an alcoholic—that's what I am." He turned uncertainly toward the door. "Maybe you're right." He nodded painfully. "That's the simple answer to everything. Maybe I ought to see Glenn."

"But don't leave yet." She moved ahead of him, with a serpentine grace, to stand in front of the door—and again he thought she limped very slightly on the same ankle she had injured in his dream. "I hope you aren't offended," she added softly. "That was only a suggestion from a friend."

He paused unsteadily, facing her, and caught her faint perfume—cool and clean as the scent of mountain pines in the dream. A hot yearning seized him for the ruthless power of the saber-tooth; and he was shaken with a sudden futile anger at all the frustrating complexities of this gray half-life of the waking world. He had failed to solve the riddle of April Bell. Even her grave solicitude seemed to conceal a secret mockery, and he wanted to escape again.

"Come back to the kitchenette," she was urging. "Let me make you a cup of coffee—and scramble us some eggs. If you feel like breakfast. Please, Barbee—coffee ought to help."

He shook his head abruptly—if she had won that hidden game, concealing all her guilty knowledge of the white wolf bitch that had lured him to attack blind Rowena Mondrick and hiding her sinister share in the murder of Rex Chittum, then he didn't want her gloating over his tortured bewilderment now.

"No," he said. "I'm going."

She must have seen his last resentful glance at the magazine and the gold cigar case on the stand beside the chair he thought was Troy's.

"Anyhow, have a cigar," she begged him sweetly. "I keep them for my friends."

She moved with feral ease to bring the heavy case; but he saw that disquieting suggestion of a limp again and blurted impulsively:

"How'd you hurt your ankle?"

"Just tripped on the stair as I came back from driving Aunt Agatha to the airport." She shrugged lightly, offering the cigars. "Nothing alarming."

But it was alarming, and Barbee's lean hand began to shudder so violently over the cigar case that she lifted one of the strong black perfectos and clasped it in his fingers. He muttered his thanks, and stumbled blindly toward the door . . .

For all his disturbance, however, he had contrived to read the engraved monogram on the gold case. It was *PT*. The black cigar, thick and tapered, was the same imported brand Troy had offered him from the humidor on his desk. He opened the door clumsily and tried to thaw the hurt stiffness from his face and turned to face the girl.

She stood watching him, breathless. Perhaps the dark light in her eyes was only pity, but he imagined a hidden glint of sardonic glee. The green robe had opened a little, exposing her white throat, and her revealed beauty hurt like a knife driven in him. Her pale lips gave him an anxious little smile, and she called sharply:

"Wait, Barbee! Please—"

He didn't wait. He couldn't endure the pity he saw or the mockery he fancied. This dull gray world of doubt and defeat and pain was too much for him, and he yearned again for the tiger's ruthless power.

He shut the door hard behind him and threw down the fat cigar and ground it under his heel. He felt sick, but he pulled himself up straight and marched defiantly back toward the stairs. He shouldn't feel hurt, he told himself. What if Troy were old enough to be her father? Twenty million could make up very easily for twenty years. And Troy, besides, must have seen her first.

Barbee walked slowly down the stairs through a gray mist of pain. Not caring whether the clerk saw him now, he staggered aimlessly out of the lobby. Perhaps she was right, he was muttering to himself—perhaps he should go to Dr. Glenn.

Because he didn't know how to get back into the joyous freedom of his tiger dream—and that escape was only possible at night, anyhow, since daylight damaged the structure of the free mind web. He couldn't endure this waking half-life any longer, with its intolerable tangle of horror and grief and pain and bewilderment and fatigue and wild longing and tormenting uncertainty and staggering panic.

Yes, he decided, he must go to Glenn.

He didn't like mental institutions; but Glennhaven was classed with the nation's best, and young Dr. Archer Glenn, like his father, was recognized as a distinguished pioneer in the new science of psychiatry. *Time* had given him three columns, Barbee recalled, for his original research in the correlation of mental and physical abnormalities and for his own brilliant additions, while he was serving with the Navy during the war, to the revolutionary new psychiatric technique of narcosynthesis.

Like his father, Barbee knew, Archer Glenn was a stalwart materialist. The elder Glenn had been a friend of the famous Houdini, and until his death his favorite hobby had been investigating and exposing sham mediums and astrologers and fortune-tellers of all kinds. The younger man still continued the campaign; Barbee had covered lectures of his for the *Star*, in which he attacked every pseudoreligious cult founded on a pseudoscientific explanation of the supernatural. Mind, Glenn's motto ran, was strictly and entirely a function of the body.

Who could be a better ally?

13

Private Hell

Barbee walked nine blocks, back to the parking lot where he had left his car. The exercise cleared the alcoholic fog rising in his brain, and made his queasy stomach feel easier. He drove north again on the new river road, over the narrow Deer Creek bridge where he had nearly crashed against a truck on the day before, and on to Glennhaven.

Standing secluded from the road behind gay walls of red-and-yellow autumn color, the buildings loomed sternly forbidding. Barbee shivered when he saw them, and tried to put down that old asylum dread. These grim fortresses, he told himself stoutly, were citadels of sanity against the unknown terrors of the mind.

He parked his car on the gravel lot behind the main building and started around to the front entrance. Glancing through an opening in the tall hedge that walled the lawn beyond, he saw a patient walking stiffly between two white-skirted nurses. His breath caught.

The patient was Rowena Mondrick.

Muffled in black against the chill that lingered in the sunny air, she wore black gloves and a black scarf knotted over her white hair and a long black coat. Her flat black lenses seemed to look straight at him as she turned between the nurses—and he thought he saw her start and pause.

In a moment she went on again, walking straight and proud before the women at her elbows, somehow dreadfully alone. A burning pity swept Barbee, and he knew he must talk to her. Her sick mind, he thought, might still hold the answers to all the monstrous questions that stalked his own shadowed thoughts.

On abrupt impulse, he turned back toward her. He wanted terribly to help her, as well as himself—and it might be, he told himself hopefully, that she was caught in the same dreadful web of coincidence and contradiction and ambiguity that was smothering him. The truth, he felt, might free them both.

The blind woman and her two alert attendants were walking away from him now, toward the bright clumps of trees along the river. He ran after them through the hedge and across the dew-dampened grass, his heart hammering painfully to his sudden frantic eagerness.

"—my dog?" He caught Rowena's voice, sharp with anxiety. "Won't you even let me call poor Turk?"

The tall nurse seized her angular arm.

"You may call if you wish, Mrs. Mondrick," the stout nurse told her patiently. "But it's no use, really. We told you the dog is dead, and you may as well forget—"

"I don't believe it!" Her voice turned thinly shrill. "I can't believe it, and I need Turk here. Please call Miss Ulford for me, and have her put advertisements in all the papers to offer a good reward."

"That won't help," the stout nurse said gently. "Because a fisherman found your dog's body floating in the river yesterday morning, down below the railroad bridge. He brought the silver-mounted collar to the police. We told you last night, don't you remember?"

"I remember," the blind woman whispered brokenly. "I had just forgotten—because I need poor Turk so very much—to warn me and guard me when they come to kill me in the dark."

"You needn't worry, Mrs. Mondrick," the tall nurse assured her cheerily. "They won't come here."

"But they will!" the blind woman cried breathlessly. "You don't know—you won't see them when they come. I warned my dear husband, long ago, of all the shocking danger. Yet I couldn't quite believe all I knew—not until they killed him—but now I know they'll come. No walls can keep them out—no barrier but silver—and you haven't left me much of that."

"You have your beads and bracelets," the stout nurse soothed her. "And you're quite safe here."

"They tried to kill me once," she whispered desperately. "Poor Turk saved me, but now he's dead and I know they'll come again. They want to stop me from warning Sam Quain—and I must do that."

She stopped abruptly, clutching with thin imploring fingers at the tall nurse's arm. Barbee checked himself behind her. He hadn't intended to eavesdrop on her, but now the shock of this accidental revelation had frozen him, speechless. For her lost dog must have died in his first dream.

"Please, Nurse," she begged frantically. "Won't you telephone Mr. Sam Quain at the Research Foundation and ask him to come see me here?"

"I'm very sorry, Mrs. Mondrick," the tall attendant told her gently. "But you know why we can't do that. Dr. Glenn says it's bad for you to see anybody until you get better. If you will just relax, and try to help us get you well again, you can soon see anyone—"

"There's no time!" she broke in sharply. "I'm afraid they'll come back tonight to kill me, and I must talk to Sam." She turned desperately to the stout nurse. "Won't you take me to the Foundation? Now!"

"You know the rules," the nurse reproved her.

"You know we can't—"

"Sam will pay you!" she gasped desperately. "And he'll be glad to explain to the doctors—because my warning will save his life. And so much more—" Her thin voice caught, and she started sobbing. "Call a cab—borrow a car—steal one!"

"We'd like to help you, Mrs. Mondrick," the stout girl said indulgently. "We'll send Mr. Quain any message you like."

"No!" Rowena whispered. "A message won't do."

Barbee gulped and started forward again, about to speak. The two nurses still had their backs to him, but Rowena had turned so that he could see her staring blind lenses and her stricken face. Pity for her caught his throat: tears blurred his sight. He wanted urgently to help her.

"Why not, Mrs. Mondrick?" the tall nurse was asking. "And what could harm Mr. Quain?"

"A man he trusts," the blind woman sobbed.

Those words halted Barbee, like a glimpse of something dreaded leering from the dark. He couldn't have spoken, because terror clutched his throat. He retreated, silent on the damp lawn, listening unwillingly.

"A man he thinks a friend," Rowena gasped.

The short nurse looked at her watch and nodded at the other.

"We've walked long enough, Mrs. Mondrick," the tall girl said pleasantly. "It's time for us to go back inside. You're tired now, and you ought to take a nap. If you still want to talk to Mr. Quain this afternoon, I think the doctor will let you call him on the telephone."

"No!" she sobbed. "That won't do."

"Why not?" the nurse said. "Surely he has a telephone."

"And so have all our enemies," the blind woman whispered hoarsely. "All those monsters, pretending to be men! They listen when I talk, and intercept my letters. Turk was trained to sniff them out, but now Turk's dead. And dear Marck's dead. There's nobody left for me to trust, except Sam Quain."

"You can trust us," the tall girl said pleasantly. "But we must go in now."

"Very well," Rowena said calmly. "I'll come—"

She started to turn, as if in quiet obedience. As the two nurses relaxed, however, she pushed at them desperately, twisted savagely free, and darted away.

"Now, Mrs. Mondrick! You mustn't do that!"

Both the startled nurses ran after her, but she moved with a frantic agility. For a moment she gained, and Barbee thought she might reach the trees above the river. He had almost forgotten her handicap, but she tripped on the nozzle of a lawn sprinkler before she had run a dozen yards and fell hard on her face.

The two nurses picked her up carefully. Holding her lean arms with a gentle firmness, they turned with her back toward the building. Barbee wanted to run when he knew they would see him. For Rowena's madness matched his own peculiar dreams too well, and he

158

was shaken with a sudden terror of the cold frantic sanity he thought he glimpsed beyond her wild disturbance.

"Hello, Mister." The tall nurse looked at him keenly, keeping a firm grip on Rowena's angular elbow. "What can we do for you?"

"I just left my car." Barbee nodded at the parking space behind him. "I'm looking for Dr. Glenn."

"Back through the hedge, please, sir." The tall girl smiled watchfully. "There's a walk around the building to the front door. You should see the girl at the desk about your appointment."

Barbee scarcely heard. He was watching Rowena Mondrick. She had stiffened at the first sound of his voice, and now she stood silent between the two nurses as if in frozen fright. The black glasses must have been lost when she fell, for her empty eyesockets were uncovered and hideous, turning her white stricken face to a dreadful mask.

"It's Will Barbee." He didn't want to talk to her now. He had overheard enough to know that anything she told him would only drag him deeper into that dark web of monstrous doubt. He felt cold and ill with terror of her—but he couldn't stop his own hoarsely rasping voice.

"Tell me, Rowena—what's your warning for Sam Quain?"

She stood facing him, tall and gaunt in her black, shrinking back from him almost as if those ghastly scars were eyes that looked upon intolerable horror. She shuddered so violently that the two nurses gripped her scrawny arms. Her pale mouth opened as if to scream, but she made no sound.

"Why did that black leopard attack you in Nigeria?" That question seemed to gasp itself out, with no volition of his own. "And what kind of leopard was it?"

Her white lips set.

"What was Dr. Mondrick really looking for—there and in the Alashan?" He knew she wouldn't answer, but he couldn't stop the breathless questions. "What did he and Sam bring back in that wooden box? Who would want to murder them?"

She cowered back from him, shaking her dreadful head.

"Stop it, Mister!" the stout nurse reproved him sharply. "Don't annoy our guest. If you really want to see Dr. Glenn go on around to the front."

The two nurses turned hastily away, with the shuddering woman between them.

"Who are those secret enemies?" Barbee couldn't stop himself from running after her, or choke his frantic croaking. "Who are those killers in the dark? Who would harm Sam Quain?"

She twisted in the strong arms that held her.

"Don't you know, Will Barbee?" Her dull, shuddering voice seemed as hideous to him as her scarred face. "Don't you know yourself?"

Terror seized Barbee and took his voice.

"Better stop it, Mister," the tall nurse warned. "If you have any business here, go on to the front. If you haven't, get off the grounds."

The two marched hurriedly away, with the blind woman stumbling limply between them. Barbee turned shakenly back toward the opening in the hedge, trying not to wonder what Rowena meant. He clung to the feeble hope that Dr. Glenn could help him.

In the reverent hush of the cool, austere reception room, that slim dark priestess of old Egypt turned gracefully from her switchboard with a dreamy little smile of welcome to her temple. Barbee was shivering still; he couldn't forget Rowena's dreadful face, nor shake off his old vague terror of mental diseases and mental institutions.

"Good morning, Mr. Barbee," the priestess cooed. "May I assist you today?"

Barbee gulped in vain for his voice, and whispered that he wanted to see Dr. Glenn.

"He's still very busy," she purred serenely. "If you've come about Mrs. Mondrick, I believe she's responding splendidly. I'm afraid you can't see her, though. Dr. Glenn doesn't want her to have visitors, quite yet."

"I just saw her," Barbee rasped grimly. "I don't know how splendidly she's responding, but I still want to see Dr. Glenn." He swallowed hard. "It's—about—myself."

Her misty smile was a dreamy caress.

"Wouldn't Dr. Bunzel do? He's the staff diagnostician, you know. Or Dr. Dilthey? The head neuropathologist. Either one, I'm sure—"

Barbee shook his head.

"Tell Glenn I'm here," he interrupted hoarsely. "Just tell him I helped a white wolf bitch kill Mrs. Mondrick's dog. I think he'll find time for me."

The exotic, long-skulled girl turned gracefully. Her swift ivory fingers plugged in a line at the switchboard, and she breathed into the transmitter at her throat. Her dark, limpid eyes came back to Barbee, luminous and unsurprised.

"Dr. Glenn will see you right away, Mr. Barbee." Her voice was a liquid minor melody. "If you will just wait a moment, and go with Nurse Graulitz, please."

Nurse Graulitz was a muscular, horse-faced, glass-eyed blond. Her nod was a cold challenge, as if she intended to administer bitter medicine and make him say he liked it. Barbee followed her down a long, quiet corridor into a small office.

In a muffled foghorn of a voice, she asked him a series of questions, among them who was responsible for his bill and what diseases he admitted having had and how much alcohol he drank. She wrote his answers on a cardboard blank, and made him sign a form he didn't try to read. Just as he finished a door opened behind him. She rose and boomed softly at Barbee:

"Dr. Glenn will see you now."

The famous psychiatrist was a tall, handsome man, with wavy black hair and sleepy hazel eyes. He held out a tanned, well-kept hand, smiling cordially. Barbee stared at him, caught with a curious, fleeting impression of forgotten close acquaintance. He had met Glenn, of course, when he covered those lectures for the *Star*. It must be only that, he told himself; yet he couldn't quite shake off the feeling of something older and more intimate.

"Good morning, Mr. Barbee." His voice was deep and oddly restful. "Come along, please."

His office was expensively simple, airy and attractive, with few things to distract the attention. Two big leather chairs, a couch with a clean white towel over the pillow, clock and ash tray and flowers in a bowl on a little table, a tall bookcase filled with formidable medical volumes and copies of the *Psychoanalytic Review*. Venetian blinds gave a view of the brilliant woods and the river and a glimpse of the highway where it turned.

Barbee seated himself, mute and uneasy.

Glenn dropped carelessly into the other chair and tapped a cigarette on his thumbnail. He looked reassuringly competent and unworried. It was queer, Barbee thought, that he hadn't felt that sense of recognition when he interviewed Glenn at the time of those lectures. The feeling expanded swiftly into a confident liking.

"Smoke?" Glenn said. "What seems to be the trouble?"

Barbee took courage from his calm, and blurted, "Witchcraft!"

Glenn seemed neither surprised nor impressed. He merely waited.

"Either I've been bewitched," Barbee told him desperately, "or else I'm losing my mind."

Glenn exhaled pale smoke.

"Suppose you just tell me about it."

"It all started Monday night, out at the airport," Barbee began speaking, awkwardly at first and then with growing ease. "This red-haired girl came up to me while I was waiting for the Mondrick expedition to land in their chartered plane—"

He told about Mondrick's death, and the strangled kitten, and the rather inexplicable fear of the surviving men who guarded that box from Asia. He described the dream in which he had run with April Bell as a wolf and the dog Turk had died—watching Glenn's dark, smooth face, he could see only a calmly sympathetic professional interest.

"Last night, Doctor, I dreamed again," he continued urgently. "I thought I was a saber-toothed tiger—it was all queerly real. This girl was with me again, telling me what to do. We followed Rex Chittum's car to the mountains, and I killed him on Sardis Hill."

The horror of that strange nightmare and its shocking aftermath had diminished a little in the telling; he thought he had caught something of Glenn's dispassionate calm. Yet now, as he finished, his hoarse voice shuddered again.

"Rex is dead—exactly as I killed him in the dream." Desperately he searched Glenn's blandly handsome face. "Tell me, Doctor," he begged huskily, "how can any dream fit reality so well? Do you think I really murdered Rex Chittum last night, under a witch's spell? Or do you think I'm already insane?"

Carefully Archer Glenn fitted his fingertips together.

"This is going to take time, Mr. Barbee." His dark head nodded gravely. "Yes, a good bit of time. I suggest that we arrange for you to stay here at Glennhaven for at least the next few days. That will give our staff the best opportunity to help you."

Barbee rose shuddering out of his chair.

"But what about it?" he croaked frenziedly. "Did I really do those things I thought I dreamed? Or am I crazy?"

Glenn sat still, watching him with calm sleepy eyes, until he collapsed weakly in his own chair again.

"Things that happen often aren't so important as the interpretation that the mind—consciously or unconsciously—places upon them." Glenn's deep voice sounded lazily matter-of-fact. "One point about your narrative, however, seems to me quite significant. Every incident you have mentioned, from Dr. Mondrick's fatal asthmatic attack to Chittum's car accident—even the death of Mrs. Mondrick's dog—has a perfectly natural explanation."

"That's what is driving me mad." Barbee peered at him, trying desperately to discover some reaction behind his deliberate unconcern. "It all might be coincidence—but *is* it?" Barbee's strained voice went higher. "How did I know of Rex Chittum's death before I was told?"

Glenn unlaced his long fingers and tapped a new cigarette carefully against his thumbnail.

"Sometimes, Mr. Barbee, the mind deceives us. Especially, under unconscious stress, we are likely to distort the details of sequence or causation. Such faulty thinking isn't necessarily insanity. Freud wrote a whole book, you know, on the psychopathology of everyday life."

Lazily, he lit the cigarette with a flat gold lighter.

"Let's take a calm look at your case, Mr. Barbee—without attempting any offhand diagnosis. You've been driving yourself pretty hard, I gather, at a job you aren't well adjusted to. You admit you've been drinking more than you can assimilate. You must have realized that such a life must end in collapse, of one kind or another."

Barbee stiffened.

"So you think I'm—insane?"

Glenn shook his handsome head judicially.

"I'm not saying that—and I do feel that you're putting an undue emotional weight, Mr. Barbee, on the matter of your sanity. Because the mind isn't a machine, and mental conditions aren't simply black or white. A certain degree of mental abnormality is entirely normal, in fact—and life would be pretty flat and dull without it."

Barbee squirmed unhappily.

"So let's try not to jump at any hasty conclusions until we've had time for a complete physical and psychiatric examination." Glenn shook his head lazily, carefully crushing out his unsmoked cigarette. "I might comment, however, that Miss Bell evidently disturbs you—and that Freud himself describes love as normal insanity."

Barbee squinted at him uneasily.

"Just what do you mean by that?"

He slowly laced his manicured fingers together again.

"In all of us, Mr. Barbee," his casual voice explained, "there are hidden unconscious feelings of fear and guilt. They arise in infancy and color our whole lives. They demand expression, and find it in ways we seldom suspect. Even the sanest and most completely normal individual has those secret motives working in him.

"Don't you think it may be possible in your case—at a time when your conscious restraints happen to be weakened by the unfortunate combination of extreme fatigue and violent emotion and too much alcohol—that those buried feelings in yourself have begun to find expression in vivid dreams or even in waking hallucinations?"

Barbee shook his head, suddenly uncomfortable. He shifted in the chair, to look out at the reds and yellows of the hills beyond the river. Beside the dark water a field of corn lay golden; and the silver vanes of a windmill beyond were flashing in the sun.

A dull resentment smoldered in him against Glenn's shrewdly dispassionate probing. He hated this small room, and Glenn's neat little theories of the mind. He didn't want all his own private shames and fears laid out on Glenn's compact diagrams. Fiercely he began to yearn again for the free escape and the splendid power of his dreams.

Glenn's deep voice droned on.

"Perhaps you blame yourself in some way, unconsciously of course, for Mrs. Mondrick's present grave mental illness—"

"I don't think so!" he interrupted sharply. "How could I?"

"The very violence of your protest gives added weight to my random guess." Glenn's lazy smile seemed to reflect a brief, kind amusement. "It will take time, as I told you, to trace out the mechanism of your major complexes. The general pattern, however, is already apparent."

"Huh?" Barbee swallowed. "How do you mean?"

"Your college studies in anthropology, don't you see, must have given you a wide knowledge of primitive beliefs in magic and witchcraft and lycanthropy. Such a background is enough to account for the unusual direction of your fantasy expressions."

"Maybe," Barbee muttered, unconvinced. "But how do you think I could blame myself for Mrs. Mondrick's illness?"

Glenn's sleepy hazel eyes were suddenly piercing.

"Tell me—did you ever consciously desire to kill Dr. Mondrick?"

"What?" Barbee sat indignantly straight. "Of course not!"

"Think back," Glenn insisted softly. "Did you?"

"No!" Barbee rapped angrily. "Why should I?"

"Did he ever injure you?"

Barbee twisted uneasily in his chair.

"Years ago, when I was in college—" He hesitated, peering longingly at the bright world beyond the window. "Old Mondrick turned against me, at the end of my senior year," he admitted grudgingly. "I never knew why. But he dropped me, when he was forming the Research Foundation, and took Sam Quain and Rex Chittum and Nick Spivak. For a long time I was pretty bitter about that."

Glenn nodded, with a pleased expression.

"That fills out the picture. You must have wished Dr. Mondrick's death—unconsciously, remember—to avenge that old slight. You wished to kill him, and he eventually died. Therefore, by the simple timeless logic of the unconscious, you are guilty of his murder."

"I don't see that," Barbee muttered stiffly. "It all happened a dozen years ago. Anyhow, it can't have much to do with your statement that I'm to blame for Mrs. Mondrick's illness."

"The unconscious ignores time," Glenn protested gently. "And you misquote me. I didn't say that you're responsible for Mrs. Mondrick's tragic illness—I merely ventured a suggestion that perhaps you blame yourself. What you tell me bears out that suggestion."

Barbee blinked angrily. "How?"

"Her unfortunate breakdown," Glenn droned calmly, "is an obvious consequence of her husband's unexpected death. If you feel unconsciously responsible for that, it follows that you must also bear the burden of her own mental disintegration."

"No!" Barbee stood up, shuddering. "I won't endure that—"

The dark handsome man nodded pleasantly.

"Exactly," Glenn told him softly. "You can't endure it consciously. That's why the guilt complex is driven down into your unconscious—where, in your memories of the courses in anthropology that Dr.

Mondrick himself taught you, it finds very fitting guises in which to haunt you."

Barbee stood shivering, gulping mutely.

"Forgetting is no escape." Glenn's sleepy hazel eyes seemed implacable. "The mind demands a penalty for every adjustment we fail to make. There's a kind of natural justice in the mechanisms of the unconscious—or sometimes a cruel parody of justice—blind and inevitable."

"What justice?" Barbee rasped harshly. "I don't see—"

"That's the point exactly." Glenn nodded genially. "You don't see, because you can't bear to look—but that doesn't stop the operation of your unconscious purposes. You blame yourself, apparently, for Mrs. Mondrick's insanity. Your buried sense of guilt demands a punishment to fit the crime. It seems to me that you're unconsciously arranging all these dreams and hallucinations just to seek atonement for causing her breakdown—at the ultimate cost of your own sanity."

Glenn smiled, as if to a lazy satisfaction with his own argument.

"Don't you see a kind of blind justice there?"

"No, I can't follow that." Barbee shook his head uneasily. "Even if I could, it wouldn't explain everything. There's still the saber-tooth dream—and Rex Chittum's death. My thoughts about Mrs. Mondrick couldn't have much to do with that, and Rex had always been my friend."

"But also your enemy," Glenn suggested suavely. "He and Quain and Spivak were chosen for the Foundation, you told me, when you were rejected. That was a cruel blow, remember. Surely you must have been jealous?"

Barbee caught his breath angrily.

"But not murderous!"

"Not consciously," Glenn droned smugly. "But the unconscious has no morals. It is utterly selfish, utterly blind. Time means nothing, and contradictions are ignored. You had wished harm to your friend Chittum, and he died. Again, therefore, you must bear the consequences of your guilty wish."

"Very convincing!" Barbee snapped. "Except you forget one point—I dreamed the dream before I knew Rex had been killed."

"I know you think so," Glenn agreed. "But the mind under stress can play odd tricks with cause and sequence. Perhaps you really invented the dream after you learned of his death, and inverted the sequence to change effect to cause. Or perhaps you expected him to die."

"How could I?"

"You knew he would be driving down Sardis Hill," Glenn said smoothly. "You knew he would be very tired, and in a hurry." The sleepy eyes narrowed slightly. "Tell me this—did you know anything about the brakes on that car?"

Barbee's jaw sagged slightly.

"Nora had told me they needed fixing."

"Don't you see the picture then?" Glenn nodded cheerfully. "The unconscious is alert to every suggestion, and it seizes every possible device for its own expression. You knew when you went to bed that Chittum had every probability of an accident on Sardis Hill."

"Probability." Barbee whispered that word, shivering. "Perhaps you're right."

Glenn's sleepy hazel eyes dwelt upon him.

"I'm not a religious man, Mr. Barbee—I reject the supernatural, and my own rational philosophy is founded on proven science. But I still believe in hell."

The dark man smiled.

"For every man manufactures his own private hell and peoples it with demons of his own creation, to torment him for his own secret sins, imagined or real. It's my business to explore those personal hells and expose their demons for what they are. Usually they turn out to be much less terrifying than they seem. Your werewolf and weretiger are your own private demons, Mr. Barbee. I hope they appear a little less dreadful to you now."

Barbee shook his head uncertainly.

"I don't know—those dreams were very real." Almost savagely he added: "You're pretty clever, Doctor, but there's more going on than just hallucination. Sam Quain and Nick Spivak are still guarding something in that wooden box. They're still fighting a desperate battle against—I don't know what. They're my friends, Doctor." He gulped hard. "I want to help them—not to be the tool of their enemies."

Glenn nodded with an air of satisfaction.

"Your vehemence tends to establish my suggestions—though you mustn't give too much weight to my off-hand comments at this exploratory session." He shifted lazily, to look at the clock. "That's all

the time we have just now. If you wish to stay at Glennhaven, we can meet again tomorrow. I think you had better rest a day or two, before we schedule your routine clinical examinations."

He nodded toward the door, but Barbee kept his seat.

"I'll stay, Doctor." His voice quivered urgently. "But there's one more question I've got to ask right now." He searched Glenn's bland brown face. "April Bell told me that she once consulted you. Has she any—any supernatural powers?"

The tall psychiatrist rose gravely.

"Professional ethics forbid me to discuss any patient," he said. "If a general answer will make you feel any easier, however, I can tell you that I helped my father investigate thousands of cases of so-called psychic phenomena of all kinds—and I have yet to see the first case in which the ordinary laws of nature fail to apply."

He turned firmly to open the door, but still Barbee waited.

"The only real scientific support of extrasensory and psychokinetic phenomena has come from such studies as those at Duke University," he added. "Some of the published results purporting to show the reality of ESP and the mental manipulation of probability are pretty convincing—but I'm afraid the wish to demonstrate the survival of the soul has blinded the researchers to some grave flaw in their experimental or statistical methods."

He shook his head, with a sober emphasis.

"This universe, to me, is strictly mechanistic. Every phenomenon that takes place in it—from the birth of suns to the tendency of men to live in fear of gods and devils—was implicit in the primal superatom from whose explosive cosmic energy it was formed. The efforts that some distinguished scientists make to find room for operation of a free human will and the creative function of supernatural divinity in such apparent defects of mechanistic determination as Heisenberg's principle of uncertainty—those futile efforts are as pathetic to me as the crudest attempt of a witch doctor to make it rain by sprinkling water on the ground. All the so-called supernatural, Mr. Barbee, is pure delusion, based on misdirected emotion and inaccurate observation and illogical thinking."

His calm brown face smiled hopefully.

"Does that make you feel any better?"

"It does, Doctor." Barbee took his strong hand and felt again that

169

sense of puzzled recognition, as if he had found some strong forgotten bond between them. Glenn, he thought, was going to be a powerful, loyal ally. "Thanks," he whispered fervidly. "That's exactly what I wanted to hear!"

14

As a Serpent Strikes—

Nurse Graulitz was waiting for him in Dr. Glenn's outer office. Surrendering wearily to her competent control, Barbee telephoned Troy's office and told the publisher he wanted to spend a few days at Glennhaven for a check up.

"Sure, Barbee!" Troy's rasping voice sounded warmly sympathetic. "You've been killing yourself—and I know Chittum was your friend. Grady'll get the *Star* out. I believe in Archer Glenn. If there's any difficulty about financing your treatment, have him call my office—and don't worry about your job."

Barbee stammered his thanks, choked with a sudden tightness in his throat. Preston Troy wasn't altogether bad, he decided. Perhaps he had been a little too severe in his own judgments on the Walraven campaign and that rather sketchy circumstantial evidence in April Bell's apartment.

Yielding again to Miss Graulitz, Barbee decided that he didn't need to drive back to Clarendon for his toothbrush and pajamas, or even to attend Rex Chittum's funeral. Obediently he followed her along the covered walk from the main building to a long red-tiled annex.

She conducted him through the library, the music room, the games room, the hobby room, and the dining room. She introduced him casually to several persons—leaving him uncertain which were staff members and which patients. He kept watching uneasily for any glimpse of Mrs. Mondrick, and presently inquired about her.

"She's in the disturbed ward," the nurse boomed softly. "That's the next building, around the quadrangle. I hear she's worse today— something upset her when she was out for her walk. She doesn't have visitors, and you won't be seeing her until she's much better."

Nurse Graulitz left him at last in a room of his own on the second floor of the annex, with the injunction to ring for Nurse Etting if he wanted anything. The room was small but comfortable, with a neat little bath adjoining. He had been given no key for the door.

The windows, he noticed, were of glass reinforced with steel wire, steel-framed, adjusted so that nothing much larger than a snake could escape through them. But all that would scarcely be enough to imprison him if he should dream again—he grinned wryly at the fleeting thought—because they hadn't been clever enough to use silver wire.

So this was madness!

He washed his face and sweaty hands in the tiny bathroom—noticing that everything was cunningly designed, with no sharp edges any- where, or any support for a noose. He sat down wearily on the side of the bed and loosened his shoelaces.

He certainly didn't feel insane, he reflected—but then did any lunatic, ever? He merely felt confused and utterly exhausted from his long struggle to master situations that had finally been too much for him. It felt good just to rest for a while.

Barbee had wondered about insanity, sometimes with a brooding dread—for his own father, whom he scarcely remembered, had died in the forbidding stone pile of the state asylum. He had vaguely supposed that a mental breakdown must be somehow strange and thrilling, with an exciting conflict of horrible depression and wild elation. But perhaps it was more often like this, just a baffled apathetic retreat from problems grown too difficult to solve.

He must have fallen asleep in the midst of such gray reflections. He was vaguely aware of someone trying to rouse him for lunch, but it was after four by his watch when he woke. Somebody had slipped off his shoes and spread a sheet over him. His nostrils felt stuffy and his head ached faintly.

He wanted a drink. Perhaps he could have smuggled in a pint. Even if whisky had put him here, he still had to have a drink. At last he decided, not very hopefully, to try Nurse Etting. He sat up and pushed the button that hung on a cord at the head of his bed.

Nurse Etting was rangy and tanned. She had a comic-strip buck-toothed face, and she appeared to have wasted unavailing pains on her mouse-colored hair. Her rolling walk suggested that her athletic legs were bowed, reminding him of a rodeo queen he had once interviewed. Yes, she told him in her flat nasal voice, he could have one drink before dinner today and not more than two afterward. She brought him a generous jigger of very good bourbon and a glass of soda.

"Thanks!" Surprised to get the drink, Barbee still felt a dull defiance toward the smug assurance of Dr. Glenn and the briskly courteous efficiency of the staff. "Here's to the snakes!"

He tossed off the whisky. Unimpressed, Nurse Etting rolled out with the empty glass. Barbee lay back on the bed for a while, trying to think over what Glenn had told him. Perhaps that ruthless materialist was right. Perhaps the were-wolf and the were-tiger had been all hallucination—

But he couldn't forget the peculiar vividness of his sensations, padding over crisp frost through the fragrant night, seeing the starlit hills with such wonderful sharpness through the eyes of that mighty saber-tooth. He couldn't forget the warm feel of the naked girl astride him, or the savage power of his leap, or the hot, sweet-smelling spurt of Rex Chittum's blood. For all Glenn's convincing arguments, nothing quite so real as that dream had ever happened to him awake.

The drink had relaxed him again, and he still felt drowsy. He began to think it would be very easy for a snake to slide out through the futile glass-and-steel barrier of that window as soon as the daylight had gone. When he went back to sleep, he decided, he would just change into a good, big snake and go back to call on April Bell. If he happened to find the Chief in bed with her—well, a thirty-foot constrictor should be able to take care of a fat little man like Preston Troy.

The radiator snapped, and he flung himself off the bed with a startled curse. Such notions wouldn't do at all—Glennhaven was supposed to cure him of those dreams. His head was choked up and still throbbing slightly, but he couldn't have another drink until after dinner. He washed his face in cold water and decided to go downstairs.

Barbee had always wondered about mental institutions. He thought of taking notes for a feature story on this adventure; but Glennhaven, as the evening wore on, began to seem remarkable for utter lack of anything noteworthy. It began to appear as a fragile never-never land, populated with timid souls in continual retreat from the real world outside and even from one another within.

In the music room, when Barbee got a news bulletin on the radio about a traffic accident, a thin, pretty girl dropped a tiny sock she had been knitting and hurried out, sobbing. He played checkers with a pink-faced, white-bearded man who managed to upset the board every time Barbee crowned a king and then apologized profusely for his clumsiness. At dinner, Dr. Dilthey and Dr. Dorn made a painful and not very successful effort to keep a light conversation going. Barbee was glad to see the early autumn twilight thickening outside the windows. He went back to his room, rang for the nurse, and ordered his two permissible drinks at once.

Nurse Etting had gone off duty, and a pert, painfully vivacious little brunette named Jedwick brought his two jiggers of bourbon and a mushy-looking historical novel he hadn't asked for. She fussed needlessly about the room, laying out pajamas and felt-soled slippers and a red robe for him and straightening the bed, obviously trying to be cheery. He was glad when she left him alone.

The two drinks made him very sleepy, although it was only eight by his watch and he had slept most of the day. He began to dress for bed and stopped to listen uneasily. Somewhere far away he had heard a thin, strange howl.

Dogs on the farms about Glennhaven began barking savagely, but he knew it wasn't a dog that had howled. He hurried to the window to listen, and caught another eerily quavering howl. It was the sleek white wolf bitch. She was down by the river, waiting for him.

Barbee examined the steel and reinforced glass of the window again. He saw no trace of any silver anywhere—Glenn, in his dogmatic materialism, must have rejected all the evidence for the mental determination of probability. It ought to be easy enough to change into a satisfyingly formidable snake and go down to meet April Bell. He heard her howling again and went breathless with a trembling eagerness.

He turned toward the high, white hospital bed—and cold dread stopped him. By the rational scientific logic of Dr. Glenn, he must cherish an unconscious jealous hatred of Sam Quain and Nick Spivak. In the mad logic of his dreams, April Bell was still resolved to destroy them because of the unknown weapon they guarded in that wooden box.

He felt sick with a shuddering fear of what the snake might do.

He delayed going to bed. He scrubbed his teeth with a new brush until the gums bled. He took a deliberate shower and carefully trimmed his toenails and put on white, too-large pajamas. Wrapped in the red hospital robe with *Glennhaven* embroidered across the back, he sat up in the one chair for an hour trying to read the novel Nurse Jedwick had brought. All the characters, however, seemed as gray and flat as the people he had met downstairs—

And the she-wolf was howling again.

She was calling, but he felt afraid to go. He wanted to close the window, to shut out her wild cry and the angered barking of the dogs. He started impatiently across the room and a fainter sound checked him, shivering. It was a woman's screaming, muffled and somewhere near, monotonous and dull, dreadful with a full abandonment to horror and despair—and he knew Rowena Mondrick's voice.

He slammed the window hastily, and took his book to bed. He tried not to listen for Rowena screaming in the disturbed ward, or the white wolf calling from the river. He tried to read again and fought the pressure of sleep. But the words made no sense. He hated the dull bleak world of crushing frustration where the blind woman screamed, and yearned for the bright release of his dreams. He surrendered, suddenly, to that new reality, and reached eagerly to snap off the light.

The book slipped out of his hands—

Only he didn't have hands. He glided away from the gaunt empty

175

thing that lay breathing very slowly in the bed. He let his long body flow across the rug and lifted his flat, triangular head to the window.

The glass dissolved as his free mind reached out to find the linkage of probability and grasp the shivering atoms to be a part of himself as he passed. The embedded steel wire yielded more slowly, and there was no silver. Laughing silently at Glenn's mechanistic philosophy, he poured out silently over the sill. He dropped on the lawn in a mound of powerful coils, and went twisting down toward the dark trees by the river.

The white bitch came trotting to meet him out of a clump of willows, her long slanted eyes shining eagerly greenish. He flicked out his slender black tongue to touch her icy muzzle, and the shining scales of his thick body rippled to the strange ecstasy of that kiss.

"So it was too many daiquiris," he jibed, "that made you feed me that witchcraft yarn?"

She laughed, her red tongue lolling.

"Don't torment me any more," he begged. "Don't you know you're driving me insane?"

Her mocking eyes turned gravely sympathetic.

"I'm sorry, Barbee." Her warm tongue licked his flat snout affectionately. "You must be bewildered, I know—the first awakenings are always painful and disturbing, until you learn the way."

"Let's go somewhere," he urged, and a shudder ran along his coils. "Rowena Mondrick is screaming back there in her room. I can't bear it. I want to get away from here and all this uncertainty. I want to forget—"

"Not tonight," the she-wolf interrupted. "We'll have fun, Barbee, when we can. But tonight we still have work to do. Three of our great enemies still live—Sam Quain and Nick Spivak and that blind widow. We've got her where she can't do anything worse than scream, but your old friends Spivak and Quain are still at work. They're learning. They're getting ready to use the weapon in that wooden box."

In her eyes blazed a sudden feral fury.

"We must stop them—tonight!"

Reluctantly, Barbee shook his broad black head.

"Must we—kill them?" he protested faintly. "Please—think of little Pat and poor Nora—"

"So it's poor Nora now?" The she-wolf mocked his tone maliciously.

Her fangs nipped at the loose, scaled skin of his neck, half playfully and yet with a savage force. "Your old friends must die," she told him, "to save the Child of Night."

Barbee objected no more. In this glorious awakening from the long nightmare of life, all his values were changed. He whipped two turns of his tapering tail around the white bitch's body and squeezed until she gasped.

"Don't worry about Nora," he told her. "But if a dinosaur happened to catch Preston Troy in bed with you, it might be just too bad."

He released her, and she shook her white fur primly.

"Don't you touch me, snake in the grass." Her voice was honey and vitriol.

He reached for her again. "Then tell me what is Troy to you."

She sprang away from his reaching tail.

"Wouldn't you like to know?" Her white fangs grinned. "Come along," she told him. "We've got a job to do tonight."

The undulations of Barbee's body thrust him forward beside her in flowing waves of power. The friction of his polished scales made a soft burring sound on the fallen leaves. He kept pace with the running wolf, his lifted head level with her own.

The night world was oddly different to him now. His scent was not so keen as the wolf's had been, nor his vision so sharp as the saber-tooth's. He could hear the gentle sigh of the river, however, and the rustle of mice in the fields, and all the tiny sounds of sleeping animals and people in the dark farm buildings they passed. Clarendon, as they approached it, became a terrific din of drumming motors and screaming tires and raucous horns and howling radios and barking dogs and droning, wailing, bellowing human voices.

They left the highway at the Cedar Street intersection and turned across the dark grounds of the Research Foundation. Light shone yellow from the ninth-floor windows of the gray tower where Spivak and Quain fought their secret war against the Child of Night; and a faint, noisome fetor was evil in the air.

The locked front door made a path for them as they reached together to grasp it, and they came into the painful brightness of the central hall. That poisonous reek was stronger inside, but the snake wouldn't be so sensitive to it, Barbee hoped, as the gray wolf had been.

Two sharp-eyed men, both too hard and old for their university sweaters, sat wearily playing casino at the information desk outside the elevators. As the silent wolf and the great snake approached, one of them dropped his dog-eared cards and felt apprehensively for the police special at his hip.

"Sorry, Jug, but I can't tell clubs from spades." His voice was hoarse and anxious. "I tell you, this Foundation job is getting on my nerves. It looked pretty good at first—twenty bucks a day just to keep people out of that laboratory—but I don't like it!"

The other gathered up the cards. "Why not, Charlie?"

"Listen, Jug!" The big man tilted his head. "Every dog in town has suddenly gone to howling, and I can't keep from wondering what this is all about. These Foundation people are afraid of something—and it is right funny, come to think of it, the way old Mondrick died and Chittum got killed. Quain and Spivak act like they know they're next on the list. Whatever they've got in that mysterious box—I wouldn't look at it for forty million!"

Jug peered down the shadowy hall, past the creeping wolf and the crawling snake, reaching unconsciously to loosen his own revolver.

"Hell, Charlie, you just been thinking too much. On a special job like this, you ain't supposed to think. It's all legal and easy—and twenty bucks is twenty bucks." Jug stared bleakly through the wolf and the snake. "But I'd like to know. Me, I don't take much stock in this story about any curse the expedition dug up in those old graves—but they did find *something*."

"I don't know," Charlie insisted. "I don't want to."

"Maybe you think they're crazy." Jug's peering eyes roved toward the closed doors of the elevators and the stairway, and upward toward the vague, muffled sounds the snake could hear from the ninth floor. "Maybe they are. Maybe they just stayed off in them damn deserts too long. Maybe—but I don't think so."

Charlie blinked uneasily. "What do you think?"

"I think they found something worth hiring special guards for." Jug caressed the grips of his revolver. "Me, I'd like to see what they've got in that precious box. Maybe it's really worth forty million." His voice dropped. "Maybe it was worth a couple of neat little murders to Mr. Spivak and Mr. Quain."

"Deal the cards and forget that box," Charlie muttered. "This Foundation is a respectable scientific outfit, and twenty bucks is twenty bucks. We don't know what's going on upstairs, and we ain't paid to guess."

He didn't see the sleek white wolf that trotted across the corridor in front of the desk, or the huge gray-and-black-patterned snake that writhed after her. She paused before the locked door to the stairs, and it became a path for her free mind web and the snake's. Jug sat staring after them, snorting his weary impatience with Charlie's apprehensions and mechanically shuffling the cards. He didn't seem to see the opening in the door.

The snake followed the wolf up eight dark flights. That musty malodor was thicker at the top of the stairs, a strange sweetness, sickeningly vile. The white wolf shrank and cowered from it, but the great snake rippled on. Another door turned misty as Barbee grasped it, and he beckoned with his flat head for the quivering bitch to follow him into the ninth-floor rooms.

One of the rooms had been fitted with bench and sink and glass apparatus for chemical analysis. The burning fumes of reagents in it were drowned beneath the lethal reek that came from a pinch of gray powder drying on a paper filter. That room was silent except for the slow drip of water from a tap. The wolf and the snake recoiled from its deadly fetor.

"See, Barbee!" The white bitch grinned feebly from her swaying illness. "Your dear old friends are trying to analyze that old poison, so they can kill us all."

The next room they entered was a museum of articulated skeletons, hung smiling whitely from steel stands. Barbee peered about it uneasily with the great snake's eyes. He recognized the neatly strung bones of modern men and modern apes, and the white plastic reconstructions of the apelike frames of Mousterian and Chellean and Prechellean types of early man. Others puzzled him, however; the restored bones were too slender, the sneering teeth too sharp, the staring skulls too smooth and long. He crouched back from those strange skeletons, and something sent a shudder flowing down his armored coils.

"See!" the white wolf whispered. "They're looking for measurements—for clues to find us—so they can use that poison."

The room beyond was dark and silent. Colored wall maps showed the continents of today and those of the past; the edges of the ice fields in the glacial ages were drawn like battlelines. Locked glass cases held the notebooks and journals Dr. Mondrick had always kept—Barbee recognized his bold red lettering on the covers.

The white bitch bristled suddenly, and Barbee saw that her greenish eyes were fixed on a frayed scrap of medieval tapestry, framed in glass and hung above the desk beside the window as if it were a special treasure. The faded pattern showed a gray, gigantic wolf snapping three chains that bound it to spring upon a bearded old man with one eye.

Puzzled at the she-wolf's snarl, Barbee lifted his flat head to study the ancient fabric. The huge wolf was Fenris, he recognized, demon of the Scandinavian mythology. Old Mondrick, he recalled, had once discussed the myth, comparing the Norse demonology to that of the Greeks. Offspring of the evil Loki and a giantess, the giant wolf Fenris had grown until the fearful gods chained him; he broke two chains, but the third magic bond held him until the dreadful day of Ragnarok when he broke free to destroy Odin, king of the gods—represented as an aged, one-eyed man. The white bitch had bared her fangs, retreating from the frayed tapestry.

"Why?" Barbee whispered. "Where is any danger?"

"There!" she growled huskily. "In that weaving, and the history it represents—and in all the myths of the wars and the marriages of men and gods and frost giants, that most men think are only fairy tales. Old Mondrick knew too much, and we let him live too long."

She paused to sniff that lethal, fetid sweetness.

"We've got to strike—now!" Her sleek body shivered. "Before these other fools rediscover all Mondrick and his wife knew—and turn this place into another trap to catch us." Her silky ears lifted, listening. "Come along, Barbee. They're just across the hall—those dear old friends of yours!"

They crossed the dark hall. Still no silver barred their path, and the long snake flowed ahead of the she-wolf through the locked door of a small corner room. Barbee stopped, lifting his flat black head in cold alarm at sight of Sam Quain and Nick Spivak.

"Why so jumpy?" The sleek bitch laughed at his start, her long eyes cold with a triumphant ferocity. "I think we're in time," she whispered. "These fools must have failed to guess the identity of the Child of Night—and your black-widow friend can't have got her warning to them yet—because they've put up no silver foil or silver wire to keep us out. I think we can put an end to these human monsters now and save the Child of Night!"

The two men in that little room didn't look so very monstrous to Barbee. Nick Spivak was wearily propped at a desk, writing. His stooped, flat-chested body seemed drained of life. He lifted his head, as Barbee peered at him, with a nervous start. Behind his thick-lensed glasses, his eyes were bloodshot and haggard and feverish. Black with a stubble of neglected beard, his thin face was gray and haunted. It would wrench Mama Spivak's heart, Barbee thought, to see him now.

Sam Quain lay sleeping on a canvas cot against the wall. Drawn and grim with an utter exhaustion, his tanned, red-stubbled face was bleakly stubborn even in sleep. One of his strong arms was stretched from under the blanket, and his hand grasped a leather handle of the iron-bound coffer, even as he slept.

The box was padlocked. Barbee made a groping mental effort toward its contents and felt that heavy silver lining inside the iron and wood— a barrier that struck a cold chill through him. He recoiled uneasily, groggily aware of the sweetish lethal reek seeping from the box. The white bitch crouched beside him, ill and frightened.

"Watch your old friend Spivak!" she was gasping faintly. "He's our meat tonight."

Nick Spivak had turned apprehensively at the desk. His terrible red eyes looked straight at Barbee, yet he didn't seem to see the snake or the snarling wolf. Shuddering a little, his narrow shoulders hunched as if with cold, he turned back to his work.

Barbee let himself flow nearer, lifting his long, flat head to look over that thin, bent shoulder. He saw Spivak's quivering fingers absently turning a queer-shaped fragment of age-yellowed bone. He saw the frightened man pick up another object on the desk, and an unpleasant numbness stiffened his coils.

The object was white plaster. It looked like the cast of a disk-shaped, deep-graven stone. A part of the curved rim of the original must have been worn flat; it must have been cracked, he saw, and a little segment lost. That sweet fetor clung to it in an evil cloud, so powerful that Barbee had to draw his flat head stiffly back.

The white bitch peered fearfully at it, swaying where she stood.

"A cast of the Stone, that must be," her dry whisper rasped. "The

181

Stone itself must be in that box—the secret that destroyed our people engraved on it and protected with that stinking emanation. We can't get at the Stone tonight." Her long tongue licked her fangs uneasily. "But I think we can stop your scholarly friend from reading that inscription."

Barbee rose in a black-patterned column to look again. Nick Spivak, he saw, had copied all the inscriptions from the plaster disk with pencil rubbings on soft yellow paper. Now he was trying to decipher them, no doubt, for the queer characters were spilled across his pages in rows and columns, mingled with his notes and guesses and tabulations in ordinary script.

"You're very strong tonight, Barbee," the she-wolf was gasping. "And I can see a certain probability of Spivak's death—a linkage close enough for you to grasp." Her red lips curled wickedly. "Kill him!" she urged. "While the link exists."

Barbee swayed uncertainly toward the stooped figure at the desk, and caught that evil sweetness again. It turned him giddy with illness, and he recoiled into a compact heap of defiance. His flat eyes shifted toward the narrow cot as Sam Quain turned a little in his sleep. A faint sympathy stirred in his cold body. He could sense the desperate purpose that armed these two lonely men in their strange citadel against the Child of Night, and a sudden pity welled up in him for Nora Quain and pink-faced little Pat.

"I won't hurt them," he whispered. "I won't touch Sam."

"This might be a good chance to get Sam out of your way with Nora." The white bitch leered at him. "But he's too near the thing in the box, and I can't find any linkage that might bring about his death tonight. Spivak is the one—and you must stop him before he unriddles that inscription."

Stiffly, painfully, Barbee thrust himself back into the lethal sweetness that hung in a paralyzing cloud around the white plaster cast on the desk. He pressed his scaled coils heavily toward the small man writing. For the man was an enemy of the Child of Night, and things were different now.

He could see the wailing desolation of Papa and Mama Spivak when they should hear the news. But the fat little tailor and his fatter wife, with their shop on Flatbush Avenue, were creatures of a remote dead dream. They weren't important any longer, any more than old Ben

Chittum in his shabby newsstand. The real things, the things that mattered now, were his own savage power and the awaited arrival of the Child of Night and the fierce love of the green-eyed wolf.

Nervously, Nick Spivak was shuffling through his sheaves of yellow sheets. He flung them down impatiently and bent to frown through a pocket lens at the plaster cast, as if searching for some error in his copy. He shook his head, lighted a cigarette and crushed it out again, and frowned apprehensively toward the cot where Sam Quain slept.

"God," he muttered, "I'm jittery tonight!" He pushed the cast away and hunched grimly over his papers again. "If I could only determine that one damn character." He chewed his pencil, his pale forehead wrinkled. "The disk makers licked those devils once, and their discovery can do it again!" His narrow shoulders lifted resolutely. "Let's see again—if the alpha character really stands for unity—"

That was all he said. For Barbee had thrust his flat head between the man's wan face and the cluttered desk. Three times his long body whipped around. Then, constricting, he grasped with all his power for the linkage of probability to make himself manifest.

Nick Spivak's thin, hollowed face stiffened with horror. Behind the glasses, his red eyes popped. He opened his mouth to scream, but a savage blow from the side of Barbee's long head paralyzed his throat. The breath hissed out of his collapsing chest. He clawed with his hands and tried to stand up. The coils drew tighter and his chest caved in. His groping fingers, in a final frantic effort, caught the plaster disk and dashed it feebly against Barbee's ribs. The cold shock of its touch numbed and sickened Barbee, and the fearful sweetness clinging to it turned him groggy. His shuddering coils relaxed a little—and this, he thought, was only the cast; slipping inertly toward the floor, he wondered dully what the original Stone itself could do.

"Tighter, Barbee!" the white bitch was whispering. "Kill him while you can."

But Nick Spivak must have been already dead. The brittle plaster disk dropped out of his fingers and shattered into dusty fragments on the floor. Barbee recovered a little from its shocking touch and its clinging malodor and squeezed again. Bones snapped. Blood spurted across the papers on the desk.

"Quickly!" the she-wolf warned. "Quain's waking up!"

She trotted to the window, and Barbee reached to help her grasp the

glass and wood and putty and steel to open a path. She shook her slender head.

"Not that way," she breathed quickly. "We must raise the sash. There's no screen, and I believe your old friend Spivak had a way of walking in his sleep when he got overtired. He was very tired tonight. That's the linkage I found to help you kill him."

Feebly, ill from that foul sweetness, she scratched at the catch. Barbee tried to help her and swayed weakly back, sinking in a shuddering pile on the warm, broken corpse. The she-wolf toiled frantically with supple paws and prying fangs, and the window came up with a bang. Sam Quain seemed to hear it, for he moved heavily on the cot.

"Nick," he muttered thickly. "What the devil's going on?"

He didn't get up, however, and the white bitch whispered sharply: "He can't wake now—that would break the linkage."

Clean, cold air, pouring in through the open window, began to dispel that evil sweetness. The she-wolf caught her breath and shook out her fur, and Barbee felt revived. He started rolling awkwardly toward the window, moving his crushed, still-pulsating burden. It left a reeking trail of spattered blood on the floor.

"Drop him!" the white bitch gasped. "While the linkage lasts."

It wasn't easy to move even so slight a form as Nick Spivak's, not when you were wrapped around and around it. Not when you were faint with the venom of the Stone. The cold air was clean and good, however, and Barbee's flowing strength returned. He hooked his flat head outside the window and caught the desk with his tail, lifting the broken body toward the windowsill.

"Quickly!" April Bell was urging. "We must get out of here before Quain can wake—and I've still some writing to do."

She trotted past the fallen chair, sprang lightly to the desk, and grasped the dead man's pencil in her pliant paws. Barbee had paused to ask what she wrote when Sam Quain groaned on the cot. Desperately he tightened his coils and toppled the limp weight of the crushed body over the sill. His coils slipped on a smear of blood, and he fell with it. The white bitch must have seen him fall, for her anxious voice floated after him:

"Get away, Barbee—before Quain wakes!"

Hurtling downward through those nine stories of darkness, Barbee unwound his coils from the dripping, still-twitching thing that had been Nick Spivak. He flung it beneath him. Frantically he groped for the hateful husk he had left on his bed at Glennhaven, sick with fear of Sam Quain's awakening.

Beneath him, he heard the broken body crunch again on the concrete walk in front of the Foundation tower. The dull sound of yielding bone had a flat finality, and he had time to see that the last shudder of life had ceased in the misshapen frame sprawled flat in the puddle of red. Faintly, his sensitive ears caught the weary nasal voice of the guard called Charlie, inside the building:

"Hell, Jug, you ain't supposed to think. I tell you again, the cause of Mondrick and Chittum dying is the coroner's business, and I don't want to know what's inside that box. Twenty bucks a night is twen—"

Barbee came crashing down—

But not upon the concrete walk beside Nick Spivak. For he had grasped his body as he fell, and that flowing change was quicker and less painful now. He fell on the floor beside his bed in the room at Glennhaven, and clambered stiffly upright.

He was a very ordinary biped, rusty with sleep. His head was choked with cold, and it throbbed from the bump against the floor. He wanted a drink. His stomach was fluttering. A dull weariness ached in him. Dr. Glenn, he thought, would doubtless tell him that he had merely rolled off the pillows on which he had propped himself to read, that all his dreadful dream had arisen afterward, from the unconscious effort to explain his fall.

15

The Human Side

All the ruthless elation of that dream had drained away, and Barbee was flooded with a dull sickness of horror in its stead—for a stunned conviction gripped him that Nick Spivak was really dead, lying flat and broken on the walk in front of the Foundation tower.

He stood beside the bed, swaying with a gray illness, rubbing at the bruise on his temple. He fingered a smarting scratch on his neck, and remembered that the white wolf's fangs had nipped him there. He caught a long breath, and shook himself stiffly. He couldn't get rid of that sick certainty that Nick Spivak had really died in that dream.

Dazedly he snapped on the light and looked at his watch. It was two-fifteen. He reached for the clothing he had left on a chair, but the night nurse must have removed it; he found only the red robe and soft slippers. Trembling, clammy with sweat, he pulled them on. He pressed the call button, and shuffled out impatiently to meet the nurse in the hall—Miss Hellar had a gorgeous fluff of pale bleached hair and the physique of a lady wrestler.

"Why, Mr. Barbee! I thought you were asleep—"

"I've got to see Glenn," he told her. "Right now."

Her broad, alarming face broke into a gentle smile. "Of course, Mr. Barbee." Her masculine voice tried to be soothing. "Why don't you just go back to bed, while we see—"

"Lady," Barbee interrupted grimly, "this is no time to show off your maniac-buttering technique. I may be crazy and I may not—I hope that's all I am. Crazy or not, I've got to talk to Glenn. Where does he sleep?"

Nurse Hellar crouched a little, as if she faced an opponent in the ring.

"Don't get fresh," Barbee advised her sharply. "I imagine you know how to handle common lunatics, but I believe my case is just a little different." He thought she nodded in uneasy agreement, and he tried to leer malevolently. "I think you'll run when I turn into a big black rat."

She retreated, turning a little pale.

"All I want is to talk to Glenn for five minutes—right away," Barbee told her. "If he doesn't like it, let him put it on my bill."

"That would come pretty high," Nurse Hellar warned. Barbee grinned at her, dropping to all fours. "But I won't try to stop you," she said shakily. "I'll show you his house."

"Smart girl!"

He stood up again. Nurse Hellar stepped back watchfully and waited for him to walk ahead of her down the hall to the stairs—he couldn't put aside a disquieting idea that she really believed he could turn himself into a rat. From the rear door of the annex she pointed out Glenn's dark mansion, and he thought she seemed relieved when he left her.

Lights sprang on in the upper windows of Glenn's brick house before he reached it, and he knew Nurse Hellar must have telephoned. The tall, suave psychiatrist himself, clad in a rather barbaric dressing gown, opened the front door before Barbee had found the bell. Glenn looked sleepier than ever.

"Well, Mr. Barbee?"

"It has happened again," Barbee blurted. "Another dream—that I know is more than just a dream. This time I was a snake. I—I killed Nick Spivak." He paused to catch a rasping breath. "I want you to call the police. They'll find him lying dead under an open ninth-floor window in front of the Humane Research Foundation building—and I'm his murderer!"

Barbee mopped his wet forehead, peering anxiously to see Glenn's reaction. The psychiatrist blinked his heavy-lidded hazel eyes, and shrugged easily in that splendid robe. He smiled a little, sympathetically, tilting back his tousled, curly head—and something in the movement woke in Barbee that warm, inexplicable sense of recognition.

"Won't you?" Barbee insisted sharply. "Won't you call the police?"

Calmly, Glenn shook his head. "No, we can't do that."

"But Nick's dead!" Barbee shivered. "My friend—"

"Let's not be hasty, Mr. Barbee." Glenn lifted his tall shoulders lazily. "If there is really no corpse, we should be troubling the police department for nothing. If there is, we might find it awkward to explain how we knew about it." His brown face smiled likably. "I'm a strict materialist—but the police are brutal materialists."

Barbee's teeth chattered. "Do you think I—I really killed him?"

"By no means," Glenn told him smoothly. "Hellar assures me that you were sound asleep in your room until a few minutes ago. However, I do see another very interesting possibility, which might explain your dream."

"Huh?" Barbee caught his breath. "What's that?"

Glenn blinked sleepily.

"You've been trying to solve a mystery which surrounds the behavior of your old friend Quain and his associates in the real world." Glenn's deep voice was casual and slow. "Consciously, you have failed to reach any certain solution. But the unconscious, remember, is often more astute than we ordinarily suspect."

Deliberately, he set the tips of his long brown fingers together.

"Unconsciously, Mr. Barbee," he continued gravely, "you may have suspected that Nick Spivak would be thrown out of a certain window tonight. If your unconscious suspicion should happen to tally neatly enough with reality, the police might find his body where you dreamed it fell."

"Nonsense!" Barbee stiffened angrily. "Only Sam was with him—"

"Exactly!" Glenn's handsome head made a slight I-told-you-so nod. "Your conscious mind rejects the notion that Sam Quain might be a murderer—and even your rejection has an emphasis which appears significant, because it suggests that unconsciously you may want Sam Quain to die for murder."

Barbee clenched a gaunt, hairy fist.

"I—I won't have that!" he choked hoarsely. "That—that's diabolical." He thrust himself forward and gulped for his voice. "That's insane. I tell you, Doctor, Sam and Nora Quain are two of my best and oldest friends."

Softly Glenn asked: "Both of them?"

Barbee knotted his sweaty hands again.

"Shut up!" he croaked. "You—you can't say that to me!"

Glenn retreated hastily into his lighted doorway.

"Just a suggestion, Mr. Barbee." He smiled disarmingly, and nodded again. "Your violent reaction indicates to me that it reaches a pretty tender spot, but I see no need to discuss it any further now. Suppose we just forget all our problems for tonight and go back to bed?"

Barbee caught an uneasy breath and thrust his hands into the sagging pockets of the red hospital robe.

"Okay, Doctor," he agreed wearily. "Sorry I bothered you." He started to leave and turned suddenly back. In a low, shaken voice he added desperately: "But you're dead wrong, Dr. Glenn. The woman I love is April Bell."

With a faint, sardonic smile, Glenn closed the door.

Barbee walked slowly back through the starlit frosty night toward the dark bulk of the buildings where only two or three windows were palely alight. He felt somehow strange to be moving on two awkward legs, seeing only formless shapes with a man's dull eyes, unaware of all the revealing sounds and odors of his dreams.

The neighborhood dogs, he noticed, had stopped their angry barking. He paused to listen for Rowena Mondrick's screaming, peering uneasily across toward the disturbed ward. New windows lit as he watched, and he wondered if some fresh emergency had aroused the ward. That hopeless, horror-choked screaming, however, had ceased.

Uncomfortably, he plodded on back toward the annex. Glenn was a fool—or possibly worse. No honest psychiatrist, Barbee felt, would be quite so reckless with his tongue. It was true, he had to admit, that he had once loved Nora before she married Sam. Perhaps he had seen her more often than was altogether wise in the years Sam was gone—but Glenn's revolting conclusion was absurd. There was nothing Sam shouldn't know, nor any sane reason why he should wish harm to Sam.

About calling the police, however, he decided that Glenn was right. Any such call would brand him as either madman or murderer. Yet he couldn't shake off that shocking certainty that Nick Spivak lay dead beneath that window. He clenched his clammy fists again and drew a long sobbing breath of the chill night air, shivering to Glenn's diabolic suggestion that Sam Quain might be accused of the murder. He had to do something about it.

He hurried back to the second floor of the annex building. Nurse Hellar rather apprehensively let him use her office phone, and he called Nora Quain. She answered at once, as if she had been waiting for the instrument to ring, and her voice seemed sharp with fear.

"Will—what's happened now?"

"Sam has a phone at the Foundation?" His own hurried voice was a breathless rasping. "Please call him right away. Wake him up. Have him—have him look for Nick Spivak."

"Why, Will?" she breathed faintly.

"I believe something has happened to Nick," he said. "I believe Sam is in great danger now because of it."

For a long time she didn't speak. He could hear the uncertain whisper of her troubled breath and the ticking of the desk clock in the study where he knew the telephone was, that measured sound queerly calm and slow. At last she asked, in a tight, choked voice:

"How did you know that, Will?"

The clock ticked on, maddeningly grave and slow.

"Just routine, Nora," he muttered uncomfortably. "Confidential sources—that's my business, you know." He gulped. "So you had already heard?"

"Sam just called me," she whispered. "He sounded wild, Will—nearly out of his mind."

"What—" No voice came, and Barbee tried again. "What about Nick?"

"He fell out of a window." Her voice was flat with horror. "The window of their special lab, on the top floor of the Foundation tower. Sam says he's dead."

The clock ticked, and he heard her harsh breathing.

"That's what my sources said," Barbee muttered hoarsely. "I want you to warn Sam, Nora. I believe he's in danger."

"How could he be?" Hysteria quivered beneath the tight control of her voice. "Sam thinks he fell asleep and walked out—he always walked in his sleep, you know. But that couldn't happen to Sam."

Agony shuddered in her voice.

"Will—what do you think—could happen to Sam?"

The clock kept ticking, while Barbee tried to swallow the rasping dryness in his throat.

"Sam and Nick were alone in that tower room," he muttered briskly. "They were guarding something that seems to be very valuable in that wooden box they brought back from the Gobi. Two of the men who knew what was in it are already dead—and the deaths of Mondrick and Rex Chittum are going to look pretty funny, now with Nick's added."

"No!" Nora's whisper was a voiceless scream. "No, Will—no!"

"That's the way it's going to look," Barbee told her. "I know cops. They're going to think Sam killed Nick for his interest in that box. They're going to keep on thinking that, at least until they learn what is in the box—and I don't think Sam will want to tell them."

"But he didn't!" Nora whispered frantically. "Sam didn't—"

Her whisper died. The ticks of the clock were slow ripples in a dead silence. At last he heard Nora breathe again. The sound was a long, weary rasp.

"Thank you, Will." Her voice was dull with a stunned bewilderment, and hot pity caught Barbee's throat. "I'll call Sam right back," she said. "I'll warn him." A sudden protest shuddered in her voice. "But he *didn't!*"

She hung up, and Barbee shuffled heavily back to his room. All this, he thought bitterly, had surely been enough for one night. Surely the white wolf bitch—or his own unconscious terrors, if she were only the symbol of them—would let him finish the night in peace.

He flung off the robe and slippers, and dropped wearily in bed. He tried to sleep, but a dull disquiet possessed him. He couldn't help staring at the steel-meshed glass that had melted before the flowing snake, or stop remembering the brittle feel of Nick Spivak's bones snapping in his closing coils. He rang for Nurse Hellar and had her bring a sleeping pill. But still he hadn't slept when he heard the white bitch whispering:

"Will Barbee!" Her thin far voice seemed taut with trouble. "Can you hear, Barbee?"

"I hear you, April," he murmured sleepily. "Good night, darling."

"No, Barbee." He thought he heard her sharp protest. "You must change again, because we've more work to do."

"Not tonight!" Resentment jarred him back toward wakefulness. "We've murdered Nick tonight—and left Sam Quain to be accused of the killing. Isn't that crime enough for tonight?"

Her far whisper seemed fainter, as if his arousing had all but snapped some slender bond between them.

"That was neat," she purred. "But not enough—"

"I've had enough," he told her. "I don't intend to dream again, and I know I don't hear you, really."

"But you do," her whisper insisted. "You can't kid yourself, Barbee—these aren't dreams. I know the change is easier when you sleep, but that's just because the human part of you still dominates your waking mind. Now please relax and listen."

He turned restlessly in bed, muttering drowsily:

"I don't hear, and I won't dream—"

"This isn't any dream," she whispered. "The ESP researchers at Duke University found evidence enough of such extrasensory perceptions as this—they could find better, if they knew how to pick subjects with more of our blood. I know you hear—don't kid me!"

He shook his head on the pillow.

"But I won't listen—"

"Barbee!" Her far voice turned sharply imperative. "You've got to listen—and change and come to me. Now! And take the most frightful form you can find—because we've a greater enemy than little Nick Spivak to fight."

"Huh?" he muttered heavily. "What enemy?"

"Your blind widow friend!" the wolf bitch breathed. "That Mondrick woman—supposed to be safe in Glenn's laughing academy, where nobody would mind her ravings. She's out, Barbee—trying to warn Sam Quain!"

Barbee felt an icy tingle along his spine, like the feel of his stiff hair rising when he had been a tall gray wolf. But he was human now, he assured himself uneasily. He could feel the cool smoothness of the sheets against his smooth human skin, and hear the hospital sounds muffled with his dull human hearing: other patients breathing in their rooms, and the distant quick footfalls of Nurse Hellar, and a telephone somewhere buzzing impatiently. He was entirely human, and almost wide awake.

"Warn Sam?" he echoed heavily. "What does she know?"

Terror shivered in that ghostly whispering.

"She knows the name of the Child of Night!"

The shock of that aroused Barbee again. Shuddering uneasily, he lifted his head to peer about the dark room. He found the pale rectangular glow of the window and the thin streak of yellow light beneath his door. He was still quite human, he informed himself, and surely he was quite awake. Yet his breathless voice came taut and dry with dread.

"The man they fear?" he said. "This conspirator—murderer—secret agent—whatever he is—that old Mondrick was talking about when he died?"

"Our awaited Messiah," the whisper said.

Barbee lay stiff and shuddering.

"Who is he?" he demanded harshly. "What's his name?"

"Really, Barbee!" Faintly, far away, he thought he heard April Bell's purring laugh. "Don't you know?"

He caught his breath impatiently.

"I think I can guess," he muttered suddenly. "I think it must be your good friend, Mr. Preston Troy!"

He waited for her answer, and it didn't come. He was alone in the dark room, awake and unchanged. He could hear the racing tick of his watch, and see the luminous dial—the time was four forty. The dawn was still two hours away, but he wasn't going to sleep until he saw the sun. He didn't dare—

"No, Barbee." That tiny whisper turned him almost ill with shock. "The Child of Night isn't Mr. Troy, but you must prove your right to know his name. You can do that tonight—by killing Rowena Mondrick!"

He stiffened in the bed, angrily pushing back the covers.

"You can't make me hurt her," he insisted bitterly. "Dreaming or awake! Anyhow, I don't think she's out. I could hear her screaming in her room earlier tonight. She's in the disturbed ward, behind locked doors, with nurses on duty. She couldn't get out."

"But she did." The whisper had thinned to the smallest possible thread of thought. "And she's on her way to warn Sam."

"She'll never find him," he scoffed. "An old blind woman, out of her mind—"

"But she isn't!" that remote whisper reached him. "No more than many another, confined because they know too much. Asylums are very convenient prisons, Barbee, to hold such enemies. But your little black widow is stronger than I thought—because she's kin to us, and she has powers that are a little more than human."

"She's old!" he gasped. "She's blind."

"I know her eyes are blind," the white bitch purred. "Because we ripped them out! But she has developed a different vision—keen enough to discover the Child of Night. She worked with old Mondrick, and she knows too much."

"No—" Barbee choked hoarsely. "I won't—"

He sat up on the side of the bed, trembling, clammy with sweat, violently shaking his head.

"Come, Barbee!" Still he couldn't snap that tugging thread of thought—or was it merely madness? "Take the deadliest shape you can," the she-wolf urged. "Bring claws to pull her down, and fangs to slash her throat. Because we've got to kill her—"

"I won't!" he shouted hoarsely, and then dropped his voice lest Nurse Hellar should hear. "I'm through, Miss April Bell!" he whispered bitterly. "Through being the tool of your hellish schemes—through murdering my friends—through with you!"

"Are you, Barb—"

Shuddering, he surged to his feet, and that taunting whisper died. His fury and alarm had broken that dreadful thread of illusion—and he certainly didn't intend to harm Rowena Mondrick, in his dreams or wide awake. He walked uneasily about the room, still gasping weakly for his breath and damp with the sweat of his panic.

That monstrous whispering had really ceased—he paused inside his door, listening to be sure. Near him he heard a gurgle and groan and sob, gurgle and groan and sob—the white-bearded man who had upset the checker board was snoring across the corridor. That was all he heard, until a man shouted something in a harsh brittle voice on the floor below.

He opened his door, listening. Other men were shouting somewhere. Women raised excited voices. Feet pounded hallways. The door of a car slammed hard. A starter whined. A motor roared suddenly and tires screamed as the car raced too fast around the curving drive toward the highway.

Rowena Mondrick had really gotten away—the certainty of that struck him with a numbing, cold impact. He knew—how, he wasn't sure. Perhaps—as suave Dr. Glenn would doubtless explain it—his own troubled unconscious mind had merely translated all the muffled sounds of alarm and search into the white bitch's whispering.

Silently he put on his slippers and the robe, pausing to stuff his thin pocketbook and his keys into the sagging pockets. He didn't know what was fact and what illusion. He couldn't define the danger to Rowena— he dared not believe that whispering. But this time he intended to take a hand in whatever happened—and not as a pawn of the Child of Night.

Something checked him at the door. Some dim unease drew his eyes back to the high bed, and he was somehow vastly grateful to find it empty. Relieved to see no vacant human husk behind, he shuffled cautiously out into the corridor. It was deserted. He ran silently to the head of the rear stair and paused there when he heard Dr. Bunzel's metallic voice twanging angrily:

"Well, Nurse?"

"Yes, Doctor," a frightened girl whispered.

"What's your excuse?"

"I have none, sir."

"How the blazes did that patient escape?"

"I don't know, sir."

"Better find out," Bunzel rapped. "You had her under restraint, in a locked ward, with particular orders to watch her. You knew she had been trying to get away." Scorn oiled his voice. "Did she vanish through the wall?"

"I think so, sir."

Bunzel uttered an incredulous roar.

"I mean, sir—" the girl stammered, "I don't know how she got out."

"What do you know about her?"

"Poor Mrs. Mondrick—" The girl sounded as if she were trying not to sob. "She was terribly upset, you know—ever since her walk yesterday morning. She had been awake all night, begging me to let her go to this Mr. Quain."

"So what?"

"The dogs started howling—that must have been about midnight—and poor Mrs. Mondrick started screaming. She wouldn't stop. Dr. Glenn had ordered a hypo if she needed it, and I decided she did. I went to get it ready. When I came back with it, just a minute later, she was gone."

"Why didn't you report this sooner?"

"I was searching the ward, sir—she isn't there."

"Look again," Bunzel rapped. "I'm going to organize a systematic search. She's acutely disturbed—I'm afraid of what she'll do."

"I know, sir," the girl sobbed. "She's dreadfully disturbed."

"Caution everybody not to alarm the other patients," Bunzel added. "And don't let any word of this get outside the building. Such affairs can result in very unfortunate publicity. I sent Dr. Dorn to check with the police. That woman must be found."

Their voices had receded toward the front of the building, and Barbee didn't hear the girl's reply. Silently he slipped down the rear stair, and peered along the lighted corridor. The frightened nurse was following the bristling little doctor into an office room. He waited until they were gone from sight and walked out the back door.

Grim elation steeled him, and cold purpose hurried him. Rowena Mondrick had really escaped, as the whispering bitch had told him—but this time he wasn't running with her monstrous pack to pull the blind woman down. He had triumphantly defied her evil call—or was it just his own sick unconscious?

He was fully awake, anyhow, and in his true human shape. He knew Rowena's danger—from the same cunning killers who had murdered her husband with a black kitten's fur and Rex Chittum with a wreck on Sardis Hill and Nick Spivak with a fall from the Foundation tower. But this time he would be no reluctant tool of April Bell and her unknown accomplices in witchcraft—or was it only common crime?

Still he didn't know all the rules of this strange game, or the stakes, or the players. But he was a rebel pawn, and now he meant to play it to the finish, for himself, on the human side.

16
The Most Frightful Shape

Breathless in the frosty dark, shivering a little in the red cotton robe, Barbee found the shabby old coupe on the gravel lot where he had left it, behind the main building. He dug for the keys in his pocket, and started the cold motor as silently as he could. A floodlight came on suddenly as he was backing toward the drive; and a heavy man in wrinkled whites darted from the building, shouting at him.

He didn't stop. He let the car lunge forward to the racing motor, swerved narrowly past the gesturing attendant to reach the drive, and came skidding recklessly to the dark highway. Anxiously he peered into the little rearview mirror; it showed no pursuit, and he slowed as much as he dared, turning back toward Clarendon along the new river road and watching breathlessly for the blind fugitive.

He was afraid to drive too slowly, for he had to find her first. Before the attendants came to drag her back to scream her life out in the disturbed ward at Glennhaven. Or before she died, as her husband had, slain by a hand from mad nightmare.

He held the car at forty, desperately scanning the dark roadsides. He could see the glow of distant headlamps along the main highway to the west, but he met no traffic on the river road. Once the eyes of some animal winked yellow in the dark and vanished as they turned. Nothing else moved, and his hope ebbed when he saw the concrete barriers of Deer Creek Bridge.

For that narrow bridge—where the truck had almost killed him as he drove back from his first vain attempt to see Rowena—was a full two miles from Glennhaven. Surely she couldn't have come so far, blundering unguided. Perhaps she was blinder than the white bitch had whispered—

He saw her then, near the bridge. A gaunt lonely figure, angular and tall, stalking on with frenzied haste. The black she wore made her oddly difficult to see—he tramped hard on his brakes, shaken with the thought that he had almost run her down. But he hadn't struck her.

She was safe. He breathed again, in immense relief, slowing the car behind her. The monstrous danger hovering over her was still suspended. He was in time to help her—and defeat one scheme of the hidden Child of Night. The little car was rolling to a halt a dozen yards behind her when he saw the headlamps in the rearview mirror.

They had swung into the road from the grounds of Glennhaven, but he thought he still had time enough. He would pick the blind woman up, he decided, and carry her straight to Sam Quain at the Foundation. That cool purpose steadied his sweaty hands on the wheel, and rekindled hope began to banish his shadowy terrors.

Such an open gesture, he felt, would surely erase Rowena's insane mistrust and allay Sam's unreasonable suspicion. It might do more. Rowena had once shared Mondrick's researches; perhaps she really had something to tell Sam Quain. Perhaps she could yet turn a light upon Barbee's own dark dilemmas—and even really identify the Child of Night.

Ahead of him, the thin woman must have heard the squeal of his brakes, for she fled frantically down the white cone of the headlamps. She stumbled on the edge of the concrete abutment, fell to hands and knees, and staggered up again as he opened the car door and leaned out to call:

"Rowena! Wait—I want to help you." She seemed to start and crouch, turning back to listen. "Just let me help you into the car," he called, "and I'll take you on to see Sam Quain."

She came back toward him, still taut and doubtful.

"Thank you, sir." Her voice was hoarse and breathless. "But—who are you?"

"I'll do anything to help you, Rowena," he told her softly. "I'm Will Barbee—"

She must have recognized his voice, because she screamed before she heard his name. Her wide mouth was black as the lenses over her eyes, and her cry was a sobbing rasp of insane fear. She stumbled back from him, blundered against the concrete railing, groped over it to get her bearings, and ran wildly across the bridge.

Barbee sat stunned for a moment, but the headlamps behind were growing in the little mirror. His time was short before that pursuit should overtake them, and he knew the blind woman could never reach Sam Quain without his aid. He shifted into low gear and stepped on the accelerator—and cold consternation shook him.

He saw the white she-wolf.

He knew she shouldn't be here, because this certainly wasn't any dream. He was entirely awake; and his gaunt, hairy hands shivering on the wheel were clearly human. But the sleek white bitch seemed as real as the lean black shape that fled, and much easier to see.

She sprang gracefully out of the shadows beyond the abutment and sat on her haunches in the middle of the pavement. The headlamps gleamed on her snowy fur, and flamed luridly green in her eyes. The light must have been painful to her, but she laughed at him, long tongue lolling.

He slammed his foot against the brake pedal, but he had no time to stop the car. No time even to wonder whether she were something real or only a laughing phantom of delirium tremens. She was too close, and he swerved automatically to avoid her.

The left fender struck the concrete barrier. The wheel drove back hard against his chest, and his head must have gone over it against the windshield. The scream of tires and crash of metal and jangle of glass all dissolved into quiet darkness.

The blow against his head must have dazed him, but only for an instant. He sat back behind the wheel and got breath into his painful lungs again and felt his throbbing head. He could find no blood.

He felt gone. Shivering weakly to the chill of the night, he shrugged the thin robe closer around him. The car had stopped diagonally across the bridge. The motor was dead, but the right headlamp still burned. He could smell a faint reek of gasoline and hot rubber. Surely he was now too wide awake to see that hallucination any longer, but he couldn't help peering uneasily ahead.

"Good work, Barbee!" the white bitch purred softly. "Though I hadn't expected this to be your most dreadful shape!"

He saw her then, leering greenly at him over a quiet black form outside the white path of the lone headlamp. He couldn't make out that huddled thing—but nothing moved on the bridge beyond it, and his straining ears caught no echo of Rowena's frenetic feet. A dazed dismay drove out his breath again.

"What—?" Horror choked him. "Who—?"

The slim she-wolf sprang lightly over that unmoving form, and came trotting lightly to the side of the car. Her long eyes burned with a triumphant glee. She grinned at him, licking at the fresh pink stains on her muzzle and her fangs.

"Neat work, Barbee!" she murmured happily. "I could feel the linkage when I called you a while ago—a blind woman on the highway, clothed in black and too afraid to listen for the cars, carries a strong probability of death. We grasped it very skillfully. I think the shape you brought was as frightful to her as any could have been. She broke the string and lost her silver beads when you made her fall—and I don't think she'll be telling Sam Quain the name of the Child of Night!"

The white bitch turned her head, fine ears lifted to listen.

"Here they come, Barbee—the blundering human fools from Glennhaven." The pale rays of the still-distant headlamps struck her, and she sprang warily back toward the shadow-clotted roadside. "We had better go," she urged. "Drive on—just leave the dead widow where she lies!"

"Dead?" Barbee echoed hoarsely. "What—what have you made me do?"

"Only your clear duty," she purred, "in our war against mankind—and such mongrel traitors as the widow, who try to turn the powers of our own blood against us! You've proved yourself, Barbee—now I know

201

you're fully with us." Her greenish eyes peered back down the road. "Drive on!" she called sharply. "Before they find you here!"

She sprang silently off the pavement into the dark.

Barbee sat numbed and breathless until the lights of the approaching car flashed in the mirror again. An urgency of sharp alarm stirred him at last from his apathy of unbelieving horror. He stumbled out of the car and lurched dazedly to the flat thing the laughing bitch had left.

That huddled form sagged limply when he lifted it. He could feel no pulse or breath. Warm blood wet his hands, and torn black garments showed him all the dreadful harm the she-wolf's fangs had done. Shock and pity turned him ill, and suddenly the dead woman was too heavy in his shuddering arms. He laid her back on the pavement as tenderly as he could. There was nothing else to do.

Falling long and black across her body, his own shadow moved. Turning dully, he saw the approaching headlamps descending the last slope to the bridge. The wind struck his hands, and he felt the blood turn stiff and cold. He stood beside the body, waiting, too sick to think.

"Drive on, Barbee!" That sharp warning startled him, whispered from the dark. "Those fools from Glennhaven don't understand the mental manipulation of probability, and you shouldn't let them find you by the widow's corpse." The white bitch's whispering turned soft, huskily urgent. "Come on to my place at the Trojan Arms—and we'll drink to the Child of Night!"

Perhaps that was only his own terror whispering, and his own sick desire, cloaked in the symbolism of his own unconscious. Perhaps it was something more dreadful. He had no time left to ponder such riddles of the mind, for the lamps of the slowing car illuminated his own ghastly predicament.

Rowena Mondrick lay dead in front of his battered car on the narrow bridge. Her literal blood was on his hands, and the nurse at Glennhaven could swear in court she had feared him desperately. He couldn't tell the jury that a white were-wolf had killed her.

Panic took hold of him. Half blinded by the approaching lights, he scrambled into the car and kicked the starter. The motor roared, and he tried to back away from the bridge railing. The steering wheel refused to turn. He tumbled desperately out again, in the white glare of the nearing headlamps, and found the left fender crumpled against the front wheel.

Shuddering and breathless in his panic, he climbed on the bent bumper and stooped to grasp the crumpled metal with both hands. His wet fingers slipped. He wiped them on the cold enamel, and strained again. Groaning, the torn metal yielded.

The other car stopped close behind them, crunching gravel.

"Well, Mr. Barbee!" The annoyed voice twanging from behind the blinding headlamps sounded like Dr. Bunzel's. "I see you had a little accident."

Fumbling beneath the bent fender, Barbee found it high enough to clear the tire. Shading his eyes against the glare, he ran back around the battered car, shivering with grief and terror.

"Just a moment, Mr. Barbee!" He heard quick footsteps on the pavement. "You're entitled to every possible courtesy so long as you're our guest at Glennhaven, but you ought to know you can't check out this way, in the middle of the night, without Dr. Glenn's permission. I'm afraid we'll have to—"

He didn't wait to listen any longer. A voiceless dread flung him back into the car. He slipped it into reverse and stepped hard on the gas, bracing himself for the crash. Bumpers grated and glass tinkled. The lights of the other car went out. The wheedling voice of the man on the ground changed to an angered roar.

"Barbee—stop!"

But Barbee didn't stop. He shifted into low gear again, and the light car swerved around the ragged, flattened thing the white wolf had left. The wheels skidded on something slippery, and the twisted fender grazed the barrier. It didn't catch, however. He recovered control and roared across the bridge.

The lights of the rammed car behind him stayed out. It might take Dr. Bunzel half an hour, he thought, to walk back to Glennhaven and a telephone. By dawn, he knew, the police would be looking for an insane hit-and-run killer in a red hospital robe, driving a blood-stained coupe.

Uneasily he watched the leap and crouch of shadows outside the feeble beam of his single headlamp, but he failed to discover the white she-wolf. The old coupe began pulling crazily to the left as he shifted into high; the smash, he supposed, must have bent something. He gripped the wheel against the demon in it and pushed the wheezing motor to forty, trying numbly to think.

A bitter and dreadful loneliness had seized him. Rowena Mondrick lay slashed to death behind him, but he couldn't stop the perversity of horror that brought his thoughts again and again to the university years when he and Sam Quain had boarded at her house. She used to play anything they liked on her piano, and have Miss Ulford serve them cookies and milk, and listen with her calm, blind patience to all their small troubles. That time, in the sick nostalgia of his thoughts, seemed the brightest of his life. She had been a true and gracious friend, but she couldn't help him now.

April Bell smiled in the darkening shadows of his mind, haunting in her green-eyed allure. The white she-wolf, he remembered uneasily, had asked him to come to the Trojan Arms and drink to the Child of Night. A frightened impulse moved him to go to April Bell. She had wanted to make coffee for him once, and perhaps she could help him yet. He was slowing to look for her street when the exotic smile of the tall redhead in his mind changed to the pink-smeared grin of a white-fanged wolf. Shivering, he drove straight on.

He had nowhere to go, and his brain seemed too dull for thought. He turned left off the river road and drove out to the end of an empty side street and parked among brush-thicketed vacant lots until the cold of the dawn had seeped in through his red cotton robe and its glow was bright in the east.

The day alarmed him from that gray apathy of stunned bewilderment. He couldn't help shrinking away from the greenish dawn, recalling the she-wolf's dread of light and the pain of it to the gray wolf he once had been. It didn't hurt him now, but it did reveal the twisted left fender of the old coupe—and the police would be looking for that.

He started the car again, shuddering from the cold, and drove back across the river road and on through the emptiest streets he could find toward the university. Once he saw headlamps behind him, yellow in the dawn. He drove straight on, not daring to speed or turn, and sobbed with relief when they stopped and winked out.

He parked again in an alley behind a lumber yard, half a mile east of the campus. Fumbling in the gray half-light, he found pliers under the seat and drained enough of the scalding, rusty mixture of antifreeze and water from the radiator to wash the dark, stiffened blood from his hands. He left the car there and limped hastily on through the waking streets toward Sam Quain's little bungalow.

He had to check a frantic impulse to dive into another alley when he saw a newsboy riding a bicycle to meet him, hurling folded papers at doorways. He caught his breath and forced himself to wait calmly at the curb, trying his best to look like a sleepy resident and fingering the coins in his pocket to find a dime.

"*Star*, mister?"

Barbee nodded easily. "Keep the change."

The boy handed him a paper and hurled another at the sleeping house behind him and pedaled on. But Barbee had seen him glance sharply at the red hospital robe and the gray felt slippers. He would remember, when he heard about the manhunt.

Carefully standing so the boy couldn't see the fatal *Glennhaven* embroidered across the shoulders of the robe, if he happened to look back, Barbee unfolded the paper as steadily as he could. His breath stopped and the damp newsprint rustled as a black headline struck him with the impact of a club:

PREHISTORIC "CURSE"—OR HUMAN KILLER— TAKES THIRD VICTIM

Nicholas Spivak, 31, anthropologist associated with the Research Foundation, was discovered dead this morning beneath an open ninth-floor window of the Humane Research Foundation building near Clarendon University. The body was found by special guards, employed by the Foundation after sudden death had claimed two other Foundation scientists this week.

Did a prehistoric curse follow the recent Foundation expedition back to Clarendon from the mounds they exhumed in Asia? The surviving members of this private research group deny all rumors that they dug up anything so exciting from the supposed birthplace of mankind in what is now the desolate Ala-shan desert, but Spivak's death raises the toll to three.

Dr. Lamarck Mondrick, founder of the organization and leader of the expedition, fell dead as the explorers left their chartered plane at the municipal airport Monday evening. Rex Chittum, a younger member of the group, died early Thursday morning when his car left the road forty miles west of Clarendon on Sardis Hill.

Samuel Quain, another Foundation associate, is being sought

for questioning in connection with Spivak's death, according to police Chief Oscar Shay and Sheriff T. E. Parker, who hinted that his testimony is expected to throw new light on the oddly coincidental previous deaths.

Laughing at the curse theory, Shay and Parker hinted that a green-painted wooden box which the explorers brought back from Asia may hold a more sinister explanation of these three fatalities.

Quain is believed to have been alone with Spivak in the tower room from which Shay and Parker state that he fell or was hurled to his death—

The paper dropped out of Barbee's cold fingers. Perhaps murder had been done—he shuddered at the recollection of Dr. Glenn's diabolical suggestions, and shook his bare head frantically. Sam Quain couldn't be the killer—that was unthinkable.

Yet a killer there must be. Rowena Mondrick made four dead—too many for mere coincidence. Beyond the grotesque web of contradiction and enigma, he thought he could distinguish a ruthless brain working cunningly to bring about these seeming accidents. The Child of Night—if that phrase meant anything.

But who—he shrank from that question, shivering in the first cold sunlight; and he hurried on along the quiet streets again toward Sam Quain's house, trying to look as if a morning stroll in a flapping red robe were quite an ordinary event.

The chill autumn air had a smoky crispness. The world, as it came to his senses, was entirely normal and believable. A milk truck rattled across the street in front of him. A woman in a vivid yellow wrapper appeared briefly on a doorstep to pick up the morning paper. An overalled man with a black lunch pail, probably a bricklayer waiting for a bus at the corner, grinned amiably as Barbee came by.

Hurrying on, Barbee nodded to the workman as casually as he could. His skin felt goose-pimpled under the thin red robe, and he couldn't help shivering to a colder chill than he felt in the frosty air. For the quiet city, it seemed to him, was only a veil of painted illusion. Its air of sleepy peace concealed brooding horror, too frightful for sane minds to dwell upon. Even the cheery bricklayer with the lunch pail might— just might—be the monstrous Child of Night.

His heart stopped when a siren split the morning hush. A police car

206

lurched around the corner ahead and came drumming down the pavement toward him. He couldn't breathe and his knees turned weak, but he set his face in an empty grin and stumbled blindly on. He waited for the cold official voice to hail him, but the car didn't pause.

He shuffled swiftly on, his feet numb and aching in the thin felt slippers. The police radio, he knew, must already be snarling out the orders to pick him up. Probably his abandoned car had already been reported, and that prowl car was racing to investigate. The hunt would spread from there, fast.

He walked two more blocks, and still the police car hadn't come back. He limped breathlessly around the last corner into Pine Street, and stopped when he saw the black sedan parked in front of Sam Quain's small white house. Terror made a hard constriction in his throat, for he thought the police were waiting for him here.

In a moment, however, he saw the lettering on the car door—only the name of the Research Foundation. He had almost forgotten Sam Quain's grim predicament in the desperation of his own, but Sam was also wanted. He must have come here, it occurred to Barbee, to wait with his family for the law.

Barbee managed to breathe again. A glow of hope thawed his consternation, and he limped hurriedly up the walk to the door. Sam Quain would surely talk to him now, in this hour of their mutual extremity. Together, they might break the monstrous web that had snared them both. He knocked eagerly.

Nora came instantly to open the door. Her round freckled face was pale and tear stricken, swollen for need of sleep. He shuffled quickly past her, anxious to get off the street before that prowl car came back, yet trying not to show his terror. He looked hopefully about the neat little living room, and failed to see anything of Sam.

"Why, Will!" A tired relief lighted her blue-circled eyes. "I'm so glad you came—it's been such a dreadful night!" She looked at his own haggard desperation, and gave him a wan little smile of sympathy. "You look worn out yourself, Will. Come on to the kitchen, and I'll pour you a cup of coffee."

"Thank you, Nora." He nodded gratefully, aware that his teeth were chattering with cold. He wanted that warming coffee urgently, but a closer necessity made him pause. "Is Sam here?" he asked breathlessly. "I've got to talk to Sam."

Her swollen eyes turned away.

"Sam isn't here."

"I saw that Foundation car," he said. "I thought Sam would be here."

Her colorless lips tightened stubbornly.

"Sorry—I didn't mean to pry." His shivering hands opened in a gesture of appeal. "I just hoped Sam would be here—because I'm in trouble too, and I think we could help each other. Please—may I have that coffee?"

She nodded silently, and he followed her back through the small house. The shades were down, the lights still burning. He shivered to something more than the aching cold in him as they passed the door of Sam's study, where the deadly thing in that wooden box had almost trapped him once.

His human nostrils couldn't smell that lethal sweetness, however. He knew the box was gone, and he could see that Nora's stiff mistrust was melting. Tiptoeing as they passed the nursery door, she touched her quivering lips—she was almost sobbing.

"Little Pat's asleep," she whispered. "I thought she'd surely wake when the police were here—they stayed for hours, trying to make me say where Sam went." She must have seen his apprehensive start. "Don't you worry, Will," she added softly. "I didn't tell them anything about you phoning me to warn Sam."

"Thanks, Nora." He shrugged wearily in the loose red robe. "Though I don't suppose it matters—the police are hunting me for something more than that."

She didn't ask any questions. She just nodded for him to sit at the white-enameled kitchen table and poured strong hot coffee from the percolator on the stove and brought cream and sugar for him.

"Thank you, Nora," he whispered huskily. He gulped the fragrant, scalding bittersweetness, his eyes blurred with tears of gratitude and pain. His solitary desperation thawed, and a sudden impulse made him blurt the thing he hadn't meant to say:

"Rowena Mondrick's dead!"

Her swollen eyes looked at him, dark with shock.

"She escaped from Glennhaven." A numb puzzlement dulled his voice. "She was found dead on Deer Creek bridge. The police think I ran her down. But I didn't." His quavering voice went on too high. "I know I didn't!"

She sat down heavily across the little white table. Her dark weary eyes dwelt upon his wild face for a long time. She nodded at last, with a faint, tear-blotted smile.

"You sound just like Sam did," she whispered. "He was so frightened, and he couldn't understand, and he didn't know what to do." Her dark-shadowed eyes searched his own drawn face again. "Will, I think there's something very dreadful behind all this. I think you're the innocent victim of it, as much as Sam is. Do you—do you really believe you can help him?"

"I think we can help each other, Nora."

Barbee tried to stir his coffee again, and had to lay down the spoon and fold his hands to stop their shuddering when he heard a siren wailing. Nora frowned at that noise; she went to listen at the nursery door, and silently poured more coffee for him. That droning scream receded at last, down some other street, and he dared to pick up his spoon.

"I'm going to tell you about Sam." She tried to swallow, as if agony choked her. "Because he does need help—so terribly!"

"I'll do all I can," Barbee whispered huskily. "Where is he?"

"I don't know—really." She shook her blonde, disheveled head, her reddened eyes dull with a hopeless bewilderment. "He didn't trust me to know—that's the dreadful thing." She gulped again, and whispered: "I'm afraid I'll never see him again."

"Can you tell me what happened?"

Her plump shoulders quivered and then stiffened angrily, as if in vain defiance of her sobs.

"I called him right back," she said. "Right after I talked to you. I told him you said the police would be looking for him to explain how Nick was killed." She watched Barbee with a brooding puzzlement. "His voice sounded funny, Will, when I told him that. He wanted to know how you knew anything about it." Her tight voice sharpened uneasily. "How did you, Will?"

Barbee couldn't meet her tortured eyes.

"Just my usual newspaper connections." He shifted uncomfortably, repeating that feeble lie. "I've got to protect my sources." He tried to lift his cup, and brown coffee splashed in his saucer. Desperately he muttered:

"What else did Sam say?"

Nora lifted the corner of her white apron to daub at her wet eyes.

"He said he had to go away—and he couldn't tell me where. I begged him to come home, but he said he hadn't time. I asked why he couldn't just explain to the police. He said they wouldn't believe him. He said his enemies had framed him too cunningly." A puzzled dread hushed her sobbing voice. "Who are Sam's enemies, Will?"

Barbee shook his head blankly.

"It's a frightful plot, Will!" A stricken, uncomprehending terror was in her whisper. "The police showed me some of the evidence they've found—trying to make me talk. They told me what they think. I—I just won't believe it!"

Barbee rasped hoarsely, "What evidence?"

"There's a note," she murmured faintly. "It's written on a piece of yellow paper in Nick's handwriting—or a good imitation. It tells how they quarreled on the way back from Asia over the treasure they brought in that green wooden box. Sam wanted it for himself, and tried to make Nick help him get it—that's what the note says, Will."

Her head shook in frantic protest.

"It says Sam gave Dr. Mondrick an overdose of his heart medicine, to kill him at the airport—just to keep him from putting that treasure in the Foundation museum. It says Sam tinkered with the brakes and steering gear of our car so that Rex Chittum would be killed on Sardis Hill—it does seem funny Sam would have him borrow our old car, when the Foundation has better ones." Her dry, dull voice was horror-haunted. "And finally it says that Nick was afraid Sam was going to kill him, to keep the secret of the other killings and get all the treasure for himself."

Nora gulped, and her voice turned high.

"The police think he did. They believe Nick really wrote that note. They say Sam and Nick were alone in the room. They found a broken chair and a trail of blood to the window. They think Sam killed him and threw him out—but you know Nick used to walk in his sleep." Her voice was flat with horror, unconvinced. "You surely remember that?"

Barbee nodded, and saw her desperate hope.

"I remember," he said hoarsely. "And I don't think Nick Spivak wrote that note."

The sleek she-wolf must have written it, he thought, when she sprang upon Nick's desk and took his pencil in her paws while that

210

great armored snake was dragging Nick's body to the window. But that was madness—he dared not speak of that.

"Didn't Sam come here at all?" he asked faintly.

She shook her head dazedly, and then she must have caught the meaning of his nod toward the sedan parked in front of the house.

"Oh—that car!" She caught her breath. "Sam had a man bring that from the Foundation garage yesterday for me to use in place of ours—the one Rex was killed in." Her brooding eyes clung to Barbee's face. "Sam said on the phone he thought the enemy wouldn't know our car, but somehow they did."

Barbee dropped his eyes and stirred his coffee.

"Do you know what Sam did?"

"Only that he went away." She jabbed angrily at her tears again. "I don't know where. He said something about the deaths of Dr. Mondrick and Rex and Nick leaving him with a terribly important job to do alone. He wouldn't say what. I told him to take this car, but he said he hadn't time to come home. He said he would take a station wagon that belongs to the Foundation. He wouldn't tell me where."

She blew her nose hard on a paper napkin.

"Will," she whispered huskily, "what *can* we do to help him?"

"We've got to find him first." Barbee lifted his quivering cup, trying to think. "But—I think I can," he whispered slowly. "I think I can find him—because he knows every officer in four states will be looking for that station wagon by noon. I think I know where Sam would go."

She leaned across the little white table, desperately.

"Where, Will?" she sobbed hoarsely. "Where is he?"

"Just a hunch." Barbee shrugged uncomfortably in the red hospital robe. "Maybe I'm wrong—I don't think so. If I'm right, it's still better if you don't know. I imagine the police will soon be here again—looking for me as well as Sam."

Her white hands flew to her throat.

"Police!" she gasped. "You wouldn't—lead them?"

"Of course not, Nora." He tried to smile at her concern. "I'll take precautions—my danger is as great as Sam's. Now, suppose you gather up some things he'll need. Rough clothing, boots, sleeping bag, matches, frying pan, a few groceries, a light rifle—maybe you have the light personal equipment he brought back from the expedition?"

She nodded, rising eagerly.

211

"I'll need that car," he added, "to get to where he is."

"Take it," she said. "Take anything you need—and let me write a note for Sam."

"Okay—but step on it," he told her. "The cops are after me too, remember." He stood up, facing her gravely. "Nora, I've had just the vaguest glimpse of what's behind this, but I think it's worse than it looks—and it looks pretty ugly. We've got to help Sam, for a lot more than just his own sake. He's the last hope—against something worse than most men ever fear."

She nodded slowly, clutching the edges of the little table.

"I know that, Will." Her dark-circled eyes were very wide, and she shuddered. "Sam wouldn't ever tell me—not even after the dreadful night when he had the box here and something killed Pat's little dog. I could see that made him sick, and I've felt something wrong ever since that plane landed with them." Her dry voice dropped. "Something waiting just out of sight, silent and grinning and dreadful, too hideous to have a name."

But it did, Barbee thought. It was named the Child of Night.

17
Not All Human

Listening breathlessly for the whine of the prowl cars, Barbee went in the bathroom to change the felt slippers and the hospital robe for walking shoes and khakis of Sam's, making the shoes fit with two pairs of heavy socks. Nora had gathered blankets and clothing and food and equipment. He made a pack as heavy as he could stagger under, while she wrote her note to Sam.

"Don't tell the cops you've seen me," he warned her harshly. "Don't tell them anything—for all we know, they may be working with these enemies of Sam's."

"I won't." She swallowed hard. "Help him, Will!"

He looked up and down the quiet street again and tossed his pack into the back seat of the Foundation sedan. It started easily. He waved at Nora's white face in the doorway, grinning with a hope he didn't feel, and drove down Pine Street at a careful eighteen miles an hour.

Once a siren howled somewhere behind him, but he drove on quietly and managed at last to breathe again. He turned south on the first through street to Center, and west on Center toward the state highway. Still he kept to an inconspicuous legal speed, and he heard no other siren. Ten miles west, he turned north on a rutted dirt road toward the hills.

Driving, he had time to try to analyze the hunch that he could find Sam Quain. Quain was an outdoor man who had roughed it on four continents. Expecting the police to broadcast a warning for him, he would want to get off the roads. His boyhood had been spent on a ranch in these hills, and his instinct would be to seek them.

Quain would be burdened, no doubt, with the box from Asia—surely he wouldn't abandon that. It was heavy—whether or not it was actually lined with silver. Barbee recalled the way Rex Chittum and Nick Spivak had stooped to its weight when they carried it off the chartered plane. Unaided, Sam couldn't carry it far. He would choose some secluded refuge that he could approach by car.

Barbee knew the spot!

Perhaps there were flaws in the logic of his explanation. That didn't matter. The hunch itself had been a sudden, certain intuition. The bungling effort at analysis must have left out much of his unconscious reasoning—if hunches were that. But he knew where Sam would be.

A vivid picture of the place had flashed across his mind while he sat in Nora's kitchen. On a Christmas vacation, one mild winter when the snows were light, he had been riding with Sam and Rex up a little-used road that twisted through the hills to where an abandoned sawmill had gone to rust, when Sam reined in his pony to point out a smoky streak on the bare, iron-reddened cliff above Laurel Canyon. That dark streak, Sam said, marked an Indian cave.

Barbee knew that cave would be the place. Far from any used roads, it was yet accessible to such a driver as Sam. There was timber enough to hide the station wagon, even from search by air. There was firewood, shelter enough, water in Laurel Creek. He would be able to carry that precious box up to the cave, and it was still a natural fortress as it had been a thousand years ago. Such were the reasons Barbee found, but the conclusion had gone before. Sam had to be there.

Twice he parked for an hour where the black sedan would be concealed and climbed to where he could watch the lonely track behind. He saw no hint of any pursuit—but the fresh tire-pattern in the weedy ruts assured him that Sam Quain must really be ahead.

Noon had passed before he reached Bear Canyon. The morning had turned warm, but heavy clouds had hidden the sun again and a rising south wind promised rain. He drove harder, fearful of a downpour that would turn these neglected ruts into a river.

Beneath the tall red cliffs above Laurel Canyon, the station wagon had been so deftly hidden, screened with weeds where the trail twisted between a granite boulder and an overhanging tree, that he almost rammed it before he saw it. He left the sedan hidden beside it, and started the climb with his pack.

Ascending Laurel Canyon, he walked boldly in the open. He knew Sam Quain—and knew that any attempt to stalk him now would be suicidal. Dull human senses brought him no clues, but an intuition as keen as the senses of the gray wolf he had been told him that Sam Quain held his life suspended.

"Sam!" Apprehension quivered in his hail. "It's Barbee—with supplies."

He gasped with alarm and quick relief when the fugitive stepped out of a red-splashed clump of scrub oak, unexpectedly near. Quain's bronzed and haggard head was bare, his shirt muddy and torn. His rawboned body seemed to droop with a dead exhaustion, but the level revolver in his big hand looked as deadly as his hard voice sounded.

"Barbee—what the devil are you doing here?"

"I just brought some things you need." Barbee turned hastily to show the pack, holding up his hands. "You don't have to worry—I hid the car, and my trail is as safe as yours. Nora sent a note."

Quain's drawn, red-stubbled face failed to soften.

"I ought to kill you, Barbee." His voice was thick and hard and strange. "I should have killed you long ago—or Dr. Mondrick should. But I guess you aren't all bad—your warning to Nora saved me from the police last night, and I do need that pack."

Barbee tramped on, with both hands lifted, until the gun beckoned him to stop.

"Sam—can you trust me now?" Pleading quivered in his voice. "I want to help—if you'll only tell me what this is all about. Yesterday I went to Glennhaven. I thought I was losing my mind. Maybe I am—but I think there's something more."

Quain's red-rimmed eyes narrowed watchfully.

"There's more," his hard voice grated. "Plenty more."

Darkening clouds had lowered about the peaks, and now the strong wind that blew up Laurel Canyon seemed suddenly cool and damp. Thunder rumbled dully against the cliffs above, and the first huge raindrops crashed against the red hanging oak leaves and splashed their faces, cold as ice.

"Take the pack," Barbee urged. "Read Nora's note—and please let me help."

At last, reluctantly, Sam Quain gestured with the gun.

"Come on out of the rain," he muttered harshly. "I don't know how much of this black deviltry you've done—consciously or not. I don't know how far to trust you. But I suppose it can't make things much worse to tell you what I know."

The cave itself was invisible from below, although that thin stain of ancient smoke betrayed it. Sam Quain pointed the way with his gun, and waited for Barbee to stumble ahead with the pack. They climbed half-obliterated steps in a water-cut chimney, where one armed man might hold off a hundred.

A long horizontal fissure above that narrow stair, the cave had been gouged by the chisel of time between two strata of hard sandstone. The roof was black with smoke of ancient fires. Hidden in the deepest corner, where the roof sloped down to the floor, Barbee saw the battered wooden box from Asia. He dropped the pack, hopefully eyeing that crude coffer.

"Not yet," Quain rapped harshly. "I've got to eat."

As soon as he had got his breath back from the climb, Barbee unrolled the pack. He made coffee on a tiny Primus stove, fried bacon, and opened a can of beans. Using a flat stone for a table, Quain ate and drank avidly. Stationed warily between Barbee and the box, he kept the gun near his hand. His narrowed, bloodshot eyes roved restlessly between Barbee and a bend of the Laurel Canyon trail that lay visible beneath the rock chimney.

Barbee waited impatiently while he ate, uneasily aware of the thickening storm. The dark ceiling of ragged clouds crept lower about the peaks. Thunder crashed above and boomed and rumbled in the gorge below. Gusts of wind blew icy rain into the cave. Heavy rain, he knew, would flood the trails and trap them here. Quain cleaned his tin plate at last, and Barbee prompted anxiously:

"Okay, Sam—tell me."

"Do you really want to know?" Sam Quain's feverish eyes scanned him. "The knowledge will haunt you, Barbee. It will turn the world into a menagerie of horrors. It will point unspeakable suspicions at every friend you have—if you're actually as innocent as you pretend. It may kill you."

"I want to know," Barbee said.

"It's your funeral." Quain tightened his grip on the gun. "Do you remember what Dr. Mondrick was saying Monday evening at the airport, when he was murdered?"

"So Mondrick was murdered?" Barbee murmured softly. "And the means was a little black kitten—garroted?"

Quain's unshaven face went pale and slack. His mouth hung open. His glittering, bloodshot eyes dilated, fixed on Barbee in a vacant stare of horror. The heavy gun jerked up in his hand, and he rasped hoarsely:

"How did you know that?"

"I saw the kitten," Barbee said. "Several ugly things have happened that I can't understand—that's why I thought I had lost my mind." He peered uneasily at the carved wooden box beyond Quain—the combination padlock looked bright as if actually plated with silver. "I remember the last words Mondrick said: "It was a hundred thousand years ago—"

The cruel blue flicker of lightning made the dull gloom of the storm seem darker. Rain drummed on the ledge above the rock chimney, and a fresh gust of wind blew cold mist into the cave. Barbee hunched his shoulders, shivering in the old wool sweater of Sam's that Nora had given him. Thunder crashed and echoed and subsided, and Sam Quain's worn voice resumed.

"It was a time when men lived in such settings as this." His cragged head nodded into the smoke-blackened cavern. "A time when all men lived in a nightmare terror that is still reflected in the myth and superstition of every land and the secret dreams of every man. For those early ancestors of ours were hunted and haunted by another, older, semihuman race that Dr. Mondrick called Homo Lycanthropus."

Barbee started, muttering:

"Werewolf-man?"

"Wolf-man," said Sam Quain. "Dr. Mondrick named them that for certain distinguishing characteristics of bone and skull and teeth— characteristics you see every day."

Barbee shuddered on the damp stone where he squatted, thinking of the long skulls and queerly sharp teeth and oddly slender bones of those articulated skeletons the giant snake and the she-wolf had found in that strange room in the Foundation tower. But he didn't speak of that—Sam Quain, he thought, would surely kill him if he did.

"A better name," Sam Quain added slowly, "might have been witch man."

Barbee felt a prickling numbness along his spine, like the feel of the wolf's hair rising. He couldn't help shivering and he was glad for the excuse of the wet, gusty wind. Water gushed in a foaming yellow fall down the rock chimney outside and began dripping from the roof of the cave. Quain paused to drag his precious box to a drier spot.

"That rival race wasn't ape-like," his hoarse voice resumed, dull as the continual rumble of far thunder. "The path of evolution isn't always upward, you know—the Cro-magnons were finer specimens than you can easily find today. Our human family tree has put out some pretty funny branches—and those witch-folk must have been our strangest cousins."

Barbee peered out into the roaring rain, trying not to show the breathless desperation of his interest.

"To find the real beginning of that racial tragedy, you have to look still farther back," Quain's dead voice was rasping on. "Half a million years and more—to the first of the two major glacial ages of the Pleistocene epoch. The first ice age with its less frigid intermission lasted nearly a hundred thousand years, and it created the witch people."

"You found the evidence of that," Barbee whispered uncomfortably, "in the Ala-shan?"

"Part of it." Sam Quain nodded. "Although the Gobi plateau itself was never glaciated—its deserts turned humid and fruitful during the ice ages, and our own eolithic ancestors were busy evolving there. The witch folk sprang from another kindred type of Hominidae who were trapped by the glaciers in the higher country southwest, toward Tibet.

"Dr. Mondrick had found remains of them in a cave he excavated before the war, beyond the Nanshan range. What we found under those burial mounds in the desert on this last trip, pieces out the story—and it makes a pretty shocking chapter."

Barbee watched the gray veils of rain.

"A neat example of challenge-and-response, as Toynbee might phrase it." Quain plowed grimly on. "Those trapped bands faced the challenge of the ice. Century by century the glaciers flowed higher and the game was less plentiful and the winters turned more cruel. They had to adapt, or die. They responded, over the slow millennia, by evolving new powers of the mind."

"Huh?" Barbee gasped to a shock of cold alarm, but he didn't say anything about free mind webs or Heisenberg's indeterminacy principle or the linkage of mind to matter through control of probability. He didn't want Sam Quain to kill him with that ready gun.

"Really?" he muttered uneasily. "What kind of powers?"

"It's hard to be precise about that." Quain frowned at him. "Dead minds don't leave fossils in the ground, you know. Dr. Mondrick thought they did, however, in language and myth and superstition. He studied such race memories, and he got more evidence from such experiments in parapsychology as Duke University researchers have begun."

Barbee couldn't help staring, jaw sagging.

"Those ice-bound nomads survived," Quain went on, "by evolving powers that enabled them to prey on their more fortunate cousins in the Gobi country. Telepathy, clairvoyance, prophecy—certainly those. Dr. Mondrick was convinced they had a more sinister gift."

Barbee had trouble breathing.

"The evidence is nearly universal," Quain was saying. "Almost every primitive people is still obsessed with the fear of the *loup-garou*, in one guise or another—of a human-seeming being who can take the shape of the most ferocious animal of the locality to prey upon men. Those witch people, in Dr. Mondrick's opinion, learned to leave their bodies hibernating in their caves while they went out across the ice fields—as wolves or bears or tigers—to hunt human game."

Barbee shuddered uncontrollably, glad he hadn't told about his dreams.

"So, in their own diabolical way, those trapped Hominidae met their challenge and conquered the ice," Quain went on. "About the end of the Mindel glaciation—some four hundred thousand years ago as the evidence shows—they overran nearly all the world. In a few thousand years, their dreadful powers had overcome every other species of the genus Homo."

Barbee uneasily recalled those huge maps of the vanished past he had seen at the Foundation, but he dared not ask about them.

"Homo lycanthropus didn't exterminate the conquered races, however—not except in the Americas, and that was their own undoing here. Usually they let the defeated breeds survive—for their slaves and their food. They had learned to like the taste of human blood, and they couldn't exist without it."

Shivering on his rock, Barbee remembered the fragrant hot sweetness of Rex Chittum's blood foaming against the fangs of the great saber-tooth. He couldn't help shaking his head in mute protest, hoping Sam Quain wouldn't see his clammy horror.

"For hundreds of thousands of years, all through the main interglacial period," Quain's harsh voice continued, "those witch-people were the hunters and the enemies and the cruel masters of mankind. They were the cunning priests and the evil gods. They were the merciless originals of every ogre and demon and man-eating dragon of every folk tale. It was an incredible, degrading, cannibalistic oppression. If you've ever wondered why the birth of any real human civilization took so long, there's the ugly answer.

"Their monstrous power lasted until after the cold came back in the Riss and Würm glaciations of the second main ice age. But they had never been very numerous—no predators can be as numerous as the animals they feed on. Perhaps the ages had finally sapped their racial vigor.

"Anyhow, nearly a hundred thousand years ago, the ancestral types of Homo sapiens revolted. The dog had been domesticated—probably by hardy tribes that followed the retreating ice to escape the rule of the witch-folk. The dog was a staunch ally."

Recalling Rowena Mondrick's dog Turk, that he and the white wolf-bitch had lured to death on the railroad bridge, Barbee couldn't stop himself from shivering again. Uneasy before Sam Quain's fevered, hollow eyes, he moved farther back from the cold driving rain.

"We found the evidences of that strange war under those burial mounds in the Ala-shan," Quain continued. "The true men seem to have learned to carry nuggets of alluvial silver as charms against attack by the witch-folk, and later wore silver jewelry. Dr. Mondrick believed there must be some scientific basis for the belief that only a silver weapon can kill a were-wolf, but he could never establish that."

Silver atoms, Barbee recalled, had no linkage that the energy complex of a free mind web could grasp to control the incidence of probability; but he didn't mention that. He tried not to think of the quaint old silver rings and beads and brooches that had failed to save Rowena Mondrick's life.

"We read the history of that rebellion, and brought back objects enough to tell it." Quain's drawn head nodded at the box behind him. "Silver beads and blades and arrowheads. But silver itself wasn't enough—the witches were cunning and strong. The men of the Ala-shan invented another, more effective weapon, that we found buried under those old mounds with the bones of dead witches—no doubt to keep them dead."

Barbee wondered forebodingly if the free mind web could detach itself from a corpse and rove at night to feed upon the living; such an unpleasant fact might be the basis of many a superstitious dread—if superstitions were actually fossil fears. He wondered what that weapon was which killed witches and kept them dead; and he shivered to the memory of that seeping malodor from the wooden box that had almost killed him and the white wolf bitch in Sam Quain's study. That same lethal sweetness had clung to the disk-shaped plaster cast whose inscriptions Nick Spivak had been deciphering when the great snake crushed him. Was the original of that cast the weapon?

"Men won," Quain's tired voice was rasping on. "Not all at once, nor easily. The witch people were clever and they clung to their old dominion. That frightful war lasted on through Acheulean and Mousterian times. The Neanderthalers and the Cro-magnons died— victims of the witches, Dr. Mondrick thought. But the progenitors of Homo sapiens survived and carried on the war. The use of the dog spread, and the knowledge of silver, and the power of that other weapon. Before the dawn of written history, the witch-folk had been almost exterminated."

Barbee moved uneasily, whispering, "Almost?"

"The witches were hard to kill," Quain said. "One of their last clans must have been the first priests and rulers of old Egypt—the evidence seems clear enough in the animal and half-animal gods the Egyptians worshipped and the demons and the evil magic they feared. I've seen excellent portraits of long-skulled Homo lycanthropus types on the walls of Egyptian tombs. But even that clan was finally conquered—or absorbed—about the time of Imhotep."

Lightning showed the grim tension on Quain's haggard face.

"For the blood of the conquerors was no longer pure." His glittering eyes peered hard at Barbee. "That was Dr. Mondrick's dreadful discovery.

"We're hybrids."

Barbee waited, too numb to breathe.

"That ugly fact is hard to understand." Quain frowned, shaking his bleak head. "The two species were always deadly enemies, yet somehow that mixture happened. The Black Mass and the Witches' Sabbath, Dr. Mondrick believed, are survivals of bestial ceremonies in which the daughters of men were forced to take part. There are other clues, perhaps, in the superstition of the incubus and all the myths about unions of gods and human women—those witch men must have been strangely passionate! Anyhow, it happened."

Against the boom of thunder echoing in that dark cave, Quain's tired voice was a slow, hoarse chant.

"Down out of the terrible past, a black river of that monstrous blood flows in the veins of Homo sapiens. We aren't all human—and that alien inheritance haunts our unconscious minds with the dark conflicts and intolerable urges that Freud discovered and tried to explain. And now that evil blood is in rebellion. Dr. Mondrick found that Homo lycanthropus is about to win that old, hideous war of the species, after all!"

18

Rebirth of the Witch Folk

Barbee sat up straight on his damp stone seat. He thought of many things—of April Bell and the Child of Night and the laughing she-wolf licking the pink stain of Rowena Mondrick's blood from her muzzle. He shivered and opened his mouth and shut it again. Thunder snarled and bellowed outside the cave, and the lightning-torn rain curtains darkened again.

"I know it's pretty hard to take," Sam Quain's saw-toothed voice resumed. "But you can see the evidence all around you—even the Bible, you recall, wisely commands the destruction of witches."

Barbee thought of April Bell's disturbing confession of her childhood struggles with her mother's indignant husband, and tried not to let Sam Quain see his shudder.

"The Biblical story of the Garden of Eden, in fact," that weary man went on, "appears to be nothing more than a symbolic condensation of the history of that tragic war of the species. The serpent was a witch man, obviously. The curse his cunning brought upon the human woman Eve and all her seed is clearly the lycanthropus inheritance we all still carry. The serpents of our time have got tired of eating dust, however; they want to rise again!

"The witch folk have left a wide trail of evidence down all the ages. There's a paleolithic painting in a cave in Ariège in southern France, dating from the actual reign of the witches, that shows the transformation of a witch man into an antlered stag—such harmless shapes must have been assumed to impress the obedient human worshipers without terrorizing them too far.

"The witch people were still plotting to recover their lost dominion of Egypt in the reign of Rameses III. Some officers and women of his harem were tried, a surviving record relates, for making wax images of the Pharaoh with magical incantations to harm him. Their genes must already have been pretty well scattered, however, and their ancient arts almost forgotten, for them to need any such childish devices to concentrate their destructive powers.

"Greek mythology, as Dr. Mondrick discovered, is actually largely a folk memory of another lycanthropus clan. The god Jupiter, carrying away the daughters of men to become the mothers of less powerful gods and heroes, is obviously a witch who hadn't lost his powers—or his passions. Proteus, the strange old man of the sea who could change his shape at will, was another master lycanthrope.

"That same terrible history is repeated in Scandinavia—as in the folk memories of every other people. The giant wolf Fenris was born of another unnatural union, to become the demon of the Norsemen. Sigmund the Volsung was another mixed-blood witch, who found it necessary to put on a wolf skin to help him become a wolf."

Barbee shuddered again, and resolutely said nothing of April Bell's fur coat.

"The witch covens of the Middle Ages, finally forced completely underground by the just wrath of the Inquisition, were nothing more than a few surviving clans of mongrel witches, trying to keep alive the arts and ceremonies of that old pagan breed. The devils they assembled to worship usually took animal form—they were transformed witches. The notorious Gilles de Rais, tried for his heresy in the fifteenth century, was probably about a quarter lycanthropus—too weak and ignorant to escape the hangman for his lurid crimes. Joan of Arc, burned for witchcraft in the same century, was no doubt another mongrel lycanthrope, whose human side was finally dominant."

Barbee shifted uncomfortably on his hard stone, thinking of Rowena Mondrick.

"In more recent times," Sam Quain said, "the witch hunters of the Zulus still carried on the necessary work of the Inquisition. Even in Europe, that monstrous pagan cult was never fully extirpated—*la vecchia religione* is a pathetic survival that still has followers today among the peasants of Italy."

Emphatically, Sam Quain shook his head.

"No, Barbee, you can't escape the evidence. Dr. Mondrick found it in every field of knowledge. The inmates of all our prisons and asylums are the victims of that dark legacy, driven by the criminal urges of their lycanthropus strain or insane with the conflict of witch and man—that's what splits a personality!

"Blood groups and cephalic indices yield more evidence—nearly every man you examine shows some physical characteristics inherited from lycanthropus. Freud's exploration of the unconscious revealed another well of dreadful evidence—that he failed to recognize.

"Then there are all these recent university experiments with parapsychology—although most of the researchers don't yet suspect the unpleasant facts they are about to uncover, and naturally the witches are trying to minimize or discredit their amazing findings.

"The evidence turns up in every land and every age. Dr. Mondrick used to keep a reminder of that on his desk—a little Roman lamp whose design showed the she-wolf caring for Romulus and Remus. He used to call that a clever bit of witch propaganda.

"There's all that—and volumes more." Sam Quain nodded heavily at the Oriental box behind him. "Not to mention the very convincing exhibits we have there."

Numbed with an increasing dread, Barbee shook himself uneasily.

"I don't quite get it," he muttered. "If Homo lycanthropus was really exterminated—"

"You know Mendel's laws of inheritance—we studied them together under Dr. Mondrick." Quain's drawn face almost smiled, and Barbee was pierced by a painful longing for the unsuspecting pleasures of those dead student days. He shook his head uncertainly, and Sam Quain explained:

"The units in the germ cell which govern inheritance, you remember, are called genes—the number in man is several thousand, and each causes or helps to cause a certain characteristic to appear in the individual; one dominant gene, for instance, causes dark eyes. Each baby inherits a double set of genes from its parents—sex is really a device for reshuffling the genes, and the laws of probability insure that every person will be unique."

"Probability—" Barbee couldn't help echoing that word in a brooding whisper, or wondering what unguessed possibilities might lie in the mental control of probability.

"Genes, you recall, can be either dominant or recessive," Quain went on. "We receive our genes in pairs, one from each parent, and the dominant gene can hide the presence of a recessive partner—one dominant gene for dark eyes can conceal the recessive gene that causes blue eyes. That one happens to be harmless, but some are sinister."

Barbee sat licking at his dry lips.

"One such ugly recessive," Quain said, "is the gene that makes deaf-mutes. Normal hybrid deaf-mutes—that is, people with one recessive gene for deafness and one dominant gene for hearing—can't be distinguished from normal people by any ordinary test. They are carriers of deaf-mutism, however. If two such carriers happen to marry, the chance reshuffling of the genes will make one child in four completely normal—inheriting a dominant gene for normal hearing from each parent. Two more children, on the average, will be normal hybrids—carriers, with one recessive gene for deafness and one matching gene for hearing which is dominant and so conceals the taint. The unfortunate fourth child, on the average, will be born a deaf-mute—condemned to live and die in silence because of the chance inheritance of two recessive genes for deafness."

Barbee shifted uncomfortably to whisper:

"What has that to do with witches?"

"Quite a lot," Sam Quain said. "Human blood—or germplasm, to use a more accurate word—still carries the taint of Homo lycanthropus. The witch folk aren't really dead—because their genes live on, handed down with those of Homo sapiens."

Barbee gulped, nodding unwillingly.

"The case is a little more complicated than that of deaf-mutism—and somewhat more sinister. Several hundred recessive genes are involved, according to Dr. Mondrick's results, instead of one. He found that it requires the combination of several pairs of lycanthropus genes to reproduce completely such a gift as extrasensory perception—and most of the lycanthropus genes happen to be recessives."

Barbee shook his head violently and abruptly stiffened again—afraid that mute denial had betrayed him.

"Throwbacks are born," Quain was saying. "Not often—so long as nature is left alone. It's all a matter of probability, and you can see the odds. But every man alive is a carrier, and most throwbacks are only partial. Literally millions of variations are possible between pure Homo sapiens and pure lycanthropus."

"Huh?" Barbee gasped. "How's that?"

"The chance matching of the genes can reproduce one gift of the witches and not another," Quain told him. "The partial reversions, those inheriting perhaps one sixteenth of the witch genes, possess such powers as ESP. They are psychic. Moody, tense, unhappy people, generally—because of the unconscious conflict of their hostile heritages. They are your religious fanatics, your spiritualistic mediums, your split personalities, your pathological criminals. The lucky exception may be a genius—you know the vigor of hybrids."

Barbee shivered in the damp wind, listening dazedly.

"Those born with a stronger inheritance are usually better aware of their unusual gifts—and more careful to conceal them. In the Middle Ages—so long as the Inquisition kept alive the ancient arts of witch-hunting—they were usually found and burned. Nowadays they fare better. They're able to realize their gifts, and organize, and plot to regain their lost supremacy. They must spend a lot of their time cultivating the modern scientific skepticism of everything supernatural—even that's a propaganda word. Dr. Mondrick used to say, that really means superhuman."

Barbee sat thinking numbly of April Bell and her strange confession. She must be a throwback, actually a witch—and he had come under her spells.

"A few outstanding individuals in each generation must inherit approximately a quarter of the lycanthropus genes," Quain was saying. "They are quarter-breed witches—still not usually aware of what they are. They have increased perceptions, some bungling and half-unconscious use of their strange ancestral powers, some of the surprising vigor of hybrids. The key to their lives is the conflict of two species. Evil is mingled with good, fighting good, cloaked with good—their twisted lives take strange directions."

The truth was dawning on Barbee, and it seized him with the chilly grasp of something colder than the spray-laden wind that whipped into that storm-darkened cavern.

"Dr. Mondrick spent a lot of time looking for a definite test for the lycanthropus genes," Quain went on. "He wasn't very successful. It's easy enough to identify such physical traits as skull shape and blood grouping, but unfortunately they aren't linked very closely with the more dangerous mental traits. Some of his tests were indicative, none was conclusive."

Barbee caught a long, gasping breath.

"Was that—?" he whispered, and couldn't finish.

Quain nodded in the gloom, his harsh face almost sympathetic.

"Don't let it worry you, Will," he said quietly. "The tests did indicate that you carry a strong lycanthropus taint, and Dr. Mondrick let you go—he couldn't afford to take chances. But the results aren't conclusive. Even if they were, many part witches make very good and useful citizens. Dr. Mondrick told me once that his tests showed a considerable taint of lycanthropus in his own wife."

"In Rowena?"

Barbee breathed that, and slowly nodded. It must have been the witch blood in the blind woman, and her witch's gifts, that made her so dangerous to other witches. That dark heritage, it must have been, that sent her to Glennhaven and then to her death. But Barbee didn't want to talk about Rowena Mondrick.

"The full-blood witches?" he whispered uncomfortably. "Who are they?"

"There shouldn't be any," Sam Quain said. "You can see the impossible odds against the complete regrouping of all those hundreds of pairs of recessive genes. Even the three-quarter-breeds oughtn't to occur more than one to the generation, and they would be much too clever to allow themselves to be suspected—especially in such a country as America, where the people are the nominal rulers and the actual instruments of power are newspaper chains and banks and holding companies and legislative lobbies."

Lightning etched Quain's face again, stark and harsh against the darkness of the cave behind him.

"There should be no full-blood witches alive today—but I believe there is one." His red-rimmed eyes stared hard at Barbee. "Dr. Mondrick uncovered evidence of a secret leader of the witch people, born with a vast heritage of that evil power. A veiled satan, moving unsuspected among humanity, plotting to restore the dead dominion of his dark kind!"

Barbee shifted uncomfortably before Quain's savage eyes.

"The Child of Night?" he muttered uneasily. "I remember that phrase of Mondrick's." He tried to swallow. "But how can the witches recover their power," he protested faintly, "when the throwbacks occur only by chance?"

"They don't," Sam Quain told him grimly. "That was Dr. Mondrick's last, most alarming discovery—the one he was trying to announce to the world when the witches murdered him. The throwbacks have begun to gather into secret clans. By mating among themselves, they have upset the random odds, and increased the probability of reversion."

Barbee nodded slowly. The mental control of probability might play a sinister role in that, it came to him, manipulating the reshuffle of the genes to insure the birth of a full-blood witch—but he dared not speak of that.

"The plot must have begun generations ago," Sam Quain went on. "A few secret clans of the off-breed witches, Dr. Mondrick believed, have always handed down the memory of their lost dominion—and the determination to get it back. They work underground, cautious and desperate. Having their own black powers, it is easy for them to do what Dr. Mondrick's tests failed to accomplish—to detect that hidden strain in 'humans' who may not know they possess it. They are finding the carriers and using the modern science of selective breeding—with doubtless some improvements of their own—to filter out the dominant genes of Homo sapiens and so give birth to this powerful leader they're waiting for—the monstrous Messiah they call the Child of Night."

The Child of Night—that odd phrase echoed painfully in Barbee's numbed brain. Sam Quain's fevered eyes seemed to peer at him too searchingly. He squirmed and shuddered on the wet rock where he squatted, and his own fearful eyes went back to the iron-bound box beyond the other man. He tried to swallow, and croaked rustily:

"May I see—what's inside?"

Quain's big hand leveled the revolver.

"No, Barbee." His narrowed eyes were cold and his weary voice rapped hard. "Maybe you're okay. But I can't afford to trust you now—any more than Dr. Mondrick could when he saw that test. What I've told you can't do any harm—I've been pretty careful not to spill anything that the leaders of the witch clans don't already know. But you can't look in the box."

Quain seemed to see his shrinking hurt.

"I'm sorry, Will." Briefly, his voice turned almost kind. "I can tell you a part of what's in it. There are silver weapons, that men used in that long war against the witches. There are charred, cracked bones—of men who lost their battles. There is a complete skeleton of Homo lycanthropus from one of those burial mounds—and the weapon left to keep it there."

His voice went savagely grim again.

"That weapon defeated the witches once," he rasped bleakly. "It will again—when men learn how to use it. That's all I can tell you, Barbee."

"Who—" Barbee shivered, and his faint whisper grated, "Who is this Child of Night?"

"He might be you," Sam Quain said. "By that, I mean he might be anybody. We do know the physical appearance of Homo lycan-thropus—the delicate bones and pointed ears and long, rounded skulls and low-growing hair and pointed, peculiar teeth. But the physical and mental characteristics are not strongly linked in inheritance, Dr. Mondrick found—and even the Child of Night might be not quite a thoroughbred."

A brooding horror shadowed Quain's stark face.

"That's why I came out here, Barbee, instead of making a fight in the courts. I can't trust anybody. I can't stand—people. Most of them are mostly human, but I've no sure way of finding out the monsters. I could never be quite certain that Nick or Rex wasn't a spy of the witches. It seems hideous to say, but I've wondered even about Nora—"

Sam Quain's sick voice trailed away.

231

Huddled away from the wet, gusty wind, Barbee tried to stop his own shivering. He wanted to ask how a red-haired witch could snare a normal man, and what he should do to escape her spells. Could silver save him now, or a dog? Or even that weapon in the wooden box? He licked his lips and shook his head—Sam Quain would surely kill him, if he asked all the questions in his mind.

"You'll let me help you, Sam?" he asked huskily. "I want to. I need to—to save my own sanity—since you've told me this." Desperately he watched Quain's cragged face. "Can't we somehow identify the Child of Night and expose the witch folk?"

"That was Mondrick's idea." Sam Quain shook his head. "It might have worked—four hundred years ago, before the clans discredited their last enemies in the Inquisition. Nowadays the witches in university laboratories can prove there are no witches. The witches who publish newspapers can make a fool of anyone who says there are. The witches in the government can put him out of the way."

Barbee shivered again, peering out into the rainy dusk. The damaging radiations of the daylight would soon be gone so that mind webs could rove free. He knew that April Bell would call, and he would change again—and knew Sam Quain should be the next to die.

"Sam!" A frantic urgency quivered in his voice. "What can we do?"

Sam Quain lifted the gun a little as if unconsciously, his gaunt, square face soberly reflective. His sunken eyes studied Barbee, and at last he nodded slightly.

"I can't forget that test," his dull voice grated. "I don't like your looks, Barbee—or your coming here. Sorry if that sounds hard, but I must protect myself. I do need help, however—you can see how desperately." His haunted eyes went briefly to the wooden box behind him. "So I'm going to give you one chance."

"Thank you, Sam!" Barbee whispered fervidly. "Just tell me what to do."

"First," Quain told him, "there's one condition you must understand." Barbee waited, watching the steady gun. "I must kill you at the first hint of treachery."

"I—I understand." Barbee nodded and gulped convulsively. "But you don't believe that I could be a—hybrid?"

His breathing stopped as Quain nodded.

"Probably you are, Barbee. While the human genes predominate, a thousand to one, nearly every man alive carries some slight taint of lycanthropus—enough to cause some unconscious conflict between the normal human instincts and that alien heritage. That's something the psychiatrists have overlooked, in all their theories of psychopathology."

Barbee tried to relax, and managed to breathe.

"Mondrick's test indicated that you carry more lycanthropus genes than most men," Quain said. "I can see signs enough of the conflict within you—but I don't believe the human part has yet surrendered."

"Thanks, Sam!" A warm tightness hurt Barbee's throat. "I'll do anything."

Sam Quain frowned thoughtfully. The drum and rumble of the storm had paused, and the slow drip of water seemed loud in the dark cave. Barbee sat shivering from the damp chill, waiting breathlessly. A pitiless illumination had dispelled the shadowy uncertainties of his waking life and explained the haunting horror of his dreams. He thought he understood the savage conflict in him, the war of humanity and diabolic monstrosity. The human side had to win! He clenched his fists and caught his breath and listened hopefully.

"Dr. Mondrick had a plan," Sam Quain said quietly. "He tried to take the witch clan by surprise—to broadcast a public warning and gather the human masses behind him. He hoped to arouse the people and their governments, and establish a scientific equivalent of the Inquisition to stop the Child of Night. But the witches murdered him and Nick and Rex—and now I think we must try a different plan."

He rubbed his red-stubbled jaw, and peered hard at Barbee again.

"The public war has failed, and now I think we must launch a private campaign. I'm going to gather a small, secret group—one man at a time. That doesn't require that I identify the hybrids, but merely that I find a few who don't belong to that black clan. Any witch man who learns about us must be eliminated."

Barbee nodded mutely and closed his sagging mouth.

"Now I want you to go back to Clarendon," Sam Quain said. "I want you to make the first contacts for me with those we pick for our own secret legion—I must stay here."

He glanced at his precious box, and Barbee whispered, "Who?"

"We must pick them as carefully as the Child of Night selects his witch pack. They must have money or political influence or scientific skill. They can't be weaklings—this job is tough enough to kill the best

man alive." His glittering eyes flashed back at Barbee. "And—they had
better not be witches!"

Barbee tried to breathe.

"Have you anybody—in mind?" He tried to think. "How about Dr.
Archer Glenn? He's a scientist—a dogmatic materialist. He has reputa-
tion and money."

Stubbornly, Sam Quain shook his head.

"Precisely the type we can't trust. The type who laughs at witches—
perhaps because he's a witch himself. No, Glenn would just lock us in
his disturbed ward, along with poor Mrs. Mondrick."

Barbee stiffened and tried to relax, glad Quain hadn't heard of the
blind widow's death.

"We must pick a different type," Quain was saying. "The first man on
my list is your employer."

"Preston Troy?" Barbee blinked with astonishment, relieved to
forget Rowena Mondrick. "Troy does have millions," he admitted, "and
a lot of political drag. But he's no saint. He's boss of the city-hall ring.
He planned all the crooked work Walraven ever did, and collected
most of the loot. His wife has locked him out of her room for the last
ten years. He's keeping half the pretty women in Clarendon."

"Including some certain one?"

Quain's face showed a passing glint of amusement.

"That doesn't matter," he went on gravely. "Dr. Mondrick used to say
that most saints were about one-eighth lycanthropus—their saintliness
just an over-compensation for the taint of evil. Suppose you tackle
Preston Troy tonight?"

Barbee started to shake his head. The police net he had just escaped
would be spread wide by now. Preston Troy himself would doubtless
be eager to detain him—and get an exclusive story for the *Star*. His
sick mind could already see the black headline: STAR NABS CAR KILLER.

"Anything wrong?" Quain was asking.

"Not a thing!" Barbee stood up hastily. It was far too late for any
confession that he was wanted for running down Mondrick's widow. He
had to go back to Clarendon. But Nora Quain wouldn't have told the
police about the Foundation car, he thought hopefully. He might reach
Preston Troy. He might even—just possibly—win that brutally realistic
prince of industry for Quain's strange cause. He tried to veneer his

dread with a smile. Stiff with the cold in him, stooping beneath the black roof of the cave, he put out his hand.

"Two of us," he whispered, "against the Child of Night!"

"We'll find others—we must." Quain straightened wearily. "Because hell itself—every legend of men degraded and tormented by demons—is only one more racial memory of the witch people's reign." Quain saw his offered hand, and gestured him back with the ugly gun. "Sorry, Barbee, but you'll have to show me first. Better get moving!"

19

On Sardis Hill

Numbly reluctant to face the flooded roads and the incredulous scorn of Preston Troy and the things that would whisper to him after dark, Barbee left Sam Quain crouching with his gun beside the wooden box from Asia—how weary and feeble a champion of mankind against those inhuman hunters!

The rain had turned to icy mist, but a cold yellow torrent still poured down from the cliffs, through the narrow rock chimney that was a stair to the cave. He scrambled stiffly down through it, drenched and shivering—yet queerly relieved to escape the presence of Sam Quain and that ominous box.

The dusk was thick by the time he came splashing through ice-cold water to the parked Foundation car. It started easily, and the road was better than he had hoped. He could hear the rumble of rolling boulders as he crossed the Bear Creek ford, but the car plowed steadily through the foaming water.

He had to turn on the lights before he came back to the highway, but nothing whispered from the dark. No sleek she-wolf sprang into the road ahead, and no police siren wailed behind him. It was eight o'clock when he parked the car on the drive beside Troy's long mansion at Trojan Hills.

Barbee knew his way about the house, for he had been here on political stories. He let himself in through the side entrance. The dining room, to his relief, was dark. He climbed the stairs silently and rapped on the door of Troy's second-floor den. The publisher's leather-throated voice asked who the devil he was.

"Chief, it's Barbee," he whispered apprehensively. "I've got to see you right away—because I didn't run over Mrs. Mondrick."

"So you didn't?" Troy's voice, rasping through the door, sounded unbelieving. After a brief delay it added, "Come in."

The den was a huge room with a brass-railed bar across one end, decorated with hunting trophies and long-limbed nudes in oil. The air had a faint aroma of stale cigar smoke, leather upholstery, and financial importance, and Troy had boasted that more history was made here than in the governor's mansion.

The first thing Barbee saw was a white fur jacket on the back of a chair. A greenish glint caught his glance—the malicious malachite eye of a tiny jade wolf pinned in the fur. The jacket was April Bell's. His hands tried to clench, and it was a moment before he could go on breathing.

"Well, Barbee?" In shirt sleeves, with a fresh cigar in his mouth, Troy stood beside a huge mahogany desk cluttered with papers and ash trays and empty glasses. His massive, pink-jowled face had a look of wary expectancy. "So your car didn't kill Mrs. Mondrick?"

"No, Chief." Barbee made himself look away from April Bell's coat and tried to smooth his shuddering voice. "They're trying to frame me—just like they did Sam Quain!"

"They?" Troy's reddish eyebrows lifted interrogatively.

"It's a terrible, tremendous story, Chief—if you will only listen."

Troy's eyes were pale and cold.

"Sheriff Parker and the city police would be interested," he said. "And your doctors out at Glennhaven."

"I'm not—crazy." Barbee was almost sobbing. "Please, Chief—listen to me first!"

"Okay." Troy nodded, poker-faced. "Wait." He waddled deliberately behind the bar and mixed two Scotch and sodas and brought them back to the desk. "Shoot."

"I did think I was going insane," Barbee admitted, "until I talked to Sam Quain. Now I know I've been bewitched—"

He saw Troy's wide-mouthed face turn harder and tried to slow his nervous, hurried voice. He tried desperately to be convincing, telling Sam Quain's strange story of the origin and extermination of Homo lycanthropus and the rebirth of the witch folk from the genes.

He watched intently, trying to see how Troy reacted. He couldn't be sure. The thick cigar went out and the tall forgotten glass made a wet ring on the desk, but Troy's shrewd, narrowed eyes told him nothing. He caught his breath, and his dry, tight voice finished urgently:

"Believe me, Chief—you've got to believe!"

"So Dr. Mondrick and the other Foundation men were murdered by these witches?" Troy laced his pudgy fingers together in front of his paunch, and chewed reflectively on his dead cigar. "And now you want me to help you fight this Child of Night?"

Barbee gulped, and nodded desperately.

Troy peered at him with blank blue eyes.

"Maybe you aren't crazy!" A slow excitement seemed to take fire behind the stiff, ruddy mask of his face—and Barbee began to feel a breathless agony of hope. "Maybe these witches are framing you and Quain—because this theory of Mondrick's explains a lot. Even why you like some people on sight and don't trust others—because you sense that evil blood in them!"

"You trust me?" Barbee gasped. "You'll help—"

Troy's bald, massive head nodded decisively.

"I'll investigate," he said. "I'll go back with you to that cave tonight and listen to Quain and maybe have a look in that mysterious box. If Quain's as convincing as you are, I'm with you, Barbee—to my last cent and my last gasp."

"Thanks, Chief!" Barbee whispered huskily. "With you to help, we may have a chance."

"We'll lick 'em!" Troy boomed aggressively. "You've come to the right man, Barbee—I don't get beaten by anybody. Just give me half an hour to get ready. I'll tell Rhodora that I'm mending political fences—and she can go alone to Walraven's party. Use the bathroom there if you want to wash up."

Barbee was appalled by what he saw in the bathroom mirror. He looked as gaunt and tired and bearded and begrimed and torn as Sam Quain had been. And there was something else—something that somehow made him think of those smiling skeletons of Homo lycanthropus the giant snake had found. He wondered if the glass were faintly discolored and slightly curved—he was sure he had never looked quite like that.

An unpleasant hunch jarred him out of that brooding puzzlement. He hurried back into the den and carefully picked up the telephone on the long desk. He was in time to hear Troy's voice.

"Parker? I've got a man for you. This Barbee, that got out of Glennhaven and ran down the Mondrick woman. He used to work for me, you know, and now he's come to my house at Trojan Hills. No question the guy belongs in the state asylum—he has been trying to feed me the queerest yarn I ever heard! Can you come after him right away?"

"Sure, Mr. Troy," the sheriff said. "Twenty minutes."

"Be careful," Troy said. "I think he's dangerous. I'll try to keep him in my den on the second floor."

"Right, Mr. Troy."

"Another thing, Parker. Barbee says he has seen Sam Quain—the man you want for the Foundation murders. He says Quain is hiding in a cave up Laurel Canyon, above Bear Creek. It might be a good tip—Barbee and Quain are old friends, and they might be in the plot together. With a little persuasion, Barbee might lead you to the cave."

"Thanks, Mr. Troy!"

"That's all right, Parker. You know the *Star* stands for law and order. All I want is the first look inside that green wooden box. But hurry, won't you? I don't much like Barbee's looks."

"Okay. Mr. Troy—"

Silently Barbee replaced the receiver. The lush nudes on the walls were dancing fantastically, and a gray mist seemed to thicken about him in that long room. He stood numbed and swaying, shivering to the chill of it. He knew he had betrayed Sam Quain—perhaps even to the Child of Night.

For this frightful blunder was all his own fault. Of course Sam Quain had sent him here—but he hadn't dared tell Quain that April Bell was a witch and Preston Troy her intimate. There was too much he had been afraid to tell, and it was too late now.

Or was it?

A hard new purpose steadied him. He listened and slipped off his shoes and padded silently out of the den. The door of Troy's bedroom across the hall was slightly ajar, and he glimpsed the squat publisher turning from a chest of drawers with a flat automatic in his pudgy fist.

The picture of a red-haired girl, standing on the chest, drew Barbee's eyes from the gun. The girl was April Bell. Savagely, for a moment, he wished that he were the great snake again. But no—he shuddered away from the very notion. He didn't intend to change again.

He ran noiselessly down the stairs and slipped out through the side door. The mud-splashed Foundation car stood where he had left it on the drive. Quivering with eagerness, he started the motor as quietly as he could and drove back to the highway before he clicked on the lights.

He turned west and tramped on the accelerator. Perhaps he could still undo his blunder. If he could get back to the cave ahead of Sheriff Parker and his deputies, Sam Quain might listen to his warning. Perhaps they could carry the precious box back to the car and escape together. Now that Troy knew of Quain's plan, they must go far from Clarendon—because Preston Troy was very likely the Child of Night.

The lightning had ceased with the fall of darkness, but the cold south wind blew steadily, laden with fine rain. The windshield wipers slowed as he stepped on the gas, and it was difficult to see the wet road. Panic gripped him, for one skid on the slick pavement could mean defeat for Sam Quain.

He was already slowing for the rutted side road that led toward Laurel Canyon when he knew that he was being followed. The steamy blur of the rear vision mirror showed no lights behind, but his cold intuition was too imperative to be ignored. Afraid to pause or turn, he drove on, faster.

He knew what was behind—as certainly as if he had seen the feral flash of greenish eyes following. April Bell was after him, probably in the guise of the white were-wolf. She hadn't interfered with his visit to Preston Troy because Troy was a leader of the clan. But now she was going back with him to kill Sam Quain.

The Child of Night had won.

A cold sickness of despair took hold of Barbee, and he shivered at the wheel. His dazed mind refused to make any rational effort to grasp and follow the details of their dark conspiracy, but he knew the reborn witch men were invincible. He couldn't go back to Sam Quain and let April Bell use him for her killer again. He couldn't return to Clarendon—that would mean a padded cell in the state asylum. A hopeless panic drove him blindly on.

He pushed the car on west toward the hills, just because he couldn't go back. The headlamps made a white blur in the rain, and he saw a strange procession marching through it. Mondrick's blind wife, tall and terrible, leading her tawny dog and clutching her silver dagger. Old Ben Chittum, fumbling with gnarled hands and failing to light his pipe, struck dead inside. Fat Mama Spivak, wailing on the shoulder of the fat little tailor. Nora Quain, her blonde hair disheveled and her round face swollen with tears, leading little Pat, who was trying stubbornly not to cry.

The speedometer climbed to seventy. The vacuum drive wipers stopped as he mounted the first foothills, and rain fogged the windshield. The roaring car lurched and swayed on the wet pavement, flinging white wings of water out of puddles. A farm truck with no lights burst suddenly out of the mist, and he whipped narrowly around it.

The needle touched eighty.

But the sleek white bitch, he knew, was following close behind him—a free mind web, riding the wind and swift as thought. He watched the misted mirror, holding the accelerator down. There was nothing his eyes could see—but his mind felt the malice of greenish eyes leering.

The hills rose higher and the curves were steeper, but he didn't slow the car. This was the way the great saber-tooth had chased Rex Chittum. He recalled the night-cloaked hills as the tiger's eyes had seen them, and his nightmares began to haunt him.

Once again he was the shaggy gray wolf, cracking the backbone of Pat Quain's little dog in his jaws. He was the giant snake, flowing up into the Foundation tower to crush out Nick Spivak's life. He was the tiger, with the naked witch astride him, racing up this same road to slash Rex Chittum's throat.

241

He held the accelerator down and held the pitching car on the twisting road, trying to run away from those evil dreams. He tried not to think of Sam Quain waiting for help in that dripping cavern—until Sheriff Parker's men should come. He watched the steamy mirror, and he tried to get away.

For a terrible sick eagerness was creeping upon him, more dreadful than the sleek white wolf he felt behind. In the corner of the mirror was a little sticker cut in the outline of a pterosaur—that winged, reptilian monster of the geologic past was the emblem of an oil company; and the sticker was marked with the mileage when the car was last greased. The image of that flying saurian began to haunt Barbee.

Such a gigantic winged lizard, he felt, would make a satisfying change of shape. He would have fangs and claws to destroy all his enemies, and pinions to soar away from all this unendurable confusion of troubles, along with April Bell. He wanted to stop the car—but that urge was insanity, and he fought it desperately.

He held the roaring car on the road, racing to escape his fears, but the sheets of rain glowing white in the headlamps seemed to make a kind of prison in which no motion moved him. He tried to overtake his lost sanity—to find some solid reality his mind could grasp—but his fevered thought ran on endlessly, like some frantic creature shut in a treadmill cage, and reached no goal.

Had April Bell really snared him with black magic—or only with a normal woman's lure? Had all the dreadful knowledge that he tried to flee come from the cruel Ala-shan in that wooden box—or merely in a bottle from the Mint Bar? Was he maniac or murderer—or neither? Could Sam Quain really have been the killer, his motive some treasure in that box, all his story of the witch folk merely the clever invention of an expert anthropologist turned to crime? Or was it truth and Preston Troy the Child of Night? Had Mondrick's blind widow really been demented? What was the warning she had died trying to bring Sam Quain?

Barbee tried not to think, and tramped harder on the gas.

Sam Quain, he recalled wearily, had warned him of all this. Knowledge of Homo lycanthropus was horror and madness. Now he could never rest. He could find no haven, anywhere. The secret hunters would trail him down, just because he knew their secret.

The car lurched over the last dark crest and roared down the grade beyond. A yellow sign flashed in the headlamps, and he knew this was Sardis Hill. His mind could see the treacherous hairpin turn ahead, where the great saber-tooth had caught the linkage of probability to slash Rex Chittum's throat. He could feel the wet tires already skidding on the pavement; he needed no special perceptions to see the stark probability of his own death here, but he didn't try to slow the plunging car.

"Damn you!" he whispered to the sleek she-wolf that he knew was close behind. "I don't think you'll catch me now!"

He laughed a little, triumphantly, at her crimson grin and Sheriff Parker's men and that padded cell in the state asylum. He glanced at the rain-blurred mirror, smiling defiantly at the Child of Night. No, those secret hunters would never catch him now! He pushed harder on the gas pedal and saw the hairpin curve flash out of the rain.

"Damn you, April!" He felt the wheels slide and didn't try to stop them. "I don't think you can make me change again."

Skidding swiftly sidewise, the car was going off the wet pavement. The wheel twisted viciously in his hands, and he let go. The car shuddered against some boulder at the edge of the asphalt and went spinning into the dark chasm beyond. Barbee relaxed happily, waiting for the crash.

"Good-bye," he breathed to the white were-wolf.

20

The Child of Night

The pain was less than Barbee had feared. The silence of the long spinning fall ended suddenly when the car struck a hard granite ledge. Tortured metal screamed hideously, as if in mockery of human agony. His body was seized and torn and crushed. For an instant the torture was unendurable, but he scarcely felt the final impact.

After the merest second of darkness, he was conscious again. One front wheel of the car still spun above him; he could hear the diminishing purr and click of the bearings. Liquid was splashing near him. The fear of fire took hold of him when he smelled the raw reek of gasoline, and he dragged himself feebly from beneath a cruel weight of wreckage.

A brief elation lifted him when he found that no important bones were broken. Oddly, his bruised and aching body wasn't even bleeding. Shuddering from the icy bite of the rain-laden wind, he was staggering back toward the pavement when the white bitch howled above him.

He tried to run from the eerily triumphant quaver of her wail, but a trembling sickness had taken his strength. He stumbled on the wet rubble and couldn't get up. Cowering helplessly back against a dripping boulder, he lay staring up at the sleek she-wolf.

"Well, Barbee!" She had paused at the edge of the road where the car had left it on the curve above, peering down at him with greenish sardonic eyes. Her voice was April Bell's, bright with a kindly malice. "So you tried to get away?"

He caught up a handful of gravel and flung it at her weakly.

"Damn you!" he sobbed. "Won't you even let me die?"

Ignoring his angered voice and the futile spatter of gravel, she came bounding gracefully down the stony slope. He tried to pull himself up the rough face of the boulder, and slipped back into gray illness. He heard the light patter of her paws and smelled the pleasant fragrance of her wet fur close to him and felt her warm tongue licking his face.

"Get away!" He sat up painfully and tried weakly to push her away. "What the devil do you want?"

"Only to help you when you need me, Barbee." She sat on her haunches in front of him, white fangs smiling. "I followed you here to grasp a linkage of probability and help you free yourself. I know it must be painful and confusing, but you'll soon feel better."

"Oh!" he muttered bitterly. "You think so?"

He relaxed against the jagged rock, staring at her. One slim forepaw was lifted, and her greenish eyes shone with a friendly amusement. Even as a wolf she was beautiful, slenderly graceful as the red-haired girl, her clean fur snowy white. Yet he shuddered back from her.

"Get the hell away!" he rapped hoarsely. "Can't you even let me die?"

"No, Barbee." She shook her delicate head. "Now you'll never die."

"Huh?" He shivered. "Why not?"

"Because, Barbee—" Her pointed ears lifted suddenly, and she turned quickly to listen with a motionless alertness. "I'll tell you," she murmured swiftly. "Sometime. Now I can feel another forming linkage that we must prepare to use—it involves your friend Sam Quain. But he can't harm you yet, and I'll come back."

Her quick cold kiss astonished him. She raced back up to the road and left him lying there. Her mocking eyes haunted him, and he was sick with a stunned bewilderment. Even death was denied him. He couldn't understand—he wished April Bell had told him more of the theory of free mind webs and the linkage of matter and mind through control of probability. Perhaps she had twisted probability to save him, as she and the great saber-tooth had twisted it the other way to cause Rex Chittum's death. He only knew that he had failed to kill himself.

He lay there a long time, shivering in the thin rain, too miserable to think. He was waiting with a sick and hopeless apprehension for the white bitch, but she didn't come back. Presently he felt stronger, and the moaning gears of a van grinding up the hill aroused him with a hope of shelter from the rain.

He staggered into the blinding glare of the headlamps, waving his arms desperately; but the grimy-faced driver merely scowled at him. He shook his fist and shouted. The driver swerved the truck as if to run him down, and then ignored him.

The heavy wheel brushed him, and the van lurched on, slowing for the steep curve above. It was empty, the back yawning open. A sudden impulse sent him stumbling after it, as it paused while the driver shifted gears. He caught the edges of the body, and flung himself puffing aboard.

The black cavern of the covered body was empty except for a pile of musty-smelling army blankets that must have been used to pack a load of furniture. He wrapped himself in them and sat huddled on the hard floor, dully watching the dark road unroll behind.

The night-clad foothills flowed back around him, and the first scattered farms, and the lonely lights at a crossroads service station. Clarendon lay ahead. He knew the police would be looking for him again, armed now with Troy's description of his borrowed clothing; but still he felt too sick to try to think of any plan.

He was vanquished, and there was no sanctuary. Even death had barred its doors. Only an animal urge to keep out of the cold rain lived on in him, and a brooding apprehension of the white she-wolf's return.

No green eyes followed, however, and a faint hope glowed again in the icy night of his mind. The dark buildings of the university slid back past him as the driver slowed for the traffic light at the corner of the campus and turned left on the north river highway. He saw then that the van would pass Glennhaven, and a sudden purpose seized him.

He was going back to Dr. Glenn.

He didn't want to go back. He didn't want the false escape of insanity, or the hard refuge of a cell in the state asylum. But the white bitch would soon be following again. He needed the comforting armor of Glenn's skeptical materialism. He waited for the van to slow again on the curve beyond Glennhaven and dropped to the wet pavement.

Too stiff to run, he fell on his face. He lumbered painfully to his feet, too dazed to feel the cold rain. He was tired. He wanted a dry place to sleep, and he had almost forgotten any other purpose when a dog yelped beside a dark house across the road, shrill with panic. That aroused him, for he thought the white were-wolf must be near.

Other dogs began to howl as he stumbled back down the highway to the square stone pillars at the entrance to the hospital grounds. Lights were still on in Glenn's big dwelling. He staggered up the walk to it, peering apprehensively behind. Still no green eyes followed. He leaned on the bell, and the tall psychiatrist came to the door. His tanned handsome face showed only faint surprise.

"Hello, Barbee. I thought you would come back."

Barbee stood swaying, licking at the numb stiffness of his lips.

"The police?" he whispered anxiously. "Are they here?"

Glenn smiled at his drenched and battered figure with a suave professional sympathy.

"Let's not worry about the law just now," he urged soothingly. "You really look all in, Barbee. Why don't you just relax, and let our staff help you solve you problems? That's our business, you know. We'll just telephone Sheriff Parker and the police that you're safe here, and forget your legal troubles until tomorrow. Right?"

"Right," Barbee agreed uncertainly. "Only—there's one thing you've got to know," he added desperately. "I didn't run down Mrs. Mondrick!"

Glenn blinked sleepily.

"I know her blood is on the fender of my car," Barbee said wildly. "But a white wolf killed her—I saw the blood on its muzzle!"

Glenn nodded easily.

"We can talk more about that in the morning, Mr. Barbee. But whatever has happened—in the reality situation or in your own mind—I want to assure you that I'm deeply interested in your case.

JACK WILLIAMSON

You appear very much disturbed, but I intend to use every resource of psychiatry to help you."

"Thanks," Barbee muttered. "But you still think I killed her."

"All the evidence is pretty convincing." Still smiling, Glenn stepped cautiously back. "You mustn't try to leave again, and you'll have to move into a different ward in the morning."

"The disturbed ward," Barbee said bitterly. "I'll bet you still don't know how Rowena Mondrick got out of there!"

Glenn lifted his shoulders unconcernedly.

"Dr. Bunzel is still upset about that," he admitted casually. "But we needn't worry about anything else tonight. You look pretty uncomfortable. Why don't you just go on back to your room and take a hot bath and get some sleep—"

"Sleep?" Barbee echoed hoarsely. "Doctor, I'm afraid to sleep—because I know that same white wolf is coming back for me. She's going to change me into some other shape and make me go with her to kill Sam Quain. You won't be able to see her—even I can't see her yet—but no walls can keep her out."

Glenn smiled again, nodding in meaningless agreement.

"She's coming!" Barbee's voice turned high. "Listen to the dogs!"

He could hear the frightened dogs howling at every farm down the wind. He gestured toward the sound, shaking with a wave of frantic panic. Glenn merely waited in the doorway, his brown face blandly smooth.

"That white wolf is April Bell," Barbee whispered huskily. "She murdered Dr. Mondrick. She made me help her kill Rex Chittum and Nick Spivak. I saw her standing over Mrs. Mondrick's body, licking her fangs." His teeth chattered. "She'll come back the moment I sleep, to make me change again and go with her to hunt Sam Quain."

Glenn shrugged again, professionally placid.

"You're tired," he said. "You're excited. Just let me give you something to help you sleep—"

"I won't take anything." Barbee tried to keep his ragged voice from screaming. "This is something more than madness—I've got to make you understand! Listen to what Sam Quain told me tonight—"

"Now, Mr. Barbee," Glenn protested blandly. "Let's be calm—"

"Calm?" Barbee gasped hoarsely. "Listen to this!" Clutching the door facing to hold himself upright, dripping muddy pools on the mat, he launched desperately into the story: "There are witches, Doctor— Mondrick called them Homo lycanthropus. They evolved in the first ice age, and haunted men until every myth and legend of werewolves and vampires and evil spirits is a racial memory of their free mind webs, preying on mankind."

"So?" Glenn nodded sympathetically, unimpressed.

"And Mondrick discovered that the human race today is a hybrid mixture—"

Barbee's troubled voice ran desperately on. Once he recalled Sam Quain's disquieting suspicion that Glenn himself might be a witch man, but he dismissed the idea instantly. That odd sense of recognition and confident liking was awake again. He was glad to see the quiet attentiveness on Glenn's gravely sympathetic face. All he wanted was the competent aid of Glenn's skeptical scientific mind.

"Now, Doctor!" A bleak challenge broke into his husky whisper as he finished. "What do you say to that?"

Deliberately, with the old reflective gesture, Glenn fitted the capable brown fingers of his two hands together.

"You're ill, Mr. Barbee," his deep voice said soberly. "Remember that. You're too ill to see reality except in a distorting mirror of your own fears. Your story of Homo lycanthropus, it seems to me, is a kind of warped hysterical parallel to the truth."

Barbee tried to listen—and shuddered when he heard the dogs still howling behind him.

"It's true that some of the parapsychology boys have interpreted their findings as scientific evidence for the existence of a spirit separate from the body that can somehow influence the probability of events in the real world and may even survive after physical death."

Glenn nodded as if pleased with his own argument.

"It's also true that men are descended from savage animals. We've all inherited traits that are no longer useful in civilized society. The unconscious mind does sometimes seem a dark cave of horrors, and the same unpleasant facts are often expressed in the symbolism of legend and myth. It's even true that interesting throwbacks do occur."

Barbee shook his head in a weary protest.

"But you can't explain those witches away," he gasped hoarsely. "Not when they're looking for the linkage of probability to kill Sam Quain right now!" He looked uneasily behind him, shrinking from the frightened howling of the dogs. "Think of poor Nora," he whispered. "And dear little Pat! I don't want to murder Sam tonight—that's the reason I'm afraid to sleep!"

"Please, Mr. Barbee." Glenn's calm voice was warmly sympathetic. "Won't you try to understand? Your fear of sleep is nothing more than your fear of those unconscious wishes which sleep sets free. The witch of your dreams may turn out to be nothing except your guilty love of Nora Quain, and your thoughts of murder only the natural consequence of an unconscious jealous hatred of her husband."

Barbee clenched his fists, shaken with a silent wrath.

"You deny such ideas now," Glenn said calmly. "You must learn to accept them, to face them and dispose of them on a realistic basis. That will be the objective of our therapy. There's nothing unique about such fears. All people express them—"

"All people," Barbee broke in huskily, "are tainted with the witch blood."

Glenn nodded easily.

"Your fantasy expression of a fundamental truth. All people experience the same inner conflicts—"

Barbee heard footsteps behind him on the walk and turned with a muffled sob of terror. It wasn't the sleek white bitch, however, but only horse-faced Nurse Graulitz and muscular Nurse Hellar. He looked accusingly back at Glenn.

"Better go with them quietly, Mr. Barbee," the tall psychiatrist told him gently. "They'll put you to bed and help you get to sleep—"

"I'm afraid to sleep," Barbee sobbed. "I won't—"

He caught his breath and tried to run. The two white-starched Amazons caught his arms, and he surrendered to a chilled exhaustion. They took him back to his room in the annex. A hot shower stopped the chattering of his teeth, and the clean bed was insidiously relaxing.

"I'll be watching the hall," Nurse Hellar told him. "I'll give you a shot if you don't go right to sleep."

He needed no shot. Sleep tugged and beckoned. It was a silken web that meshed him, a tireless insistent line that drew upon him unceasingly. It was a ruthless pressure, a driving wind, a soothing song. It became a screaming agony of need.

Yet he found it—until something made him look at the closed door.

The bottom panels were silently dissolving. The white wolf-bitch came trotting through the opening. She sat down on her haunches in the middle of the room, watching him with amused, expectant eyes. Her long red tongue lolled beside her shining fangs.

"You can wait till daylight," he told her wearily. "But you can't change me—because I'm not going to sleep."

Her greenish eyes smiled limpidly.

"You don't need to sleep." She spoke with the warm velvet voice of April Bell. "I've just told your half brother what happened tonight on Sardis Hill—and he's very happy about it. He says you must be very powerful, because even the nurses didn't notice. He says you can change when you like now, without the aid of sleep—because, you see, you no longer have any human resistance that has to be relaxed."

"What's all this?" Barbee sat up quickly on the edge of the bed, frowning in puzzlement. "What didn't the nurses notice?"

The white bitch grinned maliciously.

"Don't you know, Barbee?"

"Know what?" he rasped, annoyed. "And who's my half brother?"

"Didn't Archer tell you anything?" The she-wolf shook her slender head. "No, he wouldn't. He probably meant to spend a whole year awakening your ancestral powers, the way he did mine—at forty dollars an hour. But the clan can't wait. I cut you free tonight because we've got to do something about Sam Quain and your human taint made you too reluctant."

Barbee blinked confusedly.

"I don't get any of this," he muttered. "I don't even believe I have a half brother. Of course I never knew my parents. Mother died when I was born, and my father was soon afterward committed to the state asylum. I was brought up in an institution till I started to attend the university and came to board with Mrs. Mondrick."

"That's all a fairy tale." The she-wolf laughed silently. "Of course there really was a Luther Barbee—but he and his wife were paid to adopt you. They happened to find out what an inhuman little monster you were. That's why the woman had to be killed and the man put away—before they talked too much."

Barbee shook his head unbelievingly.

"Then what—" he muttered unwillingly. "What am I?"

"You and I are special beings, Barbee." The bitch smiled redly. "We were bred from mankind, by a special art and for a special end—but we are neither of us more than slightly human."

Barbee nodded reluctantly.

"Sam was telling me about Homo lycanthropus," he murmured dazedly. "About the taint in the blood of men and the rebirth of the witch race from the genes."

"Quain knows too much," the white bitch observed. "The technique of gathering the genes by mental control of probability was perfected here at Glennhaven," she added. "Your own famous father finished the work nearly thirty years ago."

Barbee shivered, clutching the iron bedpost.

"Who was my father?"

"The older Dr. Glenn," the she-wolf said. "That makes Dr. Archer Glenn your half brother. He is a few years older than you and a slightly less successful genetic experiment."

Barbee gulped uneasily, thinking of that odd feeling of warm kinship toward the tall psychiatrist—was it a recognition of their common dark inheritance? He whispered huskily:

"My mother?"

"You knew her." The white bitch laughed at his shocked wonderment. "She was a woman your father had selected for her genes—he brought her to Glennhaven as a nurse. She was richly gifted with our ancestral legacy, but unfortunately never able to overcome the unfortunate influence of her tragic human taint. She was foolish enough to believe your father loved her, and she never forgave him when she learned the truth. She joined our human enemies—but you were already born."

Goose flesh roughened Barbee's skin.

"She wasn't—" he gulped— "Rowena Mondrick?"

"Miss Rowena Stalcup, then," the white bitch purred. "She wasn't aware of her own ancestral powers until your father began arousing them. A bit of a prude, I believe—she was horrified at the idea of bearing you out of wedlock, even when she thought you would be human."

The white bitch snickered, and Barbee caught his breath.

"And I killed her!" he gasped faintly. "My own mother!"

"Nonsense, Barbee!" The she-wolf lolled her scarlet tongue, still laughing at him. "You needn't be so squeamish about the extermination of a mongrel traitress, but I'm the one who killed her. Your car on the bridge merely completed the linkage of probability, so that I could get her throat."

She nodded brightly, licking her cruel white fangs.

"But—" Barbee whispered strickenly, "if she was really my mother—"

"She was our enemy." The white bitch snarled savagely. "She pretended to join your father's coven and then used the arts she had learned to escape him and carry the secrets of the clan to old Mondrick—that's what first put Mondrick on our trail. Rowena worked with him until one of us tore out her eyes years ago in Nigeria, when she was about to uncover one of those Stones—those disk-shaped weapons of something deadlier than silver—that our ancient human enemies buried with our murdered ancestors to keep them in their graves."

Barbee nodded uncomfortably, recalling that lethal reek seeping from the silver-lined box that had nearly killed them in Sam Quain's study, and that malodorous plaster cast of some circular object that Nick Spivak had been working over when the great snake killed him. He clutched the bedpost with both hands until his knuckles cracked, but he couldn't stop the shudder of foreboding that swept him.

"That should have been a lesson to her," the white bitch was whispering. "But she still helped old Mondrick all she could. She's the one who warned him to test you when he was about to take you into the Foundation."

"She was?" Barbee shifted doubtfully on the bed. "But she was always so kind and friendly," he protested, "even after that. I thought she liked me—"

"She loved you, I imagine," the she-wolf said. "After all, you did have some strong human traits—that's why we decided to set you free. Perhaps she hoped you would revolt from the coven, when the time came, as she had done. She didn't know how strong your inheritance would be."

Barbee stared a long time at the wolf's red grin.

"I wish—" he whispered hoarsely, "I wish I had known."

"Don't upset yourself," she advised him. "The woman died, you remember, trying to warn Sam Quain."

Barbee blinked uneasily, breathing:

"What was it she wanted to tell Sam?"

"The name of the Child of Night." The she-wolf sat leering at him redly. "But we stopped her—and you played your own role very cleverly, Barbee, pretending to be his friend and begging for a chance to help him and trying to comfort his crying wife."

"Huh?" Barbee rose from the bed. He felt suddenly cold, and he stood swaying with a gray illness. "You don't—" he whispered breathlessly. "You can't mean—that I—"

"I do, Barbee!" the she-wolf pricked up her triangular ears, her greenish eyes dancing with a malicious pleasure in his deep perturbation. "You're one of us—the powerful one we've bred to be our leader. You're the one we call the Child of Night."

21

Into the Shadows

Barbee shook his head dazedly.

"No!" He stood shuddering, clinging to the bedpost. A sudden sweat filmed his cold skin. He tried to breathe, and gasped a faint protest: "I don't believe it."

"You will," she purred, "as soon as you grasp your powers. Our ancestral gifts are always slow to awaken—the slowest usually the greatest. They tend to lie unused and even unsuspected, hidden by the dominant human heritage, until they waken of themselves—or are awakened by such an expert as Archer Glenn. Your father blundered by telling Rowena too abruptly, and her human part rebelled."

Trembling weakly, Barbee sat back on the bed.

"I'll not be—your Black Messiah!" he whispered faintly. "That— that's insanity. Anyhow, I don't believe you! I don't even believe you're here. Just something out of a whisky bottle!" He shook a threatening fist. "Get the devil out of here—before I scream."

"Go ahead and scream." She laughed at him silently, fine ears pricked up. "My mind web isn't nearly so powerful as yours—Nurse Hellar can't see me."

Barbee didn't scream. For two minutes he sat on the edge of the bed, watching the bright-eyed, expectant wolf. If she were just hallucination, born of delirium tremens, she was still a remarkably vivid and graceful and malicious illusion.

"You followed me away from Preston Troy's tonight," he accused her suddenly. "I know you were there—in another shape, probably. I saw your white coat with that little jade running wolf pinned to it, on a chair in his den."

"So what?" Her greenish eyes smiled mockingly. "I was only waiting for you, Barbee."

"I saw your picture in his bedroom." Barbee's voice was shaking. "And I saw him let himself into your apartment with his own key. What is he to you, April?"

Laughing again, the white wolf trotted to him and put her slender white paws on his trembling knees. Her long greenish eyes looked more than ever human—April Bell's. They looked eager and glad and yet faintly mocking, and they shone with tears.

"So that's why you've been trying to run away from me tonight, Barbee?"

Hoarsely he muttered, "Maybe it is."

"So that's all it is!" Her cold muzzle lifted as if impulsively to kiss him. "You silly, jealous devil! I told you that we're special beings, you and I, Barbee. We were born for a special purpose. It would be too bad if you didn't like me."

He rubbed angrily at the tingle of her icy kiss, demanding bleakly: "Who is Preston Troy?"

"Just my father." She tittered at his shocked unbelief. "All I told you about my childhood and the brutalities of that ignorant dairyman is true—I told you he wasn't my father and knew he wasn't."

The white bitch leered at him gleefully.

"You see, Mother had been a secretary of Preston's before she married the dairyman, and she still saw him whenever she could. The dairyman suspected—that's why he was so ready to believe that I was a witch and so cruel in his punishments. He never liked my red hair."

She chuckled reminiscently.

"But Preston was always generous," she said. "Of course he couldn't marry Mother—he'd had too many other secretaries. But he used to send us money and gifts in California—Mother would tell me they came from a mythical Aunt Agatha, before I knew about Preston. He has done a lot for me since she died—he even paid for my analysis at Glennhaven." Her greenish gaze mocked him. "So you were jealous, Barbee?"

He touched her silky fur with uncertain sweaty fingers.

"I guess I was," he muttered hoarsely. "Anyhow, I can't help being glad—"

He paused as light struck him. The door was swinging open. Nurse Hellar peered into the room with an expression of mild reproof on her broad face.

"Really, Mr. Barbee!" she admonished him softly. "You'll catch cold if you sit up all night talking to yourself. Let me tuck you in bed." She started resolutely toward him, and the white bitch nipped at her muscular ankle. "Gracious, what was that?" She peered at the redly grinning wolf without seeming to see anything, and threatened Barbee in a somewhat shaken voice: "If you aren't in bed when I get back with the hypo—"

"You won't be," the she-wolf told him, as Nurse Hellar retreated apprehensively. "Because it's time for us to go."

"Where?" he whispered uneasily.

"To take care of your friend Sam Quain," purred the voice of April Bell. "He's about to get away from the sheriff's men. The high water has stopped them, and he's climbing a trail they don't know about. He's carrying that box. He has the only weapon that can ever harm you, Barbee, and we must stop him before he learns to use it. I've found a linkage of probability that we can grasp, when the moment comes."

Stubbornly, Barbee clenched his fists.

"I won't hurt Sam," he muttered grimly. "Not even if I am bewitched!"

"But you aren't, Barbee." Gently, the white bitch rubbed her silken shoulder against his knees. "Can't you realize that you're one of us?— completely, now, because your last human ties were broken on Sardis Hill tonight."

"Huh?" He sat blinking at her. "What do you mean?"

"So you still don't feel your wonderful gifts, Barbee?" She smiled up at him with a kindly mockery. "I'll show you what I mean when we come to Sardis Hill." Her tapered head nodded urgently. "Now it's time to go."

He sat back resolutely.

"I still don't believe I could be this Child of Night," he said flatly. "And I won't harm Sam!"

"Come," she whispered. "You'll believe when I show you."

"No!" Shivering in cold rigidity, Barbee clung with clammy hands to the iron bed. "I can't be any such monstrous—thing!"

"You'll be our leader, Will," she told him softly. "Our new chieftain in the long fight for our lost dominion—until a stronger one takes your place. You and I are the most powerful in generations, but a child with both our genes will have still less of the human taint."

She dropped to all fours again and nipped playfully at his knee. "Let's go."

He tried to resist, but his clinging fingers slipped from the bedpost. His wistful longing for the winged might of the oil company's pterosaur came back; it turned swiftly to a ruthless, burning eagerness. His body flowed and grew. The change was easy now, for all that awkwardness and pain was gone; and it brought him a fresh, savage strength.

The white bitch beside him was changing too. She reared to her hind feet and grew swiftly taller. The flowing curves of her white body filled, and the fur was gone, and she flung the burnished red hair back off her bare shoulders. Fiercely eager, Barbee gathered the slim woman in his leathery wings, and he kissed her cool, tender lips with the giant saurian's snout. Laughing, she gave his hard scaled head a ringing slap.

"We've another appointment first." She slipped out of his folded wings and sprang astride his armored back. "With probability and your old friend Quain."

Barbee looked at the reinforced window, and it melted out of its frame. He slithered through the opening, with the girl crouching low upon him, and perched for a moment with his mighty talons gripping the sill. He looked back, with a tiny shudder of disgust, for the ugly human husk behind him. To his faint surprise, the white hospital bed was empty. That minor puzzle didn't trouble him, however. It was good to be strong and free again, and he liked the feel of the girl astride him.

"Why, Mr. Barbee!" He heard Nurse Hellar's breathless voice and

felt the unpleasant glow of light as she opened the door. He didn't let her see him, and a comical consternation twisted her face as she looked under the bed and into the corners of the empty room, carrying her hypodermic needle. "Wherever are you?"

Barbee felt a demoniac impulse to manifest himself and show her, but April Bell's flat hand slapped his scaly flank reprovingly. Leaving Nurse Hellar to solve her own problem, he spread his black wings and launched himself awkwardly from the window.

The night was still cloudy and the brisk south wind laden with icy drizzle. The shape of things was clear to his new senses, however; the damp chill was merely stimulating now, and all his trembling fatigue was gone. He beat the rain-washed air with long easy strokes, soaring westward.

A frightened dog barked suddenly in the yard of a dark farmhouse beneath them, and Barbee dived to terrify it into whimpering silence with his own hissing scream. A joyous strength lifted his wings. This was life. All his old uncertainties and conflicts and frustrations were left behind. At last he was free.

They lifted into the west. Lights of cars moved over the flanks of the night-mantled hills below, lanterns swung, and flashlights made furtive gleams. But the manhunt, he saw with the saurian's eyes, was making slow progress. Flood waters had come tumbling down from the higher canyons since he left Sam Quain at the cave; Bear Creek and Laurel Canyon were impassable now with white water and grinding boulders. The sheriff's men were halted at the ford.

"They'll never catch him," murmured April Bell. "We'll have to use that linkage, to help him slip on the rocks and kill himself."

"No," Barbee muttered reluctantly. "I won't do that—"

"I think you will," the white witch told him, "when you see what happened on Sardis Hill."

A queer dread burdened his pinions as he flapped reluctantly westward again, following the black thread of the highway twisting up over the folds of the higher hills. He soared over the narrow saddle of the pass and wheeled low above the steep, sharp curve beyond, his strange eyes searching.

Three cars were stopped beside the pavement above the hairpin, and a black ambulance. A little knot of curious late motorists stood on the edge of the road, peering down the slope at the flattened ruin of the Foundation sedan. Two men in white beside it were expertly lifting something to a stretcher.

Barbee saw what they lifted and shuddered in the air.

"Your body," the white girl told him softly. "Your powers were grown, and you didn't need it any longer. I caught the linkage of probability, while you were driving down the hill, to help set you free."

The men were spreading a blanket over the unpleasant object on the stretcher.

"Free?" Barbee whispered hoarsely. "You mean—dead?"

"No," purred April Bell. "Now you'll never die—not if we kill Sam Quain before he learns how to use his weapon. You're the first of us in modern times to be strong enough to survive, but even so your human taint still made you weak and unhappy. It was time for you to be separated."

He staggered dazedly, on stiffened wings.

"Sorry, darling." He heard the throb of a sudden tenderness beneath the friendly mischief in her voice. "I suppose it's hard to lose your body, even though you don't need it now. But you really should be happy."

"Happy?" he rasped bitterly. "To be dead?"

"No—free!" Eagerness trembled in her husky whisper. "You'll soon feel differently, Will. For all your great ancestral powers will be awakening, now that the human barriers are gone. And now you own all the heirlooms and the precious secrets our clans and covens have kept through those dark ages when men thought they had won."

His long wings faltered, shuddering in the air.

"Darling—you mustn't be afraid!" Warmly, her fingers stroked his scales. "I guess you do feel strange and lonely—the way I felt when they first told me. But you won't be alone very long." A quiet elation lifted her voice. "You see, Archer Glenn says I am also strong enough to survive."

He wheeled slowly, on weary wings.

"Of course I must wait until our heir is born—a son pure enough to father our race again." He felt her body tighten to that indomitable purpose. "But then I can be separated, too," she added softly. "To be with you forever!"

"Huh!" He snorted dully. "Fellow revenants!"

"Don't feel too sorry for yourself, Will Barbee!" She laughed at him lightly, tossing her burnished hair back and digging her bare heels into his scaly hide. "You're a vampire now, and you might as well learn to like it. Your old friend Quain is the one in need of sympathy."

"No!" he gasped, unconvinced. "I won't believe you."

He drifted lower on leaden wings, wheeling slowly above the two men carrying the human part of him up from that smashed car to the waiting ambulance. One of them slipped on the wet rocks, and they almost spilled the thing under the blanket. He knew that didn't matter now.

"It used to give me the creepiest feeling, when Archer was first teaching me the old arts," April Bell was murmuring joyously. "To think of hiding in the dark, maybe even in your own grave, and going out at night to feed! That used to seem so gruesome, but now I think it's going to be fun."

Silently, shivering in the air, Barbee watched the two men slide their burden into the ambulance. He was wondering dully about the separate energy complexes of the mind, and he wished Sam Quain had told him a little more about what the Mondrick expedition found under those old burial mounds in the Ala-shan.

"That's the way our people used to live," the white witch chattered cheerfully, "before men learned how to fight us. It's the natural way, because our free mind webs have such wonderful powers. They can survive almost forever, unless they're destroyed by light or silver or those horrible stones men used to bury with us."

She seemed to listen, peering northeastward.

"It's time to find Quain," she said. "I can feel the linkage forming."

Heavily he flew northeast. He flapped low above the sheriff's men, waiting above the white water at the Bear Creek ford.

"Don't mind them," April Bell called scornfully. "They don't have silver bullets and they don't know how to see us. Men have forgotten how to fight us since the terrible times of the Inquisition—they don't even understand their dogs. Sam Quain is our only danger now."

He flew over the ford and up the foaming torrent that came down Laurel Canyon. April Bell's slim arm pointed, and he saw Sam Quain. Staggering to the weight of the green-painted box on his shoulder, Quain was high on that narrow, unguessed trail which twisted breathtakingly above the mad white water.

"Wait!" cooed April Bell. "Wait until we can seize the chance that he will slip and fall—that's the linkage I feel."

Barbee wheeled deliberately above the ragged ledges. Even now he couldn't help admiring Sam Quain as a brave and dangerous enemy. Defying desperate odds and long exhaustion, the man was making a splendid effort. Against any lesser antagonist, he might have had a chance.

For at last, climbing half-obliterated steps the Indians must have cut, he pushed the precious box ahead of him and dragged himself to the top of the cliff. He rested for only a moment, panting, calmly watching the lights of the sheriff's men beyond the ford. Then, with a stubborn weary strength, he lifted the heavy wooden box to his shoulder again.

"Now!" cried April Bell.

With silent black wings half folded, Barbee dived.

Sam Quain seemed suddenly aware of the danger. He tried to get back from the precipice, and swayed as he began to lose his balance. His haggard face stared up, slowly twisting into a grim, red-stubbled grin of horror. He must have known how to see free mind webs, for his mouth opened and Barbee thought he heard his own name shouted in a tone of utmost anguish:

"So it's *you*—Will Barbee—"

The talons of the pterosaur caught the iron-bound box. The seeping reek of that ancient, deadly thing in it filled Barbee's nostrils with a lethal sweetness. The very touch of the box numbed him with a strange chill. His wings were paralyzed, but he clung desperately to the box.

Torn out of Sam Quain's clutching fingers, the box fell over the cliffs. Barbee dropped with it, lifeless with that seeping emanation, until the box slipped out of his frozen talons. He spread stiffly painful wings to check his fall, great eyes fixed on the plunging box.

It struck a ledge far below and shattered into wooden splinters and twisted scraps of white sheet silver. Barbee saw blackened silver weapons, and dissolving bits of yellow bone, and a disk-shaped object that glowed with a terrible dull violet luminescence, to the eyes of the saurian, radiation more damaging than daylight.

That dreadful glow reminded him of the descriptions of an atomic accident, in which an experimenter was killed at Los Alamos. Was radioactive uranium, he wondered, the metal more deadly than silver?

If it were, the witches in charge of atomic security would see to it that none was available to such men as Quain for use in killing other witches.

That glowing disk shattered on the ledge and went down with the specimen skeleton of lycanthropus and the old silver weapons and all the rest into the grinding chaos of foam and mud and rocks and wild water in the swollen creek.

Life returned to Barbee's wings. He flapped heavily away from the spreading cloud of evil malodor that came up from the broken disk. Still weak and shaken, he alighted clumsily on the rocks above the roaring stream. April Bell slipped off his back.

"You were splendid, Barbee!" Her voice was a velvet caress. "That Stone was our only real danger—you are the only one of the clan strong enough to grasp that box; the deadly emanations of the Stone would paralyze any of the rest of us before we could get near enough to touch it." He shivered with pleasure as her electric fingers scratched his heaving, scaly flank. "Now let's finish the job, and kill Sam Quain."

Clinging with trembling talons to the wet boulder where he perched, Barbee shook his long armored head.

"What harm can Sam do?" he hissed reluctantly. "That box held his only weapon, and all the proof he could use to get any support. Now he's just an ordinary fugitive from the law, suspected of three murders. Without that box, his story is pure insanity—such witches as Dr. Glenn can take care of him."

He reached for the red-haired girl with a long leather wing.

"Suppose he does get away from the sheriff's men? Suppose he's fool enough to try to tell somebody his story? Or, more likely, write it? Suppose some unwary publisher should dare to print it—disguised, perhaps, to look like fiction?

"Would the witches worry?

"I think not. The witches who review books would doubtless dismiss it as a trivial bit of escapist fantasy. Suppose it came into the hands of such a distinguished psychiatrist as Dr. Glenn? I can see his sleepy smile. An interesting case history, he might say—and I can see his lazy shrug.

"An illuminating picture of reality, such a respected witch might add, as seen through the twisted vision of a disintegrating schizoid personality. The autobiography of a mental breakdown. The vampire legend, he might conclude, has served very conveniently for many thousand years as a conventional folk expression of unconscious feelings of aggression and guilt. In the face of such suavely sophisticated skepticism, who would believe?

"Who would dare believe?"

The pterosaur hunched his folded wings in a scaly shrug.

"Let's forget Sam Quain—for Nora's sake."

"So it's Nora Quain again?"

Archly indignant, April Bell twisted coyly out of his black caressing pinions. Her white body shrank, and her head grew long and pointed. Her red hair changed to silky fur. Only the greenish malicious eyes of the slim she-wolf were still the same, alight with a provocative challenge.

"Wait for me, April!"

With a red silent laugh she ran from him, up the dark wooded slope where his wings couldn't follow. The change, however, was easy now. Barbee let the saurian's body flow into the shape of a huge gray wolf. He picked up her exciting scent and followed her into the shadows.

About the Author

JACK WILLIAMSON has been in the forefront of science fiction since his first published story in 1928. Now in his seventy-second year as a published author, Williamson is the acclaimed author of such trailblazing science fiction as *The Humanoids* and *The Legion of Time*. *The Oxford English Dictionary* credits Williamson with inventing the terms "genetic engineering" (in *Dragon's Island*) and "terraforming" (in *Seetee Ship*).

Williamson also has been active academically. He has taught since the 1950s, and is professor emeritus at Eastern New Mexico University. Williamson recently was presented a Lifetime Achievement Award by the Horror Writers Association. He lives and works in Portales, New Mexico, where he is writing his next novel.